Abraham and Sarah

Roberta Kells Dorr

MOODY PUBLISHERS

CHICAGO

Edited by Barbara A. Lilland
Interior design: Ragont Design
Cover design: Brand Navigation, LLC
Cover images: man © Fotolia/magann; man's eyes © iStockphoto LP/Kemter; Horizontal Bar
            Pattern © iStockphoto LP/naeinabil; woman © iStockphoto LP/master2;
            Desert scene © iStockphoto LP/adamkaz; Red Head Scarf © Big Stock/belinda-bw

Library of Congress Cataloging-in-Publication Data

Dorr, Roberta Kells.
 [Abraham & Sarah, the long journey]
 Abraham and Sarah / Roberta Kells Dorr.
    pages cm
 Originially published: Nashville, Tenn. ; Moorings, 1995 as Abraham & Sarah, the long journey.
 Summary: "A splendid exploration of faith against great odds and love that endures years of disappointment.Abraham and Sarah is a masterful historical drama from the moment that Abraham strides into the pagan temple to rescue Sarah. The couple set out in search of the blessings God had promised: abundant fertile land and decedents more plentiful than the stars.But years of wandering bring the couple to Egypt where once again Abraham convinces Sarah that as sister and brother surely they will pass safely through the territory. But Pharaoh takes Sarah into his harem where she befriends Pharaoh's daughter, Hagar. Together the three are ordered to leave.Years of barrenness have embittered Sarah and she hatches a plan: Hagar must become the vessel for the child God has promised. Ishmael is born to Hagar and so is jealousy born in Sarah's heart. But God had a plan and He was right all along. This miracle unfolds with Historical authenticity leaving the reader with a better understanding of the ancient world and the life-changing faith of Abraham and Sarah"-- Provided by publisher.
 ISBN 978-0-8024-0957-7 (pbk.)
 1. Abraham (Biblical patriarch)—Fiction. 2. Sarah (Biblical matriarch)—Fiction. 3. Bible. Old Testament—History of Biblical events—Fiction. 4.   Brothers and sisters—History—Fiction. 5. Religious fiction. I. Title.
 PS3554.O694A64 2014
 813'.54--dc23
                            2013041485

We hope you enjoy this book from River North Fiction by Moody Publishers. Our goal is to provide high-quality, thought-provoking books and products that connect truth to your real needs and challenges. For more information on other books and products written and produced from a biblical perspective, go to www.moodypublishers.com or write to:

River North Fiction
Imprint of Moody Publishers
820 N. LaSalle Boulevard
Chicago, IL 60610

1 3 5 7 9 10 8 6 4 2

Printed in the United States of America

To my grandmother, Emma Benham
Sherman, who instilled in me a
love for the people of the Bible

Obedience is the fruit of faith;
patience is the bloom on the fruit.

— *Christina Rossetti*

1

*N*ahor cursed and spat. "It's just one night in the temple of the goddess. That's not going to hurt her saucy arrogance as far as I can see." He stood with his brother Haran on the river landing. It was before sunrise, and the mist rose around them, making it difficult to spot the barge as it pulled away. The brothers had just tallied a shipment of copper and diorite that was to be sent on to Dilmun in the gulf. The great city wall of Ur rose behind them in the darkness. The door leading back into their family warehouse remained open, giving the only light.

Haran didn't answer right away. He wasn't eager to face their father with the unwelcome news. He pushed his round felt hat back on his head, leaned against the railing, and pondered the dilemma. The water lapped softly against the steps leading down to the river. The odor of brine and rotting wood filled their nostrils. Somewhere in a distant courtyard a cock crowed, signaling the approaching dawn. At sunrise they had agreed to meet their father.

"The rites are cruel and you know it. You just don't want to face it," Haran said without looking up.

"Every virgin in the city has gone through this ritual, so why not our sister?"

"I'll tell you why," said Haran, whirling around to face Nahor. "Neither our father nor Abram will allow it."

"Abram isn't here and our father can be convinced." Nahor spoke with smug assurance. "Once he hears that the temple priests will buy no more idols from his shop, he'll have to give in."

Haran walked down a few steps and knelt to wash his hands in the swiftly flowing water. He lingered a moment. "The fresh water from the Zagros Mountains is beginning to flow," he said. "I can almost feel it pushing the briny water back into the gulf."

"Already?" Nahor lunged down the steps, pulled up the skirt of his robe, and squatted beside his brother. He held his hand in the river and smiled. "It's only been two days since the sacred rites were held on top of the ziggurat; just imagine, spring is already on its way."

"You believe all of that?"

"Why not?" Nahor said. "There's some kind of power there. A mystery man and the priestess coming together in a sacred marriage, and it seems to happen every time."

"But the mystery man disappears. I suspect he's sacrificed to the goddess in place of the king. At least that's what's whispered."

"But spring comes. There's fresh water to fill the irrigation ditches. The fields turn green and are filled with flowers." Nahor stood, lifted his fringed skirt, and wiped his hands. "The sun's up. It's time to go talk to our father."

Haran frowned as he walked slowly to the top of the stairs. "It's a miserable business. Our father dotes on her. Her mother's death almost killed him."

"He spoils her and you know it." Nahor stood at the bottom of the stairs, his dripping hands held out to his sides. He had never liked the new wife old Terah had taken after his own mother died. For no reason he could explain, her daughter, Sarai, was a constant irritation to him. He sneezed, rubbed his hands impatiently on his robe, and mounted the stairs. "Our mother gave him three healthy sons, and as far as I know, Father never grieved for her."

"Come now," chided Haran. "None of this is our sister's fault."

"If she doesn't make the sacrifice, it'll be her fault. We'll not only lose business, but the people of Ur will have nothing to do with us."

"I understand," said Haran. "I agree with you. It's just that I see the difficulty with our father and with Abram."

"I always say, if we're going to live in Ur, we have to do as the people here do. There's no other way."

The two brothers stood silently watching the sky slowly brighten as the mist lifted and vanished. They could see flecks of light touch clumps of palms on the far side of the river. Behind them, the night watchman whistled as he made his way along the top of the wall, no doubt heading home. The stork that had a nest at the corner of the wall stretched her wings and landed on the platform beside them. The brothers looked at each other and Nahor nodded. It was time to inform their father of their decision.

Nahor and Haran met their father as arranged in the reception room of the old warehouse. The room was plain, even austere, and had the odor of dried thyme and crushed coriander. The walls were thin, being made of sun-dried mud bricks and plastered over with mud, dung, and straw. The sagging shutters stood open as did the worn wooden door—a futile attempt to catch a little warmth from the sun. Large flies clustered around these openings and kept up a steady buzzing.

Terah was sitting cross-legged on a slightly raised dais covered with several sheepskins, his gnarled hands hovering over the leaping flame of the brazier to get them warm. He wore a motley assortment of layers, all stained and patched. The purple cloth he had wrapped around his head also served as a wrapping for his neck. His eyes were hooded and his nose an astonishing size, seeming to jut out from under the white tangle of eyebrows.

When Nahor and Haran stood before him, Terah spoke. His words shot out with a rare fierceness as he explained that as long as he had only sons there had been no problem. Now with his daughter, the very flower of his heart, he was being pressed into an impossible decision. "For Sarai," he said, "the rites would be cruel and terrifying."

When Terah stopped speaking, he motioned for his sons to sit down. They quickly obeyed and glanced at each other, not quite knowing how to begin. Finally Nahor spoke. "Our business is flourishing. We'd be foolish to let anything stand in our way." He looked from his father to Haran, challenging them to disagree. "I just hired some new artists who are clever with clay. We are in line for big profits," Nahor pressed on.

"Well," Haran fumed impatiently, "I can tell you right now Sarai won't go along with this if she knows what's going to happen."

Terah coughed and cleared his throat. His sons were immediately attentive, waiting for his opinion. They could tell by the set of his jaw, the way his eyes challenged them, and how his hands clasped and unclasped his measuring stick, that he was more upset than he had ever been in the past. "I know. I know very well the problem."

Haran fidgeted and frowned. "Up to the present we have been loyal subjects. My daughter Milcah would have taken part in the mysteries if Nahor hadn't married her."

Nahor raised his hand and interrupted. "It comes down to this. If we refuse, we can't expect the idols we make to be blessed by the goddess. If they aren't blessed, who will buy them?"

Terah's face clouded. "That's just the problem. The high priestess is standing firm on her decision. No family who refuses to make the sacrifices can continue to make idols."

"She has forgotten," Haran interjected, "we are not Sumerians, or black-headed ones, as they call themselves."

"That adds to our difficulty," Nahor said. "We're not part of them. If we want to be accepted, we must honor their customs."

Terah was impatiently jabbing at the hot coals in the brazier. "Such a strange custom. Why do they insist on it?"

Nahor hesitated, and when he spoke, there was a tone of awe in his voice. "They say it gives strength to the goddess. They swear that if a young virgin doesn't submit to the mysteries, she'll never bear children."

Terah was visibly shaken. He had forgotten this aspect of the rituals. "Then . . ." he said, "even though my daughter is beautiful . . ."

"Exactly. No Sumerian would marry her. They would have nothing to do with her, fearing she was cursed."

Terah's shoulders sagged and he dabbed at his eyes. "Now you see," he said, "it isn't simple. Not simple at all."

Nahor saw his father was weakening, and he jumped in to make the final point. "If we don't have Sarai there for the ceremony tonight, we'll lose the temple's business, and Sarai will never marry or have children."

"Then," Terah said, looking intently at Nahor, "you believe what they say?"

"Believe or not," Nahor said, "this will affect our business."

Terah had heard enough. He waved his hands wildly, signaling Nahor to stop. He wanted to end the discussion. There was a whole day before them and maybe he would think of something. He struggled to stand, and Nahor jumped up to help him.

"My father," he said, "don't worry. I have been to the temple and have chosen one of these women for a night. I couldn't see that it hurt her."

"But Sarai is so frivolous and strong-willed." Haran was now standing, and his face was twisted into a look of misery.

"I'll talk with the priestess . . . give her some silver. I'll make sure Sarai is treated right," Nahor said. "When this is over, Sarai will thank us. She can marry anyone in Ur, even a prince."

Terah had heard enough. Without another word he turned and walked out the door and headed in the direction of the temple and the market. The two brothers came to the doorway and watched him go. They stood in silence, thinking of all the complexities. Their sister Sarai was beautiful but head-strong, the darling of the entire family, and Terah—along with their older brother Abram—could refuse her nothing.

Abram was not to know of the scheme. He would never approve of it. In fact, ever since an experience none of them had been able to understand, Abram had been opposed to the family's business in idols. He wanted them to stick to trading. He'd gone back to the ways of the old religion.

"It's fortunate," Nahor said now, "that Abram is safely off on a trading venture and won't be back until the fertility festival is over. By that time Sarai will probably be happily married to a wealthy man in Ur."

To everyone's relief, Sarai did not balk at the invitation. Her brothers told her that she was to take part in the temple mysteries. When she asked more questions, they were evasive. The temple mysteries were always referred to with raised eyebrows and blushes, but the secrets were never divulged so she knew nothing of the sacrifice. She tried on the fine linen robe with many fringes, the caplet of silver leaves, and the new sandals with golden thongs and then paraded back and forth before the serving girls.

"The goddess will find you beautiful," one of the young girls said, clapping her hands in delight.

"Better that Abram were here to see me. He always treats me as a child."

A serving maid smirked and said, "He won't think you a child after tonight."

Sarai stopped preening and frowned. "No one believes me when I say I love Abram." She looked around and saw their unbelieving expressions. She felt put out and contrary. In a burst of frustration she countered, "Someday I intend to marry him."

An old woman cackled with amusement, "After tonight you won't need Abram's love. You can marry anyone in Ur." Sarai fingered the fringes and brushed a strand of hair back under the caplet. "I don't want anyone else."

"Even a prince?" the women chorused.

Sarai laughed. "A prince? A Sumerian prince?"

"Why not?" the old woman said. "Every young virgin hopes to marry one of Ur's princes."

Sarai made circles with her fingers around her eyes. "They have big eyes and ugly shaved heads, and they are all fat."

"And Abram..."

"Oh, he's handsome and strong. He isn't afraid of anything or anyone." Everyone laughed as though it was a good joke. Abram was ten years older than Sarai and her half-brother. Though he was exactly as Sarai described him, still each girl assumed, given the chance, Sarai would choose a prince.

Once more she was the center of attention. Maids whirled around the room trying to grant her every wish, and she, giddy with excitement, joked and posed in the new garments until she was bored with the whole affair.

Sarai dropped the elaborate headpiece on one little slave's head and thrust the fine robe and fancy slippers into another's lap. "I'll be back to get ready, but I have other things to do now." Laughing, she turned to leave and was surprised to see her favorite maid blinking back tears and the others turning away so she couldn't see their expressions.

"What's wrong?" she chided as she stepped back into the room. "Why is everyone so sad?"

When no one answered, she snatched up the small image that had no body but sported two large eyes. "See, no evil djinn can harm me as long as I carry the eyes of the goddess. She sees everything." She whirled around so that the eyes seemed to look in all directions.

The slaves and serving maids had to laugh. Impulsively they gathered around her, kissing her hands and the hem of her robe. "Surely only good will come to you tonight," her maid whispered. "The goddess will be merciful. She will be pleased with your offering."

Sarai tore herself away from them, and tucking the image of the eyes in the fold of her fringed robe, she joked, "Enough, the eyes have seen enough if I am to be approved by the goddess." With that she left them, and it was only later, much later, that she remembered their tears and understood.

Sarai loved attention. When evening finally came and all the women gathered to see that she was dressed as befitted Terah's daughter, she preened and paraded before them like one of the family's peacocks.

Her robe was of the finest linen brought from Egypt on one of Terah's trading ventures. Her caplet of silver leaves was the work of a royal artisan, and the jewelry she wore was chosen from the chest of family jewels hidden in the secret alcove beneath the stairs.

At last her father's concubine brought her a bracelet of copper inset with jade and lapis lazuli. "Be brave and do whatever is asked of you and all will be well. Remember it is only one night," she said.

Sarai had been so excited, she paid little attention to the words but instead went from one admiring group to another, showing off the new bracelet. It was obvious she had loved every bit of the preparation, from the anointing with fragrant oil to the procession of dancers and magicians that came to lead her to the temple of Ningal at the foot of the ziggurat.

Terah, the brothers Nahor and Haran, a few of the slaves, and Terah's concubine followed behind the procession, keeping a careful watch so that no harm should come to Sarai.

When they came to the great gate leading into the temple, the guards insisted that only Sarai and the slaves bearing her sedan chair might enter. For the first time Sarai felt a twinge of apprehension. It was too dark to see any of her family. Most of the torches had burned out, and she could make out only a large, dimly lit courtyard. The gate slammed behind her with a harsh, grating sound. Quickly she was carried through a mob of impatient men who were milling around and making crude remarks. The chair was set down in a cleared space before the venerated temple of Ningal, the earth goddess. Sarai peered into the shadows and saw a group of young women huddled together on a clay bench built out from the temple wall.

Without a word being said, one of the priestesses came and led her to a place on the bench. "What do we do now?" Sarai asked. "What does this mean?"

The priestess seemed to be surprised at her question. "I see," she said at last, "you are not one of us. You are not a Sumerian." She waved her hand toward the clumps of men. "You will wait here until you are chosen by one of them," she said. "He will pay the goddess for your favors."

Sarai had trouble comprehending just what the priestess meant. She couldn't imagine the delightful preparation and all the excitement were to lead to this. She sank down on the clay bench and turned to the young girl next to her. "What's to happen?" she asked.

"We're to sacrifice our virginity to the great goddess," the girl whispered.

"I know that," Sarai said, "but what does that mean?"

The girl looked at Sarai in surprise, then whispered, "It means we will be chosen by strangers who will pay the goddess the price of our virginity."

"And then what?" Sarai demanded with growing apprehension.

"We must go with the man into the temple. He can do with us as he pleases," the girl said, blushing.

Sarai suddenly understood enough to be alarmed. "Must we be chosen?" she asked. "Is everyone chosen?"

"If a person isn't chosen, the price is lowered until even a poor beggar can afford the unfortunate girl."

Sarai noticed with mounting disgust that the ribald crowd of men had pushed forward to look over the offerings for the night. Most of them were old enough to be her father. Some wore strange garments of other countries. They were traders looking for entertainment, and they had the money required. Others were from Ur and wore the typical fringed garment and had the usual shaved head and bulging eyes.

One old man, obviously wealthy, leaned heavily on a slave's arm while pointing with a long, bony finger at first one girl and then another.

"He's trying to decide which of us he wants," the girl next to Sarai explained. "He'll get his choice. You'll see, he'll get his choice."

Sarai was indignant. "I don't care who he is or what the priestess wants, I won't go with any of them no matter what they pay."

At that moment the old man pointed at Sarai and then prodded the young slave to lead him over for a better look. Sarai shrank back. Her hands clung to the bench with such force her knuckles turned white. The old man had to lean down to get a closer look. For a moment the torchlight glinted on his shaved head and greedy, lustful eyes. His clothes were of rich embroidery and fringed, but reeked of garlic and wine.

He was about to reach out and test the firmness of Sarai's arm when several young men pushed him aside. They, too, had settled on Sarai. With crude jokes and obscene gestures they tried to get her attention.

Sarai eyed them defiantly, but that seemed only to make them more interested. The young priestess in charge noticed and raised the price on Sarai until some of them backed off.

"It won't be so bad," the girl next to Sarai whispered. "If we are fortunate, the high priestess herself will come to bless us and give us one of the small images for good luck. There will be entertainment before we are finally chosen."

No sooner had she spoken than a sudden commotion arose near the great bronze doors of the temple. From inside could be heard trumpets, then chanting, and at last a grating, grinding sound as the huge doors slowly opened. The singing and chanting grew louder and louder. From the doorway came a great burst of blinding light and flames, then smoke billowed out into the court-yard, carrying with it the pleasant odor of sandalwood. In the midst of the smoke an apparition of female beauty appeared. Most of the men and many of the women fell to their knees and wept for joy, crying, "Inanna, Inanna, queen of heaven, give us blessing."

She wore a crown of sparkling jewels and a garment of such dazzling white that no fuller could claim credit. The garment was decorated with only a jeweled girdle, and her feet, fragile as alabaster, were enclosed in golden, jeweled slippers.

"The queen of heaven. It's the queen of heaven," whispered the people in awe.

Sarai had not bowed; instead she looked with intense curiosity at this woman who was the high priestess of Inanna, the queen of Ur. The high priestess moved out to join one of the young priestesses who carried a basket on her arm filled with small images of the goddess. The high priestess proceeded to give each young woman one as a talisman to bring her luck and good fortune in love. Each time she handed one to a girl, she would say, "May the earth goddess, Ningal, be pleased with your offering and make you fruitful."

Sarai was surprised that the hands of the high priestess belied the youthful impression she created. She was much older than she at first appeared. Looking more closely, Sarai noticed hard lines around her mouth and saw that her eyes were glazed as though she was not really seeing anything.

Sarai took the small image from her and sat studying it. To her confusion and astonishment, she saw that the image was quite familiar. She had seen hundreds like it being crafted in her father's shop.

She had no time to think about the strangeness of her discovery because at that moment the young priestess began to pass through the men with a large bronze pot. There was much discussion and at times tough bargaining as each man picked out the young woman of his choice. With a flourish he dropped the gold pieces in the pot, claimed the young girl, and disappeared into the dark, shadowed entrance of the temple.

Sarai was fifth in the line and could see that it would be but a short time before the old man would drop his coins in the pot and come to claim her. She broke into a sweat and angrily peered into the darkness, looking for a familiar face. Where were her brothers or her father? How could they leave her here? How could they desert her, knowing what they must know?

She saw the leering stance of the old man as he fumbled in his belt for the coins. He handed them to the young slave and waved his cane at the priestess, demanding that he be next.

Sarai jumped up, ready to object, and dropped the small clay image. As it hit the cobblestones of the court, one short arm broke off and rolled under the bench. Instantly the air was filled with wailing and shrieking as a dozen young priestesses rushed to pick up the broken image.

"It is an omen," they shrieked. "The goddess is angry." They turned and glared at Sarai and were about to insist that she go with the old man.

Suddenly there was a disturbance at the gate, followed by shouting. A band of armed men pushed their way into the courtyard. Their leader, who was tall and handsome and had a reckless air about him, stepped forward into the light. He looked boldly around as though challenging the crowd, and then with long, sure strides he walked to the priestess holding the brass pot.

With a thrill of recognition Sarai stepped forward. It was Abram. She hesitated as she saw him take a pouch from his belt and pour its contents into his hand. Then while they all watched in stunned amazement, he let the gold slip through his fingers slowly so they would know he was paying a good price.

For a brief moment he looked at the priestess. Turning, he strode over to where Sarai was standing. He took her in his arms, and she clung to him with all hauteur gone, only unabashed relief evident. Then holding her at arm's length, he asked if she was all right. Sarai nodded and noticed that his eyes were tender and filled with compassion.

Motioning to his men to lead the way, he started toward the gate with Sarai. Suddenly fierce-looking temple guards blocked the way, their lances drawn. At the same time everyone heard a deafening clap of cymbals and a roll of deep thundering drums. Smoke began to pour from the temple doorway. As the smoke cleared, out of the darkness emerged a figure of fearful demeanor. There was no doubt it was the high priestess of Ningal.

All talk ceased as men and women fell to their knees and bowed their faces to the ground. Only Abram and Sarai remained standing, and Sarai, terrified, cringed behind Abram and covered her eyes.

The priestess was tall and thin, with hair coiled round with snakeskins so it looked like a mass of writhing snakes. Unlike the priestess of Inanna, she was the image of power and gave off the aura of dark deeds and hidden mysteries.

Her garment was elaborately fringed, and on her head she wore a domed headpiece decorated with the horns of young bulls. From her hands hung a magical gaggle of bones, bat wings, and dried mandrake roots.

Most frightening of all was the mask of a snake's head she wore over her face, leaving only her eyes showing. They were glowing like two hot coals, and from behind the mask came a sound like the hissing of a cobra.

She came forward, all the time making the hissing sound and at times the sound of rattlers. Her movements were smooth and practiced, almost slithering. When Abram stood his ground, her eyes behind the mask became dark and foreboding, and as the hissing sound stopped, she raised her arm, pointed at Sarai, and demanded, "Where are you going with this woman?"

"She is my sister, and I'm taking her home where she belongs."

"Belongs? She belongs here. She must make the sacrifice or be cursed."

Instead of being frightened, Abram looked amused. "What or who gives you the right to curse?"

The high priestess, trembling with rage, pulled off the snake mask, revealing features hard, menacing, and feral. Her eyes blazed with indignation as she pointed one long finger at Sarai and through clenched teeth spat out her most frightening curse, "By the authority of the great goddess of Ur, I, her high priestess, curse anyone who leaves without sacrificing."

"A curse?" Abram questioned. "What curse does Ningal give to one who has done no wrong?"

"Curse! I curse her with barrenness. Her womb will be filled with evil spirits, her arms forever empty."

Abram hesitated only a moment while Sarai stood paralyzed, the burning eyes of the high priestess and the terrible word barren ringing in her ears.

Abram drew himself up until he towered over the high priestess and in a composed voice spoke, "We have no fear of your curses. We are not worshipers of your gods." With that he turned, took Sarai by the hand, and proceeded to elbow his way past the astonished guards and through the crowd as they parted before him.

Only once did Sarai look back. She saw the priestess; her feet planted wide apart, her long finger pointing ominously at her as the words she spewed burned like fire.

"Barren! I curse you with barrenness! I curse you with an eternal curse in the name of the great goddess Ningal!" Again and again she shouted, then chanted the terrible words. "You will never have a child. Ningal will never bless you. I have cursed you in her magic name." The eyes of the priestess were wild and terrible, and Sarai knew she would never be free of them or the words she had spoken.

By the time they reached home, Sarai was hysterical. She clung to Abram and at first refused to let any of the servants near her. "It was terrible," she shouted at the women. "You made it seem so exciting. You made it sound like an honor."

The women backed away, and only Terah's concubine responded. "You are back early," she said with a twinge of accusation in her voice. "You didn't make the sacrifice."

"Make the sacrifice!" Sarai said, whirling around and glaring at her. "It was terrible. Nothing exciting like you made it seem."

The concubine stood with her hands on her hips as she rolled her eyes in unbelief. "If you didn't make the sacrifice, I can imagine it was quite unpleasant."

At the concubine's words Sarai burst into tears and could not be comforted. She clung to Abram's arm and hid her face in the folds of his sleeve.

The concubine shrugged and turned to Abram. "What happened? Obviously she didn't stay for the sacrifice."

"I paid the price and rescued her," Abram said as he put his arm around Sarai as though to protect her from further attack. "I can't imagine who would do this to Sarai. She's completely devastated."

"Do this to Sarai!" the concubine sniffed. "Is she better than the rest of us?"

Abram ignored her challenge and turned to Sarai's old nurse. "Here," he said, "brew her some warm honey and herbs and put her to bed. No doubt a good sleep will help more than all this talk."

To everyone's relief, Sarai stopped sobbing and followed her nurse back to the sleeping rooms.

When they were gone, the concubine turned to Abram. "A sorry mess you've made of things," she said. "Now the poor girl will never marry, and if she ever does, she'll never have a child."

Abram didn't answer but turned and walked toward the door with long, sure strides. He stopped only once to look at all of them and to make sure Sarai had left, then he pushed through the door, letting it bang with an ominous thud behind him.

Only after Abram was assured that Sarai had finally gone to sleep did he come to face his father and the brothers. They had heard everything and were embarrassed and indignant. They felt that Abram had disgraced the family "How can we live here among these people?" Terah said with hands out pleading. "We may not understand their gods or their customs, but we are here as strangers—guests. We must try to fit in."

"It was only for one night. It wouldn't have hurt her," said Nahor.

"She could have married a rich man or a prince. Now there is no one," said Haran.

Abram looked around at them and squared his shoulders defiantly. "We are not as the Sumerians. We will never be and we need not try."

Terah spoke with a great effort. He seemed to have aged in the few minutes they had been engaged in the discussion. "If we don't fit in, it will be hard to succeed at anything here in Ur. We may even have to leave."

For a few moments Abram said nothing. When he finally spoke, it was with sadness but a note of authority that surprised his brothers. "We may have to leave but how much better to leave than have our own family destroyed by the evil around us."

"Evil?" Haran asked with a slight smirk.

"Yes, evil," Abram said, looking him in the eye until his brother turned away and his father left with drooping shoulders, greatly disturbed.

A fortnight later the family was still divided over the matter of the idols and Sarai's traumatic experience. Abram had tried to explain to them an astonishing revelation that had come to him with such force and veracity that he now saw everything differently.

Terah and the brothers tried again and again to explain to Abram that it made no difference how one worshiped or who was worshiped. The moon god Nanna was in control of many things in nature and it seemed logical to worship him. It was also noised about that men and women who prayed to the little clay images had some astounding stories of answered prayers.

"Surely so many people can't be wrong," Nahor said.

"The images are simple things of clay made by humble men," Abram objected.

"But who's to say they don't possess wonderful magic to drive away the evil spirits and bring good luck, especially when they are fashioned to the high priest's specifications and are blessed with a touch of his oil?" Terah said.

The arguments always ended with someone reminding Abram that they had lost a good bit of business already because of his foolishness, and Sarai—in spite of her beauty—would never be married. "Our most lucrative business is in images for Ningal's feasts. Now she will have nothing to do with us," they said.

Abram was frustrated that his father and brothers could be so blind. Since the new revelation, it had seemed illogical that something molded out of ordinary clay could be a god worthy of prayers and worship.

He was thinking along these lines early one morning as he made his way down to his father's warehouse and workrooms. The workrooms were at the end of a narrow lane leading into a section of the city called the Karem. Traders and artisans clustered in this section of the city. High mud walls rose on each side of the lane. Here and there were worn wooden doors that led into the courtyards, workrooms, and storage areas of the city.

When Abram came to the familiar door of his father's shop, he found the wooden bolt still in place, which meant that neither his father nor the workmen had arrived. He was familiar with the bolt, and within minutes he had the door open and was stooping down to enter the courtyard now flooded with early morning light.

He glanced into the room where the fresh clay was kept and then into the next room where the potters' wheels stood ready and waiting for the first work of the day. Finally he came to the larger room where the finished idols were displayed. There were smaller images that could be hidden in a man's hand, then larger ones that would stand in a niche by a front door. A large, well-formed image of the god Nanna was his father's prize piece and one he hoped to sell to a smaller temple for a good price.

Impulsively Abram reached out and twisted off an ear from one of the idols and held it in his hand. It was nothing but common clay, and the idol made no move to defend himself. He jabbed out the jeweled eyes of another and broke off the arm of a third. All the time he muttered, "They neither see nor hear nor speak, and none of them can feel a thing."

In a sudden burst of frustration he flung his arm out and swept all the small idols off their shelves onto the floor where he watched them break into unrecognizable bits of pottery. Then he grabbed a stick from behind the door and jabbed and pushed one after another of the larger idols off their pedestals onto the floor where they lay in miserable heaps of rubble. A wonderful feeling of elation swept over him as he felt justified in all that he had done. Surely now his father would understand. Surely he could see that one must be as wise in worship as in trading. A god so fragile was no god at all.

At that moment he heard his father coming along the narrow lane outside. Abram looked around and realized that it would be hard for his father to get any real lesson from the devastation. He would think only of the hours involved, the money paid to the artisans, and the profit lost. Quickly Abram reached for the stick and thrust it into the outstretched hands of the large idol he had not destroyed.

Seldom had anyone seen Terah surprised or caught off guard. Now he was shocked and dismayed. He kicked at pieces of the rubble and circled the rooms, all the while shaking his head in disbelief. It was almost as though he wasn't aware that anyone else was in the room. "How did this happen? Who could have done such a thing?" he muttered with a glance at Abram.

"My father," Abram replied quickly, "don't you see? The big idol did it. The stick is in his hands."

"What foolishness are you talking?" Terah said, turning with an accusing look to his son. "How could such a thing made of clay move at all, let alone destroy all the idols?"

Abram hesitated only a moment, then with a knowing look, he said, "No more foolish, I would say, than to expect this idol made of clay to answer prayers."

Terah looked surprised, then a bit sheepish as he admitted, "Maybe you have a bit of wisdom there. Perhaps we have gone too far in following the Sumerians."

"We have indeed gone too far when we offer our children to their gods and goddesses."

"Who among us would offer a child to the god or goddess of the Sumerians?" Terah stood up straight and glared at Abram with an obvious sense of indignation.

"Have you forgotten Sarai?" Abram countered with a surprising tone of defiance.

Usually once Terah spoke, no one contradicted him. He thumped his cane on the floor in annoyance and sputtered, "Your brothers are right to be angry. You thought you rescued Sarai, but you have only placed the rope of barrenness around her neck. If we were Sumerians, she would become a prostitute. That's what they do with the barren ones. My poor Sarai. What's to become of her now?" Quickly his tone changed as he sank down on the stone bench and hid his face in his hands.

"Father," Abram said, "I plan to marry Sarai myself."

Terah looked up in surprise. "How . . . I don't understand?"

"Because she is my sister? I know this isn't usual among us as it is in Egypt, but Sarai and I have different mothers. More important, we are all strangers here among these people. It is best if we marry among ourselves."

Terah smiled. He realized Abram's remark was a strike at his own marriage to a Sumerian. At the same time he saw that the marriage was right for Sarai. She wouldn't have to leave her home and her people. To give a daughter to foreigners was risky. If they didn't treat her right, one was helpless to interfere without bloodshed. Terah slowly got to his feet and embraced Abram. Then with genuine warmth he said, "My son, at times you are a puzzle to me, but I must admit you have gladdened my heart more than all my other children."

* * *

Like Nahor's marriage to Milcah, the daughter of Haran, Abram's marriage to Sarai was simple. There was no agreement between father and bridegroom, only the feasting and celebration with the formal moving of Sarai and Abram to their own rooms in Terah's large house.

Terah was happier than he had been in a long time. This marriage was obviously just what Sarai really wanted, and he knew that Abram was at last content. "Perhaps now he'll be so occupied with his new wife that he won't be bothering with the stars and our ancient God," he said to the brothers.

With the joyful event it seemed that all their troubles were at an end. But when the months and then several years went by and Sarai gave no sign of becoming pregnant, old questions returned. Not only their neighbors but Abram's brothers began to believe that Sarai was cursed and would never have a child.

Terah tried to encourage them. But he often heard Sarai weeping in the night and saw Abram looking grim and burdened.

"She cursed me, the priestess of Ningal cursed me, and I'll never have a child," Sarai said over and over as she wiped the tears from her eyes.

"It's proof the goddess has strange powers," the people of Ur would say and in time the brothers and even Terah hesitantly agreed.

Only Abram refused to go along with the pronouncement. "It isn't the moon or the moon god or Ningal, his consort, that sends children," he said. "It is Elohim, the Creator God, who holds life in his hands." He would say this, knowing that people first laughed at him, then pitied him. He chafed at their scorn. He even grew angry at times with his God, the all-powerful Elohim. He could easily give them a child, but he seemed to withhold his blessing even when it would have silenced his enemies.

Terah pondered the situation often. Whether Ningal's curse had harmed Sarai only time would tell. Now he had to live with the burden of neighbors and friends who firmly believed in Ningal's curse. "We may have to leave Ur to find peace," he concluded. Then thinking of his warehouses, the trade he had spent a lifetime building, and the comfort they all lived in, he rationalized, "It would be difficult to leave. It would be costly. We have nowhere to go. In time, people will forget, and Sarai may have a child."

The people didn't forget, and life in Ur became more and more difficult for Terah and his family. At the same time their caravans covered wide areas and brought back even greater wealth to Ur and to the family of Terah. Their business in idols prospered, even without the blessing of the priestess of Ningal, and the family found it more and more difficult to consider leaving Ur. All but Abram determined to accept the unpleasantness. "Where would we go?" they asked each other. "There's no place where a woman is welcome who cannot bear children."

It was true that at times, when tossing restlessly upon his straw mat and listening for the call of the night watchman on the wall, Terah felt what he called a divine nudge to leave. It was persistent and strong, but never with real direction as to where they were to go or why. However, the next morning with the first cock crow and the new sun rising, he would think better of it.

If it had not been for a major tragedy, an emergency of enormous proportions, they might never have left. Such a disaster came suddenly and unexpectedly, and life in Ur was never to be the same again.

2

*T*he crisis came on them suddenly. It was first rumored, then confirmed, that the fierce, barbaric Elamites from beyond the Tigris were preparing for battle and Ur was their target. The Elamites, who lived in the Zagros Mountains, had marched against Ur before and had been soundly defeated. "This time," they boasted, "will be different."

Ur was already suffering from a variety of disasters. First, the Amorites from the western desert had attacked them and claimed their outlying fortresses. Then there had been a poor harvest so they were forced to import grains and pay the inflated price of 144,000 gur for 10,000 tons. The birthing of their cattle had fallen off, and trade had slackened.

With all of these unfortunate happenings, many had been completely unnerved as they heard reports of Elamite soothsayers who foretold victory for the Elamites. "The stars," the Elamites were saying, "are aligned for our success and the readings in water and in the goat's liver confirm it."

Day by day the tension increased. It could be witnessed everyplace. The temples were crowded with supplicants. In the market and at the gates, men lingered to discuss the news while women exchanged predictions of doom as they drew water at the wells. Even the children clung to their parents and cried out in the night for fear of the Elamites.

When news came that one of Elam's most powerful magicians had taken a rope and tied it in ten knots, declaring that in ten days Ur would be decimated and their king taken captive, most of the people of Ur gave up all hope.

Despite all of this, some people in Ur trusted in their powerful moon god, Nanna. Or put their faith in the mercenaries their king, Ibbi-Suen, had sent out against the barbaric horde. "They have never been able to defeat us," they boasted. "You will see. These fiends will be turned back."

Terah and his son Abram disagreed with these optimists, but Haran and Nahor were skeptical. They tended to believe the priests of Nanna, who insisted their omens predicted a victory for Ur. According to these priests, the readings of the goat's liver, the stars, and the entrails of sacrificed animals all foretold defeat for the Elamites.

Just after sunrise, in the month of U-Ne-ku—the month of the gathering of seed—Terah was discussing the latest news with Haran and Nahor. They were sitting cross-legged on thick, goat-hair rugs in the reception room off their large warehouse. The two sons were trying to convince their father there was nothing to worry about. "In the past," said Nahor, "the Elamites have never even breached our walls."

"But as Abram says," Terah objected, "this time the Elamites are more determined and better prepared. They see us as rich from trade, and they know we have just imported more grain."

At mention of the old man's eldest and favorite son, Nahor bit his lip and nervously toyed with the measuring stick he still held in his hand. Haran stood up. "I suppose Abram's the one who has gotten you all upset," he said testily. "We'll have a good laugh when he's proven wrong."

Terah didn't answer but picked up a crudely glazed bowl filled with steaming barley gruel. Then holding it between his hands, he sipped with loud enjoyment. Both sons knew they must wait for him to finish if they were to hear his response. Finally, having set the bowl down on the reed tray, he waved some flies away and motioned for the servant.

Terah took his time wiping his mouth on the edge of his fringed robe and then leaned back and looked at his two sons. His eyes were those of an astute bargainer, while his large Semitic nose betrayed his background and kept him from totally fitting in with the Sumerians. "Abram is right. The Elamites have been getting stronger. They may not be so easy to turn back this time."

The brothers looked at each other and then back at their father. They wanted to tell him how they resented some of the things Abram had done. They and their wives had always tried so hard to fit in and be a part of everything. Act too different, they reasoned, and you just brought on enemies. Abram didn't worry about such things. He had always gone his own way and ignored Sumerian traditions.

Haran, being older, spoke, "My honored father, we know that Abram is sharp in bargaining and can outwit the cleverest trader. In spite of offending the Sumerians, they accept and even seem to prefer him at their feasts and celebrations. But to us they complain. They want to know how he can stand against all of them and their customs, even their gods."

Terah seemed not to be listening, but when Haran finished, he challenged them, "Your problem is that you don't see how clever your brother is. He's brilliant, and this sometimes gets him in trouble."

"Brilliant?" Nahor said, the frustration evident in his voice. "How's it brilliant to defy everyone and act as though you're the only one who's right?"

Terah cackled with a dry rasping tone of amusement that annoyed both brothers. "Don't you see? He's the only one who dared come out and say the idols made in my shop were nothing but stone or clay and couldn't help anyone."

"He could have kept his thoughts to himself," Haran said. "He didn't have to crush the idols. We lost valuable trade, and he barely escaped having their priests put his feet to the fire."

"It may have been foolhardy," Terah admitted with obvious smugness, "but he wasn't afraid of the people or their clay gods. He isn't afraid . . . like the rest of us."

Nahor bristled. He hated it when his father took Abram's side and even appeared to admire him for what he'd done. "There have been times," he said with an effort at control, "when it would have served us and our sister, Sarai, better if he had been afraid."

At that the old man grew terribly disturbed, waved his cane, and ordered them help him to his feet. "You know that's a subject we'll never discuss. I forbid it to be mentioned." He was shaking all over and pounding his cane on the mud brick floor. All the time he was looking at them from under his craggy eyebrows, eyes hard as flint.

Nahor knew he had gone too far. The trouble over Sarai and the priestesses of Inanna and the goddess Ningal had almost killed their father. Still, Nahor found it impossible to resist one last thrust. "I hope he's right. If not, we'll all look foolish. Already everyone is laughing at us for moving our cattle farther north and even our families out of the city."

He didn't get a chance to say more. Terah stiffened and, with eyes still blazing, thundered his frustration, "And if he's right, if the Elamites do destroy everything, we'll be the only ones prepared. You'll see how brilliant your brother is then."

Nahor was ashamed that he had deliberately riled his father, while Haran, remembering it was getting late, hurriedly excused himself. He said that he was going to the central market to hear the latest news.

As was the custom, Haran took the old man's hand, pressed it to his lips, then left. He stood silhouetted in the doorway for just a moment as though wishing to say some final word. Apparently thinking better of it, he turned and disappeared into the bright morning sunlight.

The old man sank back among the dusty cushions. He was exhausted with the effort his rage had caused him. It was not his custom to get so upset. He suffered from no illusions. He knew that both Haran and Nahor trusted in the wise men of Ur and their gods. They were always repeating the encouraging predictions and ignoring any ominous news coming out of Elam.

Just a week earlier, a trader who had come through the Elamite capital of Shushan had told how the men there had been practicing war games. They were fighting huge lions with only their daggers and shields to defend themselves and walking about the streets completely dressed for battle with their quilted helmets and large shields. "All the talk in their markets is of war," he warned.

"You mustn't get so disturbed, my father," Nahor said. "Our rulers know what is happening. They have conquered large parts of Elam. They have made agreements, even marrying some of their royal women in pledge. More than that, our walls are high, and our god is more powerful."

Terah listened, but his blood ran cold as he visualized these wild, undisciplined barbarians successfully breaching the walls and breaking down the gates. They could take over the city before anyone knew what was happening. Very few took the threat seriously, and no one was prepared. "Only Abram sees things as they are," he muttered, "and with him it isn't logic. He talks about some warning, some nudge from the Elohim, the God most people have forgotten."

Suddenly the sound of running, of bare feet hitting hard on the cobbled street just outside the door, broke the early morning silence. Urgent and fearful voices rose and fell in the distant lanes and along the wall. Then finally, clear and strong, cutting the early morning fog, came the piercing, shrieking blast of silver trumpets that signaled danger. Terah sat alert while Nahor jumped to his feet, clearly alarmed. Sounds that seemed to come from the ziggurat were answered by guards on the city's walls. The sharp, quick blasts were followed by ones more wild and eerie, a frantic call to attention and action.

As the sound grew in intensity, it seemed to come from all directions. It was the announcement of approaching disaster, the warning of victorious Elamites moving in triumph across the plain. They had not been stopped by Ur's mercenaries sent out against them.

Both Terah and Nahor were stunned. Even now the gates were probably being closed and barricaded while the walls would be alive with the bowmen of Ur.

Before either Terah or Nahor could form a plan of action, a figure loomed in the doorway. It was Abram. He was out of breath from running. "Don't be alarmed," he said. "We have to be calm and think clearly. I was with the guards on the wall. Our mercenaries are fleeing before the Elamite hordes. They cover the land like locusts."

Nahor rang his hands in fear. "What are we to do? Where are we to go?"

Abram didn't answer but calmly helped Terah to his feet and stood holding his arm to steady him. Terah looked at his son with pride. Even in the midst of this emergency Abram was dressed in every aspect like the Sumerian dignitaries. His robe had as many fringes as theirs, and he wore it as they did—fastened on one shoulder with his right arm bare.

When Abram spoke, he was calm, and his voice rang with decided authority. "We'll have to leave immediately. I have the mules ready. The women and our men are waiting for us outside the city."

"But how will we go? How can we leave?" Nahor was terrified. "It won't be safe to leave now."

Abram helped Terah mount the mule he'd brought as he said, "Terah knows the plan. We'll have to go to our grazing land up the river where I have put in supplies. We have to hurry or it will be too late."

"The gates will be closed," Nahor said as his teeth chattered in fear.

"You're right. We have to hurry," Abram said, not bothering to remind Nahor that he had urged him to leave a fortnight ago.

On every side people were screaming in panic and pushing their way through the narrow streets looking for children and family. Others, still curious, were crowded onto the rooftops or clustered on the steps leading to the top of the wall. The smell and feel of terror were everywhere.

"Where's Haran?" Abram shouted over the din as he was about to get on his own mule.

"He went to the market square to hear the news." Nahor's eyes were wide with fright, and his hands trembled as he tried to steady the mule.

"The market? Are you sure?" Abram's voice registered alarm.

Terah nodded. "It was the news. He wanted to hear the news."

Abram hesitated only a moment. He had to think fast. He couldn't leave without his brother, and yet to delay could mean they wouldn't be able to get out. "Nahor," he said, "you'll have to take our father and be in charge. I'm going to look for Haran."

Terah reached out toward his favorite son, and Nahor opened his mouth to object. But Abram gave both mules a sharp tap that sent them lunging in the direction of the western gate.

The streets were so crowded with people running, screaming, and carrying small children or household treasures that Abram couldn't ride. He had to walk.

He headed out of the Karem, the familiar section of warehouses along the river, and plunged into the narrow lanes that wove in and out among the older, poorer houses. He came at last to the western gate. Already the soldiers were trying to close it but were finding it impossible. Too many people were pushing, elbowing, and shouting as they tried to get in to where they hoped to find safety. Abram breathed a sigh of relief. Nahor and his father would have been able to escape, and he hoped they were well on their way out of danger.

As he elbowed his way through the crowds, he came at last to the market. A veritable riot was in progress. Awnings were pulled down; storage bins gaped open; the baker's oven held only dying coals; the potter's wheel was still. People fought over every morsel of food, and Abram realized they were at last preparing frantically for a long siege.

He climbed up on a low wall and looked around. If Haran were in the market, he should be able to see him. Instead he saw one of the cheese makers named Urim. "Have you seen Haran?" he shouted over the uproar but was drowned out by another blast of the trumpets from the ziggurat. They sounded wild and discordant, a warning that the walls were about to be breached.

Abram fought his way through the crowd but found that Urim had disappeared. He felt himself carried along helplessly with the force of the crowd down the main street toward the walled-in temple area. He realized the people were fleeing to the one place they thought was secure, Nanna's temple and holy mountain. He also realized that was the first place the Elamites would ravage if they could. To conquer the holy mountain and take the king and the image of Nanna captive would be to win the city with very little effort.

Glancing around, Abram spotted Urim again. He was shouting to him from the rooftop of one of the houses that overlooked the great gate leading into the temple area. While Abram struggled to hear, he found himself suddenly pulled out of the crowd and pushed halfway up the steps leading to the roof. The noise was deafening, and he could only nod his thanks.

From his new vantage point he could see and hear everything. It was no longer the sound of their own trumpets that rent the air. It was the crude, eerie blast of Elamite rams' horns. The strident wail was ominous and penetrating. It seemed to rush at the frantic people from all directions. Then above the wailing of the horns came the bloodcurdling shout of victory. It was as he had feared. The Elamites had breached the walls and were inside the city.

Immediately people pushed and struggled to reverse their direction. They had come face to face with Elamites, who advanced with poised spears ready to strike.

In wave after wave they came, their bare feet stomping on the hard-packed earth while here and there standards were raised to show the moving horde where next to attack. Most frightening was the inhuman sound of their hoarse voices thundering their victory chant.

With surprising swiftness they had raised their standard above the bronze gates to the temple area, and the barbaric hordes plunged onto the holy ground of temples, palaces, and ziggurat with no regard for its sanctity.

Abram stood and watched in amazement as the rough Elamite tribesmen swarmed over the ziggurat. They quickly climbed the steps that led to the first level, then on they rushed to the next until they had climbed the one hundred steps to the holy shrine at the top. They started tearing off the wooden doors covered with heavy gold and inlaid with agate and lapis lazuli. They snatched up the golden vessels, spilled the priceless incense and spices, smashed the delicate instruments for observing the stars, and fought over the ornate robes of the priests.

A gasp of horror went through the crowd as jubilant, strutting trumpeters, followed by a band of taunting standard bearers, advanced in front of three men carrying the sacred image of Nanna. Divested of royal robes, the god now looked like a plump, somewhat dumpy carving of cypress wood.

Though Abram had long recognized the idols for what they were, even he was astounded. How was it possible that the great Nanna, who was believed to be the all-powerful god of divination, decider of human fate, controller of the moon with its growing and shrinking, could be so unceremoniously hustled out the gate by young beardless vandals? It was an unthinkable affront to all that the citizens of Ur held dear.

Amid ribald jokes and obscene antics, one of the captains dragged Ibbi-Suen, the exalted king of Ur and greater Sumer, out to stand before the mob. He was blindfolded and in chains, tormented and spat upon.

Abram had seen enough. While the attention was focused on the events at the gate, he could move quickly to find Haran. He turned and thanked the cheese maker, then made his way down the steps. He dodged in and out among the fleeing people, pushing his way along the wall until he reached a small door. Some instinct told him that he would find Haran within the temple area. There Haran had studied the stars as did Abram, and he had enjoyed talking to the learned dignitaries of the various temples and palaces.

Once inside, Abram sought shelter behind a freestanding pillar in the great open courtyard. He noticed with surprise that only a few Elamites guarded the palace, the courtrooms, and the entire temple area. Here and there he could see some of their brigands pulling down walls or hurrying off with golden urns, brass lamps, and jars of oil and incense.

Most of the fierce-visaged Elamites had swarmed out to wreak destruction on the private homes of Ur. They had bigger things in mind than to bother themselves with one unarmed man. However, Abram intended to be careful. With a quick, cautious look around, he headed for the ornate temple at the foot of the ziggurat. Haran was most likely to have fled there with his friends.

The god was supposed to descend to this temple from time to time, and it was here the people usually came to worship. Abram stood just inside the gate and viewed the carnage in the open courtyard. Men lay everywhere, sprawled just as the Elamite swordsmen had left them. Their faces were still streaked with ashes of contrition and their clothes were rent in penance. The whole city had rapidly become a boiling cauldron of disaster.

Inside the temple it was dark and ominously empty. As his eyes became accustomed to the gloom, he saw a fearful sight. The alabaster and diorite idols that used to sit on ledges around the wall had been pushed off and smashed. The rare jewels that had been eyes or ornamental decorations had been stolen. These were the idols that had been donated by various merchants because they were too busy to come often to the temple.

The niche where the god used to stand gaped open with its embroidered curtain torn. Everything of value had been carried off. And Haran was nowhere to be seen.

At the temple of the goddesses Ningal and Inanna, where Sarai had endured her ordeal, Abram saw that the high priestess of Inanna lay where she had fallen on the broad steps. She was stripped of jewelry, wig, embroidered slippers, and ornate girdle. Blood still ran from where she had been stabbed, and her eyes stared—glazed and wide with alarm—up into the glare of the afternoon sun. Lying near her were the women known as devotees of the temple, servants of the goddess and sellers of their charms as a sacrifice to the goddess.

He edged past the carnage and went inside. The idol was gone, but before the niche lay the high priestess of Ningal. She was no longer a creature of fearful power and control. The hair with the curling snakeskins had been a wig, which she now clutched in one hand as though she had been ready to put it on. Her clothes had been ripped and torn so that her aged body was exposed. Her bald head still spurted blood. The eyes were open and staring with a look of terror that belied her supposed strength.

Abram could hardly believe this wasted fragment of a woman could ever have presented such a terrifying visage. How could her curses have seemed so frightening? The odor here was rank, and he had to cover his nose as he hurried back out into the sunlight.

Just to one side of the door, piled one on top of the other like sacks of grain, were the eunuchs. Only one young man lay apart from the rest at the base of the worn steps. Abram fell back, shielding his eyes from the fearful sight. He recognized the boy; he had known his father. It was the same youth who during the spring festival had danced in such ecstasy before the statue of the goddess that when handed the sacrificial knife, he had castrated himself. The crowd had roared its approval while the father had been held in disgrace for turning pale and vomiting.

Abram turned away. Haran wasn't to be found there either. In a frenzy of fear he approached the Dublal-makh, the great double gate that opened onto the large courtyard surrounding the ziggurat. Cautiously he crossed the Sacred Way and began to climb the stairs. For the first time he felt there was something depressing about the two lower terraces being stained black with bitumen and the third a dull red. The shrine at the top was of blue brick that on clear days blended in with the color of the sky.

He had to dodge back and forth to avoid stepping on the naked bodies of the priests who had been killed and robbed of their fine garments. He was seized by a growing apprehension that he would never find his brother alive.

If indeed Haran had sought refuge in the temple area, there was almost no chance of his having escaped. Abram quickened his climb, reaching the first level just as some Elamites appeared along the parapet.

Before he could slip into one of the small rooms, they saw him. A fierce-looking little man drew his sword and rushed at him. There was no time to think. Instinctively Abram grabbed the man's upraised arm and with a tremendous wrench twisted the sword out of his hand. It fell clattering to the tiles, and both men tussled and struggled to reclaim it.

Abram saw that the rest of the men were loaded down with treasures they had taken from the storeroom and were not willing to join in the fight. They rushed past and down the steps, leaving Abram and the Elamite to fight it out. With one swift lunge Abram recovered the sword and whirled around just in time to see the Elamite preparing to spring at him. He raised the sword in both hands and brought it down with all of his might. He had never before wielded a sword. He had been a merchant, not a mercenary. He had never known the sound of metal cleaving a man's skull or the feel of a sword cutting into soft flesh.

For a moment Abram was stunned. The enemy had been stopped in midair with the grimace of hate still on his face and his lips still moving with inaudible curses.

The thrust had swung Abram off balance, and as he regained his footing, still clutching the embedded sword, he felt a wave of euphoria. That was quickly followed by revulsion as he saw the sweaty upturned face leering at him, mouth open, displaying malodorous rotting teeth.

With a great effort he pulled the sword loose and stared at the blood dripping from the tip. He had to wipe it off. To be rid of the ugly man's blood was, he hoped, to be rid of the memory of his face and the surge of fear he had felt when the man lunged at him.

With a grimace of disgust he reached down for a loose end of the man's tunic, and with slow deliberation he wiped off the sword. He must keep the sword. He might need it again. He cringed at the realization that the handle was still warm and damp with the other man's sweat.

As he moved along the high terrace, he realized how fortunate he was to be alive. The soldiers had killed everyone they encountered.

He went from one prone body to another. Here a young man had fallen carrying a scroll. There an old man had flung up his hands in horror as he was run through with a javelin. Over and over again Abram was thankful to find that Haran was not among the fallen ones.

Finally he came to the back terrace where he saw a terrible sight. A man, faintly familiar, dressed much as Haran would have dressed, had been stabbed in the back as he looked down over the wall into the courtyard below. With great foreboding and dread, Abram approached the still figure. Even before he turned the body over, he knew it was Haran.

Abram knelt beside the still form. It seemed impossible that the mouth was motionless and the eyes stared out but didn't focus or kindle with recognition. He felt a choking sensation. Tears blinded him. His brother was gone. Such pain, such a feeling of loss, enveloped Abram that he couldn't move or think.

He tried to lift Haran but realized he wouldn't get far. The ziggurat was deserted. The Elamites were busy plundering the city below. Time passed, and he thought of nothing but his grief until the sun set and darkness descended over the Hill of Heaven.

Slowly he folded the garments around Haran, and as he did so, he noticed the family signet ring. With the ring went a blessing. Abram turned away. It was heartbreaking to see the hands, at once so familiar and yet now cold and still. He knew he should take the ring, but he couldn't bear to touch it.

He stood up. For the first time he thought of Haran's sons, Lot and Iscah, and wondered if they had escaped. Usually it was the sons' business to bury their father, but now nothing could be done as usual.

In a daze Abram ascended one more flight to the observatory where he had come so often to study the movement of the stars. He hoped to find someone to help him, but instead he found his friend, the old astronomer, dead among the smashed tablets he had spent a lifetime studying.

Looking up, he noticed that, as so often in the past, the evening star hung low on the horizon beside the new moon. He could remember the old astronomer telling them that the morning star was the star of love and beauty, but the evening star signaled hate and destruction. "One goddess exhibiting two opposing natures . . . just like a woman," he had often observed with a shy smile.

Abram leaned against one of the pillars of the observatory and wept. The Hill of Heaven was dark and quiet. For the first time the priests were not out to greet the moon and evening star with sistra balag-di drums, harps, and high-pitched nasal chants. How sad, he thought, all Ur believed that those who blessed the new moon would not die this month.

Peering over the parapet, he could see, far below him, flames bursting out in one section after another. The smell of burning flesh scorched his lungs. Faint and far away, as though in some nightmare, could be heard shouts, screams, and cursing as people were driven from their homes. Above it all, and most terrifying, was the frequent sound of the Elamite horns announcing their victory. Abram felt drained, exhausted, and unable to fully comprehend the extent of the tragedy. Everything was lost.

Gradually he began to recognize the immediate danger. The city was crawling with Elamites; the gates were closed and well-guarded. The moment he descended from the deserted Hill of Heaven, he would be accosted and taken prisoner or killed.

He who had always helped others found himself trapped in a hopeless situation. He thought of his father and Nahor, and he hoped they had safely made it through the gate and up the river to the grazing lands where he had taken the rest of the family.

He thought of Sarai, his lovely, spoiled little wife, and wondered what would become of her if he couldn't escape. After Abram's own mother had died, Terah, following their custom, had married the daughter of his uncle. She was the only mother Abram remembered. She had been gentle and loving, and he had been her favorite. In turn, when she gave birth to a daughter, Abram had loved the child with an almost fanatical love.

For a moment he forgot everything in his concern for Sarai. He had done his best to shield her from the cruel observations of their neighbors. "By now your house should be full of children," the people taunted. "What's wrong with Sarai? For sure you'll find she has a devil in her belly." Delighted in her barrenness, it was to them proof that only the goddess Ningal or Innini could grant children.

Abram had been so determined to protect her from the crude jeers that he had spoiled her beyond all logic. True, she had been indulged first by his grandfather and then their father. Now he saw no way of putting an end to it—and had no real desire to—for he loved the woman she had become.

Gradually the panic returned. There was no way out. What good had it been to rescue his family if he weren't there to lead them to safety? He sank down on the steps of a small shrine and with his head in his hands groaned,

"Elohim, Elohim, where are you? These gods have failed, and only you are left."

No sooner had he uttered the words than he remembered a day in the past. A day like no other day. It was the day he had taken a firm stand and smashed the idols in his father's shop.

He remembered how at first Terah had been taken aback, though Abram had been right in guessing the logic would please his father. However, the city's elders were a different story. They had learned nothing from the demonstration. Instead, they had been determined to kill him—and almost did.

In the very midst of the crisis, when crushed with the blackest depression, Abram had felt the presence of his God—Elohim, the God who had been nearly forgotten and few knew or worshiped.

Though Abram had seen nothing, he remembered being overwhelmed by such love and compassion that he wept for joy. Once again he felt surrounded by this same love. Such a slender thread of hope to go on. Such a strange bit of encouragement. Though he could not explain it, he knew he had been singled out and comforted. It was real, more real than the hand he held before his face, more real than the devastation all around him.

He stood up. The feeling of hopelessness had vanished. He felt vibrantly alive, and a small surge of courage began to grow. He thought first of Haran. It would be impossible to bury him, but now he knew he must go back and take the family ring that had been given to Haran. It would be a reminder of Haran and of all those from his family who had worn it in the past.

Haran still lay where Abram had left him, and the hand that bore the ring was still stretched out on the cool tiles. Abram was relieved that no one had taken it. It would have been a great loss. Abram stooped down and gently worked the ring off Haran's lifeless finger and then, with only a moment's hesitation, put it on his own. He was the older brother, and whether he wore the ring or not, he would be responsible for the family when his father died.

He stood up and looked around. He'd somehow have to escape the city to where his family waited for him. He didn't know how he would go. He knew only that he must find a way.

As he peered into the darkness, he was surprised to see a figure materialize out of the shadows. When he came closer, Abram could see it was Urim, the cheese maker. "My lord," Urim said, "if you will let me go with you, perhaps together we can find a way out."

"What do you know?" Abram questioned.

"I know that you have been planning for some time to leave Ur. I want to go with you."

"And your family?"

Urim's teeth flashed white in the moonlight as he said with a smile, "My wife and children are already with your family and servants. I hope you don't mind."

"It seems everything has already been decided. How do you propose to get out?"

"I have no plan. It looks impossible. From what I've seen we've more chance of getting speared on an Elamite javelin than escaping, but I'm ready to try."

Abram immediately liked the man. He was glad to have someone with him. If they escaped, it would be a miracle. They moved out of the shadows and Abram got a better look at Urim. The man was obviously no scholar but one of those ordinary men with an abundance of common sense. If we are to escape, Abram thought, this is the man who will find a way.

3

*S*arai had left Ur much earlier. When Abram told her they would be moving out to live in tents until the possible trouble in Ur was over, she was annoyed. When he said she must pack up everything she treasured, she was miserable. It had taken one large, cumbersome cart heavily loaded to carry her jewelry and cosmetics. Three others were filled with her ornate robes, wedding finery, exquisite woven pieces, headdresses, and footwear. Finally it took a whole string of donkeys to carry the condiments, herbs, seasonings, dried fruits, grains, and wines she used for special occasions.

She had not known that Abram was not riding with them until they were at the gate ready to leave. She was terribly upset. She would never forget the last poignant moments.

It had been dark, and though she couldn't see the marble fountain, she could hear its soft splashing on the hard granite curb. She breathed deeply of the pungent odor of the tuberoses, heard the nesting stork stir and flap its wings, and rubbed her hand over the heavy worn boards of the gate that opened out into the lane.

She reached out for Abram and clung to him, begging him to stay with her. He joked and humored her, trying to reassure her that she would be back within a few days. "It's just a feeling I've had. I may be wrong, but I don't want to take a chance," he said. She knew it was more serious than he wanted to admit, and Sarai intuited that she would never see her lovely old home again.

When they paused outside the city to look back at the Hill of Heaven, Sarai again had misgivings. On the flat plain the man-made mountain rose huge and dark within the city walls, but the temple at the top had already caught the first rays of the morning sun. She knew the priests would be mounting the steps, and the high priest would be sprinkling drops of clear water in all four directions to purify the city.

Sarai shuddered. As much as she loved her home, the place brought back memories of the fearful ordeal she endured before she was married to Abram.

She could picture all too vividly the temple of Ningal in the shadow of the ziggurat, and she would never forget what had happened to her there. She didn't like to think of it and promptly put the memory out of her mind.

There was the whir of wings as a family of bats was visible for a moment against the lightening sky. A wild dog howled and was answered by one of their trusted sheepdogs. Then the signal was given, and they moved out onto the worn roadway that bordered the irrigation ditches.

They had heard almost nothing of what was happening back in the city until Terah and Nahor had ridden in with their report of the Elamite attack and their own narrow escape. Sarai could tell by the fear in Nahor's eyes, and the way his mouth twitched when he tried to tell of all they had seen, that something unspeakably terrible had happened. "It's thanks to Abram we haven't all been killed or captured," Terah insisted.

"And where is Abram?" Sarai asked with alarm.

"And where's my father?" Milcah demanded of her husband, Nahor.

Lot and Iscah pushed forward to face their uncle and grandfather. "Yes," they demanded, "where is our father?"

Nahor glanced at Terah, who stiffened and glared at them all. His face was ashen. Though he was exhausted, he maintained the demeanor of authority. "Haran is somewhere in the city. We can only hope he is still alive."

"And Abram . . . where is he?" Sarai pushed the two men aside and clutched her father's arm in a frightened grip.

Terah's agonized eyes told the story before he spoke. "Abram went to find Haran. Both may be lost to us."

Sarai pulled back and glared at her father. "Not Abram. Nothing will happen to Abram. He'll think of something." Her voice was confident, but they could tell by the way she clutched her shoulder scarf and tossed her head defiantly that she was really frightened.

When night came and there was no news, the anxiety grew. Most of the family gathered around Terah as if needing his strength to face whatever might be in store for them. Sarai stayed in her tent, unwilling to let the others see her mounting fear and anxiety. She sat by a fire of nettles and aimlessly poked small sticks into the fire to keep the coals burning, her thoughts on Abram.

It had never occurred to her that anything really bad could happen to him. She realized with growing panic that she couldn't even imagine life without him. He was always able to make things come out right. He was fearless.

She remembered with a shiver of delight how he had dared to rescue her from Ningal's sacrifice. Then how he had smashed the idols and even dared to challenge the gods of the moon.

She would never forget how Abram had risked everything for her sake. Her father's concubine, her brothers Nahor and Haran, and even her father thought she should do as the maidens of Ur and sacrifice to the goddess. She remembered how her father's concubine had whispered, "They say that if you don't go, you will be cursed. No child will grow in your womb."

Even after all these years, she had not borne a child, and she was haunted by the priestess's curse. She had never been allowed to forget the curse for a moment because the people of Ur were always asking her why she had not made peace with the goddess so she could have a child. In that way they continued to taunt her. She knew they whispered that her barrenness had resulted from her refusal to honor the great earth goddess Ningal and her daughter Inanna.

With a conscious effort she pushed the fearful memories from her mind. She was concerned about her husband, not about the past. She moved out of the tent into the bright moonlight. Nervous and impatient, she wanted to be where she could see the road more clearly.

It was impossible for the God Abram trusted to save him. Nanna ruled in Ur, and Nanna was a jealous god who allowed no other gods. If Abram escaped, it would have to be by his own wits. His God didn't have much power, didn't control anything of practical, everyday worth. She had tested him. She had asked for a child, and nothing had happened.

From where she stood she could see a stirring by the campfire. Then Lot and his brother Iscah stood up and looked down the road. Sarai strained to see what, if anything, they could be seeing. Gradually two figures, riding hard, emerged out of the mist that hung low over the river. Identifying them was impossible. Sarai clutched the tent pole and bowed her head on her hands. She couldn't bear to look. They must be messengers with bad news.

Lot began to run as soon as he recognized his uncle as one of the riders. "Abram!" he shouted. Sarai lifted her head and saw that it was indeed Abram. He was barely recognizable. His clothes were torn and bloodstained; his face was dust-blown and streaked. In his belt he carried a sword that was covered with dry, caked blood. Only his eyes were familiar, but they had lost their sparkle and looked out at the world with a new seriousness. Before she could move he had jumped from his mule and hurried past Lot and Iscah to sweep her up in his arms.

She felt his arms tighten around her, and at the same time she felt a hard, cold object press into her side. Her hand reached for his and she realized he was wearing the ring. Haran's ring. She buried her head in his shoulder and wept.

Only after Abram was sure Sarai was all right did he agree to answer questions. He explained that the cheese maker had known of a sheep gate where animals were brought for sacrifice, and it led out of the city. They had managed to escape through the gate and found two mules tethered just outside. They had not hesitated to claim the mules, knowing their owners were probably dead.

Reluctantly he told them of his search for Haran. But long before he was able to tell of his death, Milcah began to scream. She tore her hair, scratched her face until it bled, and pleaded over and over to be allowed to go back to Ur. "I won't leave him to the vultures," she wailed. "I won't let the Elamites humiliate my father."

All the while both Lot and Iscah blamed themselves for not forcing their father to leave the city. "We should have known. It was obvious the Elamites were bent on destroying Ur."

Everyone was so upset by the news that no one took time to correct the brothers. No one reminded them of how difficult it had been to get them to leave. In the end they realized that no amount of grieving would bring Haran back, and two days later they sadly gathered up their things, ready to move on.

As usual, Sarai challenged Abram with questions. "Why," she asked, "if your Elohim is so powerful could he not destroy the Elamites and save Haran? That would have convinced everyone that he was the strongest God. Everyone would have believed in Him." She tossed her head and gave Abram a searching look.

Terah had traveled the trade routes since his youth, so he directed where they were to go now. There was no time to lose, no time for grief. In profound silence they headed up the well-known northbound route.

Within a fortnight they had covered the barren wasteland of Sumer and were edging around the affluent kingdom of Mari. A fortnight later they arrived at the confluence of the Euphrates and the Balikh. There they turned north and after a week had arrived at the city of Haran.

Terah was not well. At Haran the family determined that he was too tired and feeble to go on. They left their animals with caretakers in the grazing lands outside the city, then hurriedly crowded into whatever lodging was available. Abram and his family moved into an old stone fortress abandoned by a brigand who had become wealthy robbing caravans.

Bit by bit news of the destruction of Ur reached them. The Elamites had taken the king, Ibbi-Suen, into captivity, destroyed the lovely fountains and the intricate irrigation system, burned the almond trees, decimated the places of learning, and thrown out the clay tablets that recorded Ur's splendid history. Gradually they accepted that Ur, the only city they had called home, was gone. With that realization, as well as grief for his son Haran and worry over what was to happen to his family, Terah became seriously ill. In a short time he died, and with his death new and fearful decisions had to be made.

"I hear Abram's planning on leaving Haran," Urim's wife, Safra, said as her husband came into the courtyard with his cart and unsold cheeses. "He must be going back to Ur."

Urim was immediately interested. "He can't go back to Ur. They say the Elamites have totally destroyed it."

"Then where's he going?"

"They say he's breaking up the family. Nahor is terribly upset about it. He also accuses Abram of not honoring the old family gods."

Safra looked doubtful, "I know Terah made a show of worshiping Nanna. Even brought some fancy idols with him from Ur."

"You're right, but Abram's against those gods . . . even the family gods."

Safra was squatting in the middle of the courtyard, plucking the feathers from several pigeons they would eat that evening. She squinted into the bright sunlight as she glanced up. "It's strange," she said, "very strange. And hard to believe." Her words hung between them like vultures while she studied his face.

"Strange? What do you mean? What have you heard?"

"Lot's wife says Abram's been told to leave Haran and he's been promised land and blessings."

Urim shrugged. "Fortune-tellers say such things."

"It wasn't a fortune-teller." She looked up and saw that her little serving girl was listening. She motioned for Urim to bend down so she could whisper, "It's his God, the Elohim he worships. He's the one they say told him."

Urim drew back and stared at his wife in disbelief. "That's just women's talk. That's all."

"That's not all," she said. "He's to have descendants as the stars." She looked up in time to see the amused expression on Urim's face. She shrugged and went back to plucking one of the birds. "Well," she added, "that's what they say."

Urim strutted around the courtyard, his eyes half closed in thought. After walking back and forth several times, he came over to his wife and demanded, "To be given land and descendants? What kind of foolishness is this? Where would he go? His family is here. No one gives anybody land, and as for descendants . . . he doesn't even have one child."

"I know. That's what we all thought. That's what's so strange."

Urim stood in the middle of the courtyard, feet wide apart, mind calculating as he rubbed his chin. "Well, I'll tell you what I think. I think all this trouble has left him a bit addled. At least we must admit he's gone to dreaming." With that pronouncement, Urim started toward the door leading out of the courtyard, then turned back. "And Abram's wife . . . what does that fancy wife of his think?"

"She's spunky." Safra held the pigeon suspended in midair as she carefully examined it. "She says she's not going."

Urim laughed as he snatched up the water jug, drank from the spout, then wiped his mouth on his sleeve. "That should be interesting. I've heard she always gets her way."

Safra dropped the pigeon in the stone pot and looked up. "We're all waiting to see what happens."

Urim watched her pick up the second pigeon and begin to idly pluck the feathers. "And Nahor, his brother Nahor, is he going too?"

"No, Nahor thinks he's making a big mistake."

"Who told you all this?"

Safra hesitated as though not wanting to trust him with the information. Then thinking better of it, she said, "Nahor's wife, Milcah. She's never gotten over her father's death."

Urim again picked up the jug and tipped it ready to drink. "So Nahor's not going. That's serious. Abram's breaking up the family."

Safra seemed not to hear him. "I wish I were going someplace," she said wistfully.

Urim set the jug down so hard that it almost cracked. "That's the trouble with men like Abram. They make people discontent with where they are and what they're doing." Then he muttered, "Myself included."

* * *

At that very moment Lot was making his way with his uncle Nahor to the house of Abram. Lot knew that Nahor was alarmed. He had been upset for a long time, but now everything was coming to a head.

As the older brother, for Abram to leave and split up the family was unthinkable. As a little boy, Lot had often heard Terah say, "Families have to stick together to succeed." Everyone seemed to know that.

Another steadfast rule was to never leave the graves of your people. Terah had died and was buried here in Haran, and that meant the family should stay in this place. Lot could see that the confrontation would be bitter. He viewed it as ominous but exciting. He didn't know which side he would take. To stay with Nahor in Haran was safe, but with Abram, life would always be an adventure.

Although Lot admired and respected Abram, Nahor fascinated him. He could see in the pursing of the lips and slight squinting of the eyes just a hint of the crafty, sly nature Nahor was reputed to have. Nahor was unequaled at making a bargain, but openly admitted being void of the integrity and rectitude of Abram. He counted it an advantage that some of their customers tended to steer clear of him and asked to deal with Abram instead. "As a family we complement each other," he would say with a smirk and slight nod of the head.

Lot suspected that the furor over Sarai's rescue and then the destruction of the idols, rather than his uncle Haran's death or the invasion by the Elamites, hastened Terah's death. It was whispered among those who knew the family well that after these scandals, Terah never regained his strength. In time, Abram no longer mentioned the unfortunate confrontations, and everyone in the family agreed that the episodes should be forgotten as soon as possible.

There had been a time when Abram talked as though they would continue in the trading business. "We'll stay here in Haran until Terah recovers," he said. "It's the junction of a rich caravan route between Nineveh and Carchemish. It may prove better for trade than Ur."

From that and other statements, Lot assumed that when the time of mourning for Terah was over, they would resume the trading business, and things would get better. Though Nahor raised sheep and owned land, it was the trading business that really interested him. But could the younger brother manage without Abram?

The two men found Abram on the roof of his rambling stone fortress. It was strong and practical but lacking in the niceties that had characterized the house in Ur. Abram rose and embraced his brother and then Lot. He greeted them heartily and urged them to relax among the cushions under the palm leaf shelter. "As you can see," he said, "I'm getting supplies ready for our journey." He motioned to the piles of grain, dried figs, jars of oil, and skins bursting with ripe dates.

"Then you are serious?" Nahor said, looking around in astonishment.

"Yes, of course. I never intended to stay here."

Nahor's expression showed obvious displeasure. "I don't understand," he muttered. "Trading will go better here than in Ur. There are routes to Mari, Nineveh, Damascus, and even Egypt."

"It's not that I don't see the opportunity. We could do well here. I'm just not interested anymore," Abram replied.

Nahor stroked his chin; his eyes narrowed as he studied his brother for a moment. "It's that same old thing. The idols—you don't want to make and sell idols."

Abram grew serious. There had been too many discussions with his father and brothers about the idols. He didn't want to repeat any of that now. "It's more than that. Of course, it started with the idols, but now it is more—much more."

Nahor was leaning forward. "You're not still thinking about the old religion and the God Elohim, as you call him? You're too practical, too smart, to get carried away by that sort of thing."

Abram didn't answer right away but sat fingering the fringe on his cloak as he looked out at the stars through the dried fronds of palm that formed the roof of the pavilion. "Don't you ever wonder where all this came from? Aren't you curious? There are fixed stars that never move, and there are others that parade in an orderly fashion across the sky."

Lot could see that Nahor didn't want to discuss the stars. Nahor's opinion all along had been that most of their problems started when Abram had taken an interest in the stars and commenced sitting with some of the old astronomers in Ur.

Lot looked at Abram with concern. The face was strong and handsome, the nose large and the mouth generous, but it was his eyes that made the difference. His eyes were wide and questioning. Intelligent eyes that seemed to see more than others and yet sparkled with enjoyment at a well-turned joke.

There was an eagerness about him, an inquisitiveness that made him stop and ask questions about what seemed to be simple matters. He was always seeing things from a different angle or perspective. Lot suddenly realized that for all of his admiration of his uncle Abram, he himself was more practical like Nahor.

"I am not here to argue about what happened to Sarai or to bother you about the idols," Nahor said. "I'm here to remind you that we are family, and family ties can't be broken."

Abram turned and Lot was surprised to see that his eyes were soft with something close to pity. "Nahor," he said, "I, more than most, understand about family. There is only one thing stronger than family."

Nahor leaned forward, his jaw taut, his eyes hard and cold. "Nothing, nothing is stronger than family, and you are the oldest."

Abram stood up and walked to the parapet. His natural dignity immediately silenced Nahor. Abram seemed calm and very much in control as he glanced down into the courtyard and then out at the stars. "You know you are welcome to come with me," he said finally. "I hope Lot will decide to come."

Lot was stunned, while Nahor seemed almost overcome with frustration. Nahor closed and unclosed his fists. His voice choked with emotion. "As I hear it, you don't really know where you're going. You have only some promise of land, descendants, and blessing," he thundered. "You have taken total leave of your senses and now you expect me to go. It's foolishness. No good will come of it. It's not a trading venture. It's not a business proposition. It's merely a dream, a childish dream."

Abram listened patiently to the tirade, and when he finally spoke, it was with a twinge of regret. "I'm sorry you don't want to come. It won't be easy, but as you mentioned, I have promises."

"I'll not let you take the household gods our father left us."

"I neither want nor need them."

Nahor cringed. "You are to have blessings, land, and descendants, and you are leaving the gods behind?"

"I would have left them in Ur."

"I thought after the trouble that you would have learned."

"My brother," Abram said with quiet dignity, "I didn't want to offend you, so I said nothing. I neither need nor want those lifeless bits of clay."

"Lifeless clay!" Nahor shouted, jumping to his feet. "You call them lifeless clay! They have powers you can't imagine."

"You have no proof." Now Abram's eyes flashed dangerously.

"Aha, no proof you say. I have proof. We all have had proof, but our old father forbade us to speak of it."

Abram took a deep breath, leaned back against the rough edge of the parapet, and demanded, "You have proof. What proof? Why were you not to speak of it?"

"Our father made us promise. He said we were never to say the words."

"And now I am head of this family, and I demand that you tell me everything."

Nahor backed up, looking frightened at what he'd brought about. But then glancing at Lot, he stiffened and drew himself up, speaking quickly and boldly, "It has been noticed by our family—and indeed by all our acquaintances—that while we have many children, you have none."

"And what does that mean?"

"Why, it's obvious to all of us. You have offended the great earth mother. She has closed Sarai's womb."

Abram stared at Nahor in disbelief. The cruel words cut like a knife. Others might point out the lack, but for his own brother to mention it was devastating. "I will have children," Abram said at last. His voice was calm, and there was still a quiet dignity about him. "I have been promised children and descendants."

Nahor was totally frustrated, but he couldn't leave the subject alone. "You will have children when you make peace with Ningal. Look, I have children, the poorest peasant has children, the king has hundreds, and they all worship Ningal."

"Keep the house gods. I have been given promises," Abram said.

"Promises!" Nahor spat on the floor in a spasm of disgust. "What good have your promises been? Our homes and lands are gone, our father has died, and you have not one child to show for your promises." In a veritable frenzy he snatched up his silver-knobbed walking stick, flung his cloak over his shoulder, and strode toward the door. "You'll be back," he said through clenched teeth as he shook the walking stick. "I predict you'll be back. You can't live on dreams or depend on Elohim. You'll see."

He closed the door with a bang, and they could hear him breathing heavily as he felt his way down the dark stairs.

In that moment Lot made his decision. "My uncle," he said, "I know nothing of this God and I have very little faith in the venture, but if you'll have me, I'd like to go too."

In just such a simple way Lot decided to join his uncle. He was encouraged by the thought that Abram had some genuine promise of great blessing and that if he were there, he would get a little of it for himself.

As Lot made his way down the stairs and out into the narrow lane, he congratulated himself on his wisdom. Abram had no children of his own, and with a bit of luck it was possible that he would choose Lot to inherit all his wealth. Any way he looked at it, his best chance for good fortune lay with Abram. Lot drew in his breath with the excitement of it all. With Abram's wealth he would move to the city and enjoy all the comforts he had only imagined up until now.

* * *

Abram had not followed them down the stairs. For the first time in his life, he let himself shirk the niceties and conventions of his people. It was a small thing compared to what he'd been accused of: deserting the family. To turn his back on his own flesh and blood was almost the worst crime a man could commit. To desert his family and the household gods made by his father was beyond the comprehension of anyone he knew. He didn't blame Nahor for his strong reaction.

Of course, it all went deeper than any of them imagined. It had started in Ur with innocent questions, then the scandal over Sarai, and finally the devastation by the Elamites. Was it possible that he was the only one who watched how easily they gutted Nanna's temple and swept the god from his pedestal? Nanna, the powerful god who controlled the moon and stars, seedtime and harvest and was supposed to hold their fate in his hands. The god was helpless before the Elamites.

Abram knew he had hurt Nahor and frightened Sarai, but there was no way he could turn back. He rubbed his hand along the cold stones of the parapet and took a deep breath of the clear night air. It had seemed such a small decision . . . to keep moving, to seek Elohim's path. Now he saw that it was going to be the hardest thing he had ever done in his life.

✳ ✳ ✳

A few days later, Urim the cheese maker squeezed in among the men at the gate while Abram was discussing his plans. He wanted desperately to go too. "Can you use a cheese maker?" he asked when there was a lull in the conversation.

He saw Abram's eyes move over the heads of the dignitaries and search him out. "A cheese maker? We can always use a cheese maker," he said, obviously recognizing Urim. "If you really want to go, come and let my nephew Lot record your name." Abram's eyes crinkled into an amused smile.

In a daze of excitement Urim hurried over to where Lot sat cross-legged on a raised platform in the shade. Up close Urim could see that Lot appeared to be shrewd and calculating. He wasn't as relaxed and genial as Abram. After many questions and several conferences with his uncle, Lot had a scribe record Urim's name in wedge-shaped characters on a tablet of moist clay.

When Urim returned home, reality set in. He could answer none of the practical questions his wife asked him. He walked around the small courtyard touching the large jars of grain and olive oil, then his old plow, the yoke hanging beside it, and the cart from which he sold his cheese. He'd need to get rid of some of these things and take only the essentials.

"I'll have to take the molds and pots for making cheese," he said half to himself.

"I need my grindstones, my loom, and the dried herbs," his wife said.

In the end it was the tent that caused the most trouble and almost kept Urim from going. To have a goat hair tent made the size he needed for his family would have taken six months. There was no time for that, and finally he ended the matter by trading some of his goats to a band of nomads for one of their worn tents.

When the day of departure arrived and those who were going gathered before sunrise outside the city gates, Urim and his family were included. He sat on one donkey that was loaded down with their bedrolls. His wife sat on another that was almost covered with bags of wheat and barley. She held in her arms the precious grindstones and had her savory herbs tied around her waist. Behind them came two donkeys laden with Urim's cheese-making equipment. On each side were his four young sons herding the goats that were to produce the milk for cheese.

There was great confusion as relatives and friends came out to say good-bye. Urim had left his house and tools with his brother, and now there were last-minute admonitions and expressed concern. "I'm surprised that you're really going," Urim's brother said.

"Don't worry," Urim replied smugly. "It's the chance of a lifetime. I'm going to get rich and famous with Abram."

"We'll see," the brother said. "It's more than likely you'll be back poorer and wiser. Too bad you won't listen to reason."

The signal was given; the donkeys were prodded into a loose grouping; goats and sheep padded past with only the clicking sound of the herders and an occasional bleating. The early morning air was vibrant with excitement as the whole formation took shape and began to move. For a short time the torches flickered along the wall and at the gate, and then the city of Haran was lost in darkness.

Urim chuckled. "What a surprise my brother is in for. I'll be back in no time and rich enough to sit at the gate with the best of them."

At the same time on a rooftop overlooking the city gate, a lone figure watched everything with interest, even at times straining forward to catch the chance remarks that drifted up to him from the gathering below. It was Nahor. He had been too proud to speak to his brother since the disagreement, and he was unyielding in his determination not to say he was sorry.

He was bitterly disappointed. Abram was the older brother. It was his duty to hold the family together, to plan for them, to make a living from which they could all benefit. "He's making a big mistake, a very big mistake," Nahor muttered.

He watched until the torches at the gate were snuffed out and the last of the stragglers faded into the early morning mist. Soon even the sounds of bleating and soft, padding hooves could no longer be heard. "He'll be sorry, very sorry," he said as he turned and felt his way down the narrow stairs.

Back on his hard straw pallet he tossed and turned, trying to rid himself of the anger and resentment. "He's not one for such a venture. He's a bar-gainer, a man of important affairs, a shrewd dealer. He's wasting it all, and he's destroyed the family." He felt such anger and frustration he knew the sun would be up before he could get any sleep.

Nahor sat up and groped in the dark for the wall niche and the small, well-formed image of Nanna carefully wrapped in a woolen cloth. He ran his hands over its smooth belly and round bald head. He could feel the jewels that made up the eyes. Nanna was powerful. Nanna, god of the moon, kept the dark forces of night and evil spirits under control. Abram had done a fearful thing to divide the family this way, and worse than that, he had turned his back on the old household gods that had always protected them. "Sarai will never have a child until he makes peace with the gods," he said for the hundredth time.

That his sensible brother could flaunt the proven necessity of their household gods was unthinkable. It was frightening to live in a house without gods and even more frightening to go off on such a trek without them. "He'll be back," he muttered to himself. "He'll be back having lost everything."

Nahor raised the cold red clay god to his lips, smelled the musty odor of rose water and incense, then carefully wrapped it in the woolen cloth and replaced it in the niche. He lay back down, and within minutes he had dozed off and didn't wake until the second cockcrow.

*U*ntil the last minute Sarai had hoped that Abram would change his mind. She didn't want to leave the comforts, such as they were, of Haran. Though he didn't discuss it with Sarai, she suspected it was again some message from his God telling him to leave. With only some vague mention of promises and blessings, he had packed up all their belongings, ready to move out of their dark fortress and head out along the old trade route toward Damascus.

Sarai had begged and complained until she realized that Abram was determined to go. In the end she had given in and began collecting the treasures that would make the trip more enjoyable.

Some whispered that she was trying her husband's patience with all of her demands. It was evident that she had found Haran agreeable—not as suitable as Ur had been before all the trouble, but certainly better than living in a tent. She was annoyed with the turn of events, and her voice had a sharp edge as she inquired, "Where are we going? When are we going to settle down?"

As usual Abram was patient and unconcerned. "I don't really know," he said. "We'll see where our God leads us."

"What if it is some unpleasant place?" Her head was cocked to one side and her eyes studied his face intently.

Abram laughed. "I trust Him, Sarai. He'll pick the very best place for us."

"But what if He doesn't? Will you go back to Haran?" This question became her chant, but her husband remained silent.

It took Sarai a week to get over her pique and admit to herself that she might enjoy this new adventure after all. It took her more time to get used to riding in the large, cumbersome cart. The wooden wheels creaked and groaned. The exterior was ugly and plain, but the inside was both comfortable and attractive. Abram had seen to that.

There were bright, cheerful reed mats covering the floor with embroidered armrests and straw-stuffed pillows strewn about just as in the finest guest rooms of Haran. Overhead was a canopy of goat hair; the side pieces could be raised or lowered so the rider could see out. The exterior was drab, but on the underside stars were painted on a blue midnight background.

Sarai seldom rode alone, often inviting other women to join her. Sometimes it was Mara, Lot's wife, and at other times some of the young daughters of their herders and servants. They sang, carded wool, and spent days working on woven mats and baskets made of the tall grass and weeds they found along the way.

Though she had often heard tales of the trips her father, grandfather, and uncles had taken as traders over this same route, Sarai was not prepared for the leisurely pace. There was no schedule, no time set for their arrival at any given place. When they came to fields of green grass, Abram encouraged her to get down from her cart and wade knee deep in the fragrant thyme and mint. He paused to watch her pick the small starlike flowers called dove's dung, and often they stopped to enjoy the sharp, sweet song of a bird hidden in the thorn bushes.

Gradually, though reluctantly, she began to find solace in the peaceful rhythm. Yawash, yawash, slowly, slowly, seemed to be the words most often heard. It took a strong bashi or head of the caravan to get everyone organized for the day, but once they started to move it was a colorful procession.

Every animal was decked out by his rider and wore brightly woven saddle blankets, blue lapis lazuli beads to keep off the evil eye, and shells strung on cords so that as they clashed and clanged they made a pleasant sort of music to accompany the bumping and swaying of the carts.

Sarai especially looked forward to the camping at night. The smell of warm bread being cooked over an open fire and young lambs roasting on a spit gave promise of a plentiful feast. Later when the moon came up and the stars burst out in the blackness of the low hanging sky, she would lie with Abram's arms around her, listening patiently as he talked of his dreams for the future.

From the first she had been skeptical of the promises he held in such regard. It seemed to her that they were always getting bigger and grander. First he was to have land, perhaps a whole country where they would enjoy a home and safety, and then he was to have descendants too numerous to count. He, who was no longer young, owned no land, and had no children, believed completely in these impossible promises. It bothered her that he should seem to know this unseen God so intimately, talked to Him, and even heard Him speak.

"This is the real God, the Creator, the One people have almost forgotten," Abram explained.

"And where is this country that is to belong to you and to your descendants?" Sarai asked testily.

"We are coming to it soon now." Abram smiled as though remembering something pleasant.

"You have seen it already?" Sarai raised up on her elbow and looked at him with astonishment.

"I'm not sure. When I was very young, I went on a trading trip down to Egypt with my father. We traded finely tooled leather goods for their sheer material. We had stopped in a great fertile valley where the earth was moist and rich and the grass was the darkest green you can imagine. We camped under a great tree. The place was called Shechem."

"Didn't it belong to anyone?"

"There were a few scattered villages built of mud bricks, but the valley had no well and was hard to defend, so it was left open for herders and traders like us. The people who live there are mostly Amorites."

"How will you know if this is the place your God has promised?" Sarai asked as she shivered and drew closer into Abram's encircling arms.

He pulled the woven robe over her bare shoulder and lay for a few moments quietly thinking. "When I get there, I'll ask Him."

* * *

When they came to Damascus, Abram found a pleasant location for their camp in a garden of date palms on one of the branches of the Abana River with the brown ruggedness of Jebel Kasyun looming in the distance. As soon as possible he took several of the men into the city to gather news and replenish their supplies. They needed many things and Abram knew that Sarai would want to see the best of the jewelry, cloth, and perfumes.

"Go to the market where they sell animals and see if they have any camels to sell," he told Lot. "I'll make arrangements for some merchants to visit the caravan with their wares."

Lot knew very little about buying camels. Like Abram, he had heard the animals were being used by desert traders because they could go for days without water. Beyond that he knew little. They hadn't been used in Ur and were a novelty in Haran. To help him, Abram had chosen a young man who boasted of having traveled in a caravan made up entirely of camels and of knowing the markets of Damascus well.

The animal section of the market was near the khan or inn. It was an open area black with flies and smelling of straw, old leather, and urine. Here and there worn, striped awnings had been hoisted into place to shelter some wealthy merchants from the sweltering sun. Raucous traders milled around, shouting in hoarse voices the price and worth of their animals. Small boys ran in and out, either chasing a stray sheep or collecting the dung to be mixed with straw and burned as fuel.

Lot was amazed at the variety and number of animals in the market. Some were kneeling, others were standing, but all were held by ropes or tied to stakes. He was drawn to some fine, well-cared for camels, but his driver restrained him. He said, "They are only for riding, and the camels we need are those with the big, ugly heads."

Lot again picked four camels from a friendly, persuasive fellow who had placed a variety of fancy trappings on them. Again the driver pulled him aside. "Pardon," he said, "but you must not choose the camel by his trappings."

Lot was exasperated. He wanted to finish buying the camels, and to him, they all looked very much alike. "What then am I to look for?" he asked impatiently.

"Come," the driver said as he led him off to one side under the awning of the khan. "You must choose a camel by the breadth of his chest, the shortness of his leg, the fullness of his flank."

"Then it is impossible," Lot said. "There are so many and every owner has disguised his animal. Who can tell which are strong and which are weak?"

"There is one test that never fails. If I stand on the hocks when a camel is kneeling and he can still rise, this camel won't fall by the wayside when things get difficult."

The thought of a camel dropping behind and left to die in some desert place horrified Lot—such waste! He quickly made a decision. "You buy the camels. I'll sit here in the khan and see if I can glean some news."

Lot found many men standing or sitting in small groups in the open courtyard of the inn. He approached a group of men dressed in the long, fringed garb of men from the old kingdom of Sumer. They were sitting around watching two men play a game Lot recognized as one he had played often in Ur. The board the men were playing on was especially handsome. It was made of colorful inlay, and the playing pieces were of black-and-white ivory. When the men saw Lot, they stopped talking and eagerly made room for him with nods of respect and deference. It pleased Lot that they recognized him as a man of means and prominence.

The time passed quickly, and before he was ready to leave, the driver was back with news that he had bought the necessary camels, even two extra camels to carry some food for the other animals. "They say there is famine in much of the area through which we are going," he said. "We'll need the extra supplies."

Lot had also heard rumors of the famine and was worried. He could hardly wait to tell Abram. Surely they wouldn't go on if there was a famine in the land. However, when he arrived back at camp, there was such an air of festivity that Lot hesitated to tell his disturbing news.

Abram had found a rich merchant named Eliazer who had also fled from Ur. Upon meeting a fellow countryman, Eliazer promptly closed his shops and brought much of the contents out to the place where Abram was camping.

"Pick anything you like," Abram told Sarai. "Gather the women and let them have whatever they want as long as there is room for it."

While the women were viewing the jewelry, ointments, headpieces, and delicately carved boxes, Abram was entertaining Eliazer in his tent. Lot was surprised to learn that Eliazer was going to sell everything he owned and join them. "It won't take long. My brother and cousins will undoubtedly buy everything," Eliazer assured them.

Lot was astounded. Here was a man of great wealth and position, willing to give up everything to join them. Lot wondered what Abram had told him; he knew that Abram made things sound exciting. He could feel the air of adventure and see that Eliazer had caught the dream, just as the rest of them had.

When Eliazer finally ordered his slaves to gather up the unwanted goods and depart, Lot stayed to tell Abram the disturbing news of the famine. "The traders I spoke with," he said, "have warned of a famine. They say it has totally ravaged the land west of the Jordan. Do you think we should go on?"

Abram didn't seem to hear him. "Eliazer has a big family," he said. "They all fled with him from Ur just ahead of the armies. Fortunately they had sent some of their most precious belongings on to Damascus before the massacre."

Lot was silent for a moment as he mulled over the whole situation. Abram never had been one to fear much of anything, but this was serious.

"The men suggested that we turn back while we can."

"Turn back!" Abram was obviously not impressed. "I have faith that the God who called me out won't let a famine defeat us."

"What do you mean?" Lot questioned.

"By the time we get there, the famine will be over, or we will find it was all an exaggeration."

"Everyone says the pastures have turned to dust. We'll have to buy aliek for the camels."

Abram was interested. "And what is aliek?"

"It's a small grain like lentils, with a green husk. Here in Damascus they mix it into a dough with wheat flour and water, then press it into oblong balls. A camel needs six of these a day, and with water he'll survive."

Abram smiled. "Then it's all taken care of, and we won't worry about the famine."

Lot said no more, but the whole thing made him nervous. He had seen the expressions on the men's faces and heard the anxiety in their voices as they had spoken of the famine. Lot couldn't help but wonder whether the gods Abram had lashed out against were getting ready to punish them. People— many people—had said that Abram would be punished for defying the earth gods and destroying the idols. Everyone agreed that Sarai was barren because of it.

Lot quickly decided that whatever happened, he was not going to sacrifice his life and risk losing his flocks for Abram's dream. He would go along until he saw how things turned out. If there really was a famine instead of the promised blessings, he would quietly make other plans.

* * *

They waited some days outside Damascus until Eliazer and his large family could join them. They were happy days blighted only by the news that continued to come out of the country beyond the Jordan. Abram listened to all the reports, but refused to be discouraged. Instead he grew impatient and anxious to be back on the trail.

They left Damascus on a bright, sunny day and headed out past the western gate onto the road called the King's Highway that would take them to the foot of Mount Hermon. They couldn't move as fast as the traders who were unencumbered with families, flocks of sheep, baby lambs, goats, and herds of camels. At times they pitched their tents and camped in one place for five days before moving on. "It is necessary to move at least every ten days," the saying went among shepherds, "or the grazing land is all eaten away."

At the foot of Mount Hermon were both water and adequate pasture, and they decided to stay camped there until the new moon.

Everyone agreed it was good to be out of the wagons and camping. Lot's wife, Mara, was especially relieved. She liked the bustle of an orderly routine carried on in settled conditions. Each night the goat's milk was heated and poured into a special goatskin that had been used so often for this purpose that the skin contained enough of the curdled milk to curdle the new batch. It was then covered and kept warm. In the morning it would have become yogurt, which they ate with sweet dates and bread.

At other times the women would rise long before dawn and put the yogurt into a leben skin and rock back and forth until all the liquid was drawn out, leaving soft, butterlike balls. This delicious leben was most prized. Mara loved to wake early enough to listen as her servants stirred up the fire, baked the bread, and set up the tripod with its goatskin bag for making the day's leben. In the same way she looked forward to sunset. Then the herders rounded up their animals, and her servants rolled out the sleeping mats and gathered dung patties to hold the fire during the night.

Mara could picture the same procedure going on in Sarai's tent; the only difference was that Sarai would be up managing and directing the whole procedure. Sarai often made telling remarks about women who lay in bed until the sun was up.

On the third night in the new campsite, Mara was chilly, so she sat by her small fire of dried nettles and enjoyed the night sounds. She had put her girls to bed and was waiting for her husband. As on most evenings, he sat with some of the men around a fire discussing the happenings of the day. Mara had noted that Abram, too, was with the men, but she also knew that on occasion, he spent the entire evening with Sarai. That irritated her. It made her brood and ponder the source of Sarai's apparent charm.

Though Sarai wasn't young, she was still astonishingly beautiful. Her name meant "contention," and Mara thought it suited her well. She was willful, selfish, and outspoken. Sarai didn't contradict Abram in front of others, but they all could tell when she was displeased and they could just imagine what she said to him when she got him alone.

Mara never mentioned it to anyone, but she was smugly pleased that Sarai was cursed with barrenness. She would never have said it herself, but she enjoyed hearing others speculate as to what great wickedness Sarai had been involved in that she had been cursed with barrenness. Though Mara had borne no sons, her two daughters were at least something. Surely sons would follow.

The stars hadn't come out yet, but the wind had come up. One of the loose tent pieces flapped annoyingly while the poles creaked and groaned. Mara could hear the bleating of the sheep as they were driven into the enclosure formed by the tethered donkeys and kneeling camels, then much jostling as the ewes searched for their hungry lambs. Finally all was quiet, so quiet that she could hear the laughter of the men gathered around Eliazer's campfire.

She wondered what they talked about. She knew Lot's conversation always turned to the profit he intended to make. Since leaving Damascus, he had become more interested in the animals they owned. She had heard him say that both camels and sheep double themselves in three years. "Of course," he had added, "the male lambs will be sold or killed for food. The females we'll keep for breeding." She knew that the young male camels were always sold and only a few kept to carry the baggage.

What he didn't discuss was how heavily he counted on inheriting all his uncle's wealth. Since Abram had no children, Lot considered it was more or less understood between them that he would be his uncle's heir. Mara had taken for granted that he had agreed to go on this venture for whatever gain might be in it for them.

Mara jabbed the fire with a sturdy oak branch. They had plenty of dried nettles for the fire, and her girls had found truffles, which she considered a great delicacy. She hadn't shared them with anyone, not even Sarai. Especially not with Sarai. Sarai had everything. One didn't need to give her more.

Mara did have to reluctantly concede that Sarai genuinely loved her husband. She would defend his ideas, gloat over his success, and follow him on the most uncomfortable adventures. Such behavior was all the more amazing, since it was totally contrary to her spoiled nature.

Mara stood up and dusted off her robe. She looked around and then tiptoed to the far side of her tent. She strained to see the neighboring tents. She wanted to see if Sarai was up waiting for her husband. As far as she could tell, the tent was dark. Sarai wasn't waiting up.

Mara wouldn't go to sleep until Lot returned. It was their custom. Even in

Haran, women waited until the men came home. The men might be hungry, or more likely looking for some wifely attention before going to sleep. Then there was the news. Mara never wanted to miss that. Sarai obviously wasn't curious. She could wait.

Mara had noticed that in most things Sarai seemed to get her way. She should have been divorced and disgraced for having no children, but instead she seemed only to get her husband's added attention and concern.

That Sarai had a tent of her own further infuriated Mara. She didn't have to share her tent with anyone, and Abram didn't seem to mind. "You can't always win, Sarai," Mara sputtered to herself, jabbing all the time at the fire. "It's not natural. I'm just waiting . . . waiting to see you brought down and humbled."

* * *

Usually the men went to Abram's tent, but on that night Eliazer had planned a special celebration in honor of his benefactor. Many of the men of the tribe and others who wanted to share in the festivities sat around the fire enjoying Eliazer's hospitality. There was to be no talk of business. Instead stories were told and humorous happenings remembered. There was a feeling of well-being and expectancy.

The men usually ate together, and tonight Eliazer had ordered spits erected and lambs roasted to a succulent brown. To everyone's surprise, he was lavish with the dried dates and figs and passed the skins filled with date wine again and again. "It's time to celebrate. We may soon be coming to the place that Abram's God has promised him."

The men looked at each other, and the air grew vibrant with excitement. Finally Urim, who could wait no longer, spoke, "Are we then nearing our goal?" The ribs he had been eagerly gnawing dropped to his lap unnoticed.

All eyes turned to Abram. He sat as usual in the seat of honor on banked cushions with a tasseled canopy slung overhead, held in place by four lances that had been driven into the ground on each side. He had been talking to his nephew Lot and hadn't followed the discussion, but now with the cheese maker's question repeated, he was suddenly alert. "You must understand," he said, "I can't say with any certainty where we are going."

For a moment the words hung on the evening air in all their mystery and obtuseness. Abram was always answering like this, and yet there was such a sureness about the going itself that none of them doubted for a moment that he knew exactly where they were headed.

"But," Lot interjected, "we are following the trade route our people have always followed. Surely you can tell us now where this land is that you are to be given."

Abram took a drink of fresh camel's milk from the gourd that hung from his belt. "There's nothing like fresh, warm milk enjoyed under a full moon," he said as though oblivious of the questions.

"But, my lord," Eliazer said hesitantly, "the little bird that rests in your bosom."

"My wife, Sarai, you mean. Among ourselves we can speak frankly. We are family, are we not?"

"Well then, your wife, Sarai, has mentioned to some of the women that we are going to Shechem. The big, fruitful valley beyond the mountains of Gilboa."

Abram looked down into his cup and smiled. "So someone has plowed with my heifer, as the saying goes, and you think you have discovered something."

The men looked away in embarrassment. Very rarely did they give away the source of their information, particularly if it had come through their wives. However, they were all so anxious to discover what this man who walked among them like a god was thinking that they scrambled to get any bit of information possible. "We meant no harm," one of them mumbled.

"Of course you meant no harm," Abram said as he handed his gourd for the serving lad to wipe with the tail of his short robe before he carefully fastened it back on his belt. "You want to know and I want to know. I've only this impression, this vision that comes into my mind of the fertile valley . . . the fig trees, pomegranates, nuts, and grain for bread . . . and grass for more flocks than we can imagine. A veritable garden."

"And," Lot urged him on, "you are to be given this land?"

"That my God has spoken I know. He wanted to save me from the trouble that was coming with the Elamites and also from the evils of the new religions and their idols."

"The land . . . what about the land you are to be given?" Lot was growing increasingly anxious.

"I only know He is leading me to a place that is to belong to me and my descendants, and that my people are to be a great nation. These things I know, but the details weren't given." He got to his feet and walked out through the midst of them.

When he was gone, one of the men spoke, "Do you think it's true that he really doesn't know where he is going?"

"I think he knows a lot more than he is telling us," another man ventured. "He's certainly convinced it's going to be some wonderful place."

"Well, I'm counting on Abram's hadh, or luck as we say. He's already wealthy beyond belief. I think we can trust his instincts for success," Lot announced as if to assure himself. "You'll see, this God of his has promised to bless him, and if we are there, we'll get some of it too."

"But the famine. What about the famine?" one of them said.

Lot turned back and spoke almost fiercely, "You can be sure the famine isn't where we're going. Abram's God promised blessings." With that he said good night to Eliazer and left.

The men thanked Eliazer for his hospitality and then quietly disappeared into the star-studded night. The vicious dogs that were trained to prowl all night around the camp growled, baring their teeth until each man spoke, and then knowing the voice, they went on their way.

The night air was fragrant with the odor of wood smoke and pine. Here on the lower slopes of Hermon were pine forests and, in places, jutting rocks, caves, and bubbling streams. If it weren't such rugged country, it would be a delightful place to stay.

* * *

As Abram approached his tent, he had a feeling of well-being. Their grain bags were full, the leather satchels were stuffed with the most succulent dates, and since they had gathered the pine cones on Hermon, they had a good supply of pine nuts. He saw that Sarai had already gone to bed and was undoubtedly asleep. He could decide in the morning whether to tell her how the secret he had entrusted to her had suddenly come out in the meeting.

He smiled as he pictured her hair loose and flowing, her lashes thick and feathery like a young girl's. Her mouth still had the fullness of passion, and when she was awake, it either curved into a smile or, if puzzled or irritated, formed into a most provocative pout.

If he scolded her for her indiscretion in telling his secrets, he could just imagine how she would look at him with her whole expression gone suddenly serious. Tears might pool in her eyes and she'd say she was sorry. It had all happened before and he could never stay upset with her for long. Ever since they had been children, playing together in his father's sunny courtyard beside the house in Ur, he had not been able to keep a secret from her.

He let his serving man roll out his sleeping mat and raise the side of the tent so he'd get more of the night breeze. Then without another thought he went to sleep.

✳ ✳ ✳

Mara heard footsteps, then muffled laughter as goodnights were said. She saw the light glowing through the qata, the brightly woven cloth that divided Lot's section of the tent from hers. She called his name softly and he came around to stand by her fire. She quickly knelt and loosed his sandals, banked the cushions for him to sit, and motioned for him to relax. "Was there news? Has anyone heard just where we're going?"

It was a subject they never tired of discussing, and Lot sank down on the cushions, ready to tell what he knew.

"Did he say where we are going?" she asked again eagerly.

"He never says. He's always vague, but I have a feeling we're almost there. Maybe a new moon or two, and we'll see this land he's to be given."

"How do you know? What makes you think such a thing?"

"It's just a feeling I have."

"What feeling? What do you feel?"

"I guess it's his own excitement. You can't be around him without sensing something wonderful is about to happen."

"So you think it's all true? He's really going to have all these promises come true?"

"He's a sensible man . . . a very pragmatic man. And he believes and is even more excited than I am."

"But the famine . . . what about the famine? I thought there was a famine in the land west of the Jordan."

Lot jabbed at the fire. "Who knows? One can't always believe traders. Anyway, can you imagine Abram's God giving him some land blighted by famine? All his talk and excitement for nothing? It's hard to imagine such a thing."

Mara shrugged and looked out into the darkness. "He and Sarai would be so embarrassed. After all that talk about his God, convincing all of us to come along, even leaving the family gods behind, it would be quite devastating."

"He didn't ask any of us to come," Lot said defensively. "It was something we chose to do."

"However it was, it will be most embarrassing if there should be a famine," Mara tried to speak calmly, but her voice held an edge of malicious enjoyment that Lot completely missed.

5

*T*hey heard only rumors of the famine until they came to ford the Jordan near the city of Hazor. Here they met a straggling band of men and their families fleeing Shechem in the valley of Mukhnah. With hollow eyes and distended bellies, they spoke of famine, dust storms, and heat.

When urged, they reported that most of the people had gone to Egypt or down the Wadi Far'ah to the land east of the Jordan. "The rains should have come a month ago," one of them said. "It was just the same as last year, and the year before. Now it's even the drinking water. The streams and cisterns are all going dry."

The men in Abram's band looked at him, thinking to see some hesitancy, some reaction. Though he listened, the depressing news seemed at first to have little effect on his enthusiasm. But when the sun beat down mercilessly and the nights grew hot and suffocating, Abram became silent and thoughtful, yet still insisting that they press on toward the valley.

Finally one little boy pointed out birds of prey that seemed to be following them, and Abram became disturbed. Great vultures and hawks would come flapping their wings and then light in the dusty branches of the tall carob trees where they could look down on his company with parted beaks and hungry eyes. "That's ominous," he muttered. "Birds don't act like that without some awful carnage."

The farther they went, the more they encountered bad omens, repeated warnings of hunger, lack of water, and a terrible, debilitating heat. All the people they met seemed almost speechless, unable to tell adequately of the horror they had experienced.

Finally the men and women in Abram's company began to beg him, first gently and then insistently, to turn back or go another route. To their surprise, he pushed his headpiece back and wiped the sweat from his brow but insisted they press on. His step slowed, and his eyes began to look dark and troubled, but he continued to urge them on up through a rock-bordered pass until late one afternoon they came out onto a wide basin. "See the mountains on the right with the sun glinting on them," he said as he tried to muster some enthusiasm. "The tallest is Mount Ebal and the other beside it is Gerizim. The walled city in between is Shechem."

The large valley was surrounded by a ring of mountains. In better days it had been fertile beyond belief, but now it was a bowl of blowing dust.

They passed several small villages that showed no sign of life. When they came to a huge oak at the foot of the valley that led up to the city called Shechem, they stopped. It was obvious that the oak had been a center for various mysterious rites.

"I remember this tree," Abram said. "It was known as the Oak of the Sorceress. There used to be an old hag who sat here begging and telling fortunes. She had charms and incantations, and some even said she called up the devil and the djinn to do her bidding."

As they came closer to the enormous tree, they could see that libations of blood had been poured all over the gnarled roots. Near a broken-down altar they found bones, bits of curling hairy skins, and broken shards of pottery.

The odor of decay, death, and corruption was heavy on the air. "Things have been very bad here," Lot whispered to Abram. "The people obviously have been trying to placate Mot, so he will free Baal and they will have rain again."

Abram didn't seem to hear him. He walked around under the tree, lightly touching the standing stones with hollowed out places for oil or blood and fingering the bits of cloth tied to the bare branches of the tree.

With a sigh he looked back at the expectant faces of his people and remarked, "Such things are forbidden by Elohim, our God."

The people looked with interest at the tree and then up the valley toward Shechem. From where they stood they could tell that the city gate had once been impressive and the wall well built. Now however, the gate hung open, and the wall was crumbling with large, gaping fissures. Through these openings, they could see an odd assemblage of one-story stone and mud houses. They had flat roofs constructed of dried rushes covered with mud held in place by large crossbeams. Few of the houses had windows.

Abram chose Lot to go with him and cautioned Eliazer to hold the caravan in place until they returned. As the two men approached the city, they could see that it was depressingly dirty. Refuse had been thrown out in the streets for the goats or wild dogs. Vines and almond trees that had once lent a certain charm to their small courtyards were now standing leafless and bare, adding to the total desolate effect.

At first the city seemed deserted. However, as they came closer, beggars and a few lepers crept out with various objects supposedly for sale. The two men soon discovered that the beggars wanted to trade the decorated pottery, woven strips of bright cloth, or a few handfuls of grain for some drinking water.

Abram asked one of the threadbare urchins to get someone in authority. The boy hurried off and, within minutes, was back with an elderly gentleman. Abram noticed that he walked with a cane but carried himself with dignity. "You are welcome. You are welcome," the old man said, speaking their language with a strong Amorite accent.

He didn't smile, and Abram noticed that he kept nervously jabbing his cane into the path as though that might steady him. He wore fine robes, but they were stained and dusty, and his elegantly decorated sandals were strapped on feet that hadn't been washed for days.

"We need your permission to camp in the valley below your city," Abram said.

Instantly the man's eyes grew troubled as he looked over the crowded carts, donkeys, camels, sheep, and goats that stretched as far as he could see. "You are welcome to camp, but as you can see most of those who were able-bodied have fled the valley. The rest of us are still trying to leave."

"So I imagined," Abram said.

"You can see the streams are almost dry. The soil has turned to powder. It's blowing away." The old man motioned to the valley and then up the side of Mount Ebal where terraces once cradled vines and small olive trees.

"We'll need water," Abram muttered almost to himself as he looked back down toward the valley. "We have many people and our flocks are extensive."

The old man shook his head. "The water is scarce everywhere. We are sending mules to the wells at Dothan and over to Jezreel just to have drinking water."

Lot moved closer to his uncle and spoke in a whisper, "It would be foolish to camp here. We need to move on."

Abram frowned. "I remember this as such a green, fruitful valley. How can it all have dried up?"

The old man raised his hand and looked up at the cloudless sky. "It's said that we've offended Hadad, god of rain. We even sacrificed our children to him . . . and see, he doesn't care. He isn't going to help."

Abram frowned. When people sacrificed their children, they were usually desperate. The bigger the problem, the more precious the sacrifice demanded by the gods. A child, a young man, a beautiful young woman—all were sacrificed in the hope of getting the gods' attention.

"Is it all right if we decide to stay?"

"You can stay. Of course you can stay. I suppose there's enough dried grass for a few days. There are no wells. You'll find precious little water anyplace."

Abram thanked the old man and started back to the mouth of the valley where he had left the caravan. He was deep in thought, and Lot assumed he was deciding to move on. But when he spoke, it was involving another matter. "Lot," he said, "go down and see that the people pitch their tents near whatever water you can find."

"And you, my lord? Where will you be?"

"I am going up the mountain. I need to be alone." Abram was already looking toward the path that led up past the city of Shechem to the steep mountain heights of Ebal.

"My lord," Lot said in a tone of voice that conveyed his concern, "shouldn't we move on as quickly as possible?"

Abram seemed not to hear him. "You'll be in charge and make all decisions until I come back."

Abram turned and started up the path. He didn't look back to see if Lot was following his instructions but pressed on with a determined stride. He was soon out of the valley and climbing. The dogs and curious children eventually turned back, and at last he was alone.

He saw nothing of the carefully terraced plots now overgrown with cactus or stripped down to the bare outcroppings of rock. He was deeply troubled. He realized that all along, he had envisioned this valley as the very place God was leading him and his people. He had thought this was the land God was going to give him.

He had seen the valley first on a trading venture with his father. They were on their way down to Egypt when they heard there were armed bands waiting for the caravans along the usual route, so they had decided to come through this valley, then move up into the highlands. The valley had burst upon their travel-weary eyes as a virtual paradise. As young as he had been, he had noticed how fertile it was and how few people had settled in or around it. "There are no wells. Also it is hard to defend such an open valley," they had told him.

When he reached the top of Ebal, he sank down on a projection of rock. He felt exhausted and terribly disappointed. More than that he felt let down, tricked. Tears of frustration blinded his eyes. He'd risked everything and, worse, he had encouraged others to follow him. Now he could see it was like following a mirage. He began to doubt, to wonder if he could have imagined the promises.

It was some minutes before he looked up and was astonished at the sight before him. He stood up and shielded his eyes to see better. There was not only the valley of Mukhnah, "the encampment," but he could clearly see that the city of Shechem squatted right at the entrance to a pass that led westward, out to the coast.

Off to one side was the huge sacred oak that from this height looked no bigger than one of its leaves. His people setting up camp looked as small as ants.

The view of the valley was as nothing compared to the great distances he could see in every direction. To the south, he saw the port of Joppa and beyond it the great sea; to the east, the hills over against Luz, beyond that the chasm of the Jordan River, and on farther the plain of Hauran. His eyes followed the Jordan almost to its source and on out to the snowy peak of Mount Hermon.

He forgot how hot and tired he was. He also forgot for the moment his concern over the famine and the lack of water. There was a wind blowing, but the sky was cloudless and the air was clear, making the view all the more distinct. He drew in a deep breath of the clear, hot air and continued to pick out the familiar sights.

On that first visit so long ago with his father, he remembered an old man in Shechem telling them that Ebal was the highest point in the land and one could see almost down to the border of Egypt from its height. Now he knew that was true.

Slowly a great peace settled over him. The frustrations that had led him to strike out and climb the mountain melted away. In their place was a strange quietness. It was a quietness he had felt once or twice before. A quietness that carried with it an undercurrent of excitement. A feeling that something important was about to happen. Gradually he felt intensely alert, aware of the blueness of the sky, the grayness of the jagged rocks around him, a thorn bush, and a small yellow flower at his feet.

It was then that he heard the voice. It was the same voice and the same feeling that had caused him to leave Haran. "Abram, unto your seed I will give this land."

Abram whirled around expecting to see someone, but no one was in sight. He stood very still and listened. He heard only the wind and saw only small puffs of dirt blown around the base of the rocks. Again he heard the voice: "Unto your seed I will give this land."

He sank to his knees and then lowered his head to the ground and covered his face. The words enveloped him. They seemed to come from a great distance, and yet they were as close as his own heart. It was as though someone not only spoke the words, but also wrote them with a sharp stylus somewhere in his mind so that he heard them over and over again whichever way he turned.

He lost all consciousness of time. He was caught up in heart-rending emotion. He, a rational man, a man shrewder than most, a bargainer, and an intellectual, felt he was in the very presence of the great Creator God. The fear and doubt lifted, and in their place was a quiet ecstasy, an almost rapturous delight. The Creator God, Elohim, had spoken. Abram recognized His voice. Elohim had singled him out for this special blessing, and Abram was speechless with wonder.

Gradually the glory faded. The moment passed and Abram became aware again of his immediate surroundings. He stood up. The sun was edging its way down to the rim of Mount Carmel in the far distance, and in the valley he could see bright spots of light that must be their campfires already lit.

He lingered, still feeling the euphoria of the encounter. He had no doubt it was God who had spoken, the God he had encountered first in Ur and then in Haran. Joy flooded his entire being. He didn't want to leave. He didn't want to return to the valley. He repeated the words over and over.

He had been right. His every instinct had led him to this place, and now he knew that it was to be his.

The sun dropped lower, hovering on the horizon, while in the valley it was already dark. The vision had faded and with it came a terrible reality. This was the place, the place he'd been promised, and it was a barren, parched wasteland. Even worse, he'd brought all these people with him on extravagant promises. What would they say? What would they think when he told them this was all he was going to have?

He sank down on a jutting rock and let his head drop into his hands. "Oh my God, what am I to do? What will I tell all these people ... and Sarai? How can I tell her that this is the land you promised me, the land we have been talking about?"

There was no answer. No breeze stirred. A hawk flew overhead, balanced effortlessly on the warm air. Abram sat motionless and watched its slow, circling descent. When it finally disappeared, he stood up and with a sigh started back down to the camp.

At the base of the mountain he found Lot looking frustrated and impatient. Things had not gone well. "My lord," Lot's voice was urgent and strained. "There's barely enough water for our flocks and camels. We'll all die here if we don't move on quickly."

Abram hardly heard what he was saying. His mind was still preoccupied with what he'd seen and heard. "Pass the word through the camp," he told Lot, "that they are to sanctify and cleanse themselves. Tomorrow we will climb the mount, build an altar, and worship."

Lot frowned. "But, my uncle, there is almost no water, and our own drinking supply will soon be gone."

"Tomorrow you will see. We are going to climb the mountain and build an altar in this place," Abram said, looking around with an air of grim determination.

"An altar?" Lot asked.

"Tomorrow. It will be a time of dedication for all of us."

Lot could see that trying to dissuade his uncle would be useless. Reluctantly he relayed Abram's message to the people, then hinted that perhaps Abram had some explanation, some revelation from his God.

The next morning, before daybreak, the men gathered at the edge of the camp. Depression had given way to curiosity. As they started up the mountain, an air of excitement, then expectation, began to grow. They sang the old songs and felt the renewal of hope, of something spectacular about to happen.

The women and children huddled together in the deep shadows of the encampment and watched them go, wondering at the strangeness of it all.

At the summit the stars still hung low in the east, and the moon gave a hard, sharp light that brought the barren rocks into focus. Quickly, at Abram's command, the men picked up stones and silently piled them in the shape of a crude altar.

Just at sunrise the altar was ready and a young lamb was sacrificed as the men broke into an ancient hymn of thanksgiving and praise. When the singing died down, Abram offered a prayer to Elohim, the Creator God.

By that time the sun had risen over the summit of Gilboa, and its rays illumined the mountains beyond the Jordan. As the whole landscape became visible, there was a gasp of surprise. The long, tedious trek they had made from Mount Hermon now looked only a stone's throw away. They were filled with awe as they gazed in every direction. Most of them had spent all their lives on the flat plains of the Euphrates and could not imagine the possibility of such a view.

Abram waited until they had finished exclaiming, and then he began to point out the sights, Mount Carmel to the northwest, to the east Mount Hermon, and behind the eastern hills the Jordan, and to the south the port of Joppa.

"This land, all of it that you see, is the very land my God has promised me and my descendants." Abram glanced around expectantly, hopefully, but when he saw their sober, worried faces he grew silent.

First there were covert whispers and then overtones of displeasure. Finally Lot could contain himself no longer. "My lord," he sputtered, "do you mean that the land you have been promised is this?" His hand swept around, taking in the valley and the barren mountains.

Abram nodded, his gaze sweeping the horizon. "Yes, yes, this whole land is to be given to me and to my descendants."

As murmurs of displeasure broke out among the men, Lot spoke again, his voice bitter with disappointment, "Did you not ask your God why He has given you a land of death? One from which even the wild animals and pleasant birds have fled?"

Abram could see that they could think of nothing but the famine. He tried to encourage them. "I have seen the valley when it was green and bursting with figs, olives, grapevines, and great fields of wheat and barley," he said. "This drought will pass. It will be green again. That is the way of things."

The steady rumble of unease continued, but only Lot dared speak, "My lord, last night we were barely able to water our animals. If we aren't to die, we must move on quickly."

Abram looked from one to the other and saw their anger and frustration. He had no answers, and he didn't want to discuss anything at the moment. "We'll go back to our tents," he said, turning away so they couldn't see the hurt in his eyes. "It will become clear what we're to do."

Lot was not ready to drop the subject so quickly. "My lord," he said, "the place is impossible."

Abram turned and looked at Lot, meeting his eyes. "We may not understand, but it will become clear," he said. "The Creator God, the God of mountains and of hosts, He is the one who has made the promise, and He will show us what to do." With that Abram turned and started back down the mountain with a fast, determined stride.

* * *

The next morning when Abram ordered the old rags to be taken down from the tree of the sorceress and the ground around it completely cleared of debris, Lot questioned his wisdom. "My uncle," he said, "if we destroy his sacred place, won't the local god, Hadad, punish us?"

Abram paused a moment before replying. "This place is no longer his," he said finally. "It belongs to the living God, the God not made with hands."

Soon the great tree had been restored to its simple beauty and the area around it completely cleared. Even the air was freshened with incense. "God has spoken to me here in this place," Abram said. "This tree will no longer mark the place of the sorceress but will from this time on be called the Tree of Grace."

When Lot reported the events of the day to Mara, she could tell he was depressed, even angry. "Can you imagine," he said, jabbing the fire with a pointed stick, "he was excited. He didn't even see that it was a rotten trick."

"The people predicted Ur's god would wreak revenge on Abram," Mara said. "Now Abram's come against Hadad too." Mara's eyes were large with fright.

"To come against the moon god and the god of thunder is to invite trouble." Lot's voice registered his frustration.

"He's to have descendants. Where will he get them, do you suppose? Not from Sarai, I'm sure." In the darkness Mara bit her lip to keep from showing her pleasure. "If that promise turns out to be as empty as the others . . . well!" She saw she didn't have to say more. Lot understood perfectly.

71

* * *

Though Sarai wasn't pleased with the turn of events, she made up her mind to hold her peace and probe the subject gently. However, she was puzzled that Abram didn't seem to be angrier. His God had gotten him into this predicament, and she felt he should have been more resentful and bitter.

For herself, she wanted none of it. She secretly hoped he would give up this wild adventure and go back to Haran. It was true that, like Abram, she found the idol worship questionable at best, and the religious practices vulgar, but she had her family and so paid little attention to these things that bothered Abram so much.

She had always known that Abram listened to her, and she felt sure that if she insisted and was determined to go back, he would take her. With that bit of assurance, she ordered her maidens to lift the tent flaps so she could see the moon rise over the mountains to the east and catch any breeze.

She directed one of them to bring her a small earthen jar purchased in Damascus. She held the little jar carefully between two fingers while she gently pulled away the wax that held the stopper in place. "He chose this for me," she said as she poured a bit of the rare fragrance into her palm. She rubbed her hands together and then held them up so she could smell the heady odor of jasmine.

"He always buys the very best," she said as she proceeded to rub the oil up each arm, on each earlobe, down her neck, and around each breast.

She handed the bottle back to the maid and then dismissed all of them. Tonight she wanted to be alone. She was sure Abram would come looking for her, and she intended to be ready.

6

The next day they folded their tents and were on their way out of the valley. Although Abram was interested in seeing more of the land he had glimpsed from Mount Ebal, he was becoming more and more perplexed and deeply disturbed. He had pictured it all so differently. He had been so sure of the promises, and now he found himself wondering, pondering, almost doubting.

Listening to Sarai hadn't helped. The moment he had entered her tent and smelled the jasmine, he knew she wanted something. He was surprised when she didn't come right out and tell him like she usually did.

How subtle she'd been to remind him of the house and fields they'd left in Ur and the comforts his brother was enjoying in Haran. She had even suggested that perhaps the slaughter carried out by the Elamites was over and life in Ur was normal again. She left no doubt that she wanted to go back. She was already tired of their constant wandering, and the idea of famine frightened her.

He thought briefly of his brother Nahor and his prediction of disaster. If Nahor's gods were real, he had certainly offended them. Could it be possible that Ningal alone knew the secrets of life? Would Sarai forever be barren because she had not acknowledged the goddess's power?

While he was thinking these thoughts he was busy seeing that everything was ready to move on. He was quiet and preoccupied, easily irritated. He had no explanation to give these people who trusted him. He could see in their looks and in the silence as they kept glancing at him that they were expecting him to give some reason for their disappointment.

He squared his shoulders and looked around. Perhaps farther on he would find the prosperity and plenty he had at first envisioned. There had to be some explanation. He didn't doubt that he had heard the voice of this unseen God called Elohim, but there was so much he didn't know. If he could only meet someone who shared this same experience . . . someone who knew this God.

To his surprise, things didn't get better. They continued to get worse, much worse. They began to see hordes of locusts. The locusts buzzed and hummed, their wings vibrating in a continual whir. They landed on the tents in droves, letting their fragile legs cling tenaciously to the stiff goat hair weave, their small treacherous jaws boring holes in the sturdy stuff. They were in the sleeping rolls, on the cushions, and even crushed underfoot. Every green thing disappeared before their all-consuming hunger.

As Abram's band made their way up into the hill country toward Ai and Luz, they battled and struggled against the onslaught. Though the locusts skewered on a stick and roasted were surprisingly good to eat, the people soon tired of them. They yearned to get relief from the plague and to find fresh, sweet water, ripe figs, and grapes, but there were none.

Gradually they noticed that the soil was no longer rich and dark. Instead, hard layers of red earth barely covered the solid rock. Only in the ravines that fell away to the west would it be possible to plow or sow regular crops of grain. Most of the men were deeply disappointed. Eliazer was the only one who encouraged Abram. "Perhaps," he said, "Elohim is using the famine to drive the people out so you can have the land without shedding blood."

Abram gave serious thought to the words of his friend, though the farther they went from Shechem, the more doubts tormented him. How could it be, he wondered, that the voice was so distinct and the message so clear and still there is no guidance as to what we are to do about the famine?

To make matters even worse, the people were constantly asking questions he couldn't answer, while Sarai had grown silent. He could tell by the way her mouth was set and the impatient way she swatted at the locusts that she was at some sort of breaking point.

Finally when they reached Luz, there was a degree of relief. The nights grew cooler and the plague of locusts came mercifully to an end. At last they found some water. It was not in great abundance, but enough to sustain them if they were careful and used it mostly for drinking.

Abram obtained permission for his people to camp in the open fields between Luz and Ai. He forced himself to move among them as they pitched their tents and tried to encourage them. Instead of being encouraged, they looked at him with wide, troubled eyes, hoping for a decision that would rescue them from their misery.

When days passed and Abram had no solution to offer, open hostility sprang up among the women and then spilled over to the men. They pleaded with Lot to convince Abram of the seriousness of their situation. It was no secret that most of them wanted to turn back.

Urim, the cheese maker, was the most vocal. "We didn't know it would be like this!" he complained one day as he brought some smoked cheese to Abram's tent.

Abram had been praying, and he resented the interruption by the feisty little man. More than that, he found it irksome to be reminded constantly and now even in his own tent of the disappointment people were feeling. Despite his frustration, Abram waved Urim to a cushion and was surprised when he sat down.

Abram studied the man, realizing again that Urim was a man of action, with little ability to reason. However, he did make wonderful cheese. "It is the way of the world that things are not perfect," Abram said, hoping to silence him.

"But, my lord," Urim said leaning forward, one hand resting on his knee and the other scratching his head, "your God seemed to promise so much. Has He perhaps forgotten you?"

No one else had dared voice such a thought, and Abram found it unsettling. He had struggled to put down the same nagging thought, and now as the words hung on the air between them, he found them as real and palpable as the tent over their heads. The words had taken on form and shape, demanding a response. "Were you with us on Mount Ebal?" he asked.

"Yes, yes, my lord. I was there. I saw the land and heard all that you said. From up in the clouds it looked quite grand, but it's down here we live and here there's nothing but thirst and hunger for man and beast."

"So . . . " Abram said as he carefully studied the man, "what would you suggest?"

"Why, to me, it's quite plain. We should forget about this God awhile and use our wits." Urim never let his eyes waver from Abram's face. He seemed to be expecting some favorable response.

"And if we used our wits, what would we do? What could we do that we aren't doing now?" Abram was growing impatient, but he could see that the man prided himself on his own common sense and perhaps could be depended on to find some answer.

Abram's interest encouraged Urim. He smiled and leaned forward. "Go

75

down to Egypt like everyone else. Wait it out. It's obvious your God isn't thinking about the famine. Probably doesn't even know it exists since He's somewhere up there on Ebal. No, there are times, I always say, when one has to think for oneself."

Abram didn't answer, and Urim was always nervous when people didn't talk. He got to his feet and pushed the offering of smoked goat cheese on its circle of matting toward Abram. "There's more if you need it," he said. When Abram still didn't look up or answer, he slowly backed out of the tent, feeling satisfied that he'd said all that he had wanted to say.

* * *

That night Abram sat in his tent, not wanting to see anyone. The words of the cheese maker drummed in his head stronger than the words of his God on Mount Ebal. "Forget about this God awhile and use our wits," the man had said.

It had been a long time since he had entertained such thoughts, but now they seemed to ring with some truth. What bothered him was the fear that if he once began to rely on his wits, would he still be able to hear the voice of his God? Would he lose the promises altogether?

It grew late and his servants still waited to roll out his sleeping mat, raise the tent flaps, and bring him the silver pitcher and basin. Even with the shortage of water he could not think of retiring for the night without washing his feet and hands. As he had learned long before when traveling with his father, it took only a small amount of water when poured from the pitcher over the hands and then the feet into the basin.

He had the servants adjust the tent flaps so he could see the moon and stars, and then he dismissed them. He stretched out on the sleeping mat, but sleep wouldn't come. Instead he kept going over what Eliazer had said about the famine perhaps being Elohim's way of freeing the land from the Amorites. On the other hand, if he insisted on staying and his herds of goats and sheep starved to death and the people were thirsty, it would be too late to take the advice of the cheese maker.

He got up and went to the door of his tent. He could see the other tents clearly in the moonlight, the dried thorn hedges that marked off the courtyards and sheltered most of the animals at night.

Sarai's tent was dark. He had shared the cheese with her and had gotten a bellyful of advice. Sometimes she wasn't logical. If she had her way, they would fold up their tents and head for Egypt or back to Haran.

She was too quick for him. She made up her mind too fast and seemed to have good reasons for everything. Once she saw anything clearly, she wouldn't let it go but hung on tenaciously and tried to convince him of its rightness. He felt he had to be alone. He needed to think things through before he saw her again, and so he hadn't gone to her, even though he'd seen that she was waiting up for him.

In the distance he could see the flat-roofed, whitewashed buildings of Luz as they crowned the ridge. An owl screeched from the bare branches of a nearby oak and was echoed by a braying donkey and barking dog. He had the lonesome feeling of a stranger in a strange land.

The only thing familiar in his surroundings was the low-hanging canopy of stars overhead. As a citizen of Ur, he had made an extensive study of the stars. Now he could clearly see the familiar configurations. There was the great dragon or serpent that wound itself around one-half of the northern sky. In one of the coils of its tail was the unmoving star called Thuban, or "the subtle." The bright star in its head was called Rastaban, meaning "the head of the subtle." He knew the desert Semites called the star Al Waid, meaning "who is to be destroyed."

He always liked to think that a time would come when the promise handed down from the old religion would come to pass: "The seed of the woman will bruise the serpent's head and the serpent will bruise his heel."

His eyes next traveled to the group of stars in the form of a lamb called Taleh. From his study with the stargazers of Ur, he knew the ancient Akkadians called the figure Baraziggar. Bar meant "altar" and ziggar, "right making." Gradually a thought began to form. It was the idea of an altar. An altar would require repentance and making things right. He had noticed that Elohim was most likely to speak and give guidance when men built altars and made things right. Quickly he decided to build an altar.

With final resignation he let the tent flap fall in place. Tomorrow they would build the altar and offer a sacrifice. If they received no guidance, they could consider going down to Egypt as Urim had suggested and Sarai had urged. The move would please Sarai. He wanted to do something to please her. He couldn't stand this loneliness, this feeling of isolation from the men and his beloved Sarai as well. However, if Elohim spoke and told him to stay, he would stay . . . no matter the cost to himself.

With that thought in mind, he once again lay down and was soon asleep.

The next day he reluctantly told Sarai what he intended to do and was rewarded by her tears and loving embrace. When he told the men, he could almost hear the sigh of relief as they hurried off to gather the rough-hewn stones to build the altar.

The wood for the sacrifice was dry and brittle, but it had been hard to light and at first refused to burn. The very air was charged with anxiety and suspense rather than worship. Abram stayed until the coals burned down to glowing embers, then finally had to announce that in spite of their urgent prayers and entreaties, he had received no answer. Elohim had been silent. Glancing around, he noted a look of intense relief on everyone's face. Reluctantly he agreed to go down to Egypt until the famine was over.

Once the decision was made, he tried to put all further doubts and questions from his mind and instead made plans for going down to Egypt. He had heard the reports of trouble at the border. Too many half-starved, emaciated people were trying to slip by the guards. He had one great advantage, and he would have to make the most of it.

In the old days, when he had come with his father and the uncles on trading ventures down into Egypt, they had made the acquaintance of the pharaoh's vizier. He was an intelligent man who liked to sit in the evening and hear of other countries, their customs, and their beliefs. He had taken a special liking to these traders from Ur and had always given them a hearty welcome. They in turn had filled his hand with rare and priceless gifts.

Abram had heard that this very vizier had by some strange twist of fate become the new Pharaoh, called Amenemhet. Still more amazing, it was said that he had moved the capital of Egypt from Thebes to a place called Itjtawy in the delta. This made it much more accessible. Abram hoped Pharaoh would remember him from the past and would make things easy for them during their stay.

"We'll have to send presents," Abram explained to his men as they were warming themselves by a small fire of dried dung. He had described the unique relationship his father had enjoyed with the vizier-turned-pharaoh. "He is a man who appreciates fine things, and in return we can depend on him to be generous."

The men were immediately encouraged. They totally ignored Abram's warning of the difficulties they could face at the border and instead talked only of the rumors they had heard of life in Egypt.

Sarai especially was pleased. She quietly told Mara how Abram had been quite modest in his remarks about his friendship with the pharaoh. "Imagine," she said, "a vizier becoming a pharaoh. Who would have thought such a thing possible?" She was busy with her hand loom and didn't notice the way Mara tossed her head and smirked.

"Lot says he is from an important family that lives on an island up near the first cataract," Mara said and was pleased to see that Sarai stopped her weaving and looked up in surprise. She obviously hadn't thought that Mara would be so well informed. Neither woman knew what a cataract was, but neither was going to admit it to the other.

That night when Abram came to Sarai's tent and had eaten the freshly baked bread dipped in olive oil and thyme, Sarai asked him, "What is a cataract?"

Abram was about to bite into the steaming bread, but he hesitated in surprise. "Where did you hear of cataracts?"

"From Mara. She says the new pharaoh is from an island up near the first cataract." Sarai didn't look up but toyed with the bread she was eating. The information she sought was much more important than food.

"So you don't want to be outdone. You want to know as much as Mara." He laughed. It always pleased him to ferret out some hidden aspect of Sarai's nature.

Sarai threw down her bread and turned away. She hated when Abram pointed out the foolishness of her pride. She was even more annoyed when he didn't seem to notice her frustration. He went on dipping his bread and eating hungrily. When he had finished, he motioned for her maid to take the food away, wiped his hands on the damp towel she held for him, and then settled back in the cushions and looked at Sarai.

"How is it," he said, "that you seem to grow more lovely with time? If we were back in Ur, I'd have to find some way to protect you."

"What do you mean, protect me?" she asked rather coyly.

"Why, in a place like Ur, as it is now with the Elamites in power, they take what they want. If it's a man's wife they want, they don't hesitate to take her."

"But the husband would complain to the judges at the gate and they'd have their heads for it."

Abram had to smile, seeing Sarai's certainty at just how the husband would act. He realized that she had been rather sheltered and had no idea of the dark evils that had come with the Elamites to plague the residents of Ur. He felt that he had been remiss in not explaining some of the dangers. "I'm afraid you don't understand," he said, reaching for her warm, rather practical little hand. "They would have the husband killed."

Sarai was immediately horrified. "Killed! They would have the husband killed!" Her hands flew to her mouth and her eyes were large with the fright of such an idea. "Why would they kill him?"

"Just so they wouldn't be bothered with him and any plots for revenge."

"Are you sure?" she asked.

"Very sure."

"Have you known anyone . . ." She couldn't finish the sentence. It was too horrible to contemplate.

"Yes, Sarai, I have even heard the women of Ur have taken to wearing veils to cover their faces or they stay inside."

"How unpleasant."

Abram had to laugh at the look on her face and for a moment that broke the tension. "We may find the same thing true in Egypt. I was only there as a young man with a group of traders. Even then the vizier had a reputation for lustily gathering beautiful women into his harem."

Sarai laughed suddenly and merrily, just as she had done when they were playing together back in Ur in their father's courtyard. "Well, there's no need to fear. I'm too old to attract any man's attention."

Abram became serious. Quickly his eyes scanned her face and then her small shapely figure with the bare toes peeping out from beneath her fringed skirt. "Sarai, I must confess, I find you more beautiful now than when you were younger."

Again she laughed. "How can you be serious?"

He caught her hands and turned her around to face him. He studied her face, and she saw that he was seeing her almost as a stranger would see her. When he spoke, his words came with great effort. "Sarai, you wouldn't know, but there is a soft, glowing bit of vitality that seems to radiate from you, making you most attractive. Pharaoh is sure to find you captivating. We'll have to hide you away or cover you up while we're in Egypt."

Sarai jumped to her feet. "You mean I'll have to stay hidden away while everyone else visits and has exciting adventures?"

Abram got up and reached out to her, explaining, "We'll ask Pharaoh for a house for our families while we are there. You can invite the ladies of the court to visit, but I'm afraid it may not be safe for you to visit them."

Sarai pulled away and turned her back to him. "That would spoil everything. I couldn't stand it."

"There's no other way." Abram's voice was husky with concern.

"But they will invite us back. I couldn't endure having to refuse."

As usual Abram couldn't stand seeing Sarai so disappointed. He determined to find a way to please her without taking a chance on offending the pharaoh.

He had been thinking a great deal about Pharaoh and had already decided to send presents to him. At every stop he intended to dispatch runners with costly gifts to remind the pharaoh of their past friendship.

Abram had no idea how the man they had known as a vizier had become the exalted, most honorable, and venerated Pharaoh of both Upper and Lower Egypt. As the people said, "He has brought together the Vulture of Upper Egypt and the Serpent of Lower Egypt." He would be wearing the two crowns, the rounded white crown for the lands to the south and the red crown that fit over it for the northern section. Kemet, the black-and-red land as the Egyptians called it, was united under his rule. Their old friend was undoubtedly very powerful and would be able to help them considerably if they were careful not to offend him.

"Sarai," he said gently, "I will try to think of some solution that won't be so distasteful to you. However, we can't take a chance on offending Pharaoh."

With a little cry of joy that always delighted Abram, she spun around and impulsively flung her arms around him. "You will. You will think of something. I know you will."

Later, back in his own tent, Abram quickly put aside the happy time spent in Sarai's grateful arms and once again struggled with the problems of going down to Egypt. He seemed always to be caught in an impossible tangle. He'd promised Sarai the freedom she wanted, and he would have to think of some way without offending the pharaoh to make sure they didn't court disaster. There had been ghastly stories of wives in Ur being snatched from their homes and husbands brutally killed. What had happened in Ur could happen in Egypt, he reasoned. Beautiful Sarai could be taken and he could be killed.

Then another, more frightening thought occurred. If he were to introduce Sarai as his wife, the old question of children would be raised. If it were discovered that she was barren, there would be the usual fear that she was somehow the bearer of frightful omens and demonic entities. They would be sure she was cursed, and her very presence could bring the same curse to them and their household.

As he tossed and turned, suddenly a solution occurred to him. Sarai was his half-sister. It would be no lie to say to anyone who might inquire that she was indeed his sister, implying she was still unmarried. That would avoid any possibility of his life being in danger and any question about Sarai's barren state. With that settled he turned over and sank into a deep sleep.

Sarai readily agreed to say, if asked, that she was his sister. As it turned out the only time they were questioned was at the border going into Egypt where a contingent of Pharaoh's border guards stopped them and asked questions. A scribe jotted down all the information. When they parted the curtains of Sarai's cart and asked her name, she told them Sarai, and when they asked for her relationship to the others, she hesitated only a moment before saying, "The sister of Abram."

Abram, standing beside the scribe, breathed a sigh of relief and smiled his approval. It was only later that he began to wonder if he had made a mistake not only in asking Sarai to tell this half lie, but also in making the trip down to Egypt. He didn't know what else he could have done, but it soon became clear that Elohim had not brought him here.

7

*I*n one of the gardens of the royal palace at Itjtawy in the delta near Memphis, a group of maidens waited for Pharaoh's new favorite. They had all come from noble families with high hopes that they would be chosen to wait on Her Radiance. Among the group was a haughty young beauty who stood apart from the others and seemed sulky and out of sorts, if not outright hostile. When her turn came to have her name recorded by the royal scribe, she tossed her head and gave her name as Hajar Gameela.

The scribe looked up and smirked as he noted her arrogance. He recognized her as one of the daughters of the pharaoh by a concubine who had recently fallen from favor. "Beautiful stone," he said writing her name in small figures on a partially rolled parchment. "You can discard the fancy name. Now you are just an ordinary brown rock to be polished and shaped. Don't forget or it will go hard with you."

"Don't try to threaten me," she said, leaning over so no one else would hear. "I don't want to be chosen, and I don't intend to stay." She whirled around and with a proud lift of her chin rejoined the others in the shade of the tall lotus pillars.

The scribe threw down his reed pen, "By the feather of maat, the truthful one," he stormed, "I'll not abide such conceit. Guard!"

He motioned for one of the guards but then on second thought waved him away. However, as he went on recording names, he was no longer calm and efficient but instead glanced every once in a while at the rebellious Hajar Gameela. "You'd think the girl would realize she has no influence now. She's trouble," he muttered half to himself and half to the young boy who assisted him.

Hajar stood apart from the other young women. She was the only one not excited and eager. She glanced around furtively. She felt confident that she could easily be chosen if that was what she wanted. However, that was definitely not what she wanted, and Hajar had always managed to get what she wanted. That is, she had always gotten just what she wanted until her mother had been suddenly rejected by the pharaoh, and she herself was no longer his pride and joy.

It was due to the new favorite's clever plotting that she was here, and she was determined to do whatever was necessary to frustrate the woman's plans.

Many people had explained to her that it would be a great honor to be chosen as a maiden to wait on the women of high standing in Pharaoh's court. But she knew it was the new favorite's way of putting her down, making sure she realized she was no longer privileged.

As Hajar thought about it now, she realized that she would have been wiser to hide her love for her father, the pharaoh, from this woman. This woman, Senebtisy, who had taken her mother's place in Pharaoh's affections, was no great beauty, but she was from a powerful family. She was already noted for ridding the court of any competition. Hajar's mother had urged caution. "We no longer have any influence with Pharaoh, and if we are to stay, we'll have to accede pleasantly to this woman's wishes."

Hajar had not listened to her mother. Instead she had fought a desperate battle to be first in the aging pharaoh's affections. She had been so sure of winning her father over that she had privately taunted the new favorite in every way possible. "It's too bad," she would say with a look of concern, "he doesn't honor you as he did my mother."

Her insolence did not go unnoticed, and Senebtisy was determined to humble Hajar and rid the court of her. But how to do so was a problem. Pharaoh had always been amused and charmed by Hajar's spunk. He found her refreshingly outspoken. What others considered arrogance, he condoned as appropriate for one of royal blood.

Just when Hajar thought she had won, Senebtisy had suggested she enter the competition to become one of the young maidens stationed in the women's court. Pharaoh had thought that showed genuine affection for Hajar on the part of his favorite. He didn't suspect that it was her way of controlling every aspect of Hajar's life.

"See," she told Pharaoh, "your daughter is slim and round-eyed and has skin like an almond blossom. What else is worthy of her birth and station? She will be like a beautiful lotus blossom among my women. She will learn many things while we are looking for a suitable husband for her."

Senebtisy had already chosen the suitable husband for Hajar and only waited for the right moment to approach Pharaoh. The man she had chosen was an aged nomarch from the delta. He had ruled this area almost like a king until Amenemhet became Pharaoh and united the country. Pharaoh was sure to consider it a wise move. To have a marriage agreement with such a powerful man would assure some control over the nome he still held.

As the day wore on, Hajar had hoped she would be eliminated, but each time the chief eunuch had passed over her and other young girls were rejected. The other girls wanted nothing in life so badly as to win while she wanted only to remain a princess, a favorite of her father.

Quickly she decided she wouldn't smile. She would stand straight and remain distant. She would make no claims to brilliance in any field and then perhaps they would excuse her. She almost laughed thinking how angry Her Radiance, Senebtisy, would be.

Hajar had been so preoccupied with her own frustrations that she hadn't paid attention to anything or anyone. Now she looked around. It had been the only home she had known. She loved the fountains, the banks of flowers, and the servants always waiting to serve. To think of leaving pained her, but to stay and be under the control of the new favorite was unbearable.

In most homes there was only one small pool and a fountain that played on special feast days. Here there were numerous courtyards, all beautifully cared for with fountains bubbling constantly. The pillars that edged the lotus pool were decorated with bright designs, and the light, airy material that was strung in between to keep out the sun gave the whole portico a soft glow. Incense burned on twin braziers, and though the summer had passed, it smelled like spring because of the fragrant, spiraling smoke.

Gradually Hajar became aware of an uneasy silence. Everyone seemed to be waiting for someone or something. The young girls giggled nervously and whispered furtively to their friends. She would have been as nervous as the others if she had wanted to stay. Since she didn't want to stay, she was totally relaxed.

Suddenly there was the sound of a trumpet being blown somewhere in another courtyard or perhaps in the entrance hall. It was the signal for the two great brass doors leading into the main building to swing open. There, framed in the doorway, were the royal eunuchs. Their short skirts were carefully pleated and their headbands fashioned with gold coiled snakes, the spears they carried sharp and deadly.

Behind them came an open sedan chair that rested on delicately carved ebony poles and carried by four footmen. The group of hopeful beauties gasped as they saw the woman in the chair. She gave the illusion of youth by her erect bearing, small exposed breasts, and full black wig held in place by a cap of golden wing feathers with a cobra at its crest. The hand that seemed so carelessly draped over the chair's arm flashed with rare jewels.

She looked straight ahead until the chair was gently placed on the warm blue tiles, then with a regal lift of her chin, she gave her hand to one of the bearers and stepped down. They all noticed that she wore no shoes, but several of her toes were decorated with gold rings. Her eyes darted over the bowed heads of her slaves until they lighted on the young girl who carried her sandals.

"Layla!" she said firmly as she reached out and gave the kneeling girl a sharp thump on the head with her scepter. The girl looked up with alarm and noticed the royal one pointing at her feet. "My sandals, I want my sandals."

Quickly the girl sprang forward and deftly eased the sandals onto her feet.

"It's Her Radiance, Pharaoh's new favorite," one of the youngest girls whispered. Senebtisy looked around as though wanting to determine who had spoken. Her eyes were outlined in heavy black kohl, and her eyebrows were carefully arched. It was easy to see that at some time in the past she had been a beautiful woman. Now, though she was still slim and gave the illusion of youthfulness, close observation showed her to be considerably older than she at first appeared.

Her expression was the fixed, pleasant half-smile the members of Pharaoh's family had always worn in public. However, Hajar knew from months of observation that she was a woman who seemed pleasant on the surface but could be both bitter and vindictive. Hajar also knew from personal experience that Her Radiance could be a very hard taskmistress. Hajar was more determined than ever to fail whatever test was put to her. She moved to the back where she would be less likely to be seen.

Her Radiance began pointing to one girl after another, signaling them to come out where she could get a better look at them, then quickly decide their fate.

Her eyes settled on Hajar with recognition. She singled her out to walk back and forth before the royal chair. Hajar had deliberately walked with a swinging gait like a peasant from one of the villages of Upper Egypt. To

Hajar's disgust, that didn't discourage the woman, and in the end she was placed among those who were chosen.

At last, just as the test was finished, a frightful thing happened. Senebtisy accidentally dropped the scepter with the glowing golden ankh on the top. Her hands flew to her face as she stood looking with horror at the scepter bouncing across the bright tiles. No one moved. For anyone but specified royalty to touch the symbol of power and authority with its emblem of life and good luck on the crest could bring death, yet for Her Radiance to stoop was unthinkable.

It was a bad omen. The new favorite grew pale as she sank into her chair. No one moved. All eyes clung to the scepter.

Quickly Hajar stepped forward. She cared nothing for royal favor, nor did she fear the punishment that could be meted out to her. With a deft movement she stooped down and picked up the scepter. There was a gasp of astonishment from those who were watching.

Bending slightly in deference, then advancing in a manner that could only be considered haughty, she came forward and returned the scepter. Senebtisy took the scepter, but as their eyes met, she flashed a look of virulent hatred at Hajar. "No one but the chosen one touches the sacred ankh and lives," she said.

Hajar smiled, affecting a show of innocence. "Maybe I am chosen," she said.

A gasp went around the room while Senebtisy's eyebrows shot up dangerously. "If the gods don't destroy you, others will. Bind her," she ordered her eunuchs.

The pharaoh's favorite raised her chin and, looking down at Hajar with total disdain, ordered the eunuchs to take her to one of the back rooms and lock her up.

The eunuchs moved forward to obey. "It would be better that you had died from touching the scepter," one of them said. "Now she will see you as a real threat. You are a foolish girl."

Hajar was more surprised than she let anyone see. She had felt such hatred well up inside her that she had acted impulsively. She, better than the rest, knew the danger involved in touching the queen's scepter. Then to have suggested she might be one of the "chosen" had been total arrogance.

Hajar was locked in an old storeroom for five days and fed only water and stale bread. During that time, she received word that her mother had been sent back to her family in disgrace. At the end of the five days, Pharaoh had discovered Hajar's fate. To everyone's surprise, he was amused and thought it showed her royal bearing. "So she touched the scepter and still lives. The girl does me credit. It's too bad she wasn't a son."

With no more consideration, he ordered Hajar to be allowed to continue in training with the other maidens. That order infuriated Senebtisy. If she had been against the girl before, now she was doubly determined to have her married and out of the court. However, it was not her way to go against Pharaoh's wishes. She determined to do as he wished, but encourage the wedding as soon as possible.

Everything seemed to have changed for Hajar. The chief eunuch who came to release her was eager to please, and the young women in training viewed her with obvious envy. She was given new clothes, a beaded pectoral, and a ring from Pharaoh's treasure house. Since her hair was thick and glossy, the attendants decided not to shave her head, but cut it in the shape of the wigs most of the girls wore.

When they had finished, she was taken to join the others being shown the secrets of Pharaoh's perfumery. The perfumery was in a walled courtyard surrounded by a luxurious garden of flowers. It contained expensive secrets that required a full band of Nubian slaves as guards. The few old women who knew the secret formulas were virtual prisoners and were never allowed to leave.

Hajar and the other maidens did not have access to the secret formulas, but they were expected to learn the uses of each wax cone, every stick of incense, the contents of numerous alabaster bottles, and just what fragrant oils were preferred by Pharaoh's favorites.

Hajar learned quickly, and in two months, when she had become familiar with every aspect of the process, she was moved on to the open courtyard. There in the shade, old women squatted in groups, either picking over dried leaves that were spread out on leather mats or working with mortar and pestle. They looked up briefly to inspect the maidens but then went on with their gossip and work.

During that time, though Hajar had adjusted to the daily schedule, she was secretly determined to find a means of escape. For the first time, in the open courtyard, she saw a possible opportunity.

On the far side of the court was a well-worn wooden door that stood open. It led outside into a marketplace. Rough-looking peasants loitered beside carts laden with baskets of herbs and flowers. They shouted and joked as they waited for the old women who came out to bargain with them for their wares. If the old women could go out to bargain for herbs, it shouldn't be impossible for her to do the same and then manage to escape. Once outside she should be able to bribe a peasant to take her to the Nile where she would hire a boat to take her upstream to her mother's family. In the meantime, she would seem interested in all that was going on.

She moved over to observe one of the women working with a mortar and pestle. Hajar saw that she had some graphite soaking in water and then, placing it in the mortar, she worked to crush and pound it into a fine powder. Every once in a while she tested it with a long bony finger to see if it contained any lumps. "What are you making?" Hajar asked as she squatted beside the old woman.

"Kohl to outline the eyes and lapis for the blue shadow. There must be no small lumps or . . . " The woman shook her head and continued with the pounding.

"Or what, old woman?" Hajar asked. "If you don't grind it well, what will happen?"

For a moment the woman stopped the steady pounding movement and grimaced as she glanced up into the sunlight. Her teeth were rotting, and she was blind in one eye. The woman fixed her one good eye on Hajar and then slowly and deliberately, without a word, drew her gnarled finger across her throat. The meaning was all too plain. Hajar could see that perfection was expected, and punishment for failure was swift and severe.

She looked around at the pleasant scene. Nothing was as it seemed. People worked hard, not because they liked what they were doing, but because they feared the punishment that was meted out for any irregularity.

With a start she remembered how impulsively she had picked up the queen's scepter. Undoubtedly she had barely escaped some horrible punishment. She wasn't used to such restrictions and had never been punished for anything. As she joined the rest of the young apprentices, she swore by the horns of the goddess Hathor that she would use every means possible to escape.

She went over and over in her mind all that she had learned of the palace.

She noted especially the doors leading out and decided they were all well-guarded. There were too many people around not to notice and give the alarm if someone tried to escape. Only the gate leading to the market was a possibility. However, even there, she would need a plan and a great deal of luck.

She would have to use her wits, but for luck she would depend on her personal goddess, Hathor. Hajar had chosen Hathor, the horned cow goddess, because she was the lady of all gods and the mistress of heaven. Hajar had long ago decided she was the most powerful goddess.

Hajar kept a smooth, cleverly shaped image of Hathor with her at all times. Even when one of the delicate horns broke off, she took it to the local idol maker and had it mended. She didn't want a new one; this one had belonged to her ancestors and was supposed to be very powerful. Anytime her grandmother or mother needed anything or had any problem, they prayed to Hathor, and she was sure the goddess rarely failed them.

As a child, Hajar had been afraid of the small image. It had a woman's body, but the head of a cow with two small black stones for eyes. The eyes frightened her. They were not soft and gentle like a cow's but hard and accusing, even angry. There seemed to be a hidden strength about the very ugliness of the image, and now Hajar was depending on this strength.

Hajar wasted no time in devising a plan. She had often seen the scribe who had first recorded her name. She could tell that he genuinely hated her and would do anything to rid the palace of her. When she heard that he was once again to be in the great room recording the names of children conceived or born during the past month, she quietly stood behind the curtain until she was sure that he had finished. He was gathering up his quills and fitting them back in his case when she came out and addressed him as politely as possible. "Most learned scribe of my mistress," she said.

He looked up, squinted, then when he recognized her, frowned. "So the spitfire is tamed," he said. "It must mean that some favor is desired."

Hajar tried to resist an impulse to curse him.

He stood up and continued stuffing his reeds in the worn wooden case and rolling the parchment. "I have no time to do favors for insolent women."

"Your hate has won, for now you are to be rid of me."

For a moment he stopped gathering up his belongings and looked at her with pure loathing. "Aye, by the royal beard, to get rid of you would be an accomplishment. How's it to be done?"

She sniffed and turned up her chin. "You have only to write a permit for the guards at the gate. I am being dismissed by Her Radiance after all." She could not meet the scribe's scrutiny lest he see the cunning in her eyes.

"Aha! I knew it would come to this. She never should have chosen you in the first place." The scribe's eyes had narrowed and he smiled knowingly.

As he set out his writing equipment and proceeded to write the permit, she complained. "It's so unfair. I had such bright prospects and now . . ." she managed to sob convincingly.

The scribe smirked and then grinned as though enjoying a private joke. "I told them you wouldn't last. A sassy one as ever I've seen."

"It isn't fair," she wailed as she snatched up the permit and fled. She didn't want to stay a minute longer lest he see the smile of triumph that crossed her face.

Just before sunset she rode out the traders' gate. She easily passed the guards who were so busy hurrying the craftsmen and merchants out that they barely looked at her pass. As she rode down the crowded lane toward the dock on the Nile, she could feel the small sharp horns of the little goddess Hathor pressing into her side. She had tucked her at the last minute into her girdle as the only object she was going to take with her.

More than the scribe's pass, she was depending on the goddess to help her escape. Miraculously the goddess seemed to be with her, and within a short time she had reached the Nile. She had nothing to pay the boatman but a ring given her by her father. Parting with it pained her deeply, but there was no other way. She watched with growing anxiety as the boatman turned the ring over and over, looking at her with hooded, suspicious eyes. He went below deck and she became nervous. She could hear sounds of heated discussion and feared the man had recognized the ring and was afraid to accept it.

Minutes later the boatman sent a messenger ashore and then came to where Hajar stood. "I have sent the ring to be checked. I can't afford to get in trouble with Pharaoh," he said.

Hajar ran her fingers back and forth between the small image's horns, then took her out and held her in her hand. "I am depending on you, my beloved Hathor," she whispered over and over. She felt sure that if the ring was recognized, she would not escape without the help of the goddess.

However, remembering all the stories her mother and grandmother had told her of the great power the goddess possessed, she had little doubt that all would be well. Surely it would not be long until she would be headed for Upper Egypt and her family home.

Suddenly and without warning a black linen sack was thrown over her head, and strong hands grabbed her from behind, tying her so that she couldn't move. There was the braying of a donkey nearby, then the rattle of cart wheels. Hajar knew what was going to happen. She had taken the chance, and it was just her vile luck to get caught. Undoubtedly she would be taken in the cart back to the palace and there would be made into a laughingstock, a warning to others who might want to run away.

There was no reason to doubt that she would be executed. She had heard of others who had been publicly executed for a much less serious crime. She thought of her father, the pharaoh. He would be angry that she had tried to run away, and if he heard of the ring being used for her passage, he would never forgive her. Her Radiance, Senebtisy, would probably hold a celebration.

There was no hope. No matter what she did the punishment would not be reversed. However, she was determined to maintain her dignity. She would not plead for mercy or weep. She would be proud and defiant, not showing her true feelings.

Flooded with a mixture of despair and frustration, she also knew a growing anger that she should have been so close to escape before she was caught. The anger centered on the goddess Hathor who had deserted her at the most crucial moment. She blamed the small goddess for everything.

"You're brown and ugly and completely in my power," she muttered. "There's only a short time. If you don't rescue me, I'll know you're useless." For a moment she held the small clay figure in one hand and was about to press hard with her thumb so the head would snap off. Then she thought better of it and kept it in the palm of her hand. She would wait and see. The goddess might yet help her.

*P*haraoh had indeed remembered the traders from Mesopotamia. In the days when he was a vizier, he had depended on such men to acquaint him with the outside world. Now he welcomed Abram and his entourage warmly, and he insisted on putting several of his finest villas at their disposal. Their extensive flocks and herds and the men who cared for them would be provided a place to camp in the delta.

He seemed eager to see Abram. While emissaries from other countries waited for days to get an audience, Abram was invited right away to a feast and then a private audience with Pharaoh Amenemhet in his receiving hall. Abram was allowed to bring some of his men with him, so Lot and Eliazer with a few other retainers made their way to a bathhouse recommended to them by one of the other merchants to prepare for the big event.

"Egyptians are known for cleanliness," a merchant advised. "It would be offensive to Pharaoh to see visitors who had not spent the day at the baths."

They found to their surprise that when they arrived for the feast, they were to wear Egyptian garments and wigs. Abram alone retained his own clothes. "I want to see my old friend as he looked when he used to visit in my vizier's office," Pharaoh said.

The visit went very well. Pharaoh asked Abram to sit with him on his carved ebony throne so he could more easily ask questions. He had heard of the Elamite invasion, so he asked astute questions about every aspect. He was obviously pleased with Abram's answers. At times he leaned forward to catch every word, and at other times he fired questions so fast that Abram hardly had time to answer.

When he had exhausted the political news, he asked about the studies Abram had done. When he heard that he was experienced in stargazing and mathematics, he was delighted. He was even more curious when Abram told him of crushing the idols and turning from the old worship of Nanna and Ningal to worship Elohim, the Creator God.

"Now," he said at last, "tell me some of the wisdom of your country." He settled back among the cushions and looked at Abram with an expectant twinkle in his eye.

Abram thought a moment, then smiled. "This is one of the more common sayings, but I think it is not for kings: 'Who possesses much silver may be happy; who possesses much barley may be glad; but he who has nothing at all may sleep.'"

"Ah, but it is for kings. What king would not give everything he possesses for some good sleep? Who can sleep and have such responsibilities as I have? I must see that the Nile rises, the sun shines, the plants grow, and the people are happy."

"My lord," Abram said in astonishment, "you are in charge of the Nile and the sun?"

"Of course. If I do not perform the rituals and sacrifices, nothing would happen. The earth would become bare and dark while the people would weep and make my life unbearable."

"But, my lord, in Ur they believe the gods do these things."

Pharaoh drew himself up and assumed an air of great austerity. "Here, I am the god. I must make everything happen at the right time and in the right way."

Abram was surprised. He had forgotten much that he had known about the Egyptians. He determined to sit as often as possible with this intelligent ruler, so he could learn more about their ways and beliefs. For this reason, when Pharaoh stood and dismissed them, Abram asked that he might come again and talk with him further on these matters.

Pharaoh was pleased. "There are very few a god can talk with as a man. I would welcome your visits anytime."

With that they passed from the pharaoh's presence, bowing and kneeling at appropriate moments. When they were back out on the street, they asked one of the guards to take them to the villas Pharaoh had ordered prepared for their use.

The main villa was situated behind a high wall with grounds extending down to marble steps that disappeared into the Nile. Reeds and water lilies sheltered a quiet basin where many a princess had come to bathe or where the royal barges often docked. It was not far by barge to Pharaoh's palace.

Surrounding the villa was an extensive formal garden with grapevines, fruit trees, and flowers climbing the wall or bordering walkways. In the center was a lovely blue-tiled pond filled with fish and bordered with water lilies and spikes of papyrus. A few fat geese floated lazily on its dark surface.

Abram, Lot, Eliazer, and a few of their retainers were promptly invited to eat at the pharaoh's table and in the evenings to his private diwan where he could more freely ask questions about the world they were familiar with. The welcoming ceremony prepared at the pharaoh's command by the supreme vizier was surprisingly grand. In all, it was five days before Abram and his men were free to ride back to Tjel near the border for their wives, servants, and extensive belongings.

* * *

As Sarai and her women entered the gate of the villa and approached the house, the women hung back and let Sarai lead the way. She paused in the doorway and ran her hand over the surface of one of the columns, then leaned back to gaze at its height. She laughed with delight. "Look," she said, "it's a palm tree made of stone."

She ventured cautiously in through the door. In the main reception hall she paused to view the curious, unfamiliar sight. The roof was supported by painted wooden columns that bore a slight resemblance to upright giant bundles of papyrus. The ceiling, on closer inspection, was a marvel of geometric designs that were lighted by grillwork windows.

"How lovely!" Sarai exclaimed as she stepped from the reception room into the main living area. Its ceiling was supported by columns that ended in rather stylized capitals carved like lotus buds. It was a shadowy, quiet room. Sarai's eyes had to become adjusted to the cool darkness before she could clearly see that the walls and floor had been transformed into something resembling one of the delta's rich marshes.

Clerestory windows set high in the walls produced the only light. Strong rays pooled on the painted floor and highlighted sections of the wall rendered with lotus blooms, poppies, and cornflowers. With more light the room would have been ablaze with color. In the afternoon heat, it gave off a relaxed atmosphere.

The rest of the house contained sleeping rooms, and the kitchens, storerooms, baking facilities, and granaries were clustered near the servants' quarters. An outer stair led to the roof, and there the women found carpets of woven rushes spread under a luxurious grape arbor. Armrests, clay pots, a stack of wooden bowls and stone platters hinted that was where they would eat and spend their evenings.

"How kind of Pharoah!" Sarai exclaimed later in the day as she showed Abram the marvels of the villa. "It is nicer than our house in Ur."

"You haven't said a word about how it compares to your tent."

Sarai cocked her head on one side and studied Abram. She knew what he wanted her to say, and she had no intention of encouraging him. "I hope we never have to go back to living in a tent," she said. "This is the kind of blessing I'm sure your God had in mind from the beginning."

She didn't wait for an answer but hurried out to instruct her serving girls as to which chests were to hold her robes and where to put her perfumes and ointments.

Abram went to the parapet and looked down into the walled area and then out past it to the Nile with its reed boats and more formal falukas. Most of them were fitted with sails and headed south. He remembered hearing that the sails were used only going south against the current. Coming north, the current carried them along. How odd, he thought, that the wind should always come from the north and the current always flows north. It was evident that most things in Egypt were predictable.

There never seemed to be famine, earthquakes, storms, or barbaric invasions. From one day to the next, they could predict what was likely to happen. Even the rising of the Nile was always predictable. It came when the star Sothis was seen on the horizon just after sunrise. The only flood they knew was the Nile's gentle overflowing that left behind the rich black soil, giving their land its namesake—Kemet, the black land.

A palm tree obstructed Abram's view, and he moved so he could see the pyramids being built by Pharaoh where the green fields ended and where the desert, which they called the "red" land, began. These pyramids would not be as big or as complex as the pyramids farther down the Nile near Memphis, but to him, they were impressive. It seemed a custom unlike any other.

The dead were supposed to join the god, Re, in his sun boat, and yet there was an obsession to preserve the body. Stranger still, animals seemed to be gods, and birds like the hawk, Horns, were said to indwell the ruling pharaoh. To Abram, who had been schooled in the logic of Mesopotamia, this prevalence of conflicting beliefs and ideologies was baffling. Perhaps someone like Pharaoh Amenemhet could answer some of his questions.

Pharaoh had seemed genuinely glad to see him. Abram's gifts had not been wasted as evidenced by this villa and the invitation to eat at Pharaoh's bountiful table. Abram knew it was a great honor. Only foreign emissaries, princes, and very wealthy men ate at Pharaoh's table. With a sudden shock he realized that in Pharaoh's eyes he was wealthy.

Abram, Lot, his brother Iscah, and Eliazer, along with several of the younger men, had been enjoying the pharaoh's hospitality for several weeks before the invitation arrived from Amenemhet's mother for the women of Abram's family to visit her. Sarai was immediately excited, but Abram grew cautious. "Pharaoh is known for his shrewdness and his penchant for beautiful foreign women," he said. "I don't want you to go."

"But it's not him—it's his mother who has invited us."

"He will no doubt be somewhere observing all that goes on."

"And you think he will single me out and convince me to stay."

"Not convince you. Order you."

Sarai laughed as she snatched up a brass mirror and held it at arm's length, so she could see a larger view of herself. "How absurd to think a man who could have any woman would choose one of my age."

Abram grabbed her arm and pulled her to him. "If I'm still attracted to you, I'm sure he will be."

"You're hurting me," she pouted as she pulled her arm away and turned her back to him.

He swung her around to face him. "Sarai, this is serious. Pharaoh Amenemhet is considered a god here. His desire is law and he can take anything he wants."

"You think he'll take me and have you killed."

"He could if he wanted to."

"Remember, we agreed. I'll tell the queen that I'm your sister. I can manage everything."

Abram still felt uneasy about the visit, but he could see that Sarai would be terribly disappointed. "All right, accept the invitation. I suppose there's nothing else to do."

Sarai was delighted. She began making plans immediately.

Jewelry was pulled out and tried on. Her finest robes from Chaldea were unpacked. She even loaned some of her best rings and ankle bracelets to Mara and the other wives.

The day of the visit, the queen sent several changes of beautiful Egyptian garments for each of them. Along with the clothes came bejeweled pectorals, rings, bracelets, and ankle bracelets. The queen had also been thoughtful enough to send some of her women to help them dress for the occasion.

At first there was great consternation as Sarai and the women who were going with her struggled to arrange the filmy gowns to cover their breasts and arms. The queen's serving women scolded and argued but eventually gave in to their modesty. They agreed for them to wear the garments they had brought from Ur, but adorn themselves with the jewelry the queen had sent.

When they were finally ready, the women were surprised to learn that Pharaoh was sending two of his royal barges to transport them. None of them had ever been in a boat, though there had been boats sailing the Euphrates in Ur. They were called quffa, meaning "turnip." They resembled turnips; they were round, made of reeds, and covered with animals skins. They were for carrying goods, not for regular transportation.

Much of their enthusiasm for going was marred by their fear of the water and the boat trip. There were many protestations of feeling faint, having a severe headache, and being exhausted; however, at the last moment, they all went.

The ride in the royal barge turned out to be one of the day's more pleasant surprises. The sails were perfumed, and the couches were covered in the finest bright-colored linen. Incense burned in a copper bowl set into the prow of the ship while the queen's women, who had come to escort them, periodically waved ostrich fans to create a cool breeze. Once out in the main stream, young Egyptians sang jolly songs accompanied by their sistrums.

Sarai was charmed by everything she saw. The sun was shining. The sky was cloudless. From the first, she had been overwhelmed by the greenness of grass and trees and the loads of bright green clover piled high on the backs of donkeys. Such profusion of green she had never imagined in the dull brown lands she had known. Now she was impressed with the abundance of water. Instead of a trickle from a spring, there was a steady flow one could drown in if one weren't careful.

The scenes along the Nile were all new and constantly changing. Women washed clothes among the rocks; a water buffalo lazed in knee-deep water; white herons stood motionless, almost obscured by dark green rushes. Sarai noticed with pleasure that people in other boats saluted them because they were riding in the royal barge.

They rounded a curve in the river and caught their first glimpse of the pharaoh's white-walled palace, half-hidden among the palm trees. Marble columns, an obelisk, and banners that proclaimed the pharaoh was at home gradually came into view. It was all so huge and impressive that even Sarai was reluctant to land.

There was nothing to fear. Though at first the queen seemed a bit austere and unsmiling, she was a gracious hostess. Huge trays of dried fruits were served, costly incense was burned, and the musicians played haunting tunes. The only thing to blight the afternoon's activity was the shocking manner in which the Egyptians dressed.

When the dancing girls appeared, they had only their long hair and beads to cover their nakedness. The children of the concubines and other lesser wives wore no clothes, and this custom seemed so strange that none of the women dared look at them and some covered their eyes with their hands.

The visit was more exciting than any of them had imagined. Though they were all shy and merely smiled and nodded when talked to, they knew they had made a good impression when the queen mother invited them back again. "You must come and tell me all about the strange customs in your country and sing some of your songs for our entertainment," she said.

When they returned home, Sarai made a point of telling Abram what a wonderful time they had and how foolish it was to worry that Pharaoh might want to keep her for his harem.

"Did you tell them you were my sister?" he asked.

Sarai paused with her hands in the air as she started to lift off the elaborate headdress the queen had given her. "Yes, I told the queen I was your sister." For a moment she hesitated and then continued, "She asked if I had children and I had to tell her no. I could tell she assumed I had never been married. I almost cried. Imagine what they must think of a woman at my age still unmarried, still without a child."

Abram could see the old hurt in her eyes, and he came to put his arms around her. "Sarai, it won't always be this way. Remember, we have the promise."

Sarai pulled away from him and snatched the wreath of golden tuberoses from her head. "Don't talk to me of the promise. It won't come true. I know it won't. It's just like the land your God promised. It was dry and barren and full of those horrible flying things."

"Those were locusts," Abram reminded her.

"I don't want to hear any more about the promise. Today I saw children, so many children no one could count them. They all belonged to pagan wives who worship Re, the god of the sun, and I have seen this land bursting with good things. Their god keeps his promises better than yours." With that she burst into tears. It was late into the night before she fell asleep, and Abram stayed on the roof to sleep in peace out under the low-hanging stars. He thought about the promise and knew Sarai had a right to be upset. He prayed and waited, but there was no answer. His God seemed to have forgotten him.

* * *

Even though it was late at night, Hajar was brought into the queen's judgment hall to be "dealt with," as Pharaoh's favorite had announced. Senebtisy came close and looked at Hajar with her practiced look of serenity that was usual with the pharaohs. One of the eunuchs whispered to her, and she answered with a strong show of anger. "Yes, yes, this is the bold one," she said. "She fears nothing. Even to pick up the royal scepter didn't daunt her. It appears she makes up her own rules. We'll soon put an end to such insolence."

She motioned to one of the eunuchs who produced a scroll from his sleeve and, at her nod, began to read. The scroll contained the information that the old man Hajar was to be married to had died very suddenly. The plans for her marriage would have to be canceled.

"Shall we call the executioner?" one of her stewards asked.

"Not yet. I want to talk to her and then we'll see." Senebtisy ordered most of the court to leave and then called for the scribe who was the keeper of records. He brought with him the large scroll of recorded births.

"Who is this girl's father?" Her Radiance demanded of the little man.

He bowed and then nervously ordered his helper to bring his carpet and cushion on which the scroll rested. With the help of the young boy and cooperation from Hajar, he found the name of Hajar's mother, the date she had gone to see Pharaoh, and then the date and hour that Hajar was born. He placed his gnarled, ink-stained finger on the column and exclaimed with obvious satisfaction, "She is the daughter of Pharaoh by his former concubine."

"You fool," the favorite said, thumping him soundly on his head. "Must you record every dalliance?"

"Those have been orders . . . I . . . I," the little man sputtered.

"There's no need for every stray glance to be recorded. Strike the names from the record."

"But Pharaoh?"

"We aren't concerned with Pharaoh now. This girl has been insolent and brash enough to challenge me. I will have her name stricken from the record."

"But Pharaoh . . ."

The little man was more frightened of the pharaoh's anger than of the new favorite. He knew the former concubine had been prized and the daughter shown special favors. If Pharaoh found out that a name such as that had been blotted from the record without his approval, it could mean death for the scribe.

"Blot it out," she stormed, standing over him and thumping the offending scroll with her flail. "I will tell Pharaoh that I, and I alone, ordered it. When he hears of the arrogance of this girl, he will agree with me." Hajar felt faint, and the heavy odor of dried roses made her feel sick. This room looked bright and cheerful in the daytime, but at night most of it was engulfed in dark shadows. Only one torch gave off any light, and she felt as though she must have died and was being judged by the gods Anubis and Thoth. Even though her arms were tied, she still clutched the small glazed figure of the cow goddess Hathor in her right hand. "Hathor," she prayed quietly, "I've served you well. Now I need help. You're stronger than the scribe and stronger than this new favorite. If you are really there, now is the time to prove what you can do."

The scribe talked for a few moments with Senebtisy. She nodded and then turned and mounted to her small throne. All eyes studied her as they waited for the verdict. Slowly and with planned hauteur she held out the flail instead of the crook, and everyone knew that Hajar was to be severely punished. "For your arrogance and pride, your open hostility to me, Pharaoh's favorite, you will be chained to the wall in the court of women. You will be whipped and fed only bread and water. More important, your mother is even now being taken as a slave into one of the temples where you will never see her again. Finally, your name is to be changed to Hagar, meaning 'flight,' so everyone will remember your foolishness."

Hajar, now Hagar, had never imagined that she could cause her mother such harm. It was almost unbearable to realize that because of her impulsive, rash action she would probably never see her mother again. Now she fell to the floor and cried, "Punish me as you like, but spare my mother. She had nothing to do with this."

"What is done is done and what has been spoken will stand," the new favorite said. With that she rose and looked around at the soldiers and then at Hagar. She once again assumed the pleasant look that royalty in Egypt were accustomed to wear, and then swept from the room.

The guards picked Hagar up from the floor with difficulty. She was almost wild with outrage and animosity. They brought her to the courtyard of women where they fastened her ankles to the wall with a chain that had served this purpose before. In the daytime it would be blistering hot, and at night it would be treacherously cold. Hagar knew that, and she swore with a great oath to get even. She would rely on her own wits and ingenuity to cause trouble wherever possible. She was determined to be a thorn in the flesh of the whole court.

As soon as her hands were loosed, she raised her right hand, and to the horror of the guards threw the small image of Hathor across the courtyard where it shattered into a dozen pieces.

The guards drew back in fear. "Hathor will see that you suffer," they said to her. "Aren't you afraid?"

"Hathor's been no help to me. I'll win by my own wits. Just wait and see. I'll win." She spat out the words in an angry torrent and the guards fell back. Never had they seen any but the most hardened criminals curse the gods.

The guards left and the courtyard again became quiet. Hagar could hear the sound of a fountain splashing, a flute being played in some distant courtyard, and faint and far away laughter. It was getting cold and she had no covering. She was hungry and thirsty. She suspected that she was to be kept as miserable as possible to be a lesson to others.

She thought about her mother and was on the verge of tears. She couldn't afford to cry. She had to be strong. She had neither the gods to protect her nor friends to help her. She was alone with only her anger and hatred to keep her alive. She wanted revenge. Revenge against Pharaoh, her father, who had loved her a short time ago. Revenge against this new favorite who wielded such power. And revenge against Hathor who had deserted her in her time of need. Once she had succeeded in wreaking revenge, she could die—but not until then.

She slid down into a seated position and tried to get comfortable, but with her feet in chains it was impossible. She wrapped her arms around her knees and rocked back and forth. Hot anger burned within her.

How I hate her! She thought as she pictured the young favorite proudly holding the place her mother had held such a short time ago. She pulled at her hair and dragged her dirty fingers down her face. "It'd be worth all of this if I could just live long enough to see her suffer."

*S*arai and the women loved to visit the palace. Slowly they became used to the formalities and the new Egyptian words and expressions. Even Abram relaxed and no longer feared for Sarai's safety. A month had passed when a special invitation came for Sarai and the women to visit the ladies of Pharaoh's house. The occasion was the birth of a new child to one of the concubines.

This time Abram gave no warning, and Sarai went off with the women, lighthearted and glowing with the anticipation of a real celebration. There was no hint of disaster or any reason to suspect that things would not go as they had gone in the past. However, hours later when the women returned to the villa, Sarai wasn't with them.

Abram was called immediately. He had only to look at their faces to realize that something fearful had happened. At first they all spoke at once with words tumbling out in a torrent until Abram could hardly gather the facts. Finally Lot's wife, Mara, pushed forward and began to explain in such a forceful way that the others grew quiet.

"I tried to warn Sarai," she said, "but she wouldn't listen. She was so flattered, so impressed by all the attention the old queen mother had given her."

"I suppose she was trying to be charming and entertaining?" Abram asked.

"Oh, yes," Mara said. "That's when the old queen nodded to one of her serving girls, and they brought bracelets, rings, and earrings and put them on her. The queen kept saying, 'We want you to stay. You can have anything you want.'"

Abram questioned them until he feared that Sarai was to be groomed as either a bride or a concubine for Pharaoh. It all fit together. Pharaoh had welcomed him as a man of position and means from Ur of the Chaldees. How could he better honor him than to marry his sister?

Abram dismissed the women. He needed to be alone to think. He paced the floor as he went over all the possibilities. Maybe it was nothing serious.

Perhaps in Egypt, it was acceptable for a queen to detain someone she took an interest in. There had been no mention of Pharaoh. Perhaps he was assuming the worst when the situation would soon be explained.

He finally decided that he must get a message to Sarai. But he realized that short of some unusual circumstance, that would be impossible. The women's quarters were in a remote, very secluded, and well-guarded section of the white palace.

The next day it became evident that Pharaoh had definitely decided to add Sarai to his harem. Just after sunrise, Abram was awakened out of a troubled sleep by a loud pounding on the front gate. He hurried out just in time to see the gate being opened for a company of Pharaoh's bodyguard. They were dressed in their most festive attire, and each one carried a gift.

Behind them came men from the pharaoh's kitchens with a feast of choice roast lambs, sweetbreads, and baskets of ripe fruits.

A scribe followed the procession. He positioned himself by the gate and took from his belt a written message, broke the pharaoh's seal, and proceeded to read. Abram turned deadly pale as he anticipated the worst.

Pharaoh acknowledged having heard reports of Sarai's charm from some of the princes and then to having observed the women from his covered balcony. He was fascinated by Sarai. He intended to marry her as soon as possible, and in gratitude and as a symbol of their new relationship he was sending these small gifts as a token of what was to follow. "It is my great pleasure to make my new friend Abram rich."

Abram struggled to maintain his composure until the messengers had left. Then he turned back to the villa, numb with dread. The realization that he was hopelessly enmeshed in a tangle of lies was unbearable. It was certain that if he confessed to the truth, Pharaoh would kill both of them.

All day he mulled over the situation, seeking some kind of escape, but by early evening he knew there was none. He climbed to the roof where he could see the glistening white of Pharaoh's palace just visible between the trees. Somewhere within those walls his beloved, naïve, and saucy Sarai was being held. Was she crying? Was she frightened? Did she realize the danger she was in? He instinctively knew she wouldn't be reacting in any of these usual ways. She was probably enjoying herself.

These thoughts drove him to despair until he realized her pleasant demeanor was probably her best protection. It wouldn't do for Sarai to understand everything and get upset. She wouldn't hesitate to explain that she was already married and insist on being brought home. It was hard for her to believe that these nice people could have her killed for much less.

Abram moved along the parapet until he could see the last bright glow of the setting sun. He was always amazed at sunrise and sunset in Egypt. It seemed to happen with very little warning. For a moment the glow highlighted the half-finished pyramid of the pharaoh that loomed to the west where the desert began. Pharaoh had taken him to see the pyramid. For the first time he had clearly understood that his old friend the vizier no longer existed. The vizier had become the pharaoh, wielding the crook and flail and wearing the two crowns of Upper and Lower Egypt.

Abram groaned. The vizier could have forgiven the lie and the complications involving Sarai, but not this god-man. Pharaoh made the sun rise after the blackness of night, and by his will and strength he held the two lands together. He believed he was a god. Who would dare to toy with the affections of a god as Abram and Sarai seemed to have done?

Abram groaned and sank to the floor with his head in his hands. "Elohim, Elohim, if You can hear me calling out from this strange land, help me! I am completely helpless to rescue Sarai. Terrible tragedy can result." He waited, hoping he would hear the quiet inner voice that had once guided him. There was nothing but silence. Either Elohim wasn't in Egypt, or else he had given up on him altogether. Abram wouldn't blame him.

He bowed his head to the dried mud of the roof. Before his God he must be honest. "Whether You answer me or not, even if You're through with me, maybe even sorry You chose me, I have to admit I did this whole thing. I got myself into this and I can't get out. If You don't help me, it's hopeless."

Abam couldn't go on. He was too broken and distraught. He waited while the new moon rose and then set, and there was nothing. Finally a soft breeze blew across the roof and rustled in the branches of the palm. Abram rose and dusted off his robe, looked over the wall at the quiet scene, then glanced up at the cluster of stars hanging so low he felt he could touch them. He remembered Elohim had promised descendants as the stars, and he wondered if the promise still held. There was no way he could tell. The only small thread of hope was that he had prayed the right prayer. He had laid it all out honestly, stating his involvement in the problem. But even that could not quell the rising flood of anxiety.

Abram was weak from lack of food. He couldn't imagine how he could possibly go to his bed and sleep. He clutched the borders of his robe so tightly that the veins stood out, dark cords against the tanned skin of his hand. Fear rose in him like a swirling tornado. If his God didn't hear him, or refused to answer him, what would he do?

Abram's part in the deception loomed ominously before him. How could he have thought it better to call Sarai his sister? It was the truth, but only a small part of the truth. He could imagine Pharaoh's face, eyes flashing with indignation and hurt pride, his mouth twisted in contempt. Worse still, he could see how it would look to Pharaoh. The few times he had mentioned his God and the relationship he had with him would now seem the idiotic dream of a madman.

"I didn't mean any harm," was all he could say.

By the next evening he was exhausted. Abram had waved aside all food and had refused to see anyone. He wandered out to the pond and sank down on a marble bench. He tried to calm his fears by listening to the night sounds of the frogs and crickets. Instead of calming him, they made him nervous with their constant repetition. Finally he stood up and started toward the villa. He had come to a decision. He would at least try to settle things. I'll go to Pharaoh and try to explain, he decided. I'll set things right tomorrow.

Everyone else, family and slaves, had been sleeping for hours when he finally went to bed. Sleep evaded him. When it did come, he dreamed of the pharaoh with sharp, accusing eyes, holding out the dread flail that promised sure and terrible punishment, even death. The dreams were so real that when morning came, he had lost his resolve altogether. He didn't go to square things with Pharaoh. Instead he accepted an invitation to dine as though nothing had happened.

＊ ＊ ＊

Sarai lay in a half-awake state trying to remember where she was and what the strange disturbance was that had nudged her out of a sound sleep. She heard the soft humming sound of pigeons nearby and the whispers and then giggles of young girls passing her door. She heard the cry of the water carrier and the baker with bread. For a moment Sarai thought she was back in Ur, in her father's house. Then she remembered. She wasn't in Ur at all but in Pharaoh's palace.

Gradually it all began to come back to her. The party with the old queen mother first appearing so formal and dignified and then laughing boisterously at Sarai's antics. The wonderful cakes and luscious dates, the dancing girls and the gifts.

They had been entertained regally, but then the queen had motioned for Sarai and her women to contribute to the entertainment. Eliazer's wife and sisters and Mara, Lot's wife, drew back and hung their heads while the others did the same. Only Sarai responded. She had never been shy or self-conscious. She first showed them how the women of Ur danced. Then feeling more relaxed and at home under their obvious approval, she showed them how a shy young bride would dance. She snatched up a woven mat and held it on her head as she explained the custom of carrying a lighted oil lamp in this way by the bride. She then executed the mincing steps and shy retreating movements.

The queen's eyes sparkled as she said, "And the bridegroom. Show us the bridegroom."

Sarai by that time was glowing under the approval of these sophisticated women. She thought only a moment before she pulled up the pleated robe to resemble a man's tunic, snatched up an embroidered sash to hold it in place, borrowed a dagger from a surprised guard, and was transformed into a bridegroom from Ur.

She performed the leaping, posturing, strutting dance so well, the women were hysterical with glee. Only when she was exhausted did they let her stop, and then they wanted her to tell stories of her people's customs. Sarai loved the attention and the approval until it was time to go. Then from a curtained enclosure came a dwarf. He bowed before the queen with his head touching the ground. When she tapped him on the back with the crook, he rose and came close enough to whisper something in her ear. Without a word the queen motioned to one of the serving girls who quickly moved to detain Sarai.

"The queen wants you to stay with us awhile. She is very pleased with you," she said.

Now Sarai remembered everything. She hadn't been able to send a message to Abram, and she knew he would think the worst. She had seen nothing of the pharaoh. She felt sure the queen meant no harm. It was probably some custom, a way of honoring special guests.

She sat up, pulled the fine linen covering over her shoulders, and looked around. The room was large and ornate. It reminded her of the decorated and pillared rooms of the villa. The smell of jasmine was in the air, though it wasn't yet time for flowers to bloom.

A face appeared at a latticed window, smiled, and then disappeared. Within moments Sarai could hear the quick padding of feet along the corridor, a bolt unlatched, and the same smiling eyes peeped around the door. She couldn't understand what the young woman said, but she handed Sarai a bowl of steaming barley gruel then smiled again and disappeared.

I like this, Sarai thought, and it can't hurt for Abram to worry about me just a little. We'll laugh about it later.

She idly sipped the hot gruel and wondered what could make it taste so good. She set the bowl down and shivered as she hugged her knees.

Outside her door were new noises. Slaves shouting to each other. Bare feet hitting firmly on the baked tiles as someone ran by, breathing hard. There was a distant clanging of cymbals and chanting as though some morning ritual were being carried out. A baby cried and some small children stopped quarreling as they heard shouted instructions from the outer courtyard.

Those sounds were normal. It was the other sound that finally got Sarai up from the pallet. She shivered in the clear, cold air and hurried out into the sunshine where it was warm. Her feet moved to a sun-drenched spot where she could feel the warmth of the tiles.

There was the sound again, a clanking sound, a sound of brass on stone. She looked around and saw the reason for the noise. It came from the corner of the courtyard where there appeared to be a crumpled mass of rags. Suddenly the crumpled mass stretched, came alive, and developed large round eyes, a pointed chin, and full, pouting lips; unbelievably dirty hair snaked down over the creature's eyes. It took a moment for Sarai to realize that she was seeing a very young woman whose feet were chained to the stone wall. She had heard the chains. The young woman was making the noise on purpose just to annoy someone.

Sarai was about to leave when she noticed that the girl's eyes seemed to be following her. "Who are you?" Sarai called impulsively, moving a bit closer to get a better look.

At first the girl didn't speak but turned away with a toss of her head. Then as Sarai came closer, she ducked her head and looked out at her from behind the strands of her hair with tormented eyes. She seemed to be studying Sarai.

"You're not Egyptian," the creature said finally in a surprisingly mellow voice that belied her appearance.

"No, I'm not Egyptian, but I can tell that you are. What is your name?" Sarai said, coming a bit closer.

"Where are you from?" The girl seemed for the moment to be slightly interested but unwilling to give her name.

Sarai knew that to give your name was to give someone control over you. People could write charms or curse you if they knew your name. "I'm from Ur on the Euphrates River. It's a long way from here."

For a momen, there was silence as the two just looked at each other then the girl said, "I wish I could be anyplace but here, even in Ur."

Sarai sighed. "Oh, my dear, you don't want to wish for such a thing. Ur has been totally destroyed. I wouldn't be here if it hadn't been so completely destroyed." Sarai's bright countenance clouded and tears came to her eyes.

Seeing the tears, the girl melted and relaxed. She brushed her hair back from her eyes and then, holding it with one hand while she got a good look at Sarai, she said, "My name is Hagar. It used to be Hajar Gameela, but now it's just Hagar."

Sarai saw that there had been a slight breakthrough. This creature was a young woman who must have been quite pretty before this tragedy struck. She squatted down beside her and spoke softly, "My name is Sarai."

They studied each other for a long moment. They realized that they were from very different backgrounds, and it was obvious there was a wide age difference. Their accents were foreign and some of the words different, but they could understand each other enough to know that both were in trouble and both had suffered. Sarai was so choked up remembering Ur that she couldn't say any more, and Hagar had been so isolated that she had almost forgotten how to carry on a conversation. Nothing more was said, but each knew that a bond had been formed and each had a loyal friend in the other.

From that day on, Sarai took every opportunity to talk to Hagar. She even managed to save some of the fruits and rich food to take to her after everyone else was asleep. In the dark of the moon and then again when the courtyard was flooded with light of the full moon, Sarai faithfully made her way out to the far side of the courtyard to check on Hagar. She found her an eager listener and could depend on her to explain the customs of these people whose ways were so alien to her own.

It was Hagar who explained to Sarai the position of honor she had been put in by being chosen for marriage to Pharaoh. She also warned her that to object in any way could mean death for both Sarai and her brother. After Sarai knew Hagar well and saw that she could be trusted, Sarai confided in her that she wasn't only Abram's sister but was also his wife, though they had no children. Hagar was shocked and then afraid. Slowly she began to understand and then explained to Sarai the dangerous situation she was in. "They will think you are making light of Pharaoh's generosity," she said. "Then when he finds out that you have been married all these years and have borne no child, he will fear you have had an evil spell cast on you. They could kill you as an evil enchantress."

"I have been promised a child," Sarai said as she struggled to keep back the tears.

It was evident that the subject was delicate and painful for Sarai. Hagar looked at her in amazement. How could she be so naïve as to think she and her husband could trifle with Pharaoh's affections and not pay a terrible price? They had stumbled into the deception rather innocently, but certainly they must have known such trifling with a pharaoh's goodwill would not go unpunished. "What are you going to do?" Hagar asked, her eyes glowing with intensity even in the darkness.

"I don't know. I keep hoping Abram will think of something. I know he is praying."

Hagar asked, "To whom does he pray?"

"The living God, Elohim, the Creator God who has made many promises to him."

"Don't trust the gods. None of them can be depended on when you're in trouble. I threw mine away. She didn't help me."

"I must admit I don't depend much on Abram's God. He's not done any of the things He promised, but Abram believes."

"At the most you'll have only six or seven months until you're called. I hope your Abram's prayers work stronger magic than mine."

Sarai wanted to explain that it wasn't magic Abram depended on, but she couldn't think how to explain. She'd never had to depend on it herself. She'd always depended on Abram. Now she realized she was depending on Abram's wits to rescue her, but if it was as difficult as Hagar seemed to think, then maybe Abram's God would have to come out of hiding and help.

It was cold. Sarai put her shawl around Hagar and then without a word slipped silent as a shadow along the wall and back to her room. For the first time she was genuinely frightened. She had seen by Hagar's reaction that her situation was serious and fearful. It hadn't occurred to her that if Pharaoh found out she was married and childless, he would indeed think she was some evil thing.

A great feeling of bitterness welled up within her. Here it was again—she was to be an outcast because she was childless. It would be as though she were a leper, unclean. A person with the evil eye. Cold, icy fear choked her, and she found herself gasping for breath and sobbing. Lest the old woman who slept at her door wake up, she stuffed part of her carefully pleated skirt into her mouth and bit down hard. She couldn't imagine how she could spend another day, another hour, in this place knowing what she knew and realizing that if she weren't rescued soon, the secret could leak out and her fate would be sealed.

✳ ✳ ✳

In the meantime, Abram was getting more deeply involved with Pharaoh and his court officials. Although the pharaoh was formal and austere during the day, in the evening he dropped the mantle of the god Horus and became a man who could sit with other men and discuss the affairs of the world.

Abram had learned much of Amenemhet's daily routine. He knew that he rose at dawn, went into his private chapel called the House of the Morning, and bathed. At the same time it was believed the sun god Re was bathing in the ocean of heaven, and together they restored the vital force that flowed out with peace, prosperity, and health upon the two lands.

Then his special priests, wearing masks of Horus and the ibis-headed Thoth, anointed and clothed him, placing around his neck the royal insignia. Thus clothed in the garments of Re and Horus, he went to the temple for a ceremony that would make meaningful all the other ceremonies that would soon be celebrated in other temples throughout the land.

All must be finished at sunrise, for at the same time in the temples up and down the Nile, the same ritual was being carried out. The seals of the holy place were broken, the idol brought out and bathed, anointed, and dressed, ready for the first bright ray of the sun to travel down the dark avenue between the lotus columns to shine for a moment on its face. However, the idol was nothing without the pharaoh. Pharaoh, now the god Horus, maintained maat, the stability of the world.

The procedures seemed strange to Abram, but he was well aware that during the day, Pharaoh with his crook and flail and the royal garments did indeed seem to be a different man from the one who sat with them in the evening or went in to his wives and concubines like any other man.

Always during these times, Abram struggled to be pleasant and affable, but his heart sank as he began to fully realize the enormity of his offense against this powerful ruler. He did everything possible to please Amenemhet.

He went with him up the Nile to Abydos, Egypt's most holy place. There he watched the ritual enactment of the death and restoration of the god Osiris. On several occasions he came back to this same place with Nakht, the chief steward, to check the progress of the elaborate cenotaph Pharaoh was having built to honor his ancestors.

One day after visiting in the palace, Abram stopped as usual at the guardhouse. He always found the guards bored and talkative. They told him news and rehearsed interesting stories of life in the villages where they had grown up. On this occasion they were discussing in hushed tones the coming ceremony, when the Nile would be given a bride. When Abram asked its meaning, they looked at each other and changed the subject.

Only after the others left did the captain agree to explain everything to Abram. "You see, it has to do with maat, the order of things. We believe that if maat breaks down in one area, it will affect all others."

Abram had struggled to understand the Egyptian concept of maat. It was something every Egyptian believed in and would go to any extent to preserve. He saw that it involved harmony or balance and was chiefly the pharaoh's responsibility. There seemed to be certain things he had to do to make the sun rise, the Nile flood, and the plants grow.

"And maat is endangered?" Abram asked.

The captain was uncomfortable discussing the subject, but after some pressure, he said, "We have had rumors for some time that there have been no children born in the palace. Now we hear there have been no sacred cats born in the temple at Bast and no bulls at Saqqara. We are afraid that the Nile will also fail us. Pharaoh and the priests must stop the destruction of maat. A bride for the Nile is a last resort."

Abram could get the man to say no more, but he decided to accept the invitation and see for himself what it took to restore maat. When the day finally arrived, he stood with Pharaoh's priests on the banks of the Nile and watched in astonishment as they enacted the age-old ceremony that was supposed to make the Nile's waters rise and flood.

At last he saw the bride of the Nile that he had heard so much about. She was young, beautiful, and supposedly delirious with joy at being chosen. He later wondered if she had not been given the same drug used in Ur for such religious ceremonies. Ergot, they called it.

Accompanied by drummers and dancers, she was led to the river's edge where she danced in the midst of the chanting priests with a wild, frenzied abandon that ended when the priests raised her above their heads and cast her into the dark water. She could be seen for a moment, her golden headpiece flashing in the sun, her arms upraised, and then she disappeared. "Hapi, great god of the Nile, has accepted her," the priests shouted and the celebration took on new excitement.

Later Abram was invited to go with Pharaoh's special advisors as they watched for the dog star, Sirius, to appear on the horizon. It was the signal for the yearly rising of the Nile. It also brought in the time of secret fertility rites and the release of inhibitions as people, led by the priests, worshiped the gods of fecundity. This year they were taken more seriously because the fertility of the whole country seemed to be at stake.

Lot and Urim entered wholeheartedly into the rites and festivities, but Abram saw a dark, disturbing side to the festivals. He declined the invitations.

Abram always enjoyed sitting in the diwan of the chief steward, and took every chance offered to talk with Amenemhet in his private apartment. Now more than ever he dared not tell Pharaoh about Sarai. Though he spent nights of torture and days of despair, he could not bring himself to broach the subject lest Pharaoh decide that maat had somehow been disturbed by them and order them both killed.

During this time, Abram grew in favor to the point of Pharaoh suggesting, "Let us build a temple for your God here among our temples so you will feel more at home among us. Lot can be the priest."

At first Abram would have welcomed this interest. He had talked much of his God and the intimate relationship he had enjoyed with Him. Being most interested in the gods and knowing of no man among his acquaintance who had heard of a God actually speaking and guiding him, Pharaoh was impressed. "Lot can spend time with the priests in my temple. They can teach him, so he can become the high priest of a temple to your God."

Abram had tried to explain that his God didn't need a temple. The whole world was His. To try to coax him into dwelling in a temple would be futile. "Elohim created us and He wants to help us and guide us."

Pharaoh was fascinated by such statements, and he insisted he wanted to know more. "Have your nephew Lot visit with Senwosret-ankh, the high priest of Memphis. Perhaps he will find a way in which we can add your God to our gods."

Abram was surprised by the pharaoh's interest in his God, but he was bewildered by Amenemhet's insistence on adding him to his own gods. He knew that in Egypt every city and village had a special god, and at times they fought each other by attacking the rival god. Those who worshiped the fish would never eat fish, but their enemies would eat fish just to spite them. It was obvious Pharaoh didn't understand. To him, it was merely a matter of joining Abram's God with Re, the sun god or Apis, the bull.

In the end both Lot and Abram visited the high priest to learn more of the ways of the Egyptians. Lot was interested until he discovered that to be a priest belonging to the higher orders, a man had to have his head shaved and every bit of hair removed from his body with an annoying waxing method and, most difficult of all, to be circumcised. Lot lost all interest in the religion of the Egyptians, but Abram went often to talk with the high priest.

Abram saw much that was foolish superstition, but he always came away impressed by the personal devotion of the priests. They were set apart, special vessels with rules and traditions that constantly reminded them of their relationship with their god.

"Lot," Abram said after one such visit, "since Elohim is so much greater than these gods of the Egyptians, don't you think it would be fitting for us to show our dedication in some more visible way?"

Lot thought for a moment, then replied, "If you're thinking we should shave our heads, that's not such a bad idea. That would get rid of any fleas or lice and might be cool in the desert, but circumcision is out. I'd never do it." He got up and started for the door but turned back. "And if you're thinking of asking Elohim about it, don't do it."

That had been just what Abram had been pondering. Lot's strong opinion made him dismiss the idea. Perhaps the gods of Egypt were more particular, or was it that the priests of Egypt were more devoted to their gods? The latter thought bothered him. He hated to think that a worshiper of an ibis-headed god would be more devoted to his god than he was to his God.

The year was divided into three sections of four months each. In late summer there was the rising of the dog star, Sirius, that heralded the four months of flood when the Nile rose and overflowed its banks on its way to what was called the seven mouths of the Nile in the delta. These months had passed, and to everyone's satisfaction the Nile had risen. The next four months called the going out, when the water receded, had also gone by.

They were already in the time of sowing and harvest, and still Abram had not been able to bring up the problem of Sarai to Pharaoh. The very idea of mentioning the awkward situation became more difficult with each passing day.

Pharaoh was a proud man. He had boasted often that he and his good friend Abram were to be linked by marriage as soon as the time was appropriate. More than that, the pharaoh had been generous beyond any imagining. He had welcomed Abram and elevated him to the position of special friend. What Abram had done would seem cruel and deliberately heartless.

Abram was appalled at how much time had passed without his being able to rescue Sarai. He had prayed and agonized before his God, making rash promises and resolutions, but nothing happened. Then quite suddenly, everything changed, and it became necessary for Abram to act.

There was a crisis of such magnitude that Abram's anxiety reached fevered heights. News had come through Mara that the royal recorder had recorded no births among Pharaoh's wives or concubines. In all that time no royal cat had birthed kittens, and the great bulls had given only dead seed to the sacred cows.

It was even whispered that when the priests of Taweret applied their most effective magic, nothing happened. Taweret was the goddess of pregnant women. She was unbelievably ugly, with the head of a hippopotamus, lion's paws, a crocodile tail, and the body of a woman.

"Pharaoh thinks it is a curse on all the Egyptians," Mara said, "and it's rumored that he's going to break the spell by taking Sarai as a full wife, not just a concubine. A foreigner from Ur might break the spell."

Her words plunged Abram into torment. His first impulse was to rush to the palace, confess everything, and throw himself on the pharaoh's mercy. He paced back and forth in the pillared entryway, trying to think of just what he would say. Each time he was about to settle on an explanation, he would see that in Pharaoh's eyes there was no excuse. Amenemhet had sought to honor him by marrying his sister and had shown his friendship in a thousand other ways. To confess to such deception would not only destroy the friendship but would also make Pharaoh look foolish before his people.

Then a terrible thought presented itself. Perhaps the very plague Pharaoh was trying to avert had been caused by his taking Sarai into his harem. If he confessed to Pharaoh that Sarai was his wife and was barren, Pharaoh had every right to declare her the cause of the trouble. She would be mercilessly tormented and perhaps even killed.

With that thought, Abram fled to the roof of his house and stood for a time looking out over the trees in the direction of the palace. Tears blinded his eyes as he pounded the mud wall of the parapet with his fist in frustration. Sarai was there in the palace right now, and he was totally helpless to go to her aid. By now she probably realized the danger she was in. His poor, willful, fascinating little wife would be depending on him to extricate her from this problem. She would imagine he could pray and a miracle would take place.

To pray. That was one of the problems. He was no longer so sure that the great Creator God would hear a man like him who had acted so deceitfully. Nor was he sure that his God had any power to help him here in Egypt in the presence of so many gods.

He knelt on the hot tiles of the roof and bowed his head to the floor. He wept and groaned but could find no words to voice his prayer. It was the worst crisis of his life, and he was helpless—a foreigner in a foreign country.

Finally in desperation he poured out his heart; he uttered his complaints. The famine in the land he'd been promised. His embarrassment before his family and people. The lack of guidance or direction. Sarai's barrenness that had caused all the trouble with the pharaoh. Where was the child he'd been promised?

Only after he had exhausted his frustration was he able to think of his faults and failings. "Sarai trusted me, and I have done nothing to help her. I lied to Pharaoh Amenemhet, and he has been my friend. I have even doubted in my heart that You are the Creator God, a God above the gods of these Egyptians. When I saw their good land, their happy children, I envied them and doubted Your promises to me."

At last Abram was quiet. The turmoil subsided, and he voiced the prayer of his heart: "Oh my God, have mercy upon me. If You love me, forgive my foolishness and rescue Sarai."

That was all he prayed, but in the prayer was a challenge. Only his God could help him now.

Later that evening Abram called Lot and suggested that his wife, Mara, and Urim's wife, Safra, might go the next day to the palace and see if they could visit Sarai or at least gather some news. "Safra can take some of her cheese as a gift to Sarai and the women attending her, and Mara can take ointment and fine woolens for the queen mother. I doubt they will let them see Sarai, but we must try. It's important to know where Sarai is and what is happening to her. It's also important to find out just what Pharaoh's plans are and how soon he intends to take Sarai as his wife."

Lot agreed that it would be well to try. "I'll talk to Mara, and we can tell Urim tomorrow. I doubt that they can get much news. It really looks hopeless. Whatever happens, we don't want to offend Pharaoh."

Abram did not answer him, and Lot backed from the room and hurried home to tell Mara.

*U*rim, the cheese maker, had been amazingly successful in Egypt. Pharaoh liked the pungent smoked goat cheese that was famous in and around Haran but was not made in the delta. Once Pharaoh Amenemhet had proclaimed it his favorite, Urim was assured of basking in his special favor.

Urim had efficiently managed to set up the whole process so he no longer did the work himself. Instead he bought slaves, obtained a modest villa, and proceeded to adjust to a life of leisure such as he had never even imagined.

While Lot, Eliazer, and Abram refused to have their heads shaved, Urim reveled in the daily lathering and massage that went with the process. He found it pleasant to doff his scratchy woolen robes for the fine, pleated, linen kirtle that fastened under one arm, and gradually he added gold armbands and a neck piece of coral.

His plump little wife, Safra, found it almost impossible to squeeze into any of the clothes the queen had sent for the women to wear. She noticed that none of the Egyptian women were big boned or fat, and she began to feel awkward and ill at ease anyplace but in her own home.

"Why don't you go and make friends?" Urim asked Safra when he found her sitting with her servants, grinding grain or working the looms. "We're rich now. It isn't like before. You can stop all this drudgery and enjoy being in Egypt."

"You think I am going to the parties with this?" She pulled at her coarsely woven billowing robe in disgust.

"Don't go in that. There are plenty who will come and make garments, beautiful garments."

Safra looked down at her hands and then her feet. "It's not just my clothes," she said in a voice so low she could barely be heard.

"What is it? Why can't you change and enjoy things? This is what I've wanted, why I came along."

"You haven't seen these women." Safra almost wept. "Their hands aren't rough from shucking corn, washing clothes, and grinding. Their feet aren't calloused and ugly, and they don't cover their hair with scarves."

For the first time since they had arrived in Egypt, Urim looked at his wife critically. He saw that she was right. No matter how sophisticated and wise he had become in the ways of the Egyptians, Safra would give away his true origins. She was a woman he had been proud of because she could manage things. She made tasty dishes with a special touch even his mother hadn't been able to accomplish. She had kept his small household running efficiently, and she had borne him sons. As a servant, she would have been priceless, but as a wife of the exalted cheese maker of the pharaoh, she was lacking. That is, she was lacking unless he could in some way get her to change.

Urim had made the acquaintance of serving girls in the pharaoh's kitchens and some of the wenches who sang and danced for men in the local beer gardens. One girl named Warda seemed to take a special interest in him, and he wondered if perhaps she would help solve the problem of Safra.

In the end he decided to ask Warda for help, and he would give her permission to buy whatever was necessary to transform Safra. She came willingly and brought a sewing woman, a hairdresser, and several old women carrying baskets of ointments, lotions, and cosmetics. Urim wondered at the extent of expense and trumpery necessary to transform one woman.

Safra had agreed, but when she saw Warda and the women who followed her carrying baskets on their heads and two donkeys loaded with mysterious baggage, she first grew fearful and then rebellious. The bathing, harsh scrubbing with a luffa, and rinsing and rearranging of her hair were barely acceptable, but when Warda insisted that all body hair be removed with the sticky wax that pulled and hurt, she refused. Safra sat in the steamy tiled bathing room on a low stool totally naked for the first time in her life. She folded her arms over her ample breasts for a little covering and demanded her familiar clothes immediately.

Warda and her women tried every inducement before they gave up and called Urim. When Safra heard that they were calling her husband, she became more reasonable and agreed to everything . . . everything but the wax.

She enjoyed the rich ointments they rubbed into her feet and hands, and she found the perfumes a new, exciting experiment. But she could not endure the weight of the neck piece. She insisted it made her nervous and she kept twisting her head from side to side and pulling at it in an effort to get it into a more comfortable position. The ankle bracelets were "uncomfortable," and to have her hair loose, flowing around her shoulders, was impossible. When Warda produced the sheer linen shift that exposed all of her plump curves in a shocking fashion, Safra bolted from the room, locked herself in one of the storerooms, and refused to come out.

Warda appealed to Urim. She told him the entire situation and assured him that his wife could not be made into an Egyptian lady without her cooperation. Urim was furious. Safra had no right to resist change when it was so important. He had never really thought much about her. Until now, she had just been there doing things in quite an acceptable fashion. Suddenly he saw her as hopelessly provincial, a drag to his new position, and worst of all she had obviously shown a rebellious streak he had not thought possible.

Warda saw all of this. Being a woman who knew an opportunity when she saw it, she decided to have Urim for herself. She would immediately be elevated from the uncertainties of life as a dancing girl to concubine and maybe even wife of a prosperous foreigner. She had seen more attractive men. Urim had some rough edges that would need to be dealt with, but he was ambitious and wanted to better himself. All of that appealed to her. She determined to have him, and before the day was over, she had accomplished her goal.

The women with their baskets and the donkeys were sent away, but Warda stayed. When Safra finally ventured out of the storeroom dressed in her old dark blue gown and her hair tied up in a scarf with the offending sandals held in her hand instead of on her feet, she was appalled to find that Urim was on the roof with Warda and had left word that he was not to be disturbed.

Later when word came that Safra was to go to the palace with Mara, she again hung back. These encounters outside her home were too painful. "Let Warda go," she insisted. "I have too much to do here at home."

When Mara heard of her decision, she went to Urim and pleaded with him to convince Safra to go. Reluctantly Urim tried. But Safra agreed only on the condition that she go in her own hand-woven gown with her hair covered by her old mantle and that she not have to wear any ankle bracelets or the neck piece. Urim was livid with humiliation.

In desperation he called Abram to witness her stubbornness. For the first time Abram saw that Urim had taken a beautiful Egyptian concubine. It grieved him to see how Urim favored her and neglected, even despised, Safra. So, he thought, our coming to Egypt has complicated our lives.

"What do you want, Safra?" Abram asked.

"I am comfortable here and have much to do. Please, let Warda go."

Abram saw that Safra would indeed be out of place and perhaps feel awkward and shy if she went, while Warda would see it as an adventure. "Then let Warda go with Mara, but do your best to see Sarai and bring back some news," he told the women.

* * *

When they reached the gate to the women's court, it was Warda who managed to get them past the guards. She held her head high, balancing the cheese in its wooden bowl on her head, insisting they were expected. Once in the large court Warda singled out a frumpy, ugly dwarf and promised him one large cheese if he would take the two of them to the rooms of the pharaoh's bride in waiting. He grinned and, reaching for the cheese, motioned for them to follow him.

With the dwarf making all the explanations, Mara and Warda had no trouble getting in to the secret chambers of preparation where Sarai was staying. It was assumed that she had ordered the cheese and had permission to see the women.

The dwarf pointed to a woman sitting beside a lily pond in a small courtyard that was fragrant with tuberoses. She didn't see them at first, and they had time to notice the elegance of the room and its sparse but artful furnishings. The tiles were of warm-toned alabaster. The pillars were covered with figures and picture writing all painted in muted greens and mauve. In the center, the room was open to the sky, and under the opening was a pond surrounded by white bell-like flowers.

Slaves in the room were standing ready with huge fans, arranging big alabaster bowls of fruit, or trying to get some incense burning in one of the large brass braziers. They saw that Sarai was sitting beside the pool with her face turned away. Next to her was a strange little creature who wore only a loincloth and a pectoral of coral with a gold wrist band. "He's another dwarf," Warda whispered to Mara as they paused to stare at him.

As they came farther into the room, the slaves withdrew, but the dwarf stayed. He had been chewing on a blade of grass, and when he saw them, he took it out of his mouth and used the furry end to get Sarai's attention. Then he pointed at Mara and Warda. He either couldn't talk or didn't want to.

"Mara!" Sarai exclaimed in astonishment. Then noticing Warda, she hesitated as she looked from one to the other and waited for an explanation.

"This is Warda, Urim's new concubine."

Sarai registered surprise. She was obviously trying to understand.

Warda smiled and offered the wedge of cheese to Sarai. "Safra wanted me to come. She says she feels out of place here."

Sarai rose, hesitated, and smiled, while the two women stood and stared. There was nothing familiar about Sarai. Her hair had been cut to her shoulders, braided into a hundred small, tight braids with a cascade of pearls flowing from her headpiece. The headpiece was of golden wing feathers that bordered her face and peaked in the center of her forehead with a golden asp ready to strike.

Her gown was of the elegant sheer material only royalty wore, and they noticed with astonishment it covered only one shoulder. Around Sarai's neck she wore a brilliant golden pectoral inlaid with coral and turquoise, and when she lifted her skirt, they could see golden toe rings with small pieces that tinkled when she moved. She was slim and stood erect, giving the illusion of timeless beauty.

"How did you get in? Why did you come? What has happened to Abram?" She came toward them, eagerly asking questions.

Mara nodded toward the dwarf. She hesitated to speak freely as long as he was there.

Sarai reassured her that the dwarf was harmless. He lived only to tell funny stories and to carry messages. "He won't even understand what you are saying."

With that they sat down with her among the cushions at the side of the pool and proceeded to tell her everything. They ended with the question, "Is it true Pharaoh is getting ready to marry you?"

Sarai jumped up again and paced nervously back and forth. She seemed unable to talk about it. When she finally spoke, her voice was soft, but her words were sharp, staccato bursts of apprehension. "You must understand. For six months there have been no births. Not even wheat seeds put in bowls of urine have sprouted."

"What do you mean?" Mara asked. "Wheat seeds in urine?"

"That's the final test. They collect a woman's urine, then place seeds in it. If they don't sprout, they know the woman is barren."

"And . . . ?" Mara asked.

"They have to find a solution fast. If nothing grows, the crops will fail and the people will starve."

"And the solution?" Mara continued to press for answers.

Sarai stopped and flung up her hands in a gesture of despair. "The solution is to marry a foreign woman since they think the curse is only on Egyptians. I am that woman. Within two days I am to visit Pharaoh and within a week to be married." She turned from them so they wouldn't see her face, but they could see she was terribly upset by the way she fingered her bracelets and twisted one ring around nervously.

Warda and Mara looked at each other in consternation. "What will you do? What will you say?"

She turned and faced them, her eyes blazing with frustration. "If my husband can do nothing, and his God does not rescue me, I'll have to tell Pharaoh the whole truth. I could only bring further curses on his house."

Both women jumped to their feet and started to speak at once. They reminded her of the danger she would be in and the terrible punishment both she and Abram were sure to call down on their heads. Mara was unable to resist the temptation to remind Sarai that when they found she was not only married but was also barren, she would be blamed for the whole problem. Nothing they said seemed to move her. When it was time for them to go, they still had not convinced her.

* * *

The dwarf found Pharaoh Amenemhet relaxing on one of his royal barges. It was a method of escaping from the people constantly waiting to see him on business. The dwarf had cleverly engaged a skiff, which had quickly overtaken the barge. "I bring important news," the dwarf shouted as the skiff pulled alongside the barge.

"Tell me, and I'll deliver the message," the old priest Imhotep insisted.

The dwarf frowned. "This is a private matter," he said. "He is expecting me."

Those proved to be the magic words, and the dwarf was immediately invited aboard and into the presence of the pharaoh.

When the dwarf signaled that he had something private to share, all the friends and retainers dropped back. The dwarf ascended the few steps and leaned on the arm of Pharaoh's royal chair so he could speak quietly with him.

Though Amenemhet was relaxing, he continued to wear the double crown of Upper and Lower Egypt and a pectoral of heavy gold emblazoned with huge jewels. His girdle matched the pectoral and held his short kilt in place. He leaned over to hear as the dwarf spoke in a whisper.

His face had borne the usual pleasant expression, but as the dwarf spoke, a frown appeared, his face clouded over, and his eyes registered his surprise. He asked only a few quick questions, then rose, his eyes hard as flint and his voice clipped and harsh as he ordered the barge to return to the palace. He then called his chief steward and ordered him to bring his promised bride to see him as soon as the barge came to shore.

In the meantime, Mara and Warda returned home to find everyone waiting eagerly for their report. They spent a great deal of time describing the luxury Sarai was living in and then describing her appearance. Abram let out a groan when he heard how she was dressed. "She'll love it there. She'll never want to come home."

"No, no," said Warda. "She is very unhappy. She told us that if by the time she went to see the pharaoh, she hadn't been rescued, she intended to tell him everything."

At that pronouncement, everyone began to talk at once. They were all frightened and astounded at what they saw as her foolish bravery.

"We'll never see her alive."

"They'll blame all of us."

"They won't stop there. They kill people for less."

They all looked at Abram. "What are you going to do? You must have a plan."

Abram looked down at his hands and then stood up with a look of determination on his face. "You're right. It would be just like Sarai to tell Pharaoh everything if she's not stopped. She has no fear."

Lot jumped up. He was terribly upset. His voice was tense and sharp, "This is a time for your God to do something—if He can."

"I have prayed," Abram said, turning to Lot. "All these months that Sarai's been gone, I've prayed."

"But what will you do?" Lot asked.

"I don't know."

Lot looked boldly around the room. "At whatever cost, be sure you don't offend Pharaoh," he said. He then hesitated as though carefully weighing the words he was about to utter. "You may even have to let Sarai go. That would be better than to have all of us killed."

Abram was momentarily stunned. At no time had he thought of letting Sarai stay as concubine or wife of Amenemhet. He swung around and looked at Lot and, then without another word, left the room.

In the women's quarters of the palace, great excitement reigned. Everyone knew that Pharaoh had called for the new foreigner and that there was some ominous aspect to the summons.

Hagar was now loose from her chains and, upon hearing more details, bribed her way into the waiting room where Sarai was being readied. "You must know," she whispered, "your ugly dwarf listened to everything your friends said and then went right to Pharaoh."

Sarai whirled around with a look of surprise and shock. "But the dwarf . . ."

"I know, he seems childish and simple. Actually he is very astute and one of my father's best spies." Hagar motioned for the women in attendance to leave them alone. "Sarai, you are too trusting. I warned you. You have known how dangerous it is to confess to all of this."

"I know, I know," Sarai said impatiently.

"No, you don't know. You have no idea the ways in which women have been punished right here in this palace. I could tell you terrible stories if there were time."

"Hagar," Sarai said, holding her hands over her ears, "don't tell me. I'm not very brave."

At that moment a trumpet was blown, and the brass doors swung back, revealing the house guards with a carrying chair. They set the chair down and gave a parchment to one of the eunuchs. Within minutes the eunuch was escorting Sarai to the chair, and there was no time for Hagar to give her further advice.

Sarai had seen Pharaoh when he visited his wives. He was an older man, but strong and well built. When he came to the women's court, he dressed only in the jeweled pectoral, the wide belt, and the short kilt. He was without his double crown or the staff and scepter. He always came with a retinue of eunuchs, several scribes, fanners, and his favorite dwarves. He came as a man and not simply Pharaoh.

Sarai had guessed him to be about the age of Abram. Though she had heard that he was the representative of Horus, and at times actually the god, she had never taken it seriously. She had assumed she would talk to him much as she would talk to her husband, without the necessity of formalities.

For this reason she was greatly shocked to see Pharaoh Amenemhet sitting on his ivory gilded throne dressed in his most regal splendor and surrounded by all the pomp that Egypt could command. It frightened her. She could imagine terrible punishments being meted out by this distant and remote Pharaoh. "Oh God of my husband Abram," she silently prayed, "if You are as strong as Abram says, help me, rescue me." Though she prayed, she expected no answer.

A eunuch helped her from the chair and whispered that she must bow to the floor and stay there until Pharaoh recognized her.

Pharaoh took a good deal of time before he gave her permission to stand and come forward. She could tell that he was studying her, perhaps deciding what her punishment should be. "Sarai," he said, "is it true, as I have been told, that you are not the sister of my good friend Abram but his wife?"

"My lord," Sarai answered, "it's true that I am both his sister and his wife. My father had two wives, and I was the child of his second wife."

"And who decided to make sport of Pharaoh by hiding the truth from him?"

"My lord," Sarai said, "it was my fault. I wanted to visit the palace and your mother detained me."

"And you deceived her."

"No, my lord," Sarai said, flushing with embarrassment. "I told her the truth . . . but only half the truth. I am my husband's half sister."

"And your children? Where are your children?"

Sarai grew pale. She felt that she would surely faint if made to say the hateful words. She looked at Pharaoh and saw that he was leaning forward, his eyes dark and hooded. "My lord," she said with great effort, "I am a woman who has never had a child."

"And your husband, he has other wives."

"No, my lord."

At that Pharaoh's eyes opened in astonishment, and he looked around the room in an obvious effort to regain his composure. When he looked back at Sarai, he no longer had the firm set to his jaw and the flinty look in his eyes. "I'm going to send for your husband. If what you tell me is true, this is indeed astounding."

Sarai was taken back to the waiting room while guards were sent to bring Abram to the palace. She knew there had been a change in the pharaoh's demeanor, but she didn't understand what it might mean.

When the guards came to get Abram, he was almost relieved to at last face the dreaded ordeal. He was resigned to accepting the very worst punishment, but he had made up his mind to ask only for Sarai's freedom.

"What is this you have done to me?" Pharaoh demanded when Abram at last stood before him. He didn't wait for Abram to answer but flung more questions: "Why did you tell me she was your sister and not mention that she was your wife?"

Abram was embarrassed and ashamed. He could think of no way to explain what he'd done, no way to defend his action.

When Amenemhet saw that Abram made no effort to defend himself, he stood up. Looking around at the curious bystanders, he spoke these words: "Let it be known, this man has been my friend. Though this plague has come upon my house through him, I will return good to him for friendship's sake." With that he called to the eunuchs and asked them to go to the court of the women and bring both Sarai and Hagar to him.

Within moments the two women appeared in the door to the right of the throne. Hagar hesitated. It was obvious that she was trying to determine why she had been called. When Amenemhet held out the crook to her and there was the old look of approval in his eyes, she wondered what had happened to bring about this change. She was soon to understand and realize that her father had seized upon a plan that would please his queen, Senebtisy, and at the same time would rid the harem of a problem.

"My daughter," he said, "I have heard reports of the friendship between this woman, Sarai, and yourself. Is that true?"

Hagar's face registered suspicion. Her first thought was that she was to be punished along with Sarai. She hesitated only a moment and then said, "She befriended me." There was just the brief hint of defiance, just a tilt of the head that reminded everyone that she was not easily dismissed.

Pharaoh ignored her obvious reluctance. His mood had changed. He seemed to be quite pleased about something. He turned to Abram. "My friend, you have given me many days of happiness. Your sister-wife has entertained my mother and befriended my daughter, and though I suspect she is the one who has brought the curse upon us, I have chosen to restore maat.

That can be done only by untying the knots and bringing order out of chaos."

Abram looked surprised, and Sarai looked up to see what was happening. Pharaoh Amenemhet was holding out the crook to her. At the same time one of the eunuchs pushed her forward until she stood before Pharaoh and beside Hagar. "Since you have admitted that you have no children, and you are my friend's only wife, I am going to give you my daughter Hagar to be your handmaiden. When you choose, she will go in to your husband and will give you a fine son for him."

He called Abram to him and, embracing him, said, "You did wrong to deceive me. You destroyed maat, the eternal order of things, which to us is more precious than riches. In giving you my daughter, I've begun the restoration of maat. You must leave and go back to your country, but if the gods are favorable, our blood will yet flow together and give you a son worthy of our friendship."

"Thank you, my lord. I little deserve your generosity." Abram drew back, shock and relief coursing through him, and let the guards lead him to Sarai and this strange young woman who was to be Sarai's handmaiden. As he left the room of assembly, he looked back and noticed that Pharaoh Amenemhet had once more assumed the half smile that all the pharaohs were noted for. He understood the smile better now. When maat, the order of all things, was functioning properly, the people knew it was so by the calm, assured countenance of their ruler.

This was not the man he had known. This was the public figure, the god-man indwelt by Horus. He would miss his friend. The man who came out from behind the royal mask in the evening and entered into a rousing game of hounds and jackals or just sat looking at the stars and pondering their significance.

He knew it was a miracle that Pharaoh had not punished them severely. He could tell by the expression on the faces of the guards and the retainers that they, too, were surprised at the turn of events. "Your God has been with you," one of the old priests said as he passed Abram in the outer hall.

Abram hardly noticed Hagar. He saw only that she was shapely and spirited and then dismissed all thought of her. It was Sarai he was concerned about—nearly a stranger now. Her face was made to look Egyptian and her hair was in small, tight braids that spilled out from under one of the Egyptian headpieces. She wore a gown of sheer material that covered her breasts but left one shoulder bare. He felt completely awed by this beautiful woman coming home with him.

* * *

That same night Pharaoh Amenemhet called his builders and instructed them to make plans to build a wall above the Reed Sea. "I want no more visitors. We've had enough of them. They break our hearts and steal maat." Much later it was recorded that he told his son, "Trust no foreigner."

*B*efore nightfall of the same day, Pharaoh signed a dispatch ordering an armed escort and a fleet of barges to take Abram and his large family up the Nile to Tanis in the delta. There they were to gather up their servants and herds and leave Egypt as quickly as possible.

Abram was relieved and overjoyed at Pharaoh's decision. He viewed it as a direct answer to his prayers and proof that his God had power to change even Pharaoh's heart. He had secretly feared that the gods of the pharaoh might be more powerful or that his God had been left behind at the border of Egypt. Now he knew, actually had proof, that this was not true. He could hardly wait to share his insight with Sarai.

As it happened there had been no time for him to talk to Sarai. To make matters worse, he had noticed a subtle change had taken place in his charming little wife.

She was dressed like an Egyptian and had taken on many of their mannerisms. He noticed how she brushed the many little braids of shoulder-length hair back with one hand and kept fingering the elaborate pectoral she wore around her neck. He saw with surprise that her hands were smooth and soft with carefully rounded nails.

On the barge he noticed that she preferred the company of the beautiful Egyptian handmaiden the pharaoh had given her. They seemed to understand each other, kept to themselves, and even whispered at times in a most annoying fashion. Sarai seemed as remote and strange as a foreign woman. He turned away, wondering what other surprises he would encounter as a result of their stay in Egypt.

At dusk the barge came to a stop at an elegant wharf and in the distance loomed the great pyramids of Khufu and Khephren. Abram remembered the steward giving orders that they were to spend the last night in Egypt in one of Pharaoh's own guesthouses at the base of the pyramids. He knew Pharaoh Amenemhet well enough to realize it was not just a parting kindness but a very clever punishment. Pharaoh wanted to remind him of all that was to be lost with the loss of his friendship.

Abram was just getting ready to ask some questions of the steward when Lot and a few of his men appeared. They were very upset. "My uncle," Lot said, "it isn't safe to stop here."

Abram was puzzled. "Not stop? I thought you would be relieved to have one more night in the luxury of Egypt."

"It's not the luxury I object to. It's the evil djinn of the old pharaohs that might haunt these huge tombs."

"If Pharaoh himself isn't afraid to stay here, then I'm sure it's quite safe."

Lot bristled. "If he's not afraid, it's because his priests assured him a man's soul enters another living creature first and then waits three thousand years before entering a human body again. I'm not so sure. I think those old pharaohs are right here; we just can't see them."

Lot turned away, but he wasn't pleased. Abram looked after him and realized that there would be difficult days ahead. Lot had loved Egypt, and it was evident that he harbored deep resentments at the abrupt manner in which they had to leave.

The guesthouse they were to stay in had been built for the pharaoh and his immediate household to use during the feasts. It was equipped with servants and furnishings as fine as any in the royal palace at Lisht. It had its own chapel and a retinue of priests who offered the daily sacrifices and waited on the image of the god that dwelt in the niche behind the temple veil.

Abram was given Pharaoh's quarters, and the women were led to the rooms for the harem. Lot, Eliazer, and the rest of the men were in rooms designed for the steward and government officials.

Abram walked around the room, enjoying its simplicity and breathing in the subtle odor of incense. Everything reminded him of Amenemhet. He almost expected to see him walk into the room with his fan bearers, pages, and the ever-present dwarf. He walked out on the open balcony and rested his elbows on the parapet. As he watched the sun set, the sky darkened and the evening star gradually blossomed in single splendor much as he had observed it in Ur.

How strange, he thought. I have come so far, yet the same star shines here just as it did in Haran and at home in Ur. Perhaps I shouldn't be surprised to find the same God in charge here just as in Ur.

Again he felt a burst of joy. Sarai had not been killed or married to the pharaoh, and he had not been executed or imprisoned. They had been banished from Egypt, but there seemed something right about that. Perhaps he should never have come down to Egypt.

As he looked into the courtyard below, he realized it must open off the harem quarters. He wondered if Sarai was there getting her things arranged. Are the changes all on the outside, he wondered, or are there also subtle changes in her thinking? She had made a point of avoiding him, and on sudden impulse he decided to call her. Perhaps they should celebrate their miraculous rescue.

He went to the door and shook the servant awake. "Go to the steward and have him prepare an intimate repast of the finest dried fruits and sweet cakes with some of his prize wine," he ordered. "Then go to the women's quarter and give the old woman in charge a message for my wife. Tell her I will be waiting in my rooms for her."

He was surprised at how soon he heard footsteps in the hall and saw the dark curtain lifted as Sarai came hesitantly into the room. "My lord," she said, "you called for me."

Abram noted the new formality and winced. She stood before him barefoot but wearing a flowing robe of light Egyptian linen. Her hair, still in the shoulder-length braids, was held back from her face by a golden band that peaked with the familiar cobra. She was obviously prepared for bed but looked as foreign and strange as she had when he first saw her that morning in the palace.

"Has Egypt altered your heart as much as your looks?" he asked, perhaps too sharply.

She pouted. "I thought you would like how I look."

"We'll talk of that later. Now is the time for celebration."

"Celebration?"

"We must celebrate the miracle, the way our God rescued us." As he spoke he started to move toward her but stopped when he saw her face clouded in anger.

She spoke up in a burst of frustration, "I've never been more humiliated. They thought I was evil. They knew I had been cursed. It's all the fault of your God. I want nothing more to do with Him and His promises."

Abram was stunned. "I don't understand."

"This would never have happened if your God had kept His promise."

"His promise?"

"You said we were to have children."

"Sarai, Sarai." He reached out and tried to take her in his arms, but she pulled away from him.

"Can you imagine what it feels like to be stared at—even feared?" Sarai stomped her foot and glared at him. "They all had children, lots of children, and when I came, many were pregnant and then . . ."

"No, no, Sarai," Abram said with growing alarm. "I've heard, I know. It was our God who shut up the wombs to rescue you."

"To rescue me? If I'd had leprosy, they couldn't have been more afraid of me. None of the sacred cats had kittens, the holy cows had no calves and gave no milk, none of the concubines or wives conceived, and even the servants were smitten. All that was blamed on me."

"I know it must have been very hard for you."

"Hard for me!" She glared at him in exasperation. "I suffered . . . how I suffered."

"But Sarai," Abram spoke softly and compassionately, "don't you see that our God rescued you?"

"No, I don't. Pharaoh did more to rescue me than your God ever did."

"Oh, Sarai! How can you say such a thing?"

"He gave me a handmaiden to have a child for me."

Abram drew back in astonishment. He knew that was the custom in both Ur and Egypt, but he had never imagined Sarai would agree to such a thing. For himself, he had never lost faith in the promise. It was obvious that Sarai had changed. Egypt had changed her.

Eventually they sat and tried to eat the delicious fruits the servants brought. Dish after dish was set before them and then removed without being eaten. They could think of nothing to say to each other, and so finally Sarai begged to be excused. She insisted she would be in a more amiable mood after a good night's sleep, and Abram let her go, hoping it would be so.

After the sound of her footsteps had died away along the hall, Abram paced restlessly back and forth, thinking of all Sarai had said and wondering what he should do. He knew he couldn't sleep, and he longed for someone to talk to.

He walked over to the parapet, and this time he looked down on the other side into an enclosed sunken garden extending from the chapel. A lone figure sat beside the lily pond, and he knew it must be one of the priests. He quickly dismissed his problems and hurried down the winding stairs that led out into the garden. He wanted to see the Great Sphinx by moonlight, and he hoped the priest would have time to go with him.

To his delight, the man was just the person he was looking for. Abram had spotted him earlier in the day and remembered his face. It was kindly, and the eyes were a strange blue-green like those of the pharaohs.

The priest was meditating, but when he saw Abram, he stood up. "Can I help you?" he asked in the soft, cultured tones of Egypt's elite.

"We will be on our way tomorrow and I wanted to see the Great Pyramid and the Sphinx by moonlight. Can you show me the way out of the villa?"

"I will do more than that. I'll go with you and answer any questions."

It was not long until the two were walking across the hard-packed sand to where they could stand in the shadow of the Great Pyramid. It rose above them, giving off a silver glow in the bright moonlight. "The pyramids give off different colors depending on the time of day," the priest said. "At dawn they are gray, gold at noon, and rose colored at sunset."

"They are tombs?" Abram asked.

"You might call them tombs, but we don't think of the pharaohs as being dead. Pharaoh goes in and out at will."

"How strange. Where does he go?"

"Where he goes is known only to the priests. It is one of the secrets of the pyramids."

"So there are secrets. It is not as simple as it looks."

"Of course. They are carefully built. We know the secrets only because they have been passed down to us."

"Does Pharaoh Amenemhet know the secrets?"

The priest chuckled and said, "He insists on certain designs. There are spells and magic sacred to the pharaohs. There are incantations such as, 'You will regularly ascend with Orion from the east and descend with Orion into the west.'"

"How can he do this?"

"There is a shaft built into the pyramid that points to Orion's constellation. Once every twenty-four hours, three stars in this constellation pass directly over this shaft, and at this time the pharaoh can follow the shaft out into the sky and the celestial regions. It is also possible for the pharaoh to visit the polestar through the northern shaft. In this way he can come and go at will."

Walking on toward the Great Sphinx, Abram was impressed with its height and the awesome silence, almost palpable, that surrounded it. "They say there's a mystery about the Sphinx. No one really knows why it was made and what it is trying to tell us," he said.

"Ah, yes, it's one of the great mysteries. Some say the face is that of Khafre. If that's true, the creature would have been carved out of this limestone outcropping hundreds of years ago."

"Khafre?" Abram said, looking puzzled.

"He was one of the early pharaohs. However, others say the sphinx is much older."

"I had heard one of the priests in Memphis say it represented the beginning and end of the zodiac."

"That has at times been a popular theory, but the beginning of the zodiac is a virgin with a shaft of wheat in her hand; the end is a lion, and this face is obviously that of a pharaoh."

"Then . . ."

"For many of us it symbolizes the union of man's two natures, the physical and the intellectual."

"So it isn't Khafre."

"Perhaps not Khafre, but it is obviously the face of a pharaoh. I like to imagine this pharaoh as one who wanted to remind Re of his existence. He wanted to make it impossible for the god to forget him, so he ordered a giant image of himself constructed that will stand forever, welcoming the sun."

"But why so large?"

The priest smiled. "Don't you see? He knew Re's chariot rode high in the sky, and it would take a very large image to get his attention."

They stood looking at the enormous creature now washed in moonlight, and Abram could imagine how the sun coming out of the eastern hills would flash on the rough features of the Sphinx and bring it to life.

Neither one spoke as they turned to walk back to the palace. In contemplating the mystery of the Sphinx, Abram had for a short time forgotten his problems. When he remembered, he was too tired to mull over them. He had Sarai back, and they were on their way out of Egypt. Everything would work out in time.

The next morning Abram and his entourage set out for the Nile and the barge that was to take them on to Tanis. They had started just before dawn when on the horizon faint streaks of light appeared behind the eastern hills. The air was crisp and cool with the only sounds coming from the soft jangling of the mules' harness decorations and the muted commands of the drivers.

As they left the sandy area for the green of the Nile, the sun came up and Abram looked back to see an unforgettable sight. The morning sun, rising over the eastern hills, burst upon the great stone head with a suffusion of brilliant light. It was indeed as the priest had said, an eternal tribute to the sun god.

Abram wondered what Amenemhet would have said. He had confided in Abram that he worshiped the god Amon, the invisible god, the god of the air. "He's no doubt the same as your God, the Elohim you worship," Pharaoh had said.

Abram had found that Amenemhet had even joined the god's name to his own, meaning "Amon leads." Furthermore, he had shown Abram the plans for a small temple he intended to build at Karnak to honor the god.

All this Abram pondered as the barge sailed up the Nile. "Is the pharaoh's god the same as Elohim?" He had tried to explain about the promises and hearing his God speak, but Pharaoh couldn't understand. Perhaps the problem was that the pharaoh was too impressed with being a god himself.

* * *

Hagar was happy with the turn of events. She had miraculously escaped not only from the boredom of the palace but also from the hostility of the pharaoh's favorite. She liked Sarai and had begun to view her as a sister, if not a mother. Everything was strange and new. There seemed to be no routine, no formalities. As it turned out, even the clothes she would wear were to be very different.

Before leaving the delta where Abram's herds had been waiting, Sarai gave her some new clothes. The shift was of wool and linen with a handsome fringe around the hem. It seemed clumsy and heavy compared to the lighter linen garments of the Egyptians, but Sarai assured her that in the desert it would be cooler. They laughed as they tried various methods of wearing the fringed shawl. It didn't fit over the ornate Egyptian headdress, but neither one wanted to change her hair and the ornaments she was used to wearing.

In the end, the fine Egyptian clothes and most of the jewelry and headdresses were packed away in chests to be worn only on special occasions. The clothes they would wear were of the Sumerian design but suited life in the desert and among the local people better.

Hagar also found the food different from anything she had ever eaten before. There was roast lamb or cracked wheat and herbs with white leben made from goat's milk; the fruits were mostly dates, figs, and dried grapes. She learned to build a fire with nettles or, for a steady, lasting fire, dung patties. She loved the sense of leisure. To Hagar, who had been used to the hurry and prodding of the palace, this was delightful. Everything moved with the rising of the sun and stopped when it set.

Most interesting of all for her was the contemplation of her new role. She was to be Sarai's handmaiden. The pharaoh had said she would bear Abram the son that Sarai had not been able to provide. With that in mind, Hagar had observed Abram closely.

She had always been independent and proud. She would never give herself to any man just because it was expected of her. Even to please her new friend Sarai, she would not submit to Abram. Pharaoh was far away and would never know what happened. He would never know if she refused to comply with his decree. If she didn't like this Abram, she could easily refuse to have anything to do with him. No one had ever made her do anything she didn't like, and she was sure that this would be no different.

On this night Sarai had gone to her tent, and Hagar was left sitting alone by her fire. They had come several days journey past the border of Egypt and were in the desert with bright stars overhead and the low murmur of voices coming from other tents.

Her thoughts turned to Sarai. She knew Sarai would never have a child now. She had passed the age when a woman conceived. She no longer had her monthly visitations. That made it inevitable that at any time now, Abram would call Hagar to his tent. She was surprised to find the idea somewhat exciting. She had watched with curiosity as he had greeted his men with enthusiasm, at the same time commanding their respect and admiration. She had been amazed to find him always gentle and understanding with Sarai, even when she was most difficult. She had also on occasion noticed his love of small children, his generosity, and his hospitality.

She who prided herself on being aloof and obstinate found herself first fascinated and then close to admiration as she studied this man who was not only her master but perhaps the future father of any child she might have.

She was not eager to have a child. A child would need love and could make her vulnerable. A child was not important to her at the moment. However, if she became genuinely attracted to this man, she might need a child. A child was what he wanted, and perhaps it would be well worth the trouble to gain the attention of a man like this who walked before them like a god.

She rubbed her arms to keep warm, then held them out over the fire to feel its heat. She was waiting . . . waiting for something. She couldn't even admit to herself that it might be for a glimpse of this man she was beginning to find so fascinating.

That he had never so much as glanced in her direction annoyed her. His eyes rested on Sarai with warmth and delight, and his interest in her baffled Hagar. Sarai wasn't young, and more than that, she was obstinate and at times quarrelsome.

Hagar had to admit that for the first time in her life she felt challenged. She wanted this man to look at her the way he had looked at Sarai, and she was determined to somehow make it happen. That was a small thing. Whether she would have a child was another matter. With that settled in her mind she rose and got a goatskin wrap from the tent and curled up by the fire. She was soon asleep and didn't know that Abram passed just a few steps from her, walking tall and composed to spend the night with Sarai in his section of the tent.

When they came to Luz in the mountains above the Jordan, Abram surprised everyone by insisting that they camp and build an altar. It had been almost four years since he had last worshiped his God in this place. It was springtime and all traces of the famine had vanished. The spring rains had been abundant and the almond trees were covered with white blossoms. The spring wheat was up and the grape arbors were touched with the green of new leaves.

Their flocks covered the hillsides in every direction and young lambs were being added daily. Abram, Lot, Iscah, and Eliazer went to the village to seek permission to camp. The leaders remembered and welcomed them. Abram had been generous with food and gifts during their former stay, and the village chief, seeing their wealth, was anticipating even greater largesse this time.

In a great show of hospitality and goodwill, the chief of the village took them to the roof of his house where a grapevine arbor offered shade. When they were comfortably settled on the straw-filled cushions, he offered them heaping trays of almonds and dates. Drinks of pomegranate juice followed in large, clumsy clay bowls. Finally, settling back among the dusty cushions, he asked them for news of Egypt. They soon found the village chief was already so well informed there was little to relate, and news of the Jordan Valley took up most of the conversation.

The Elamites who had caused such devastation in Ur had, during the same period, captured the neighboring cities that surrounded the Salt Sea. They had been exacting tribute from them ever since. Now for the first time, there was resistance.

"The men of Sodom and Gomorrah are objecting to the tribute," the village chief said as he slowly stirred the juice with his forefinger. When no one spoke, he continued, "Ched-or-la'o-mer, king of Elam, is vowing to come and bring the rebellion under control." For a moment he held his bowl suspended as his eyes nervously darted from one to the other, then with a shrug he drank noisily.

"And," questioned Lot, bending forward expectantly, "what do you think their answer is going to be? Will the men of Sodom and Gomorrah give in?"

The chief again held the clay bowl suspended as he seemed to ponder the question. Then absentmindedly setting the bowl down, he wiped his mouth on his sleeve and turned to Lot. "The men of Sodom have no interest in fighting," he said. "They live only for drinking and partying. They take pleasure in every fleshly whim."

Lot leaned forward with growing interest. "It sounds like what we enjoyed in Egypt."

"Perhaps," the chief admitted. "I know nothing of the customs of Egypt, but of Sodom and Gomorrah I know. They are not what we here in Luz would call 'real men' with the normal interests of real men."

With that the conversation came to an end. Abram invited the chief and his men to visit them and then, with the usual expressions of goodwill, bade them good day.

"Now," said Abram as they made their way up the path to where they were camped, "it's time to rebuild the altar and start over again. Elohim may never have intended that we go to Egypt. I moved too fast without listening. We must not make that mistake again."

* * *

Hagar stood in the door of the tent and watched the embers slowly die on the rough pile of stones these people called an altar. From a distance she had watched the men as they built this strange edifice and then raised their hands as they prayed and sang. She was fascinated. The altars she had known were hidden in the darkest corner of the great temples and were approached with fear and trepidation. These men were joyful. Some even seemed to be dancing.

In the midst of the men was Abram, his head thrown back and a look of wonder on his face. It was no ordinary, routine procedure such as would be carried out in the temples of Egypt. It was some mysterious, reverent-yet-joyful ritual, and Abram was the leader. As the fire leaped up and the smoke rose, Abram led the men in singing. It was singing such as she had never heard before. It was hauntingly majestic and had overtones of deep emotion.

It brought tears to her eyes and, strangely enough, a reluctant admiration for this man and his God. She who had known various emotions had never felt admiration for anyone nor had she ever cried. Now she hurried into the tent so that no one would know she had been so moved.

When she was again in control of her emotions, she went to find Sarai. Sarai was in her tent with the flaps up. She was sitting on a black-and-white goatskin rug working on a basket made of reeds gathered from the Nile. To Hagar's surprise, she was facing away from the obvious view of the altar.

When Sarai looked up, Hagar could see that she was in a bad humor. She knew better than to ask questions when Sarai was so out of sorts, but she was so curious and astonished by what she had seen that she couldn't resist.

"The God . . . where is the God they are worshiping? Where is His image?" she asked.

"No one can see him," Sarai said without looking up. "He's like the wind. Not like something made with hands."

"There's no image of Him?"

"Image?" Sarai looked up in surprise. "No, there's no image, and no one has ever seen Him."

"Then," said Hagar, narrowing her eyes in speculation, "how does my lord Abram know this God really exists?"

"That's simple," said Sarai, twisting a reed to fit at the base of the basket's handle. "This God speaks to him. Tells him things, gives him wonderful promises."

Hagar was immediately entranced. "Promises? His God really speaks and makes promises?"

Sarai stopped twisting the reed and jammed it into the opening with deliberation and a show of frustration. "Yes, promises. His God has told him this land is going to belong to him and to his descendants."

"Descendants?" The word seemed so out of place, so inappropriate. Hagar couldn't resist asking, "Has the voice ever spoken to you?"

Sarai looked up quickly and paused to determine whether Hagar had meant anything by her question. Was she making some point or statement? She decided Hagar was just curious, and so she answered with a shrug, "No, I've never heard Him speak, but He's promised Abram a child, descendants. It's all foolishness. Imagine promising a child at my age?"

Hagar could hardly take in what she was hearing. What a strange thing, to actually hear a god speak. She glanced at Sarai, ready to ask more questions, but she could tell by the tight set of her lips and the way she yanked the reeds to get them to fit that it was not the time for more questions.

Hagar turned away and headed out of the tent. She wanted to be alone, wanted to think about all that was happening and had happened. Off to the right was a path that led up to a rocky ledge. Impulsively she turned and within minutes was sitting on the ledge overlooking the camp and the men who were still gathered around the altar. The sun was setting; it would soon be dark. She rubbed her bare arms to keep warm and wrapped the fringed shawl more tightly around her.

The moon came up and one star shone out of the blue-green darkness. An eagle hung suspended in space above the altar and then flew off in the direction of the Jordan River. In Egypt they would see that as a sign of something—either very good or very bad. Everything was still now except for the sound of a baby crying in one of the tents and the high, sad sound of one of the men singing an old tribal song.

"His God has promised him descendants," she whispered. "It is obvious they won't come through Sarai."

She stood up and lifted her chin in the old defiant way. She was a stranger among these people. Their ways were not her ways and their God was unknown to her. However, if she managed her situation with cleverness, she could become the mother of this tribe's next leader. It would be her child, flesh of her flesh, bone of her bones, heir of all Abram's fortune. Of course, Sarai would claim the child. It was her right, but for at least three years Hagar would be needed to nurse the child.

Her lips curved in a smile of unabashed delight. She would have to be patient. She must do everything she could think of to please Sarai. That wouldn't be hard since they were friends. She had noticed that Sarai was hot-tempered and disagreeable at times, but that was to be expected of someone who had been cursed with such a terrible curse. Who would want or need a barren woman? It was indeed strange that Abram had kept her and even seemed to love her. Undoubtedly it was because she was also his half-sister.

Slowly she retraced her steps and found her way to Sarai's tent. As she raised the tent flap, she noticed that Sarai was already asleep. She moved noiselessly past her to the back of the tent, unrolled the heavy goatskin robe, and spread it out on the bare ground. The dew was heavy in these parts, and she had learned from experience to sleep inside the tent where it was dry and safe from wild animals. She lay down and pulled the robe up to her nose. Then smelling the rancid odor of the goat hair, she flung it away.

In the darkness Hagar reached up and fumbled in the chest that held all her belongings. She pulled out the delicate linen and wool piece that smelled sweetly of balsam and jasmine. Wrapping that around her, she once again lay down and was soon asleep. Her last thoughts were of the future. She would become Abram's mistress and mother of his child. He would love her devotedly for giving him the desire of his heart and would grant her every wish. Then she decided with a triumphant smile, I'll get rid of all the goatskin covers and have only linen shipped from Egypt.

* * *

Everything proceeded in the usual routine until it became evident that Lot and his family were somehow disgruntled and at odds with everyone. Sarai noticed it first as Mara stayed in her own tent and declined every invitation to visit. Then Abram noticed that Lot did not come as usual to sit around the fire in the evenings. Finally when the difficulty had spread to the servants, Lot came with a self-righteous smirk and his walking stick jabbing impatiently at the ground, ready to discuss the problem.

He never directly accused Abram's men of confiscating all the prize grazing land, but rather stated that the servants were quarreling among themselves. He hinted that it would be best if the men separated and each managed his own flocks and herds.

Abram had heard of the trouble but had thought it would soon pass because there was plenty of land for both of them. He had not counted on Lot's continued unhappiness over leaving Egypt. The stay in Egypt had spoiled him for the lonesome, nomadic life Abram was choosing.

Abram had seen there was a strong penchant for evil in all the places where people clustered together. He would have none of it. Then after God's revelation to him, he deliberately chose to separate himself and his family from the cities and their temptations. Lot was different. Lot yearned for the fellowship, the fast pace, and the constant change of the city. Now facing each other, Abram studied his nephew's face and saw that he was irritable and dissatisfied. There would be no simple solution.

In the end Abram let Lot choose where he would go. He was not surprised that Lot chose to move down toward the cities of Sodom and Gomorrah. "The weather is always warm down there," Lot said. "The flocks won't need shelter at night."

"If you move too close to the Jordan, you will be plagued by wild animals. Even lions come up out of the wilderness of the Jordan."

"I may live in Sodom and let my servants care for the sheep in the grazing lands outside the city."

Abram frowned. "You realize that these cities are held by the Elamites. They could sweep down at any time and destroy the cities for not paying their tribute."

Lot looked down and kicked the dirt with his sandal. "The Elamites are too far away. I don't believe they'll attack. People are just exaggerating."

No amount of argument swayed Lot. He was determined to go, and many of the servants raised in Abram's house decided to go with him. Abram was surprised that even the cheese maker and his two wives were leaving. Urim realized the danger. He even confided to Abram that he was concerned about moving to Sodom. He felt the threat of the Elamites was very real. However, in the end he packed up his family and made ready to move to Sodom.

Sarai invited the wives of the herdsmen, the women of Eliazer's house, and some of the bondswomen to a farewell party. She had felt especially close to Mara and Warda since they were the ones who had come to her in Pharaoh's house. She had no idea that Mara was jealous of her, criticized her continually, and was even ready to feign sickness as an excuse to stay away from the party.

At the same time, Sarai openly complained that Lot had made the better choice and that Mara was fortunate to have such a husband. When Warda quoted this statement to Mara, Mara rose up and dressed herself to go to Sarai's tent.

From the moment she arrived, Mara was engulfed in questions. Everyone wanted to know where she would live and what the people of Sodom were like. Mara had never been to Sodom, and she had no idea what sort of house Lot had bargained for. But she answered all questions with great assurance and watched Sarai's face to see the reaction. Sarai was not one to hide her feelings, and it was evident that she was unhappy.

Warda clung to Hagar with real affection. "We are Egyptians," she kept saying. "We should be together." For the first time Hagar seemed to notice Warda, and when it was time for the women to dance, Warda and Hagar showed how Egyptian women danced. Warda obviously had more practice, and so it wasn't long before the women insisted she do the dance of her village and then show them the dances she did as an entertainer.

"Urim says they have houses in Sodom where women dance for the

145

entertainment of men," said Urim's wife, Safra, rather innocently. "Perhaps Warda will do that."

Safra's remark almost brought the party to an abrupt close. Everyone turned to look at her. She was dressed in her everyday dark blue robe with no jewelry and the plain, white mantle framed a plump, red face that constantly needed to have the sweat blotted from it. It was obvious by her expression that she meant no harm to Warda. She didn't seem to know that among most people, it was a disgrace to dance in public before men.

Warda tossed her head and laughed. "I doubt that I'll be dancing," Warda said. "I've heard that the men of Sodom prefer to have young men dance for them naked."

The women screamed in embarrassment and hid their faces. They were always being shocked by something Warda said. Only Sarai didn't react. She was too busy thinking of all the interesting things these women would be seeing and doing in Sodom.

When the women left and Sarai was putting things back into their usual order, Abram suddenly appeared in the tent door. He was cheerful and in good spirits. "I saw the women leaving. They seemed to be quite pleased. The party must have been a success." He strode across the tent floor and reached for Sarai as she turned around. Seeing the angry look on her face, he dropped his arms and backed off. "So my pretty dove is not so pleased."

"Of course, I'm not pleased. You've given Lot the best of everything. You let him take what he wanted of the flocks and choose the place he wanted to live."

"You're thinking Sodom is better than this?"

"Isn't it obvious?" Sarai's eyes flashed and her chin lifted in defiance. "There are bazaars and singing, fine clothes and travelers. Exciting things happen there."

"Then you've heard only the good and not the bad."

"Oh, I know there are people we don't approve of, but many good people must be there too. We don't have to get involved with anything bad."

"Sarai, haven't you ever noticed that when good people get mixed up with the bad, they often suffer with them when the bad people reap the punishment they've deserved?" Abram made his statement and then, before Sarai could answer, ducked out the door of the tent and let the flap down so he wouldn't hear her reply.

After Lot left, Abram spent a great deal of time pondering all that had happened to him. He had made many mistakes, but he had persisted in his belief that the great Creator God, Elohim, had spoken and promised him a place, land, and descendants. Sarai was always nagging him about the promises. She would, in a most annoying manner, count them off on her fingers and at the same time remind him that none of them had come to pass. That bothered Abram, and he longed for some proof to give Sarai, something that would convince her that the voice was real and the promises were going to come true.

In spite of his praying and petitioning Elohim for more solid confirmation of the promises, Abram heard no voice and got no answer. He had almost given up in frustration when he heard the voice again. It was clear and distinct as though Lot or Eliazer was talking to him. He was not dreaming or meditating. It wasn't even a day for deep thoughts and fervent prayers. Instead it was a bright day with the sun shining and the birds singing.

He had come to his tent door early in the morning and was enjoying the crisp air and the smell of wood smoke. Everything looked fresh and new. The rocks were etched in rich, dark colors, the olive trees fluttered their tiny leaves, and the little new lambs frolicked on patches of bright field lilies.

In this peaceful, ordinary setting, he again heard the voice. "Go," he was told, "walk throughout the land because I am going to give it to you and to your descendants forever. Your descendants will be as the stars so that no one can count them."

He could not resist waking Sarai to tell her. Later he wished he had kept it to himself. He had barely begun to explain when she turned pale with anger and raised her voice in a way that was most unusual for her. She said terrible things. She laughed at the idea of all the land he could see ever belonging to his descendants, and then she topped it off by reminding him that he was married to a woman who had been cursed with barrenness. "Your God is making sport of you, and you can't see it."

She loved him so much that to see him encouraged by what she believed were empty promises—or worse yet, dreams and delusions—was most painful. She felt she must rescue him, save him from this constant frustration. She could not believe his God would want him to suffer so. If his God cared for him at all, surely He would give him some encouragement. If his God didn't help them soon, she had decided that she was going to set a plan in motion that would make at least one of the promises come true.

Abram spent the next months walking throughout the land just as his God had instructed him. He traveled up the central ridge to Hebron and on to Shechem and finally to Gilboa and the valley of Megiddo. He stopped at the headwaters of the Jordan and then followed it down, twisting and turning to the cities of the lower valley. He saw vineyards, olive groves, fields of barley, and wheat. He ate the sweetest grapes and drank the freshest water he had ever known. It was a land of contrasts and a subtle, haunting beauty he grew to love.

Sarai had a great deal of time to think, and by the time he returned, she had made up her mind as to what should be done. Just how to carry it out, she wasn't sure.

"We are moving close to Hebron and the oaks of Mamre," Abram announced. In all his walking, he had found no better place to camp.

To him, having a good campsite is as good as owning the land he has been promised, Sarai thought in continued frustration. He's happy but not as happy as he'll be when he sees the surprise I have for him. What his God can't do for him, I, Sarai, will do.

13

*T*hough Abram was camped miles away beneath the oaks of Mamre, he was well aware of Lot's growing prominence in Sodom. Urim, the cheese maker, visited him regularly and always brought news as well as cheese. He was a very talkative fellow, and by the time he left, Abram had a good idea of how things stood with his nephew. He was not pleased by what he heard. Lot had first moved closer to the city of Sodom and finally had built a new house within the city itself.

From what the cheese maker reported, it seemed that while Lot never engaged in the wild orgies or lustful celebrations in honor of Sin, the moon god, he donated sheep for their feasts and wool for their priests. He soaked up their compliments and edged into their counsels. Eventually he was invited to become one of the honored judges who sat at the city gate. The invitation was usually reserved for princes. Reveling in his newfound status, he sent word to his uncle that he no longer needed the family patronage.

As it turned out, only a short time later Lot was in serious trouble and needed the help he had so arrogantly dismissed.

The trouble came as a surprise. Though there had been threats and warnings, no one was prepared. The news came to Abram one night soon after the campfires had been lit. The men had just finished their evening meal of bread and lentils when a desperate call broke the silence of the night.

Abram heard it first and motioned for silence. They peered into the darkness and were astounded to see the plump forms of Urim and his wife, Safra, hurrying toward them. Safra was weeping, and it was Urim they had heard calling for help.

"Urim, Urim," Abram said, trying to calm him, "what brings you here?"

"My lord, all is lost. Everything's gone." Urim's headpiece was askew, his cloak spattered with mud, and the finely worked belt gone. In the firelight his round face was grotesque. His eyes bulged, and tears ran down his round cheeks while his mouth was puffed and gaping. Safra held the edge of her mantle to her face with both gnarled hands and wept in loud, gasping sobs.

Abram took Urim by the arm and led him a short distance from the rest of the men. "Now tell me," he said, "what has happened. Speak softly. I don't want to alarm my men unnecessarily."

Urim clutched Abram's sleeve and pleaded in a hoarse, rasping voice, "They've taken Warda. Who knows what they'll do. They're evil and cruel."

Abram eased Urim's hand from his sleeve and spoke firmly, "Now, Urim, start from the beginning. Who has taken Warda and where have they gone?"

In the firelight only Urim's bulging eyes could be seen, and they were dreadful with the whites turned red and the pupils like sharp points. "My lord, it was the Elamites and their armies. Ched-or-la'o-mer with his allies. They surprised everyone. No one resisted them. They just marched in and took everything. Lot was taken from his seat at the gate, and his family members were gathered with the rest. He has lost everything."

Abram was stunned. Though he had predicted disaster, he had not expected it to come in this way. He pushed his headpiece back and stroked his chin. His thoughts flew in all directions as he quickly pieced together all he knew of the Elamites and their allies. For weeks he had heard reports of the four kings and their exploits. They had defeated the Rephaim, the Zuzim, and the Emim. They had bypassed Sodom and Gomorrah and gone on to defeat the Horites in the mountains of Edom, then came back by Kadesh. Everyone was relieved, thinking that they weren't going to bother Sodom.

Now Abram could see that the people had been purposely misled. Sodom and Gomorrah were the grand prizes being saved until the last. The Elamites and the allies wanted more than Sodom's and Gomorrah's wealth; they wanted to make slaves of their men, women, and children. The two cities had been arrogant in not paying tribute, and so this special punishment had been reserved for them.

Abram's tortured mind conjured up visions of Lot and his family stumbling along in the night, cold, homeless, without food or water, being led into slavery by the cruel Elamites. There was little time to think or plan. Something must be done immediately. "We have only 318 men," he said, forgetting Urim and thinking out loud. "If we go up against such an army and fail, we will only be playing into their hands."

"But my lord," Urim pleaded, grabbing his arm and thrusting his bloated face close enough so Abram could smell the garlic on his breath, "what about your God? If you're right about the promises, He won't let anyone hurt you."

Abram backed off, humbled by the cheese maker's words. He paced back and forth, pondering what he should do. He felt sure his God could protect him, but what about Lot? Lot had been foolish. He lacked judgment; he was vain and proud and loved luxury.

"No," he finally reasoned as he squared his shoulders and looked back at his men. He would risk so much not because Lot deserved it but because his own honor was at stake. No honorable man turned his back on his family.

"Go," he told Urim, "take your wife to Sarai's tent and then come back and ride with us."

* * *

When Safra arrived at the tent, Sarai was already up trying to calm the other women who had heard the commotion. "Safra," she said, "tell us what happened."

Safra seemed to forget her usual shyness as she described the fearful ordeal they had been through. They had been out on the hillside with their goats when the army came. They had hidden with their sons in one of the caves until the looting stopped and the long line of prisoners with their captors disappeared down the highway on the near side of the Jordan.

The women were shocked. "Did they take Lot?" Sarai asked at last.

"Lot and his whole family. We could see them from the cave."

"Did they take Warda?" Hagar asked, pushing to the forefront.

"We saw her chained to an officer's mule. She was still wearing the headdress of her dancing costume and very little else. That was when Urim went almost mad. Our sons had to hold him back. He couldn't bear to see her treated like that."

Safra had no time to say more, for at that moment Abram appeared and ordered the women back to their tents. "Our men are riding tonight and will need provisions," he said.

The women scattered with much talking and excitement. Safra sank down exhausted on one of the cushions in Sarai's tent while Hagar lingered behind, totally forgotten by her mistress. Sarai was busy on her husband's side of the tent. She was getting a pack ready for him while he was engrossed with putting on his sword, taking down his Egyptian bow with its arrows, and stuffing his sling into his belt. Hagar moved to the door on the women's side of the tent and listened.

She could hear them arguing. Sarai was trying to discourage him. "There are four kings with big armies, and you hope to go out against them with just a handful of men? Have you forgotten? These same Elamites destroyed Ur."

Hagar couldn't hear what he answered, but it was obvious he was still preparing to go.

"Abram, be reasonable," Sarai said. "Five kings from the cities of the plains went up against these foreigners, and they were all defeated."

This time she could hear him. "They weren't just defeated by the armies of the Elamites," he said. "Two of the kings and their men were fleeing when they slipped and fell into some asphalt pits. Then of course, it was easy for the victors to plunder both Sodom and Gomorrah."

"Abram, I beg you, be reasonable," Sarai was crying. Hagar could tell that Abram had not been moved by Sarai's arguments. She wondered how this man dared go against such odds. He was either a fool or very brave.

Now she heard Sarai quite plainly. "Don't go tonight," she begged. "Wait until morning. You're tired and it'll be a long and dusty ride."

Abram was unmoved, but it was obvious he had put his arms around Sarai and was trying to console her. "My dearest," he said, "you know I have to go. I can't forget about my nephew. Families have to be able to depend on each other."

There were more tears and more pleading, but Abram stood firm. Finally he said, "I have a feeling that everything will work out. I don't know what I'll do, but I'll be back and Lot and his family and Warda . . . maybe all of the people of Sodom and Gomorrah will be with me."

Hagar knew Sarai well enough to guess what she was thinking. Sarai would assume that this was another of what she called "Abram's mistakes."

After another moment of silence, Hagar felt the tent pole move as the flap on the other side was lifted. She leaned out so she could see him. It was too dark to see much, but she could make out his strong, stalwart form moving toward his men who were gathering beside the fire. How brave he is, she thought with genuine admiration.

There was only a short discussion between Abram and Eliazer as to the route they were to take and the manner in which they would travel. "Our success will depend on our ability to surprise the enemy," Abram said. "We must be swift and able to maneuver with agility."

At that moment Urim edged into their midst. He had been listening. "They didn't go up the far side of the Jordan because of the asphalt pits and steep cliffs," he said. "We can overtake them easily if we follow them up the west side of the Jordan."

They were all strong, well-built men who were used to riding long distances. Without more discussion they mounted their donkeys, gave a few sharp taps to their animals' flanks, muttered familiar commands, and were off down the moonlit road that led to the Jordan Valley.

"Yah, yah, yah," the men shouted as they drove their heels into their donkeys' flanks and hurried them on after the enemy. At the Wadi Far'ah, they could dimly see the soft clay pitted with the enemy's tracks. There were wheel marks, camels' dung, hoofprints, and evidence of prisoners in chains. They had no idea what they would do when they caught up with the army, but each man went over and over the problem in his mind. Surprise would be all-important. Without surprise they would surely be taken captive and marched along with the other prisoners.

Just before dawn their scouting party warned them that the enemy was camped just ahead in a sheltered area at the headwaters of the Jordan. There the river was only a small stream that wound around through mossy dells and large shade trees. Abram knew the area well. He quickly ordered his men to dismount and wait while he and a few of his scouts climbed the cliff behind the camp.

From the cliff they could look down and see the tents of the enemy with their banners flapping in the early predawn breeze. They were surprised to see no sentries on guard, few signs of life. There were smoldering fires with spits holding half-eaten carcasses, and from some of the tents came the sounds of drunken singing and ribald laughter.

Abram sent two scouts down to spy out the situation at close range. When they returned, one of them reported, "The prisoners are tied and sitting huddled together in a clearing. The cattle and carts of plunder are close by. When we crept close, one of the prisoners told us all that had happened. He told us that the major divisions of the army had gone on to Damascus, leaving these guards to follow more slowly with the prisoners and all the booty. The guards have been celebrating and are drunk. They even feel secure enough to leave their posts."

"And my Warda, did you see Warda among the prisoners?" Urim had squeezed in and was frantically pulling at the scout's sleeve.

The man turned and glared at Urim impatiently. "No, there were women and children and many men, but no one who sounds like the person you describe."

Abram turned to Eliazer. "We must move quickly if we are to surprise them. I'll send men to release the prisoners, so some of them can help us. The rest of us will ready ourselves to attack."

Urim decided to go with Abram since the scout had not seen Warda with the prisoners. "She is such a prize," he reasoned. "One of those vulgar Elamites must have taken her."

When everyone was in place and ready, the men attacked the camp of drunk and sleeping Elamites with all their pent-up fury. The rams' horns blared and shrieked, cymbals clashed, knives flashed in the moonlight, swords cut tent ropes, and over the entire din was the deep-throated roar of the victory shout.

Abram and a few of his men made for the tent with the king's banner, but before they reached it, a strange thing happened. A man dressed only in a loincloth dashed out wielding a sword. He was followed by some of his own men who in the darkness mistook him for an attacker. In minutes the whole camp was in an uproar. No one knew his friend from his foe and at last, in the panic that followed, they began to run. Abram, seeing what was happening, signaled his men to follow them.

While all that was taking place, Urim had gone straight to the tent where the singing had suddenly stopped. He pulled back the flap and saw, just as he had suspected, his beloved Warda tied to a tent pole. Her captors were still drinking and were in the process of casting lots for her. With a catlike spring, Urim was in the midst of the tent wielding a short sword with one hand while he cut Warda loose with a knife he held in the other. Weeping and shaking with fear, Warda clung to him. He took only time enough to snatch up a linen robe and wrap it around her.

"Come Warda," he said. "I'll show you where the women of Sodom are being held. When we finish with this sordid business, I'll be back to take you home."

He stopped long enough to see that Warda was headed in the right direction and then rushed after Abram's men.

It was told later that they chased the enemy clear to Hobah, north of Damascus, and then came back and rounded up the prisoners and the spoil and headed back the way they'd come.

Lot had not joined the men who helped Abram. He was too shaken and miserable. He kept moaning that he had lost everything, even the fine robe he had been wearing. He was left in his linen undergarment until a young Elamite, admiring the fine weave, took that from him also; only his loincloth remained. The night was cold, and he felt sure he would be dangerously ill by morning.

When the sun came up and Abram returned looking for Lot, he found a very different man. He was deeply grateful for the garments Abram found for him and the food he was given. "I have learned my lesson," he kept saying. "Sodom is not a good place. I should never have left you, my uncle."

One memorable thing happened before Abram reached home. It was to most observers an insignificant thing, but to Abram, it was of profound importance and was to have a great deal to do with all that was to happen in the future. They were coming along the valley of Shaveh, sometimes called the Valley of the Kings, just below the small village of Salem, when their procession was stopped by a richly dressed messenger. "I'm looking for a man called Abram," he said. "I have a message for him."

Abram stepped forward, and the messenger knelt in the dust and kissed the hem of his garment. "Come, come," Abram said, lifting him to his feet, "give me the message."

"My lord," the messenger said, "the king of Sodom has come up from the valley to meet you, and the king of Salem is coming to honor you."

Abram cared little for meeting the king of Sodom, but the priest-king of Salem had interested him ever since he had first heard about him. "He has no father or mother," the people told him. "He was found on the doorstep of a poor shepherd."

"He worships only one God, the Creator God," others remarked.

Looking up toward the city, Abram saw a majestic old man with white hair and beard, a gold crown, a plain tunic, and a brown cloak of fine linen. He was moving slowly down the long flight of steps that led from the eastern city gate. He was leaning heavily on a gnarled and knotted walking stick. As he came closer to them, they saw that his eyes were kind and his whole manner was one of eager anticipation. When he reached Abram, he embraced him as though he were a brother; he kissed him on both cheeks and then stepped back and studied his face with obvious delight.

Abram was puzzled. "I have heard much of you and your good deeds but how...?"

The king smiled and motioned him to a sheltered arbor under the trees beside the brook Kidron. "You are puzzled that I have greeted you as a brother, though I never met you before. Come and sit awhile, and I'll explain."

The two men ignored the king of Sodom and his men who waited impatiently just out of sight around a bend in the road. They sat down on cushions and faced each other. "First," Melchizedek said, "let me offer you some bread freshly baked and wine from our best grapes. Then I'll explain."

When the bread had been eaten and the wine taken, Melchizedek leaned back and said, "I saw in a dream that one like you would come. One who worships as I do, the supreme God, the God who created the heavens and the earth. I am to encourage you and to bless you."

"How strange!" Abram said. "I had thought I was the only one left who believed in the one supreme God."

Melchizedek sat and listened to all that had happened to Abram from the time he had first believed and had destroyed his father's idols to the promises that had not been fulfilled. The wise old man listened and advised him to be patient. "Some things take time, but be assured that the promises made by Elohim, the Creator God, will come to pass."

He then rose and called for his priestly robes. When he was ready, he turned to Abram and told him to kneel. Then placing his hand on Abram's head, he said, "The blessing of the supreme God, Creator of heaven and earth, be upon you, Abram, and blessed be God, who has delivered your enemies over to you."

Abram rose slowly, his face radiant with joy. "It is true," he said, "without Elohim's guidance and help, I would never have been victorious. You have indeed encouraged me."

He ordered his men to give Melchizedek a tenth of all the spoils. As that was being done the king of Sodom with his retainers appeared. He ignored Melchizedek and strode over to Abram. "Just give me back my people," he said with an arrogant toss of his head. "Keep for yourself the booty stolen from my city."

Abram realized he had been one of the kings trapped in the bitumen pits and had not been taken captive with the others. "I have promised Elohim, the supreme God, Creator of heaven and earth," he said. "I will not take so much as a single thread from you, lest you boast that I am rich because of you."

Abram finally did agree to accept food for his men and agreed that a share of the booty should be given to Aner, Eshcol, and Mamre, his allies.

As the king of Sodom prepared to leave, he turned to Lot. "Are you not returning with us?" he asked.

Lot hesitated only a moment before responding, "I have had enough of city life for a time. I have decided to stay with my uncle."

* * *

It had been five days since the men marched out on their dangerous mission. As they approached the outskirts of Hebron, a joyful band of women and children, singing and dancing, met them. Leading the group was a creature of such exuberance and charm that all eyes were drawn to her. She had tucked up her skirt so her bare legs were visible, taken off her sandals, setting her feet free to stomp and tap in time to the music. Her jeweled ankle bracelets tinkled in a fascinating way while her hair fell wild and free, now covering part of her face, then spilling over her one bare shoulder. Partially holding the hair in place was a garland of golden grapes.

When Abram first saw her, he was stunned by her beauty and grace. It was only as the dancers came closer that he recognized her as Hagar, the Egyptian handmaiden to Sarai.

He stopped and looked past Hagar and the other women, hoping to see his spunky little wife, but she was nowhere to be seen. He briefly wondered if she even knew of his victory and moment of triumph. Was she still angry that he had gone against her advice? He wanted more than anything to see Sarai smile again with love and approval.

The procession stopped a moment while Hagar impulsively removed her garland of golden grapes and placed it on Abram's head. He was pleased but embarrassed. "Where is Sarai?" he asked. He was surprised when Hagar didn't answer but tossed her head, lifted her chin, and with a look of arrogant pride elbowed her way through the crowd and disappeared.

Abram thought little of it until later, much later. Then he realized that Hagar had done what Sarai should have done. The wives and children of all the other men had come out to welcome them home. Only Sarai had stayed behind, tending to some weaving she wanted to finish before sundown. "She's a good wife," he told Lot. "She's always busy. She's up with the sun and bakes the best ash cakes."

Later, when Abram and Sarai were alone together, Sarai asked about Lot. "I suppose he'll be going back to Sodom," she said testily.

"No, he's not going back," Abram said. "It seems he's had enough of such places. He's learned his lesson."

Sarai laughed. "Lot will go back. You'll see, he'll find it dull here after Sodom."

Abram disagreed. He had seen Lot. Lot had suffered more than most. Abram knew he was a changed man. "No, Sarai," Abram said, "Lot has had his fill of Sodom and so has Urim. Neither one will go back."

Sarai reached out, patted his arm, and said softly but confidently, "We'll see."

*I*n the end it was as Sarai had predicted. Lot was no longer happy away from the excitement of the city. At first he made furtive visits to his old friends. Then he began to spend some time sitting with the elders at Sodom's gate. The final break came when Mara begged him to go back, saying that she missed the niceties of her stone house on the wall. Many of her fine furnishings had been taken in the raid, but she was determined to replace them as soon as possible. "I can never leave my house," she insisted.

When that approach failed to have the desired effect, she produced another more impressive argument. "Have you forgotten," she chided, "our daughters were to have married those two young men from wealthy families. If we linger here any longer, we may miss this chance for fine marriages."

When Lot came to tell Abram he had decided to move back to his old home, he found his uncle sitting before a small fire of dung patties at the door of his tent. Abram was not pleased. "I don't think the men of Sodom will make very good husbands," he said finally.

"On the contrary," Lot said, "they have land and houses. They are wealthy."

"And how do they come by their wealth? Certainly not by herding animals."

Lot smirked and twisted the fringes on his linen kirtle. "They have land and raise fine barley for beer. The pleasure groves are always ordering their beer. My daughters will never want for anything. Anyway, they are still too young. They are only being promised to them now."

Abram studied Lot for a moment. He noticed the eyes that were suddenly shifty, the weak chin and the nose that had somehow taken over his face since he had lost his teeth. He obviously had no conscience. "Do you not find it difficult," he said finally, "to live among people who think only of their stomachs and sexual games? Have you totally forgotten the God who brought us out of Ur and promised us blessings?"

Lot moved uneasily on the goat hair rug and nervously twisted his riding prod. "Of course I've not forgotten," he said, turning to look at Abram directly, "but where are these promises? We came to the land, and it was barren and ugly with drought. Sarai is just as barren. Can't you see there are men, evil men, who have their houses full of children and their fields rich with the harvest? Elohim's promises are worthless."

Abram was stunned. What Lot said was true. He had seen the worshipers of idols with children like olive shoots around their knees and their granaries full to bursting. He had no answer for Lot, and in the end he merely bade him a sad farewell.

That night when he sat with Sarai eating some large, fresh dates folded in grape leaves, he told her all that had happened. Sarai flared up in defense of Lot. "Lot has cause to think the way he does," she said, brushing the damp hair back from her face and readjusting her mantle. "I agree with him. What has your God ever done for you? How many of the promises have been fulfilled? Just think, Abram, how much time you've wasted thinking about this God and His promises."

"Sarai, Sarai," Abram sighed. "Remember it was our God who brought us safely out of Ur, rescued you from Pharaoh's harem, and Lot and his family from slavery."

"I would say you were the one who rescued Lot. Without you, Elohim could do nothing."

Abram looked at Sarai and shook his head. "I can see you don't understand," he said.

"Oh, but I do understand. What about the promises of land and a child, blessings, where are they? I've been patient. I've waited. I've gotten old waiting and nothing has happened."

For the first time Abram saw lines of bitterness around Sarai's mouth and hard accusation in her eyes. Her hair was no longer braided in the small shoulder-length braids, and instead of the golden headband she wore a fringed mantle like the Chaldeans. Her vitality and girlish slimness, the way she tossed her head or lowered it in a flirting sort of way and looked out sideways at him, the way she walked, so straight and proud with a hint of arrogance—all that gave the illusion of youth. Now Abram was seeing her as angry, resentful, and suddenly old.

It hurt him to think that he with his love of Elohim and his desire to rid himself of all the temptations and evils of the cities had brought his beloved Sarai to this.

For the first time he was angry with his God. He felt tricked, cheated, even a bit foolish. Without a word he got up and made his way out of the tent. Sarai did not call him to come back, and he stumbled on blindly until he was out of sight of the campfires and out of range of the voices. Finally, coming to a great rock, he sank down and buried his face in his hands.

He felt numb. All that he had believed, hoped, and trusted seemed to have given way. He was sure of nothing. If he had really heard his God speaking to him, why were there no results to show? How could he expect Sarai and Lot and all the others to trust if there was no proof? Ten years had passed and though he was a rich man, he had none of the things his God had promised him. Even more frightening was the realization that Sarai could no longer conceive a child.

He sat very still and looked at his hands in the moonlight. They were strong, capable hands. They were the hands of a merchant, not a herdsman. They were hands that could be depended on to accomplish any humanly possible task. For his needs that were beyond his power, he had depended on his God. Most of the people around him depended on the moon god Sin for crops and cattle and on charms, potions, or magical incantations for desired success in any venture.

Gradually the moon rose overhead and even the crickets were silent. He was about to rise and return to his tent when he had a fearful thought. What if he had offended Elohim in some way? Perhaps he had not offered his sacrifice properly. Was it possible he had not offered the right sacrifice? He thought of the men and women in every country who regularly offered even their children to placate their gods of clay and stone. He searched his heart to see if he would ever be able to sacrifice any child Elohim might deign to give him.

With this thought he leaned back against the rock. It was still warm from the afternoon sun. It felt solid and comforting. Somewhere a donkey brayed and in the distance a dog barked.

Suddenly there was a gentle stirring of the leaves on the myrtle shrub at his side. The subtle movement made him attentive, listening for he knew not what. He became conscious of a sweet fragrance and then a deep, profound silence. He held his breath, waiting. The silence was almost palpable. Then slowly out of the midst of the silence, a voice whispered, "Do not be fearful,

Abram. I will defend you and give you great blessings."

Abram sat upright and stared out into the darkness. If it was indeed the Elohim, he had questions to ask. "Where is the son You promised me? If I have no son, someone else will inherit all my wealth."

The voice continued, more distinct and with an unmistakable note of authority, "No one else will be your heir, for you will have a son." The word "will" came with special emphasis. Abram covered his face with his hands and wept. He was surprised at his own emotion. The deep need and yearning for a son had been with him day and night for so long. He wanted to believe, but it was so hard. Why did it have to take so long? Why was it so easy for other men to have their wishes granted only for him to face so much disappointment?

"Come," the voice said, "stand on your feet and look at the heavens. Now count the stars if you can. Your descendants will be like that . . . too many to count."

Abram struggled to believe, but some instinct within him yearned for something more tangible. "How can I be sure?" he asked.

"I am the God who brought you out of Ur to give you this land forever."

Abram hesitated. "Oh Lord, my God, how can I be sure that You will really give these wonderful blessings?"

There was a long silence. Abram could hear his heart beat, and his breath stopped in his throat. Everything was still. For a moment he thought he heard someone sigh, and then the voice began to speak again. "Abram," the voice said, "take a three-year-old heifer, a three-year-old female goat, a three-year-old ram, a turtledove, and a young pigeon. Slay them and cut them apart down the middle to separate the halves but don't divide the birds. Offer these on the altar."

Abram was excited to use the age-old procedure of men everywhere who wanted to make a lasting covenant that could never be broken. The animals would be separated and the parties making the covenant would walk between them, thus sealing their decision in blood. His God was willing to covenant with him in a way he could understand.

Slowly the euphoria passed. The thick silence was broken by a wolf's lonesome howl. A bat swooped low, and he dodged back into the shadow of the rock. Abram became acutely aware of his surroundings: the harsh cliffs touched by moonlight, the low stone wall circling the olive trees near the path. He stood up and wondered how long he had been out on the hillside.

Would Sarai be asleep? He wanted to share this encounter with her. Perhaps she would believe and be encouraged.

Back at the tent he saw that she was asleep and he decided to wait until morning to tell her all that had happened. He pulled the tent flap back, stepped inside, and lay down on the hard, straw mat.

In the morning he tried to tell Sarai what God had told him the night before, but she was preoccupied with building a fire. She insisted on making comments about how hard it was to make the coals come alive in the clay fire pot and even harder to make the small twigs catch fire. She did everything possible to let him know she didn't want to hear any more about visions. She did stop and look at him when he mentioned "altar." He knew she was hearing, even though she was rejecting the message.

He ate quickly and then ordered his men to help him pick the animals for the sacrifice. They had to be perfect. No blemishes would be accepted. The altar had to be enlarged so he could divide the animals, putting half on one side and half on the other. When the men asked him where the fire was to light such a sacrifice, he was at first silent and then confessed, "The Lord God, Elohim, will light my sacrifice this time, or it will not be lit." That was one of the conditions necessary to make sure it was God who was joining him in covenant. The men grew silent and concerned. Sometimes the old priests used the sun with the help of a bronze shield to light altar fires, but the men saw no such shield.

He thanked the men and then dismissed them. It was obviously his sacrifice, and he had no intention of including the rest of them in the proceedings. They stood back and watched, disturbed to see the ravens and vultures gathering. They saw Abram take off his cloak and begin to swing it at the birds, shouting, "Yah! Yah!" Some of his servants went out to herd their sheep, but when they came back hours later, Abram was still there, and his sacrifice lay just as he had placed it on the altar, unburned.

Sarai tried to act unconcerned, but in the late afternoon she had her loom moved to the door of her tent. She could see the altar, but Abram had his back to her. She could tell by the droop of his shoulders and the way his arm hung limp with his cloak dragging on the ground that he was exhausted and disappointed. She saw the vultures now joined by hawks and the frightening bearded vultures circling, then swooping down to claim his sacrifice. She moved to the tent door and leaned against the tent pole to watch.

It makes me feel guilty, she thought, seeing him out there all alone driving off the birds from his sacrifice. This will be another failure. The promises are never kept. Why won't he give up? He never gives up. She felt the tears of frustration flood her eyes, and she turned away and fingered the rough material she was weaving. She couldn't bear to watch.

"Oh Abram," she whispered, "I love you so. Why can't you be reasonable like other men? Isn't it enough that we packed and left friends, family, and our familiar idols to travel to this barren land your God promised you?"

She moved back to the door of the tent and lifted the flap so she could see everything. Her head ached with the strain and her throat was dry. She could not stand to see what was happening, and yet she could not turn away. I don't believe his God will come and light his sacrifice, she thought. What will he do? Surely he'll give up.

It was too much to think of. She paced back and forth, trying not to look out the door. Finally she came to stand again by the tent pole, but instead of looking out at Abram, she reached for a brass mirror hanging by a piece of sheep gut from the pole. She adjusted her mantle and tucked in her hair.

"I loved Egypt," she murmured. "If we could just go back to Egypt. It was like Ur with fine foods and lotus pools. We could have stayed but . . . for the problem with the pharaoh. He had so many sons, and you, Abram, with all the promises, had none."

There were questions she had pushed down into the very depths of her soul, but now they came pouring out. "Is it my fault?" she whispered with tortured, twisted lips. No tears came, but her eyes were dark with the old fear. "Is it the curse of Ningal that we have no son? I never wanted land, but, oh, the child, Abram. Where is the child your God promised?" Her hands gripped the tent pole so hard her fingers turned white and her eyes had a wild, hopeless look.

She heard more loud shouting and the sharp cracking sound of the cloak hitting on stone. She leaned out and looked toward the altar in time to see the ugly birds clawing at the cloak and Abram shouting hoarsely, "Yah! Yah! Yah!"

The sun was setting and she was conscious of others now. She knew the shepherds would be hiding their laughter and the servants buzzing with the master's final failure. Always before it had been just words, but now it was more, much more. He'd dared to do this impossible thing, to make his God do something everyone could see. He'd dared to expect his God to light his sacrifice.

"I can't watch," she said. "I'll go get Hagar. The time has come. Together we'll make plans. We'll do what Abram's God can't do. I'll give her to him for a night, and I will have my child without this endless waiting." She hurried toward the place at the back of the tent where the side pieces were lifted. She ducked down and went through and out into the growing darkness to find Hagar.

* * *

Abram was exhausted. "Lord," he said, "I don't understand You." Looking up at the sky, he stood with his cloak at his side. His hair was damp and matted, and the lines in his face had become deep grooves down which the sweat ran untouched. "Why do You have to wait so long to do everything?" he thundered in exasperation. "Sarai has lost all patience and now she is angry with me. She doesn't believe You are going to do anything. She thinks I have imagined it all."

He watched the sun hang for a moment above the distant hill and then disappear. A star shone dimly in the reddened sky. "I told her about the stars. How You said I'd have descendants as the stars. She just laughed. Not a happy laugh. It was bitter and choked with pity. She feels sorry for me. 'Look at Asa,' she says, 'he's even younger than you and he already has fifteen sons and ten daughters. Even a man without wit can see he's more likely to found a great nation than you with no son at all.' Lord, I'm the laughingstock of everyone I meet."

Once again the birds were swooping down, croaking and screaming as they dived toward the sacrifice. "You shall not eat one bite of God's sacrifice. Yah! Yah! Yah!" The birds flew off, and Abram sank down at the base of the altar exhausted.

"Lord," he said finally, "is there something wrong? You told me to build this altar and prepare this sacrifice." He began to count on his fingers. "A three-year-old heifer, a three-year-old female goat, a three-year-old ram, a turtledove, and a young pigeon. You were so exact in Your instructions."

He looked toward the tent and saw that Sarai was no longer watching. He knew she'd given up. He heard laughter in other tents and imagined they were discussing the day's events.

For a moment Abram stood with his cloak dragging on the ground. He waited for some answer, some bit of encouragement, but there was only the quiet of evening and always the birds, the big, hungry, evil-eyed birds, now circling high above the altar. Rubbing his sleeve across his face, he wiped his brow. He stood looking at the altar, clenching and unclenching his fists in frustration. "I'm just a man . . . just a man, God. I'm tired. My arms ache from driving off the birds."

He looked in all directions as if expecting some answer, but when none came, he turned back to the altar, which was now in shadows. The birds had moved to a nearby thornbush and sat watching and waiting. The time for fire to descend and light his sacrifice was long overdue. He shrugged in resignation. "You've got to take over, God. Do You hear? I can't do any more. If Your birds eat Your sacrifice, I can't help it."

He sank down beside the altar, holding his head in his hands, and wept. "You shouldn't expect so much from just a man." Dazed and numb, he stared out into the growing darkness. He felt the cool night air swirling around him in gentle gusts. He relaxed and in moments he was sound asleep. His hand loosened and the cloak slipped down on the warm stones. His head fell back and a horror of great darkness came upon him.

The voice he had come to know so well spoke, but the words were not pleasant. "Your seed, Abram, shall be a stranger in a land that is not theirs, and shall serve them, and be afflicted for four hundred years. That nation, whom they shall serve, will I judge; and after these things they will come out with great wealth.

Do not be afraid. You will go to your fathers in peace at a good old age.

But your descendants in the fourth generation will come here again and take this land, for the iniquity of the Amorites will by that time be full."

Then Abram woke to a strange sight. Darkness had settled over the land. The moon had not yet risen, and the stars were bursting out one after another, covering the dark dome of heaven. Out of the darkness came a red-hot, glowing fire pot, and Abram watched in awe as it passed between the pieces on the altar. No hand held the pot, and yet as he watched there was a great roaring, thundering sound as a pillar of fire burst out and ignited the sacrifice. He heard again the voice speaking in tones used when covenants were made: "Unto your seed have I given this land, from the river of Egypt to the great river Euphrates."

Within minutes there was shouting and pounding of feet running on hard-packed earth. The whole camp was aroused. They stood back and watched, not daring to come close. Abram stood transfixed, his arms upraised, his head thrown back. Then covering his face with his hands, he fell to his knees and prostrated himself before the roaring pillar of fire on the altar.

When at last the sacrifice was consumed in the raging flames and the fire died down, Abram raised himself and watched with unspeakable joy as the coals glowed on the crude altar. Tears ran down his face as he raised his hands high over the altar, and vibrant words of praise poured from his lips.

"Stand back, stand back," the men whispered. "It's holy ground. His God has answered him." Abram heard nothing and was not even aware of their coming, so lost was he in adoration of the Elohim.

* * *

Later some parts of what he'd been told puzzled him: Could it be true that I have not been given the land because my God is waiting, giving the Amorites time to repent? Abram also pondered for a long time the words "your seed." That meant he was to have children. How this would come about he could not imagine, and when Sarai came to him with a plan, it somehow seemed right and proper.

"My handmaiden, whom the pharaoh gave me saying she would have a child in my place, is ready. She has agreed. In fact she finds you handsome. She told me as much."

"And you don't mind?" Abram said, searching her face for any sign of hurt or holding back.

She shrugged. "It is my fault you don't have a son already. I was the one cursed, and I'm the one to set it right." Her voice had a catch in it, and Abram could see the decision had not been easy.

"The Egyptian seems independent and even headstrong. Are you sure she will agree?"

"As I said, she finds you handsome and she's my friend. She'd do anything to please me. Besides, what harm can it do? If she conceives, you'll have your son. If not, at least we tried."

"Give me time to think. Perhaps to talk to the girl. This may have more complications than you realize."

Sarai tossed her head in the old teasing way. "Talk to her, think about it, but don't pray about it. You've proved your point. The fire came and now it's time for us to act."

*S*arai had imagined a very simple procedure. Hagar would go to Abram's tent at the most propitious time when the moon was full. There would be no celebration and no long preparation. It would be only a matter of Hagar's conceiving the child. "It need not take long," Sarai insisted.

However, Hagar had a very different idea. "I'm an Egyptian," she said, "the daughter of Pharaoh Amenemhet. I can't be treated like any ordinary handmaiden." Her eyes flashed and she tossed her head in the old defiant way. Sarai saw that it could be a delicate matter. If she was to get the child she wanted, she would have to make some concessions.

Hagar was willing to give up the child, but she insisted that the formalities of a wedding be observed. It was not to be something done secretly. Everyone must know she had been given to Sarai by her father, Pharaoh Amenemhet, so that Abram might have a son.

Sarai was irritated. Such formalities would call attention to the fact that she, as Abram's wife, was somehow lacking. She wanted to object, to insist it all be done as quietly as possible, but in the end she thought better of it and managed to say nothing.

Hagar first asked that the bridal tent be erected for her use. It was a tent in which the bride was secluded for a month while preparing for the wedding. At the culmination of the wedding celebration, she would be escorted to the tent of her new husband for the night. The next day, and every day for a month, she would spend her time in the bridal tent and visit her husband only when he sent for her. At the end of the month it was assumed she would be pregnant and deserve a tent of her own.

Hagar next asked that Warda, the Egyptian concubine of the cheese maker, come to advise and help her. "She is from Egypt and will understand our customs," she said.

Warda immediately took charge of the proceedings. She ordered the mintlike patchouli oil and sandalwood from the market in Sodom, the henna from Jericho; she ground the charred pits of dates for eye makeup, and she bought rose water from a Lebanese trader.

When everything was assembled, she ordered the bathing stool be brought and the clay fire pot with its brass bowl of rose-scented water set up in the middle of the tent. For five days Hagar sat on the stool with a covering of heavy linen until the magic fragrance of the steam had cleansed and scented her skin.

Her hair was first washed like the other women's in camel's urine to get rid of any mites or lice and then was rubbed with olive oil and rinsed with henna until it glistened. Sarai came often to observe and was more than once irritated when Hagar asked to borrow several of her maidens to pound spices or fold grape leaves over spicy seeds to make pomanders for her clothes.

"Why must you have all this preparation?" Sarai asked. "It's a simple thing to sleep with a man."

Hagar didn't look up from sorting some of her ointments. "It may be simple to sleep with a man, but I am to produce a child. A special child, Abram's child. That, it seems, is not so easy." She gave Sarai a meaningful look, and Sarai, catching the meaning, tossed her head and left the tent. As much as she was irritated by all that Hagar was doing, she reasoned that Egyptians had different customs and traditions, and she didn't want to distract Hagar from fulfilling her part of the bargain.

When the lengthy preparations were completed and Hagar was ready, she called Sarai. "My dear mistress," she said, "I must have a proper celebration, dancers and singers, a procession befitting a princess of Egypt."

In growing exasperation Sarai called Eliazer and asked him to go to the neighboring town of Hebron and find some women who entertained at weddings. She requested that sweet cakes be prepared for a feast. When Abram asked about the unusual activity, she couldn't resist voicing her frustration. "Egyptians are proud and arrogant," she said with her mouth set in a hard line.

"I'm sure you can't be talking of your lovely young handmaiden. Why, she's been willing to do almost anything to please you." He had a twinkle in his eye that made Sarai even angrier. She knew what he said was right, and yet there was something about it all that she found most unbearable. She regretted saying anything because Abram could call the whole venture off.

During this time of feasting, Hagar was brought the choicest meats, largest dates, and wild honey to sweeten the steaming hot wheels of bread. At all hours women came to watch and to give advice. Hagar paid little attention but smiled coyly when asked questions. However, at night when the others were finally asleep, she talked to Warda, and Warda asked her questions. "Do you love this man?" Warda asked on the night before she would be taken to Abram's tent.

"I am in awe of him. He fascinates me, but I will never love him. I don't want to love anyone ever."

"You don't want to love?" Warda asked in astonishment.

Hagar was idly breaking off bits of incense and throwing them on the fire. For several minutes she didn't answer, just watched the little pieces of fragrance catch fire and glow. Then without turning she said, "You can never be hurt if you don't love. In loving there's danger."

Warda was surprised. "Have you never loved anyone?" she asked.

"No, I have never wanted to be controlled by anyone. If you love someone, you will do what he wishes. Isn't that true?"

"Where have you gained all this wisdom?" Warda asked in astonishment.

Hagar looked down at her new rings and toyed with her bright gold bracelets. "You perhaps didn't know that my mother was once the favorite of Pharaoh. He loved her, gave her gifts, wonderful gifts, and I, as their child, was refused nothing."

"And . . . then?" Warda asked as Hagar seemed to hesitate.

"He found a new love, a new interest. He finally sent my mother away, and because his new love could not bear the sight of me, he gave me to Sarai." Tears welled in her eyes, but she tossed her head and hastily brushed them away. "It is easier not to care about anyone."

For a moment the small thorns crackled and a slight flame leaped up, illuminating their faces. Warda poked at the fire and pursed her lips. "What about Sarai? She is pleased now, but she needs to wield control. Without it, she could become angry and jealous."

Hagar smiled and twisted the bracelets on her arm. "Sarai will never lose control. Abram'll do anything for her. The only thing Sarai can't do is produce a child. That's why she needs me."

"And does she appreciate what you are doing?"

"She's been my friend, the only real friend I've ever had. She gave me these rings and bracelets . . . even this gold necklace."

Warda didn't express her surprise, but nodded. "Be careful. You are young and spirited, while she is beautiful but getting old. Things may turn out differently than either of you thinks."

Hagar nodded and smiled. "Don't worry about me. I can manage. I was born and suckled in the palace and have seen and heard everything."

Warda brought a cover and spread it out over the straw mat. "It's time we sleep or all our preparations will go for naught."

Hagar lay down and was asleep within minutes, but Warda sat by the fire pot and thought about her new friend and all that would take place on the morrow.

* * *

The next day the feasting continued while the final preparations were carried out in the bridal tent. During the whole time, Warda said little. It was only at the last, as Hagar was ready to leave, that Warda pulled her aside and took out a small clay perfume bottle. "Hold out your hands," she said. And as Hagar held them out she poured the whole bottle of fragrant ointment into them. "Rub them together and let some spill onto your neck and crush some into your hair."

Hagar did as she was told and then leaned forward to kiss her new friend on both cheeks. "Just perfume you are giving me and no last advice?"

Warda held her for a moment at arm's length. "You are both beautiful and dangerous. Abram is sure to love you."

Hagar laughed. "Don't worry, Warda. I have no intention of loving him."

"To not love," Warda said, "is to quench the holy fragrance within. Without love we are merely clay, like this little bottle."

Hagar stooped and kissed Warda lightly on both cheeks. "Don't worry about me," she said. "There are things I want and things I'll get."

Outside the singing and dancing became louder and more raucous. With one last glance and a fleeting smile to Warda, Hagar lifted the tent flap and went out to become the center of the procession.

Hagar was relieved to find Abram's tent empty. She had thought he would be there, but it seemed that was not part of their custom. She had been led in by the Canaanite dancers amidst laughing and singing and jokes that had become suggestive and bawdy. After she was seated, they spent some time arranging her hair, touching her cheeks with rosy salve, and giving her mint leaves to chew for her breath. Finally at a signal from Warda, they danced out of the tent, and she could hear them as they went back to the fire and the celebration.

Hagar had never been on this side of the tent before. It was neat and sparse. It had the pleasant, heady odor of rare incense; goat hair rugs hid the dirt floor; straw mats covered in bright-striped linen lined a seating area. She noticed that on an inner tent pole were hung bows and quivers of arrows. Against the taut pitch of the tent stood a large shield made of rhinoceros skin. Probably a gift from Pharaoh, she thought.

There was only one chest and it was of cedar with handsome bronze fittings. It undoubtedly held his clothes and valuables. To her surprise she saw three large clay jars that held papyrus scrolls. An alabaster lamp with several hemp wicks gave off a soft, flickering light that made enormous shadows dance across the floor and up the sides of the tent.

She sat very still and listened. There was no one on the far side behind the qata or cloth of division. Sarai had obviously gone to her own tent. A cricket's insistent chirping grew suddenly loud, while faint and far away the wedding songs and steady beat of a drum lent an air of mystery and magic. As she listened, she heard clearly and quite distinctly the soft, light step of someone approaching the tent. She thought it might be Abram and quickly moved to cover the lower half of her face. The tent flap was flung back, and Sarai stood in the doorway looking at her. Hagar could tell she was surprised. As she let the tent flap fall back in place and moved toward her, Hagar dropped the veil.

Sarai stopped and stared. "You look so different. You're beautiful."

Hagar broke the sudden tension by laughing. "Did you expect the mother of your son to be ugly?"

"No, no, of course not," Sarai said, still looking at her with a puzzled expression. "I thought you would wear something Egyptian. Where are your wig, the cobra headpiece, and the pleated linen?"

"Oh Sarai," Hagar said as she stretched out a hand to her, "I thought if I were to bear a son for Abram, I must dress as your people. Remember this is not to be my son but yours."

Sarai came and took her hand, then kneeling down kissed both cheeks. "How good you are," she said as she gave her a warm and friendly smile. "I'd almost forgotten."

Sarai stood up and turned to go, then hesitated and came back. "Remember, not only is the son mine, but the husband is mine too. He's yours only for a day or two until you find his seed growing in your womb." She had spoken it in a light, friendly way, but Hagar could see by the flash of her eyes and the set of her mouth that she was serious. With that Sarai turned and was gone.

Hagar just had time to pull the light veil back across her face when she heard drumming and singing coming closer. They were all male voices, and the drumbeats were accentuated by the steady thud of bare feet pounding out the rhythm in their traditional dance. It was never considered proper to send a man off alone on his wedding night. A bride should not be left alone either. Usually the mother, sisters, friends, and family were all gathered to bring the young woman to her husband.

Hagar had none of this. She thought fleetingly of the goddess Hathor who was supposed to protect young brides and new mothers, but Hathor had proven to be worthless. She knew nothing of the God Abram worshiped, but he undoubtedly used His strength only for men.

In the few moments left she stiffened her resolve to make the most of her situation. She knew what Abram longed for and what Sarai expected. Sarai undoubtedly intended to manage everything. I must learn to be patient, she thought. I must not alienate Sarai.

There was much raucous banter back and forth, and then she heard Abram's voice. "You needn't make so much of this," he said with laughter in his voice. "I'm no young buck." Hagar heard the sounds of the boisterous men fade away as they headed back to the fire. Abram did not immediately lift the tent flap, and she wondered if he was dreading the encounter. Well, she thought, this is my time and I will make the most of it.

* * *

Abram had let himself be drawn into this whole plan because Sarai wanted it so much. Now that he was actually facing his familiar quarters, knowing that a strange woman was inside, he wanted to turn away. To make matters even worse, she was a young woman, an Egyptian, and apparently just as headstrong as Sarai. Then again he remembered her as she had looked with her hair blowing around her, wearing the golden crown, and leading the maidens in a dance to welcome him home from fighting the Elamites. She would no doubt have expectations. Egyptian expectations. He suddenly felt very old and inadequate. How had he been talked into this?

It wasn't just Sarai. It was also the Elohim. He had made promises, and Sarai was going to see that they were fulfilled one way or another.

Abram fingered the fringe on his cloak, looked back, and saw that the men had stopped to see if he was going into his tent. He knew it would be the subject of interest from now on. Surely this was nothing but foolishness. Elohim and Sarai were to blame. Why did everything have to be so difficult?

He lifted the tent flap and stepped inside. He was surprised to see the young woman sitting so demurely. There was almost a shyness about her. He had remembered her as rather brash and confident. Maybe she wasn't as sure of herself as she had seemed. It gave him a feeling of confidence. It even made him interested.

He walked over to her and sat down. When she didn't move or turn to look at him, he gained courage. He lifted her chin so he could look in her eyes. She made no move to push him away or rebuff him, and so he unfastened the edge of her veil and let it fall so he could see her face. It was an ordinary face, but the eyes were hypnotic. He looked at her mouth and then back to her eyes. Something about the eyes fascinated him. He had a fleeting thought that he must not let her cast a spell on him. She must know all sorts of Egyptian magic, and he was a man of simple tastes who didn't want to be jarred out of his comfortable situation.

He realized that it would be easy to be aroused by her. He rather liked the soft, young curve of her cheek, and the hand that lay on her knee was slim and inviting.

He reached out and ran one finger around the place where her wrist was exposed. She didn't move away but instead turned and looked at him with a slight smile. "My lord," she said. Her voice was soft, even tantalizing, the way she said "my lord" with her Egyptian accent. "In Egypt such things as this take time. We must feel comfortable with each other."

Abram studied her face for any sign of rejection. There was none. She seemed young and vulnerable. "How does an Egyptian go about feeling comfortable?"

He could see she was pleased with his question. She even turned toward him with an eager, expectant look. "It's really very simple," she said. "We must share our thoughts. We must get to know each other. We must talk."

That made him feel a bit nervous. Sarai usually wanted to talk because she was displeased about something or she had something she wanted him to do.

What could this mysterious woman want? Men and women didn't talk. They weren't interested in the same things. What could she possibly have in mind? Abram was intrigued. He had never imagined a woman to be concerned about such things. "You must show me," he said with a hint of a smile. "What questions do you have?"

"Well, for instance," she said, "you are wealthy, but you live simply, why?"

Abram studied her face and saw that she was serious. She seemed interested. "I have been a trader and have lived in cities, but I find them not to my liking. Life is not simple in most cities. People become grasping, greedy, and often even evil when they are no longer close to God's growing things." He paused for a moment. "Do you like our way of life?"

Hagar looked down and toyed with the fringe on her skirt. "I miss some things," she said, "but I've learned to like it better than living in the palace."

"What do you like?"

"The silence, peace, time to do things, to really think."

Abram was surprised. He was used to Sarai, who was always accusing him of thinking too much. "When one like you has time to think, what do you think about?" he asked.

"Mostly all the foolish, headstrong things I've done that have gotten me in trouble."

Now Abram was really interested. "What, for instance?" he asked.

She told him of her life in the palace and answered many questions about her father, the great Pharaoh Amenemhet, until the wick had grown short in the alabaster lamp. The celebration around the fire had died down and finally stopped. Hagar looked around. "The hour is late," she said. "I must go."

Abram was perplexed. "But I thought . . ." he said.

"Oh, we must see more of each other. I will go to my tent now, but if you wish to see me tomorrow night, I'll come."

"And tomorrow night, what will we do?" he asked with a twinkle in his eye.

"Getting a child is like planting a seed," she said. "If it is to grow strong, the ground must be prepared. In Egypt, the Nile covers the land, laying down rich silt, then recedes. Only then does the farmer sow his seed . . . and it always grows."

She stood up, adjusted her mantle, and with one quick movement moved to the opening in the tent and was gone.

Abram was too astonished to move. Of all the things he had anticipated, that was not one of them. As a man and tribal leader, he was the one who always dismissed people or called them to his tent. He had to admit that he found her entertaining. He wanted the encounter to last much longer and he felt cheated. For a brief period he mulled over her questions. How strange she was! How stimulating! He had not imagined that a woman ever thought of such things. As he pinched the flames out in the lamp, he smiled to himself and wondered what the next night would hold.

* * *

Early the next morning Sarai hurried to Abram's tent, pulled back the flap, and tiptoed in. She stood looking down at him and pondered the oddness of it all. He was fully dressed and the Egyptian was gone. She frowned. Is it possible that things did not go well between them?

"Abram," she said, holding the bowl of steaming groats under his nose. "Abram, where is the girl? What happened?" When he responded with only a sleepy groan, she pressed on. "Where is Hagar?"

Abram sat up and took the bowl from her, obviously enjoying her impatience. He took a sip and looked at her anxious face. "Nothing happened. I barely touched her wrist, no more."

Sarai's face clouded. "Then she is not pregnant. The child is not even conceived yet?"

"That's right."

"Does she have more demands?"

"No, no. She just says these things can't be hurried," he said, reaching out to her.

Sarai jerked away, her eyes flashing, her mantle twisted out of shape, and her mouth a hard line. "So," she said, "what did the two of you do?"

"She just wanted to talk. She said we must get to know each other before we go about getting a child."

"Oh, how hateful!" Sarai spat the words out. "First, she must have the bride's tent, then Warda must be brought and a celebration planned, now she wants to drag this whole thing out for her own enjoyment. I won't have it." She strode around the tent, going back and forth like an angry panther.

"Now, now, Sarai," Abram said. "I thought you would be glad that nothing really happened. All we did was talk."

"Talk! What was there to talk about? To get a child doesn't take talk."

"Sarai," Abram said patiently, "I don't really know what to do. This isn't something I planned. I'm doing it mainly for you."

Sarai saw that he was sincere and so she came over and knelt beside him. "Abram," she said with all the anger suddenly gone out of her voice, "promise me . . . promise me on your dead father's name and beard that you will do your best to finish with this business tonight."

Abram took her two small hands in his and looked in her eyes. "Sarai, we have no choice but to do what the Egyptian wants until we get the child. You wouldn't want me to offend her, would you?"

Sarai agreed reluctantly. More than anything she wanted the child. "Of course, you must humor her. Just don't let her manage things." With that she turned and left the tent.

That night, just as the moon was coming up, Abram sent one of the old women in the camp to bring Hagar to his tent. Before he heard footsteps he smelled the faint odor of patchouli and knew it was Hagar. He settled back, leaned casually on the armrest, and waited for the tent flap to be drawn. Suddenly she was standing in the opening, drenched in moonlight, and smiling as though she was pleased to be there. He rose slowly and took her hand. It was soft and small; the nails were clean and well-shaped. She studied his face, and Abram wondered what she was thinking.

When they were seated, he leaned toward her and asked, "So, my Nile beauty, what are we to do tonight?"

To his amusement she laughed. Her laughter was unaffected, but displayed a hint of nervousness. That put him at ease. He waited while she arranged her sash and straightened the fringe on her shoulder. "Tonight, again we must talk," she said, tilting her head and looking at him sideways. "There are still many things we need to understand."

"And when will we . . . ?" he paused, not knowing how to put such a delicate matter into words.

"Oh, that will come quite naturally at the right time."

"And what is left to be talked about?" he said, displaying some impatience.

"My lord," she said, "I want to know about the Elohim you worship. Sarai says you have never seen Him, and yet He has talked to you and made promises."

He swung around quickly to face her. He expected to see some slight mockery in her eyes or a superior toss of her head. Instead he saw eager anticipation. He hesitated, and when he spoke, it was with restraint. "He is the Creator God," he said, "the sustainer of all life."

"No, no," she said. "That is not what I am interested in. I want to know about the promises. Sarai said He had made promises."

Abram was immediately disappointed. She was interested only in a

God who could promise wonderful things and bless those who worshiped Him. "He has made promises," he said hesitantly, "but as yet I have received nothing."

"Yet you don't doubt?"

"No," he said with an abruptness that was intended to close the subject.

She ignored his hint and asked, "You can't see your God. How do you know He is there?" She leaned back and studied him intently.

"I feel His presence. He talks with me."

For a moment she twisted the tassel of fringe on her mantle and then said slowly and thoughtfully, "Your God, is he a God for Egyptians or just for your people?"

Abram smiled. For the first time he took her seriously. "He is Creator of all things and all people," he said, "so He must be a God for Egyptians too."

She looked skeptical and hesitated as though reluctant to ask the next question. Finally she dropped the bit of mantle and looked at him directly. "Your Elohim, is He a God for women too?"

Abram was taken aback. He had never thought about his God in that way. "I don't know," he said, "I just don't know."

"Tell me," she said earnestly, "does He see me?"

No woman Abram knew asked about such things. They left such questions to the men. When he didn't answer, she asked another question: "In Egypt there are gods for men and goddesses like Hathor for women. Who do I pray to for this child?"

"We have only the one God called Elohim. He is the God who told me to look at the stars and try to count them. When I couldn't, He told me I would have descendants as the stars, and I believe Him."

Hagar sighed. "How will I know if your God favors me?"

At that Abram smiled. "All that we know of Elohim has been told us by our fathers, or we have learned by watching what he does. He has promised me a son and land, and we will see what comes of it."

There was a long silence. A wind came up. The flame in the alabaster lamp flickered and almost went out, a baby could be heard crying, and somewhere down toward the campfire came the sound of a shepherd's flute. Its notes rose and fell in a familiar tune for hopeless lovers.

Slowly Hagar turned and looked at Abram. He had been studying her and had noticed the faint resemblance to his friend the pharaoh. There were

179

the same well-shaped nose, large eyes, full mouth, and royal demeanor. He had thought her face ordinary, but now he saw a haunting beauty about her. The beauty was illusive. It was not the beauty of Sarai but a much more sensual beauty that moved him deeply.

He experienced strong emotion, and it frightened him. He had not intended to feel anything for this woman. He loved Sarai and nothing must sully that love. She was of his family. She was of the same blood. She understood him. He suddenly feared that he might be carried beyond himself, led out to some new experience that would touch him at some deep level of his being. He struggled to resist the feeling, but with Hagar's upturned face and the look of admiration that had melted her haughty stance, he forgot his caution. He reached out and drew her into his arms. He was filled with exquisite delight to hear her softly breathe, "It's time. Oh, yes, it's time."

* * *

A month, then two months passed before Hagar could announce a change had taken place. By the time of the third new moon it was almost a sure fact that Hagar was expecting a child. Abram was elated. He acted like a young man in love, jovial, swaggering a bit, relaxed. He ordered special food for Hagar, music to be played, celebrations in her honor, and several serving girls given to her for personal use. It was difficult at first to tell whether he was just happy to be expecting a child or whether it was more than that.

Sarai knew right away. Abram, who had been unswerving in his love for her, had somehow changed. Her first thought was that he had been bewitched. She suspected the Egyptian of casting some strong spell on him. He no longer noticed her in the same way as before, but instead his eyes followed the Egyptian with obvious approval. It was more than delight at the prospect of a child. It was as though he'd totally forgotten Sarai in favor of the Egyptian.

To make matters worse, Hagar was different. Her eyes shone with some new fire, and even her walk was more sure and arrogant. "I am with child by Abram," she said with a proud toss of her head as she joined the women at the well.

"I conceived so quickly. It's not at all difficult," she said, looking toward Sarai. The women sat together spinning thread to be woven into new tents. She seemed to be expecting Sarai to treat her with new respect and deference.

Sarai was furious. From the moment Hagar had announced her pregnancy, Sarai had grown more and more resentful and angry. She was angry with Hagar for her arrogance, with Abram for his delight, and most of all with Abram's God for giving Hagar, an Egyptian, a child so quickly and so effortlessly.

She resented all of her ardent prayers for a child, the concoctions she had swallowed, the new moons and the full moons, counted and observed. Most of all she was bitter, thinking of the times she had waited expectantly with unswerving faith that she would conceive. She had left nothing to chance, and still she had not become pregnant.

Then another thought occurred: Perhaps Abram's God is not a God for women. Perhaps one needs the blessings of the earth goddess after all. The one certain fact was that she had been rejected by Abram and his God. Sarai had always been a sure, confident person, and this new feeling was devastating. Quickly following this feeling was a violent hatred toward Hagar.

She could see that Hagar expected her to be overjoyed at the turn of events. Of course, Abram was to blame for making so much of the girl's accomplishment. If he hadn't repeated over and over the promise and then accepted Hagar's condition as the wonderful fulfillment, all of this could have been avoided.

The more she thought about it, the more it seemed Abram's fault. He was the one who had lingered over the meetings with Hagar. He was the one who had flattered her and made her feel that she had been chosen by the Elohim to have the promised child. He was the one who had elevated Hagar to a place of prominence.

Without a moment's hesitation she called one of the young men and told him to go quickly and bring Abram to her tent. While she waited, she paced back and forth, getting angrier and more resentful. She would confront him, make him reject Hagar.

* * *

Abram was bewildered to find Sarai in such a state of anger. He had known she was spirited and hot-tempered, but he had thought she would be pleased. She had wanted a child so badly. The idea had been hers. He could not untangle the perplexities of her reasoning. She kept saying it was his fault. He was to blame, but he could not understand what he had done.

He stood and watched her frenzy grow to frightening heights. He tried to interrupt and soothe her anger with reason, but she would not listen. In one last effort to calm her, he said, "She is your handmaiden. Pharaoh gave her to you, and you may do with her as you please." With that he turned and strode from the tent.

From that moment Sarai regained her composure. She was relieved that Abram didn't defend the Egyptian. He obviously didn't love her. He was simply using her to gain the promise. She didn't admire him for his callousness, but nevertheless she was relieved.

Sarai now decided it wasn't her husband's fault at all. The fault lay with the girl Hagar. She had posed as such a friend, and now she had turned out to be capable of such cruelty. Sarai could not forgive her for her arrogance and thoughtless bragging.

She sent for Hagar and was surprised to see her enter the tent smiling and confident. Sarai glared at her and spoke sharply, "What charms have you used to get a child by my husband?"

Hagar was confused. "I used no charms," she spoke hesitantly, not sure what Sarai meant.

"You have deceived me. You have worked Egyptian magic to get this child and to alienate my husband."

"I have done only what you asked. I thought this was what you wanted."

"Oh yes, you had to have the bridal tent, feasts, and special attention, and then you had to spend all those nights with my husband. You are evil beyond my imagining. I trusted you and you've deceived me." Sarai's eyes flashed and her voice was strident.

"My lady . . . Sarai." Hagar backed away and a look of bewilderment crossed her face.

"Well, things are going to be different. You can stop your bragging about the child and putting on airs about how fast you were able to conceive. From now on you will live like the humblest servant. You will go out with the goats in the morning and come in at night and milk them. You will draw the water and grind the wheat. You will wear only a servant's crudely spun clothes and eat after the others are finished."

While Sarai spoke, Hagar began to back away. "My lady," she said, "you forget the child."

With mention of the child, Sarai's anger became unbearable, and she slapped the Egyptian with the palm of her hand, raising a red welt. "There, you see, I am not to be trifled with," she said, rubbing her sore hand on her thigh.

Hagar backed to the tent door, holding her hand to her face. "In Egypt it is an imprisonable offense to slap a princess."

"We are not in Egypt now, and you are my handmaiden. I can do as I please."

"You forget I am carrying my lord Abram's child. He will defend me."

Sarai grew livid with rage. "You foolish one," she said, "it was Abram who told me I may do with you as I like."

Hagar let out an anguished cry. "I don't believe you!" she said.

Sarai's laugh was harsh and held a note of triumph. "Go, foolish one, and ask him. He himself will carry out my orders."

Hagar backed away, feeling the sting of Sarai's words sharper than the sting of the bruise on her face. She groped for the opening to the tent and plunged out into the moonless night. Would Abram truly not speak for her, defend her? Hagar knew Abram had always done whatever Sarai requested, but certainly he would not allow the mother of his child to be treated so badly.

Sarai's cruel words echoed in Hagar's ears, reminding her that despite the child she carried, Hagar remained merely a handmaiden, forced to do the bidding of her mistress.

Hatred flared up in her, and she began to run through the loose sand, stumbling and falling, picking herself up. With each step she felt the urgent need to escape. She ran aimlessly down the path that led south, away from the camp.

She had no idea where she would go. It didn't really matter. Just to lose herself, to find a place where she could hide from these ones who had crushed her joy. She fled through the darkness, avoiding any familiar path that would lead to the campfires of shepherds or nearby villages. She stumbled and ran, feeling the jagged rocks pierce her light sandals. Thornbushes tore at her skirt and legs, and the cold, the creeping cold of the spring night, penetrated her thin mantle. Her head throbbed, and she felt a strangling, choking sensation, an unrelenting pain somewhere in her chest.

When she began to slacken her pace, hurt and outrage boiled to the surface. She clutched at knotted roots and twigs to climb rock barriers and slid down gullies, tearing her clothes. Branches of wild fig caught her uncovered hair and held her hostage until she could pull loose. She had no idea of where she was or where she was going. She knew only that she must escape.

Hagar finally sank down at the base of a small tamarisk tree and waited for the moon to come up. The light from the moon revealed the vast, barren expanse of the Negev stretched out before her. She stood up and tried to determine how far she had come, and then hurried along at a slower, less-frenzied pace.

By morning she was beyond the planted, walled terraces of farmers and was looking out over a wide stretch of rolling sand and small bushes. She was exhausted. She sank down under an acacia bush and drank a bit of the precious water from her goatskin flask. She was soon asleep.

When she awoke, a subtle change had taken place. A hot wind blew from the south, and the sky had grown overcast. Hagar feared it was the dread Sherkiyeh, a wind that blew with the force of a furnace and stirred up sand until one could not see even a few steps ahead. There would be only a short time and the light would fade and the sand would begin to blow. She had to find shelter fast. All thought of her recent ordeal faded before her new problem.

Hagar found an outcropping of rock just in time. In great bursts the wind dug at the hillocks of sand and sent them billowing and rolling in ominous clouds until even the nearest bush was blotted out. She could see no sky and no solid ground. She covered her face with her mantle and still found it difficult to breathe. The heat was oppressive, the air dry and hostile. She tasted the gritty sand on her lips and, reaching up, felt her hair caked with it. Her skin was pummeled by small particles, and she seriously began to fear that she would suffocate alone in this wilderness, far from any familiar face.

She hid her face in her hands and gasped for air. In spite of her discomfort, she began to worry about the child she was carrying. She thought briefly of Sarai. Sarai desperately wanted the child and so did Abram. It would spoil all their plans if anything happened to the child she carried. Her death in this desert or her disappearance would punish them both. What other chance had they for the child they wanted so badly?

The old Hagar, the one who had caused Pharaoh's favorite such trouble, would have taken great delight in getting even. Abram and Sarai would assume she had died in the sandstorm and perhaps even shed tears of remorse. They would see how cruel they had been and spend the rest of their lives feeling guilty.

The sandstorm pounded and shrieked around the rocks where Hagar hid, but her thoughts were consumed with the delightful prospect of revenge. She had loved Sarai and had grown closer to Abram, and they had betrayed her. She would never forgive them. As an Egyptian, she prided herself on being strong enough to wreak revenge on those who dared to hurt her.

She felt the sand pounding her relentlessly even when she pressed herself into the hollow of the rock. The heat stifled her, and the terrible roar of the wind deadened all but her bitter thoughts. Despite her anguish, the desire for revenge rose up in such strength that she no more wished to die. I'll live, she thought, but they will never see this child.

*A*s the wind continued, Hagar's flask emptied out. Soon she became obsessed with her craving for water. At times her thirst gnawed at her with more force than her struggle to breathe. Though the huge rock partially protected her from the worst of the storm, she began to take seriously the idea that she might not escape from this ordeal alive. All of her spunk and brash bravado, even her desire for revenge, began to fade. They were of no avail against such odds.

Cowering in the niche, she felt small and powerless. Some god in charge of the desert must be punishing her. Perhaps it was the evil djinn that liked to torment humans. She vaguely remembered stories she had heard as a child about the evil spirits that lived in the deserts and deserted places of the earth. For the first time she was afraid.

She began to fear for the unborn child she carried. This was her child, not Sarai's or Abram's. If she died, this child would die too. She was the only one who could keep them both alive, and suddenly, inexplicably, she wanted the child to live. Abram's God, Elohim, had promised Abram a child. Perhaps he would help her for the child's sake.

No sooner had she thought of Abram's God than she was reminded of the taunting words she had spoken that had so angered Sarai. The Elohim was perhaps to be reckoned with in all of this. What if Abram's God saw her as cruel and spiteful?

For the first time she admitted reluctantly that she had been pleased to see the torment in Sarai's eyes. She had known that her smug delight would crush Sarai worse than a millstone dropped on her. Now she felt small twinges of remorse for what she had done. It had not been necessary for her to gloat so over getting pregnant. For a moment she saw herself as the evil one who had deliberately spoken hurting words, and she wished for a chance to make things right.

Gradually the storm began to abate. Hagar could see her surroundings, first faintly and then more distinctly. She still had to keep her mantle pressed against her face in order to breathe, but the heat was lifting and the sand no longer stung her skin. She realized that the night had passed, and it must be midday. There was a dull orange look about things. She stirred from her cramped position and tried to shake the sand from her clothes and hair.

Just as she began to move out from the niche in the rock, she was smitten once more with a terrible wrenching thirst. She tipped her water skin up to her mouth, but nothing came. She ran her tongue around the rim and found it dry. She had lived through the worst of the storm, but she could not live long without water. She knew nothing of the wells in this desert, and there was no oasis or clump of trees in sight. She saw nothing but rolling sand, thornbushes, and here and there a small acacia.

Abram would no doubt call upon his God for help, but what God would help a woman? Hathor had proved useless, and Abram's God was probably not a God for women or Egyptians. She remembered how surprised she'd been when she first heard that Abram's God actually spoke to him. Abram talked to Him as though he were a friend. What harm would it do to at least call out to Elohim and see if He would help? She thought of the child and instinctively put her hands on her stomach. For the child she must try.

The wind had died down, and in its place was heat rising from the sand and pushing up from the south in hot gusts that made the sand rise periodically in small puffs. Hagar spread her mantle on the sand as she had seen Abram do and knelt upon it with her face touching the earth. She had seen men bow before Pharaoh in the same way. "Elohim," Abram had said, "was the Creator of all things." He created the sand, and He created the water she so desperately needed.

Her prayer was simple: "Oh Lord God, named Elohim, creator of all things and friend to Abram, I carry Abram's child and both of us will die without water. Do You see me? Can You give me water in this desert?"

That was all. She sat back and looked around. There was nothing. The same treeless expanse. The same dry heat. She slowly stood to her feet and shook the sand from her clothes. On impulse she climbed the rock that had sheltered her and looked around. At first she saw nothing, then her eyes settled on a round stone a short distance away. It had been covered by sand until the wind had blown it clean. Hagar had seen such stones on the way up from Egypt. They usually covered wells, but most wells were owned by tribes who would not welcome a stranger making use of them.

Hagar didn't hesitate to climb down and investigate. She feared that if it was indeed a well, the rock would be too heavy to move. She knelt down and pushed, then tugged and pulled until the large stone moved just enough for her to grasp the rope that hung from a projection inside the well. With trembling hands she fastened her water skin to the rope and then tried to move the rock far enough to lower the skin into the well.

It was impossible. The rock would not move. She sat back on her heels. There was a faint stirring in the thornbush that grew beside the well, and at the same time she had the feeling that someone was watching her. She stood up and looked around. If the owner appeared, he could refuse to let her have even one drop of the precious water. There was no one.

She knelt down again and in feverish desperation pushed at the rock. To her surprise, it moved quite easily, almost as though someone were helping her. With trembling hands she fastened the water skin to the rope and lowered it into the well. She almost laughed when she felt it hit the water. She quickly pulled it up and stood drinking the water in great gulps, ignoring what ran down her face and spilled over her clothes.

She was about to lower the skin again when there was a movement behind her and a voice said, "Hagar!"

Hagar whirled around to see who had spoken. Who knew her here in this wilderness? Who could speak her name?

There, half hidden in shadow, was a figure leaning against the rock. She strained to get a closer look, to be sure someone was really there. In the desert with the blowing sand, people often imagined they saw unusual things. She backed away and listened in astonishment. "Hagar," she heard Him say, "I know you are Sarai's maid."

She strained to see just who had spoken. Who knew so much about her? As she backed away she heard Him ask, "Where have you come from?"

"I'm running away," she said with a defiant toss of her head. "I'm running away from my mistress." She turned and started walking, and to her surprise, the person didn't try to stop her.

He asked, "Where are you going?"

For a moment there was silence as she looked at the vast expanse of wilderness before her. She saw no path and no sign of a living thing, only blowing sand and silence. She hesitated. The anger that had made her flight possible had abated. She realized that she was hopelessly lost in a desert with wild beasts, blistering heat, and no other water.

She turned and saw that the stranger was still there, still hidden in the shadows. She wanted to ask him for help, but was too proud. He seemed to read her thoughts. "Hagar," he said, "you have no choice but to return and submit to your mistress."

At those words Hagar's face clouded. Her eyes flashed with frustration and anger. "Never . . . I can never submit to Sarai. It's impossible. You don't know how I've suffered." She paused, but sensing thatHe was not convinced, continued with even more anger, "She hates me for no reason. I can't go back. I won't submit."

For a moment there was silence. When the stranger spoke again, it was with great tenderness and compassion. "Hagar," he said, "the Lord has heard all your troubles. He knows all that has happened to you."

Hagar was astonished. This stranger was no ordinary person. For a moment she wondered whether the heat or the desert sand had conjured up such a vision. As she leaned forward, peering into the shadows, the figure stepped out, and she was aware of His eyes, only His eyes. They were most astonishing. She had never seen eyes that radiated such strength and infinite compassion.

She had barely regained some composure when He spoke again, this time with authority that made her wonder whether He might not be the God of Abram. "Hagar," he said, "you will bear a son and shall call him Ishmael because the Lord has heard you."

"A son, I am to have a son," she whispered as wonder and joy rose within her.

He held up his hand, signaling that there was more. "I," He said, "will make of your descendants a great nation."

"Ishmael," she whispered. "I am to call his name Ishmael, 'God hears.' "

As though to guard against too great an expectation, he continued to speak rather sadly and yet matter-of-factly. "He will be a wild, impulsive man," he said. "He will be against everyone and everyone will be against him."

Hagar started to speak, to object and question, but again the hand was raised. He hadn't finished. "And," he said, "he will live near the rest of his kin." The message came to an end, and the stranger looked long and tenderly at Hagar then turned and slowly walked away.

Hagar stood, watching him go. Could she have imagined it all in a delirium caused by the heat?

Her eyes followed him as he went toward the east. She noticed that his sandals cast up small puffs of sand. "No mirage or vision would have done something like that," she reasoned.

She watched as he walked steadily on, then suddenly he vanished, leaving only the wide expanse of empty sand and sky. "I have seen Abram's God and lived," she said in amazement.

The great rock stood solid and strong just as before; the sand had already begun to cover the well stone as she knelt and ran her hands around the rim. "I shall name this well, the Well of the Living One Who Sees Me," she said.

As she stood up, a great wind began to blow. It puffed the sand in small peaks and spirals and made a noise like a rushing, mighty wind. There was something strong and joyful about it, though it blew her clothes taut against her and made walking almost impossible.

Hagar hardly noticed the strength of the wind for the joy and delight that rose up within her. "He knew me," she murmured over and over again. "He saw me and saw all my troubles."

She had only a vague idea of where she was or how to find her way back. Perhaps when the stars came out, they would help her. She would have to go north, since the desert and wilderness had always been to the south of where they were camped.

While finding her way back was difficult, it was not as difficult as the order to submit. The word held layers and layers of meaning. No Egyptian was ever known to submit to anyone. She, a princess, would find it harder than most. Submission went against her very nature.

As she hurried along she made plans. "If indeed it is a boy that I carry, I will name him Ishmael. I will tell Abram that we must name the boy Ishmael. When he asks why, I will tell him about the heavenly being and how He said Elohim had heard me, and so I must name the child 'God heard me.'"

Hours later Hagar found Abram with some of his most trusted men out looking for her. He was obviously worried and distraught, and he said Sarai was back at camp, weeping with grief. Only when Hagar told him of the astounding encounter with the heavenly being did his eyes dance with delight. "So," he said, "Elohim isn't just concerned with the affairs of men, and He does hear a woman's prayer, even an Egyptian woman's prayer."

* * *

When the child was born on Sarai's lap as was the custom, Hagar asked quickly, "My lady, is it a boy?"

"It's a boy," Sarai said, "and we will name him Asa."

Hagar was about to object, but she remembered that the stranger had told her to go home and submit to Sarai, and so she said nothing. However, when the child was carried in to Abram, he said, "This child shall be called Ishmael because God heard and answered, and we must remember forever that God hears even a woman and sees her trouble."

Hagar loved the child as she had never loved anything before in her life. She had not known the meaning of love. Her most precious moments were spent with the small greedy little face pressed into her breast, depending on her for his very life. She delighted in each thing the child did but hid her delight so Sarai would not grow envious.

When the child wrapped his small fingers around one of her fingers or studied her face with wide, serious eyes and then finally smiled a half-crooked smile, she wanted to run and tell everyone. She wanted to brag outrageously when she saw how clever he was, but she wisely held her peace.

* * *

Sarai delighted in the child. She seemed to have totally claimed him as her own and took pride in his handsome little face, his first words calling her Ummi, and his affectionate nature.

Yet several things clouded Sarai's joy. She resented the fact that Abram's God had spoken to Hagar when He had never spoken to her. It did not help that the girl had gotten with child so soon. Even all that she could have accepted but to have Abram say the child's name was to be Ishmael, the name Hagar had given him, was impossible.

She wanted to find fault with Hagar, but the girl was totally different. She was always pleasant, never rebellious as she had sometimes been in the past, and she seemed to have left her old arrogant nature back in the desert.

Sarai could find no fault with her. Even at times when she noticed Abram glance at her with approval, Hagar never seemed to notice. It was as though Hagar carried some wonderful secret that gave her peace and a quiet joy.

Sarai could not imagine what the secret could be, but Abram knew. He knew, and he pondered the ways of Elohim. He couldn't understand all of it. He really hadn't thought Elohim would notice and take so much trouble for a woman, and an Egyptian woman at that. "Well," he finally decided, "it's like I told Hagar, we only know about Elohim by noticing what He does. He always surprises us just when we think we have Him figured out," he said with a laugh. "Ishmael, we'll never forget this lesson."

With all his joy in the child, Abram could not bear to see Sarai with Ishmael. He could not endure seeing the subtle change that seemed to have taken possession of her. Having no child of her own was like a thorn that would keep her wound fresh and bleeding.

The child seemed to notice the difference too. Ishmael was serious and obedient with Sarai but laughing and playful with Hagar. He didn't relax with Sarai but was always the good child, the proper child, when he was with her. Sarai bragged on his ability to please. Sometimes Abram saw her watching him with a sad, thoughtful look, and at such times she would call the child to her and demand, "Who is your dear mother?"

The child would look at her with his serious large eyes and say, "You are my mother."

"Who do you love most?" she would ask, studying him with profound seriousness.

He would always give her the answer she wanted. "You, Ummi, it is you I love most."

She would gather him into her arms and hold him tight with tears of relief coming to her eyes.

for thirteen years life moved on at the same leisurely pace with no difference from one day to the next. In that time not much thought was given to Elohim or his promises. Each person seemed to have settled for some form of compromise. Abram was pleased with the development of his son Ishmael, Sarai no longer grieved openly over her barrenness, and Hagar was content seeing that each day Ishmael was being groomed to inherit all that his father owned.

Then quite suddenly everything began to change. It started one cool spring night when Abram, unable to sleep, walked out under the stars and sat down on a projection of rock where he could see both the starry heavens and the campfires of his shepherds on the distant hillsides. The air was fragrant with new budding and blossoming things and the pungent odor of damp earth working its magic on roots and seeds.

As Abram sat and meditated, he began to study the stars. They were brilliant. They hung so low, they seemed like a giant tent cloth covering his world. His eyes wandered over them, and he realized once again how impossible it was to try to count them. How difficult it was to think his descendants would ever be that numerous.

As he pondered these things he slowly became aware of a familiar presence. He looked around and saw no one. He felt a rush of wind and then dead stillness. He held his breath and waited. Every nerve was tense. His fingers opened and closed, his feet shifted slightly on the smooth rock, but there was only the unusual silence. Then in the midst of the quiet he heard a voice and the sound of the voice was like thunder.

"Abram," the voice said, "you have known Me as Elohim, but now you will know Me as El Shaddai, the almighty God."

Abram felt such a power and presence of majesty that he fell prostrate on the ground with his face in his hands.

The voice went on to reaffirm the agreement and covenant that would make Abram the father of many nations. "You will no longer be Abram," the voice said, "but Abraham, exalted father." The name was spoken with such force that it seemed to echo and reecho all around him.

Abram was about to speak and ask what his part of the contract was to be when the voice continued: "Abraham, you must obey Me. As a permanent sign of this covenant between us, you and all your posterity must be circumcised. Each male must have his foreskin removed on the eighth day after birth. This will be proof that you and those who come after you accept the terms of this covenant."

Then the El Shaddai added, "And as to Sarai, your wife, she will no longer be Sarai, meaning 'contention,' but Sarah, meaning 'princess.' And I will bless her and give you a son by her. She will be the mother of nations and kings."

Abraham got to his knees but still could not uncover his eyes. He was awed by the solemnity of the moment but also embarrassed and appalled to find himself secretly laughing at the ridiculousness of the promise. Sarah, a mother at her age? Surely I have heard wrong, he thought. Then he said, "Oh Lord God Elohim, I do believe in Your blessing to Ishmael."

There was silence, and when the voice spoke again, it was with great might and power, "I am El Shaddai, the Almighty. As I have said, Sarah will bear you a son and you are to name him Isaac, 'laughter.' It is with him and his descendants I will sign my covenant forever."

Abraham was immediately concerned for the son he had come to love so deeply. "What of Ishmael?" he asked.

El Shaddai continued, "As for Ishmael I will bless him also, just as you have asked Me to do. Twelve princes will be among his posterity, but My covenant is with Isaac, who will be born to you and Sarah next year at this time."

With that the presence was gone as quickly as it had come, and Abraham was alone. He got slowly to his feet and looked around. The same stars shone out of the dark blue curtain of the sky, and the same fragrances and soft breeze filled the air around him. He brushed off the dust from his robe and stood thinking aloud.

"Laughter, so he is to be called laughter." Then he marveled, "He already has a name. It seems the almighty God can even make an old man and his wife fruitful." He laughed again, but this time it was with joy.

He started down the path to his tent, his feet taking off in a happy, shuffling jig. He felt young and spirited. He was going to be a father again, and

Sarah was to be a mother at last. Suddenly he paused. "Isaac, laughter," he repeated. "He doesn't want me to ever forget that He is the El Shaddai who can do anything. Wait until I tell Sarah."

With mention of Sarah he paused. Perhaps, he thought, I should wait to tell Sarah. She will surely think I dreamed it all. She will never believe she can become a mother at her age.

Then as he continued on his way back to the camp, another thought crowded out all other considerations. "I must also tell Sarah and Hagar that Ishmael must be circumcised with the rest of the men," he muttered. "They will think thirteen is too young and beg and plead. If he is to be part of the covenant, then he, too, must be circumcised. I must not linger about it. I'll have the flint knives sharpened, and we'll do it tomorrow before anyone thinks up excuses."

* * *

Abraham, as he now insisted on being called, did not tell Sarah about anything but the necessity for circumcision. As he had feared, he found her opposed to having Ishmael circumcised with the men. "He's but a child," she insisted.

"In the future," Abraham told her, "every child born in our camp will be circumcised by the eighth day."

"If that's true," Sarah sputtered, "it's well that I'm childless."

Abraham saw how disturbed she was and decided there was no need to tell her of the promise. It would give her more reason to be upset. He would wait and see what came of the promise. After all, years had passed since the first promise was made.

Hagar accepted the necessity for the circumcision better than Sarah did. "The priests of Egypt have this mark on them," she said. "For them it is a sign of dedication and honor."

The circumcision took place without Lot. He gave the excuse that he would come later. He was busy with important matters. His businesses were prospering and his daughters were getting married.

When they came to circumcising Abraham's menservants, Urim appeared. He had hurried up from Sodom to be part of the ritual. "I have always considered myself to be one of your servants," he said, "and if they are to be circumcised, I don't want to be left out."

Ishmael surprised everyone by being braver than most, even proud to be considered old enough to be included.

* * *

It was on a hot day in early summer, near the oak grove at Mamre where Abraham was temporarily camped, that he was again reminded of the promise. It was a day much like any other. The huge sprawling oaks gave shade but little relief from the heat. The tent flaps were up, and Abraham sat in the opening hoping for a cool breeze. The air was still and dry with dust blowing in spirals. The grass was brown and brittle.

Looking toward the north, Abraham saw three men coming down the road. He could tell they had come a long way because they wore garments of a simple but curious make. As they came closer he noticed their sandals were worn and their feet covered with dust. He was immediately concerned. Being noted for his hospitality, he hurried out to welcome them and urge them to come into the shade for rest and refreshment.

They glanced at each other and then, smiling, accepted his invitation. He quickly ordered cushions to be brought, carpets to be laid, and basins of water for washing their feet.

While the servants were making them comfortable, he hurried back to the tent and called for Sarah. "We have strangers," he said. "We'll need the cakes you make with your best flour."

Sarah was careful with her flour. It took twice as long to grind, and she used it only on special occasions. "Who are these men?" she asked with a frown.

"I don't know who they are or where they have come from, but they are strangers as we also are strangers here."

Sarah shrugged and hurried off to make the cakes with her own hands. She was flattered that no one else made cakes as delicate and fragrant and that Abraham always bragged about them.

While Sarah was busy mixing the good flour with oil and spices, Abraham was hurrying out to where his flocks were grazing. He selected one of the fattest calves and ordered a servant to butcher and roast it.

Then, when everything was ready, he added some cheese Urim had brought him and had the whole feast carried out and set before the men.

When they had finished, they turned to him, and one of them asked,

"Where is Sarah, your wife?"

Abraham was astounded that the man knew Sarah's name. "She's in the tent," he said, motioning to one side where the tent stretched out seemingly dark and empty.

The stranger busied himself with wiping his hands on the damp towel one of the servants had brought. "Next year at this time," he said, "you and Sarah will have a son."

Abraham's eyes grew large with wonder and surprise. He glanced toward the tent, sure that Sarah, though hidden from view, would be listening.

The guest glanced toward the tent and then at Abraham. "Why," he asked, "did Sarah laugh?"

Abraham had heard nothing, but he was sure that Sarah, if she heard, would laugh. Even he found it hard to believe that Sarah, as old as she was, could have a child.

"You know," the guest continued, "Sarah did laugh. And furthermore she said to herself, 'Can an old woman like me have a baby?'"

Abraham was speechless. That was exactly what Sarah would say. Who was this guest who knew even the thoughts of someone like Sarah?

The guest stood up and motioned to the others that it was time to leave. "Abraham," he said, "is anything too hard for the Lord? Next year, just as I told you, Sarah shall have a son."

Abraham knew that Sarah had heard. He wondered what she would think of these ordinary-looking men making such promises. Furthermore, he wondered what she would think of their knowing so much about her, even that she had laughed.

As was the polite thing for any host, Abraham walked with the guests until they came to the edge of his encampment and he saw that they were going toward Sodom. Two of the men went on, and the other lingered for a while with Abraham.

* * *

Later when Abraham returned to the tent he found Sarah waiting for him. He was so disturbed by what the stranger had told him about Sodom that he had forgotten all else. She plied him with questions but found him strangely quiet. He said he could eat nothing and kept walking out to where he could look down the road leading to Sodom. She had expected him to discuss the visit of the men and their prediction but instead he sat with his head in his hands and seemed not to be aware of her presence.

That night Abraham stayed up late sitting by the fire, saying very little, but with an air of alertness even his men noticed. From time to time he stirred the fire with a stick and watched the sparks fly up and disappear. He didn't listen to their usual banter but seemed to be waiting for something or listening expectantly.

He had been sitting like that for some time when they all heard the sound of people approaching on the road. Abraham immediately stood up, as though he had been expecting someone, and they noticed that he was disappointed when it turned out to be Urim with his whole family.

When they reached the fire, Urim jumped from his donkey and came and fell at Abraham's feet. He was badly shaken, and it took some coaxing to get him to rise and tell what had happened.

"My lord," he said, "I have much to tell you of Sodom and Lot." When Abraham heard these words, he turned pale and pulled Urim to one side to question him.

The story Urim told was frightening. He had been at the gate when the two men arrived and had seen Lot take them home with him. Urim had gone around to the back of Lot's house to see if he could help in the entertainment. He was quickly sent off to bring his best cheese.

When he returned, he could not get near the house because there was such a riot. The men of Sodom had noticed the visitors and wanted Lot to bring them out so they could enjoy them. Urim hesitated; he was too embarrassed to go on. Finally he said, "You understand the sort of enjoyment the men of Sodom had in mind."

"Yes, yes," Abraham said. "I understand, though I would not have thought it would have gone so far."

"Oh, my lord," Urim said, "the men of Sodom have no shame."

"And . . ." Abraham said "what has happened to Lot and the men?"

"Well, Lot came out and pleaded with the men. He even offered to give them his two virgin daughters!"

"He offered his daughters?" Abraham was shocked.

"Don't worry. It was just a gesture. The men didn't want his daughters and Lot knew it."

"Oh Lot," Abraham whispered. "Can this be true?"

Urim grabbed his sleeve. "You haven't heard the worst. Before I knew what was happening, those men lunged at Lot and were going to take him. 'Who do you think you are?' they said. 'We let you settle here and now you want to tell us what to do. We'll do far worse with you now than what we intended to do with those other men.'"

"What happened to him?" Abraham turned away to hide his anxiety.

"Don't worry," Urim said in distress at Abraham's concern. "The two strangers saved him. They opened the door a crack and pulled him in just as the men grabbed at him. Then a strange thing happened. If I hadn't seen it, I wouldn't have believed it. Those men of Sodom seemed to lose their sight. They couldn't see a thing, and that is how I escaped."

Then Urim told Abraham how he had heard the two men warn Lot that the city would be destroyed. Urim told how Lot had made excuses and his wife had refused to leave her house and all her fine belongings when there seemed to be no danger. "I don't know what Lot will do, but I hurried home, packed up my family, and here I am. I believed those men."

Abraham was so disturbed, he didn't sleep that night but paced back and forth until Sarah came and urged him to go to bed and get some sleep. He didn't seem to notice her or hear what she was saying until at last she clung to him and begged him to tell her what was the matter. All he could say over and over again was "I'm afraid Lot will be destroyed with Sodom."

When she asked what made him think that Sodom would be destroyed, he grew thoughtful. "I'm afraid those men couldn't find even ten righteous people in all of Sodom."

"Ten people? Ten righteous people? What does that have to do with Sodom?"

Abraham didn't hear her but bowed himself to the ground and wept.

The next morning dawned with a brilliant sunrise, but there was an ominous stillness in the air. No birds sang, no wind blew, and the sky was clear and cloudless. The quiet made everyone in Abraham's camp uneasy.

Birds of every variety flew by as though it were the season for migration. Sparrows, mourning doves, hawks, and vultures raced overhead with urgency. Wild animals on the horizon ran as though instinctively sensing some danger.

Without warning a great shaking made their tents buckle and fold, followed by a blast, rolls of thunder, and flashes of light that cut across the sky. In minutes the sun was blotted out by towering black clouds that boiled and rumbled up out of the distant Jordan rift. The women screamed and hid their faces, and the children cried. Abraham stood looking toward Sodom and grieved for Lot.

Abraham assumed that Lot was dead. He blamed himself for not going with the strangers to warn him. "I could have forced Lot to leave," he said.

"If those men couldn't convince Lot, you wouldn't have succeeded either." Sarah was badly shaken by what had happened, but she had also grown impatient. Abraham was so concerned with Sodom, he hadn't even mentioned the prediction the men had made about a child. He was sitting alone on his side of the tent, and she knew he was grieving. It wouldn't do to rush in and ask for explanations. She would have to be more subtle. In the end she brought him a wooden bowl filled with some sweet dates and plump figs. Abraham knew very well what she wanted, so he said rather abruptly, "You did laugh, didn't you?"

Sarah backed off in confusion. "Well, imagine someone saying I would have a child. Imagine it at my age."

"And you not only laughed but you thought just as the man said, 'Can an old woman like me have a baby?' "

"What if I did?" she said defiantly.

"You have to admit he knew you laughed. He even knew what you were thinking. That's astonishing."

"I was embarrassed."

"But you were also excited when you started to think about it. Did you also hear him say, 'Is anything too hard for the Lord?' "

"I heard him, but what does it mean?"

"Some time ago, before the circumcision, Elohim came and spoke to me. He told me the same thing. He even gave me a new name. I'm to be called Abraham, father of many nations. He said your name was to be changed, too."

"My name?"

"Yes, you are now to be called Sarah, 'princess.'"

"Father of many nations and princess?" Sarah was curious, if not still skeptical.

"He also has a new name, El Shaddai, the almighty God. He is no longer just Elohim, the Creator God, or El Elyon, the Most High, but He is almighty. He can do anything."

"If I were to have this child," she said, cupping her breasts in her hands,

"I would need milk for him too. How could these sagging old breasts ever be plump again?" Her eyes challenged him to answer.

"I already have the child's name," Abraham said.

"You know his name?" Sarah was instantly alert. She sank down beside him. "You even know the child's name?"

"Of course. It was given by El Shaddai himself. He's to be called Isaac, 'laughter.'"

Sarah's hand flew to her mouth. "Because I laughed."

"No Sarah," Abraham said, "because I laughed."

At that Sarah broke into peals of laughter. "You laughed too?"

"I couldn't help it," Abraham said, breaking into uncontrolled laughter. "It did seem too ridiculous," he said when he could stop laughing long enough to talk.

Sarah was suddenly serious. "Was it the same men who warned you about Sodom?"

"Yes, both times it was the Lord."

"And Sodom was destroyed?"

"No one has been able to get close enough to see anything, but I'm sure Sodom no longer exists."

"Then if he was right about that . . ." Sarah hesitated, afraid to believe something that seemed so impossible, even ridiculous. "Of course," she added, "if I should really have a child, it would prove that Elohim or El Shaddai must be stronger than the old earth goddess and her curse. How strange!"

"We don't have long to wait," he said. "Next year at this time, they said. We'll see what happens."

*A*braham questioned numerous shepherds and various people fleeing from the devastation around the Sea of Salt. Some had been outside Jericho; others on the far side of the Jordan. All of them reported that anyone in or near the two destroyed cities could not have survived. The stench and fumes of fires that still burned made it impossible to go near the cities.

Though Abraham found it hard to believe that Lot was dead, he finally had to admit that Lot and his whole family seemed to have disappeared. No amount of questioning or searching turned up any news. Eventually Abraham gave up all hope of ever finding them alive.

Sarah grieved for Mara and the girls. She was constantly remembering things out of the past. How young they had been when they left Ur. How strange their new life had seemed. Most of all she wondered why such a terrible thing had to happen to such good people. "Mara was greedy," she said sadly, "but she didn't deserve this. I wanted to go to Sodom," she added, "it could have been me."

Hagar and Sarah's maidservants did not expect to see such grief. "She doesn't know how Mara envied and criticized her," they whispered.

In the days that followed it became evident that Abraham and his people would have to move. The sky was so overcast, they could no longer see the sun. Only a dull orange light let them know that another day had dawned. At night the moon and stars had vanished, and man and beast suffered from a choking, coughing reaction to the small particles in the hot blasts of air.

It was a difficult decision. The area to the north was too settled, and the vast, relatively empty area to the south was barren desert—not rolling sandy desert but a desert of low thornbushes, tamarisk, acacia, and some scrub oak. It was rough, lonely country, often mountainous, with such high places as Mount Paran and Jebel Magharar.

During the rainy season there were flowers, wild grasses, and gushing wadis that rushed in torrents from the high, rocky ledges. However, when the rains stopped, only the most tenacious shrubs survived.

Going from the villages above Mamre, where Abraham was camped, was a track called the Way of Shur. It led south. Abraham proposed to travel along that track. Followed to its final destination, the Way of Shur led down to Egypt. The route was not as popular as the Way of the Sea, but it was often used by people wanting to go down to Egypt from the cities such as Hebron, Bethlehem, and Jericho.

As soon as possible Abraham contacted the ruling dignitaries, asking permission to camp and let his animals graze on the open areas. He sent gifts and offered various favors. The most favorable reply came from the king of Gerar, named Abimelech. He held his position by the authority of the pharaoh of Egypt.

Reluctantly Abraham and his people gathered up their belongings and drove their cattle south to the desert lands of the Negev between Kadesh and Shur. Though the grazing there was good during the rainy season, it was now midsummer. They found nothing green except in places beside a brook or farther south along the River of Egypt. Abraham's herders traveled over a wide, open area of desert just to find food for their animals.

* * *

Urim found the city of Gerar quite pleasing. It was situated between the Way of the Sea and the Way of Shur, so it enjoyed many distinguished guests from Egypt and had the benefit of news and goods from important places. It sat at the mouth of the Wadi Besor—a rushing stream in the rainy season, but now in early summer, it was almost dry.

Abimelech's steward immediately encouraged Urim to settle among them, and it was not long before Warda was called in to entertain special guests from Egypt.

Gerar had many of the refinements of Egypt. Its houses were of cut stone, and it had quiet courtyards filled with flowers and pools. However, the king was often bored, and at such times he sought out people who could distract and entertain him. Urim soon became one of his favorites. It was always the same request; he wanted to hear more of his many adventures. Most of all he plied him with questions about his travels with the rich and wise tradesman known as Abraham.

On this particular day, Urim had come up from his camp to Gerar and was stopping by the palace before going home. He had brought some aged-to-perfection cheese to the open courtyard that was used as the king's kitchen.

He could tell they were expecting a special guest. There were spits with whole sheep turning on them and bakers shaping and thrusting bread into hot clay ovens. Over in a sunny corner, some old women sat picking the stones out of cracked wheat that would be mixed with drippings from the lamb and cooked with bread in the hot ovens.

Urim placed the cheese before the burly fellow in charge of the cooking. "Who is the favored guest this time?" he asked.

"Some very rich, very important fellow who has sent the king wonderful gifts of honey, sheep, and choice figs."

Urim was curious. "And this 'very rich' man's name?" he asked as he picked up a circle of bread, opened it, and drizzled into it olive oil followed by a sprinkling of herbs. Urim liked good food. As he went from place to place marketing his cheeses, it pleased him to stop in good cooking areas to taste the specialties for the day. He knew better than to sample the special food being cooked for the king and his guests, but bread, olive oil, and herbs were plentiful and he was welcome to as much as he wanted.

"Some wealthy man named Abraham," the baker said, holding the basting stick in midair while he talked. "He has tents like a small town and flocks that graze over the whole countryside. He has been very generous with the king."

Urim smiled and took two big bites to finish the bread, then quickly wiping his hands on his robe, he excused himself. "So, at last the king is going to meet the man he is most curious about," he chortled, "and I'm the one who can give him all the information he wants. He'll be glad to see me today."

Being a person who moved cautiously among his betters, Urim took care to send a message to the king, suggesting that he had important news for him. As he had thought, it was not long before he was ushered out to the king's balcony. The king, an elderly man of great size, who spilled over the edge of the large cushion he sat on, was checking the household business with his steward.

"Urim, my friend," he said, without looking up from a clay tablet he was studying, "what important news do you bring?"

"I see you are at last having your wish to entertain the mysterious trades-man who camps out under the stars." Urim rubbed his hands together nervously. "I think you envy him his freedom."

Abimelech frowned. In spite of his gray hair and beard that suggested a ripe old age, his bare arm showed muscles that still rippled, and his legs were strong and as well shaped as those of a younger man. He was robust and hardy and was noted for keeping all twelve of the women in his harem constantly pregnant. He had more than one hundred children and an untold number of grandchildren. However, for all his prowess and strength it was his wit and wisdom that made fast friends of all who knew him.

"I don't envy anyone living in tents," the king said. "I'm surprised he didn't stay in Egypt. I hear he had connections with the pharaoh. So why did he leave?"

Urim recognized this question as a probe for information, and he skillfully tried to avoid saying anything Abraham would not approve of. "What connections do you mean?" he asked.

"Why, I've heard his sister was actually taken into Pharaoh's harem and also that he was given one of Pharaoh's own daughters as a concubine."

"Yes, yes," Urim said, trying to edge away from such a dangerous subject. "He was a special friend of Pharaoh."

"I have also heard that he has had a son by the Egyptian woman. This would, of course, be a grandson of Pharaoh."

"Amenemhet favored him above all others."

"What is there about this man that a pharaoh should be so interested in him? Was it his wealth?"

"At first," Urim said with an air of importance, "it was his wealth and the fact that he was well versed in the wisdom of Chaldea. Later, after the pharaoh knew him, he himself was the fascination."

"Ah yes, he's not just a scholar. I heard how he rescued the kings of Sodom and Gomorrah from the Elamites. It's indeed amazing. Melchizedek has told me all about it."

"Melchizedek," Urim said, "you know him?"

The king didn't answer but continued to study the clay tablet. Finally, when it was obvious that the cheese maker was getting very uncomfortable, he said, "You have done well at avoiding my question. There must be some very interesting scandal connected with our illustrious trader, his sister, and Pharaoh. Am I right?"

The king looked up at him with a penetrating gaze that totally unnerved Urim. He backed up and bowed as though to leave but was surprised by two eunuchs who suddenly appeared behind him. He was trapped. The question was one he dared not answer.

"So I'm right. It was the sister that made them leave Egypt. No doubt she's ugly and plain."

"No, no," Urim objected, "it's quite the opposite. She's very beautiful."

"I know how it is. Pharaoh wanted to have the closest ties with Abraham, family ties, but . . ."

"Sarah," Urim sputtered, "she's very beautiful. Too beautiful."

"Then what went wrong?" The king was getting impatient with Urim.

Urim saw that it would be no time at all before the king would have the information out of him. Abraham would never forgive him. He had to think fast. "My lord," he said, "these are private matters a simple cheese maker is not privy to."

The king studied Urim for a few minutes and then waved him aside. "Never mind. I intend to invite Abraham and his family to live in Gerar. I intend to give them houses and servants or whatever they want or need. You can be sure that I will make a point of seeing this sister who is so beautiful."

That evening as Abraham and some of the men from his camp sat with the king of Gerar in his roof pavilion, they were impressed with his generosity. He had spared nothing in his effort to make them welcome and comfortable.

Abraham feared that the king would object to so many people with their tents and animals moving into the free lands and using the wells. However, he received nothing but words of welcome. More than that, the king asked him to consider spending some months in the city of Gerar. Abraham could not understand why the king put such an emphasis on their moving to the city. Stranger still, he made bold to mention that their women would be welcome at the palace.

Gradually Abraham understood his motives to be above reproach. Undoubtedly the king felt that they could be a help to each other. He could supply the king with food, and in return the king could let him stay with his flocks and tents on the Negev's free land.

Three months had gone by since Abraham's encounter with the mysterious visitors. In that time only one of the predictions had come true. Sodom and Gomorrah had been completely destroyed, but the other prediction of a child for Abraham and Sarah didn't materialize. Sarah noticed a few encouraging signs, but when nothing further developed, she told Abraham, "I'm probably wanting it so badly I've imagined the symptoms." She had known several childless women who had imagined a pregnancy. Their bellies had grown huge and they had the sickness, but nothing ever came of it.

"Even if I were expecting a child, who would believe it?" she said. "I would be scorned and laughed at."

Nevertheless Abraham made a special effort to please Sarah. When she wanted certain wild herbs to season her bread, he had the whole camp searching until they found them. When she wanted fresh figs, he bartered with a man who owned a fine fig tree. When she wanted to accept the king of Gerar's invitation to move into the city, Abraham could not refuse her. "Perhaps it is better to live in a comfortable house. If there is to be a child, this would be better."

At that time a great, unforeseen tragedy overtook the house of Urim. He was at the height of his popularity and prosperity, but life for Urim would never be the same again. There had been many caravans coming from various places with an assortment of travelers. Some were traders, others miners being taken to work in the mines of the Sinai, and still others diplomats from the court of Pharaoh. The trouble occurred during one of these visits by a diplomatic entourage.

Because they were from Egypt and spoke only Egyptian, Abimelech asked Urim to bring Warda to the palace to help entertain the wives of the prominent men. One of the dignitaries, an older man with cold, calculating eyes, came to the court of the women and watched Warda with growing fascination. "How is it this beauty is found so far from Egypt?" he finally asked the king. "Who is her husband?"

The king quickly informed him that she was married to a cheese maker, a clever fellow who had come by her while in Egypt. "She is indeed the joy of his life and the delight of his heart."

"Do you think he would consider parting with her?"

"He has little use for gold, and Warda is his prize possession. I doubt that you would be very successful."

"But the girl, she is wasted here. In my house she would have the clothes, jewelry, and servants that she deserves."

The king shrugged. "You could talk to him, but I would guess he would never consider such a thing."

"So he would be difficult, you think."

"Very difficult."

"Then it may take other means. I have thought of nothing else since I first laid eyes on her."

The king leaned back among the cushions and studied the Egyptian for a few moments. "I see that you have indeed been charmed by her beauty."

The Egyptian fingered his pectoral jewels. "Perhaps you have in mind to take her for yourself," he said with narrowed eyes.

The king motioned for his cupbearer and drank leisurely, wiping his mouth finally on his sleeve before answering. "I do not choose women for their beauty," he said. "I have my harem full, and each one has come with some political or practical advantage."

"Then you do not lust for her?"

"No, no, I'm too ambitious and cool-headed to look twice at a woman who could bring me only cheese."

The Egyptian was momentarily puzzled. "Then you have already decided not to have her."

The king handed his cup back to the cupbearer in one slow, deliberate movement, "Of course, I don't object to a woman's being beautiful, but my first concern is the advantage she can bring me."

"I don't understand," the Egyptian said. "You are a king. What can any woman give you that you don't already have?"

The king folded his hands over his protruding stomach and leaned forward, his eyes bright with the challenge of the Egyptian's question. "First," he said, "I look for a woman who can give me information. A woman who has lived in some great leader's harem, a woman who knows all his secrets. Next, I form alliances by marriage. They are the strongest, the most binding agreements. You might say the woman is almost a hostage if things go wrong."

"Then, of course, you are not interested in the concubine of the cheese maker."

"No, no," the king said, leaning back among the cushions, "I have other, more interesting projects in mind."

The Egyptian didn't forget Warda. His desire for her grew into a veritable fever, and he could neither sleep nor eat for thinking about her.

As he realized his entourage would be leaving in two days, he became frantic. He first sent a messenger to Urim, stating his desire to take Warda with him and promising to pay whatever the cheese maker might demand.

To his surprise, the servant returned, saying that Urim simply laughed and said no amount of gold would tempt him to give up Warda.

When the Egyptian heard that, he was more determined than ever to have her. In a frenzy of frustration he sent one of his wives to the palace where Warda was entertaining some of the wives. "Persuade her to come with us," he told her, "and I will give you whatever you ask."

Warda simply smiled at the Egyptian wife's request. "I am content," she said. "I love Urim and his wife. I have many friends here."

When Warda returned home and told Urim, he was disturbed. "The man isn't to be trusted," he said. "You must not go to the palace for any reason until they have gone. Tomorrow they will leave and things will be back to normal."

Warda did as he suggested. She spent the evening with Safra and Urim, counting the round smoky cheeses and labeling them. When it was dark, Warda and Safra pulled out a pallet and lay down to sleep in a corner of the courtyard while Urim went to his special place on the roof.

* * *

Later when Safra tried to tell what had happened, she said she remembered nothing until she heard a great pounding at the gate, followed by shouting and splintering of the wooden door frame. She saw men, at least five, burst into the courtyard with torches. They had stern, cruel looks and demanded that Warda come with them.

Warda was still half asleep when they snatched her from the pallet and hurried her out the door. Urim looked over the parapet and let out a roar of anger. He plunged down the steps two at a time, shouting that he would make fast work of them if they did not let Warda go immediately. He dashed out the gate as Warda screamed. There were the sounds of scuffling, shouting, and the dull thud of something hitting hard against the wall.

Within minutes the struggle was over. The men were gone, taking Warda with them. Urim lay limp and bleeding; his head had a great gash in it, and he was unconscious. Safra forgot everything but reviving him. She pulled him inside the gate. Unwrapping Urim's headpiece, she washed and bound up the wound. He remained unconscious for several days.

Warda was taken directly to the old Egyptian's rooms in the palace. She had her hands tied and her mouth bound with a piece of cloth torn from her elegant dancing skirt. She couldn't talk or scream as she came to stand before the old man. He had not gone to bed in anticipation of her arrival. "Ah," he said, rubbing his hands together in satisfaction, "she is indeed a beauty."

Warda motioned that she wanted to have the bands removed so she could talk. "Not yet, my pretty," the Egyptian said as he walked around her, so he could see her from every angle. "I want you to know all that I intend to do for you: the gifts you will receive, the treasures you will wear, and the exalted position you will hold in my house. When you hear all of this, you will see that it is better that you come with me than to have remained with that odoriferous goat man."

Warda struggled to get free so she could answer, but the Egyptian smiled with pleasure at her discomfort and held up his hand. "I regret having to keep you bound, but it is necessary until we are well on our way tomorrow."

He ordered an old woman to bring an Egyptian wardrobe, pectoral, girdle, and wig and see that Warda was dressed according to her new rank. "My dear," he said, running his hand down along her arm with obvious approval, "you will be the envy of all other women when I finish with you."

Warda could see that it would do no good to struggle.

She was outnumbered. There was nothing she could do. She watched the old man leave the room, leaning heavily on his steward. His robes were of the finest Egyptian linen, the rings on his gnarled fingers were huge, and the jeweled bands on his arms were of excellent craftsmanship. He was obviously wealthy.

After he had gone, the old woman freed Warda's hands, but left her mouth bound. Warda let her put the fine garments on her without a protest. All the time she listened to everything the old woman had to say about the Egyptian. "He's rich beyond anything you can imagine," the woman said. "He buys women like most of us buy bread, but then he tires of them." She stood back to look at Warda. Her eyes grew slotted and speculative. "I'll give you a month," she said. "By the time we're back in Egypt he'll be bored with you, just as he's been bored with all his other women."

The old woman didn't see how Warda bristled at her words. She went on talking about her master and the wonderful good fortune Warda had in being chosen by him.

When Warda was finally dressed and seated on one of the cushions next to the old man's place, she had already sized up her situation. There was no way she could escape. This man was too powerful and influential. She would have to play for time and decide what she could do. She must do all within her power to please him, or she would be in the most hopeless situation of all, a concubine languishing alone and forgotten, locked in his harem for the rest of her life. He must not become bored with her as he had with the others.

When the old man returned, he was obviously pleased with her appearance. "My dear," he said, "if I have the bands removed so you can talk, will you be happy?"

Warda nodded and tried to look submissive. He ordered the old woman to remove the bands. When it was done, he walked around her and looked at her. Finally he grimaced and rubbed his hands together. "I hope you will not be foolish enough to seek revenge," he said, looking long and hard at Warda.

"My revenge," she said with a look of proud scorn, "will be to never let you be bored."

"Ha, ha, ha, he, he, he," he laughed until he coughed. "So I will not be bored. We'll see. We'll see. But for now what marvelous threats you make."

Warda didn't smile. She almost felt a twinge of pity for this proud, arrogant, and selfish old man. By the time he realized his folly, he would have lost control completely, and she would be in charge.

* * *

When Abraham heard the news, he went immediately to visit Urim. He found him still unconscious, with Safra weeping by his side. "It is better a woman be plain and ugly," she said. "Poor Urim may never recover."

Abraham had to admit there was some logic in her statement. He had known situations where the husband had been killed so some more powerful man could have his wife. His old fear had been revived. In his eyes Sarah was still beautiful and charming. "I must remind Sarah to tell only that she is my sister if anyone asks," he muttered as he hurried back home and called for Sarah.

*W*arda's abduction left Abraham feeling wary. However, when on one of his visits to the king of Gerar, the king dropped a subtle hint that he would welcome closer ties with Abraham's family, Abraham suspected nothing.

Again when the king singled him out after a large dinner party, Abraham was not suspicious of any ulterior motive. "With your wealth and knowledge and my position," the king said, "we could engage in many successful ventures." He gave a knowing smirk, and his eyes grew narrow with speculation. He waited expectantly for some response, but when Abraham gave none, he backed off to wait for a more propitious time.

On another occasion, the king motioned for Abraham to sit beside him. He ordered the steward to bring his friend the choicest meats and the finest wine. Then very cautiously, he again edged up on the subject that most interested him. "I believe you have a sister," he said as he looked over a cluster of grapes and deliberately picked one or two before turning to get Abraham's answer.

Abraham looked bewildered for a moment, and then his eyes widened in understanding. "A sister, you say? Oh, yes, yes, I do have a sister," he hedged.

"And," the king continued in a light, bantering fashion, "is it not true that she was once actually chosen by Pharaoh for his harem?"

Abraham studied the king carefully before answering. He wondered what he had in mind. What had he heard? "I do have a sister and what you say is true."

Abraham looked around as though getting ready to leave, but the king put his hand on his arm and leaned forward. "Would it not benefit us both," he said, "if I should honor you, my friend, by taking your sister for my wife?"

Abraham was appalled. He looked at the king and saw his eyes gleaming with anticipation and his small teeth glistening in his gray beard. Abraham wondered what to say. How could he explain? He had never been good at explaining things, and this was unbelievably difficult.

The king seemed to think that Abraham was speechless with gratitude, and so with a conspiratorial look he turned to his other guests and Abraham escaped into the night.

The next day a messenger from the king arrived at Abraham's house. Not an ordinary messenger, but one of the king's chief counselors. The man came with servants bearing gifts from the king and some lovely young slaves to serve Sarah.

Abraham had not spoken to Sarah about the king's proposal. He had thought there would be more time. He had hoped the king would be busy with other matters and forget about establishing a bond between their two houses. Now he realized that the king was serious and determined. There was probably very little time, and he would have to tell Sarah immediately.

Abraham was filled with apprehension. For all his fears he had not really expected such a development in Gerar. In the first place Sarah was too old. How could it be that the king even thought of such a thing? More than that, what if it should come about that she was really pregnant? How could he ever explain that to the king?

He was so stunned, he didn't answer until the messenger grew nervous and started fidgeting with the fringe on his mantle. "I realize," the messenger said, "that you are overwhelmed with the great honor the king has bestowed on you. He has not seen your sister, but he has heard of her beauty. He knows she has spent time in the harem of Pharaoh. Having her in his own harem would be like adding a priceless diadem to a lovely necklace."

By that time Abraham had regained some of his composure. He remembered the recent trouble of the cheese maker, and he decided to proceed cautiously. "I've not told my sister," he said.

"The king is understandably impatient," the messenger said. "I'll come tomorrow and escort your sister to the palace. You can draw up the agreement later." The messenger rose from the cushions and bowed.

Abraham reached out to detain him. "Is it not the custom in your country," he asked, "as it was in mine, to draw up the agreement first?"

The messenger smiled as he straightened the folds on his long, full sleeves. "Of course, that is the usual procedure. However, the king is so eager for this alliance, he is willing to meet any demands you might have. So there is no need to wait."

As Abraham led the man to the gate he felt as though cold, dark fingers of fear were strangling him.

As soon as the man was gone, Abraham hurried to the women's quarters to find Sarah. She was in the courtyard, questioning the six young serving girls the king had sent. Sarah had just found out that they had been given her from the king as a wedding gift. She was puzzled. When she saw Abraham's troubled expression, she quickly called Hagar and asked her to take the young women and find a place for them to sleep.

When they were gone, she faced Abraham. "What is this all about?" she asked with a dangerous edge to her voice.

"My dear, we'll find a solution," he said, trying to take Sarah in his arms.

"A solution to what?" Sarah backed away and stood tense and suspicious.

"There has been a slight misunderstanding and . . ."

"What kind of misunderstanding?" Sarah insisted.

"It's the same thing that happened in Egypt. I let the king believe you were my sister, and now he has his heart set on taking you into his harem." Abraham blurted out the words and then turned as though to leave.

Sarah sprang after him and grabbed his arm. "And did you tell him?"

"Sarah, I wanted to tell him, but I remembered Urim. If he wants you, he can take you by force."

"You think . . . ?" Sarah was instantly apprehensive. "But what if I'm pregnant?" she urged.

"If I should even suggest you might be pregnant, it would unravel the whole tale. Where's your husband? Whose wife are you? If you are Abraham's wife, why did he say you were his sister?"

"And you think if we tell him I'm your wife, he may kill you and take me."

"That happened to Warda. Urim could have been killed."

Sarah's face clouded. She grasped Abraham's arm and clung to him. For a moment she struggled to regain her composure and then tilted her head back and looked at him. "When they come tomorrow," she said, "I'll go with them. There's nothing else to do."

She dropped her head to hide tears. Touched by her feeling, Abraham tilted her chin so he could look in her eyes. "We must take courage." he said. "If the Elohim helped me rescue all the people of Sodom and Gomorrah, surely he'll help me rescue you."

"Don't depend on the Elohim," she retorted with some of her old bravado. "I might never get home if we wait for Him." She turned and went into her courtyard to pack a few of her things. With a heavy heart Abraham stood looking after her.

The next day when the escort came, Sarah was ready. She had given instructions to the serving women and threatened the cooks lest they slacken off. Last of all she had called Ishmael to her. She tousled his hair and spoke with a catch in her voice. "You must be brave now," she said. "When I come back, we'll go out to see the young lambs and find birds' nests in the tamarisk trees."

"Where are you going?" he said, standing very straight and twisting the cord of his slingshot round and round his finger. His eyes were troubled and anxious.

For a moment she held him tight. When she released him, she managed to say, "Be a good boy, my love, and I'll be back as soon as possible."

At the last when the carrying chair was brought, she was calm, regal, and resigned. She was prepared to accept anything if it would keep Abraham out of trouble. There was one moment of anxiety as she stepped into the chair. She happened to look back and saw Hagar standing between Abraham and Ishmael. There was a look of satisfaction on her face that troubled Sarah.

However, once she was settled in the chair, Abraham came and paced back and forth, deciding on solutions and then changing his mind, mounting a pinnacle of hope and then plunging into total despair. He lingered by the carrying chair, saying words of encouragement, making promises, and raising last-minute questions. When everything was ready, he closed the curtains on Sarah's beloved face and backed away.

He followed the small procession out the gate and stood looking down the narrow, dusty road that wove in and out between the stone houses. When the wedding procession disappeared around a bend, he ran to the roof. He could see only the waving banners and faintly hear the wedding songs as they approached the palace gates. The banners disappeared and the songs ceased, and he realized that Sarah would be locked away from all outside contact within the women's quarters of the palace.

He went over and over the situation in his mind, blaming himself for cowardice, fearing for what might happen to her, and realizing that if Sarah was pregnant, the king would undoubtedly claim the child as his own. It was too hopeless, too complex, and too impossible. He had come so close to happiness, to having the most important part of the promise fulfilled, and now by his own cowardice he had spoiled everything.

Surely the Elohim was disappointed in him. How could he ask to be rescued a second time for the same bit of foolishness? On the other hand, why did the Elohim allow such things to happen? He buried his head in his hands and sank into utter despair.

* * *

When Sarah passed through the huge wooden gates leading into the court of the women, she entered a very different world. It was a world of barefoot slaves, dark-eyed, heavily jeweled women, and children running and jumping, with everyone shouting and talking at once. When they saw Sarah, all movement stopped. No one spoke and even the children gathered in little clusters to point and stare. All eyes focused on her. One or two women whispered and smirked as their eyes followed her every movement.

An old woman led her across the courtyard to a door on the far wall. The woman indicated that the rooms were to be hers. Stepping through the door, Sarah was surprised to find herself in a dark room with one window through which a shaft of sunlight poured. She could see the hard-packed mud floor, a large incense burner in one dark corner, and two big jars set in a clay frame in the other. Lifting the lids, she found that one contained water and the other grain to be ground for her portion of bread. A smaller jar contained oil.

One maid immediately began to measure out the grain; another went out to borrow grindstones; a third went to complain that they had no oven and no fire pot.

Sarah went to the doorway and looked out into the courtyard. A fountain played in the middle of a worn flagstone terrace. It was summer and several fig trees gave off a bit of shade. A large grapevine with dusty gray leaves grew over a trellis. Clay pigeon houses were attached to the far wall, and several peacocks dragged their lovely spotted tails across the yard.

All these things Sarah noticed at first glance. After that she looked closely at the women. They were all either pregnant or very fat. Some of them could barely walk, and others sat under the shade trees fanning themselves, too enormous to move.

An old woman sat motionless on a platform that sported a striped awning and had large armrests with banks of straw-filled cushions. Sarah noticed that her deep-set, birdlike eyes were focused on her; then slowly and with great effort, she raised her hand and motioned for Sarah to come to her.

The woman was wrinkled; her skin, like tough leather, hung from her slight frame in folds resembling an old familiar cloak. Her mouth opened and closed convulsively as though she were trying to say something. "You are the new wife," she said at last with great effort. "The king will not be pleased when he sees how thin you are."

Sarah stiffened. She supposed she did look thin and poorly fed to these women who obviously were so proud of their size. "Who are you and why is everyone so large?" Sarah countered.

The old woman stuffed a few summer figs in her mouth. Only when she had finished chewing and swallowing did she answer. "I'm the king's mother," she wheezed. "How does it happen you didn't know this?"

"No one told me."

"Why should you have to be told?" the old woman scolded. "Everyone knows I'm the king's mother."

Sarah could see she was going to get into trouble if she tried to explain, and so she went back to her rooms where the fragrant odor of baked bread greeted her. "Why are all these women so big?" she asked one of the maids.

"Don't you understand?" the girl said, looking at Sarah's trim figure critically. "Only women of great wealth and leisure can eat and enjoy themselves. Most men want such women for wives. The rounder they are, the more desirable. A richer dowry is given."

Sarah went back to the doorway and watched the women. Their jewelry was dazzling, their perfume suffocating, and their hair glistened with oil and fragrant herbs, but they were almost helpless, trapped in layers of fat. None of them moved, but instead constantly ordered the maids to do even the slightest errands.

Sarah looked down at her trim, firm body and wondered, Perhaps the king will send me back because I'm too thin. How awful it would be to depend on others to do everything! To never make your own bread or throw the shuttle on a loom or nurse a young lamb back to life. How sad their lives must be!

In the days that followed, Sarah discovered that the king preferred women who could bring him some advantage. She was of interest because she had been in the harem of Pharaoh. That gave her great status, even though her slimness was out of fashion.

217

She also discovered that he prided himself on having all of his wives pregnant as often as possible. As long as he could father children, he didn't fear getting old. "The king has so many children he can't even count them," one wife told Sarah.

Another wife confided, "If you think there are a lot of children here, you should see the reports from the king's trips into the neighboring villages. Most of the children he leaves to be raised by their mothers' families. Of course, he pays the families well. It is considered quite an honor to have borne the king a child."

Before two weeks had passed, Sarah had seen the king several times, and he had mentioned her brother. He had even asked her outright if she was really Abraham's sister.

She had told him she was and then had worried about it. What would he do? Why did he want to know?

The king had set the date given by his astrologers for the celebration of their marriage. He had personally arranged for entertainment and a great feast to be held in the public square. He had planned special gifts for Abraham and his family and friends. As each day passed his plans grew more elaborate, and Sarah grew more disturbed.

She had hoped that Abraham would have thought of some means to rescue her by this time. The memory of Hagar standing beside Abraham haunted her. More and more she began to fear that the two of them were together. Perhaps they were so happy, they didn't care whether the king of Gerar did marry her. Fear had grown to enormous proportions as the day before the final celebration dawned. She had given up all hope of rescue. She had done everything she knew to do, and nothing had persuaded the king to give her up. She had prayed to Abraham's God and still nothing changed.

Just when all hope was gone, something peculiar happened. King Abimelech had a dream.

* * *

It was on a night when the king had received news that both frightened and puzzled him. His chief eunuch had brought word that none of his wives had conceived during the past weeks. That news was followed by a report that two of his wives had miscarried. "It's as though some god or evil djinn has closed their wombs," a wise old midwife reported.

The king pondered all this. Certainly it was a message. Some evil was afoot. Some god had suffered an affront, or he himself had lost his virility. If such news got out, his subjects would lose respect for him.

He paced the floor and finally, when he went to bed, slept fitfully until he dreamed.

The dream was so real and so threatening that in the early morning when he woke, Abimelech called together all of the palace officials. "I've had a dream," he said. "If it's true, I'm in great danger."

"Tell us the dream," one of the wise men urged, "and we'll determine whether it's true or not."

"As I slept, during the fourth watch of the night, the great Creator God came to me and said these words, 'You are a dead man, for that woman you took is married.'"

"Which woman?" his chief counselor asked.

"The woman said to be the sister of my friend Abraham," he responded.

All the counselors and wise men began to talk among themselves, expressing amazement at this revelation. "Tell us everything," one of the wise men said finally. "Leave out nothing, for this is indeed a strange matter."

The king walked back and forth across the room in a highly agitated state. He stopped and fingered his beard as his eyes narrowed. "I explained to the God that if indeed she is his wife, both the woman and her husband had misled me. He told me that she was his sister, and she also said that he was her brother."

Again there were expressions of astonishment and disbelief, each person asking questions but not waiting for an answer. One old man raised his hand and insisted they be quiet so they could hear what happened next.

Slowly the king lifted his head and looked around at them as though trying to read their reaction before he told them more. Satisfied that they were sympathetic, he continued, "Then the Lord said to me, 'That is why I held you back from sinning against me and didn't let you touch her. Now go and give her back to her husband, and he will pray for you and you will live. He is a prophet.'"

The king paused. He seemed too overcome with emotion to go on. Again the counselors and wise men whispered and discussed the problem. Finally one of them spoke. "And," he said, "if you don't give her back, what will happen?"

"He said that if I don't give her back, I'm doomed to death along with all my household."

Immediately there was a great uproar. No one could hear himself, let alone anyone else. Each man had an opinion of what the king should do. Some were ready to see Abraham punished; others wanted Sarah humiliated and driven from the court. One man gained the floor and in a loud voice demanded silence. "It's obvious," he said, "that this Abraham and his wife are somehow favored and protected by the gods. Whatever is done, these two must not be harmed."

With this wise advice ringing in his ears, the king called Abraham to the palace to demand an explanation.

"Why have you done this vile thing to me? What have I done to deserve this? How could you even have thought of such a thing?" the king demanded.

Abraham was embarrassed and ashamed. "Well," he stammered, "I assumed I was in a godless place. I thought you might be like those strong men who will kill a man if they want his wife. Sarah is my half sister, and we've agreed to call each other brother and sister lest we run into some trouble in foreign countries."

Abimelech for the first time saw his friend as a man without a country. He saw that he had great wealth and knowledge but no strong protection other than this God he worshiped. This God was different from most gods. He was evidently ready to go to a great deal of trouble to help Abraham. He determined to ask Abraham more about his God.

He called his chief steward, "Bring my friend sheep and oxen and add servants, both men and women. When that is done, go to the court of the women and bring his wife and give her to him."

When Sarah was brought into the long hall, she was apprehensive. She had been told only that the king had called for her. When she saw Abraham before the king's throne, she expected the worst. With a great effort she stifled the impulse to run to Abraham. To her surprise she heard the king say to Abraham, "Look over my kingdom and choose any place you want to live."

Then he motioned for her to come forward. "See, I'm giving your brother a thousand silver pieces to compensate for any damage or embarrassment. I want this matter settled between us."

Though Sarah didn't understand what was happening, she knew enough to realize that her ordeal in the king's harem was over, and she could go home with Abraham. She bowed down to the ground. The king came and raised her to her feet and handed her to Abraham. "Now," he said, "justice has been done."

Abraham thanked him and offered to pray that the king's household would be cured of the curse of barrenness that had come upon them. The king promptly ordered his family and the whole court present to kneel, and then he knelt before Abraham. In the custom of the country, Abraham loosened his girdle, lifted the short kirtle or ephod he wore over his robe, and placed it over the head of the king. Then with one hand on the king's head and the other raised, he prayed a simple prayer asking that the king and his people be cured.

News of Sarah's miraculous release reached the house of Abraham long before he returned home. The wife and children of Eliazer led the servants and slaves with their children in a rousing welcome. Drums, reed pipes, and joyous yodels echoed up and down the street, spilled over the wall around the house and off the roof. When Sarah arrived, the women led her into the receiving room, all the time begging her to tell them everything about the king's palace. Sarah was tired and exhausted. "Where are Ishmael and Hagar?" she asked, looking around the room.

"They are back in their tent beside the brook of Besor," one of them said.

The thought flashed through Sarah's mind that Abraham had put them there on purpose. He didn't want the king to see Hagar, lest he take her too. Thinking of his concern for her handmaiden bothered her.

Later when she was alone with Abraham she begged him to take her back to their tent in the desert. "I've had enough of city life and palaces," she said.

When they arrived back at their tent, a surprise was waiting for them. Hagar came out to meet them with news of Lot. "He's come back with his daughters," she said.

"He's alive?" Abraham was overjoyed and ready to welcome him immediately.

"There's something different about him," she said.

"How different? What do you mean?" Abraham searched her face, trying to catch some hint of meaning.

Hagar shrugged and looked down as the toe of her doeskin sandal nervously dug in the sand. "Lot has grown old and his daughters are quarrelsome and jealous. They're both pregnant."

"Pregnant?" Abraham was surprised. "They must have gotten married after all."

"No, my lord," Hagar said as she hesitated and then turned away, giving the impression that she didn't want to answer more questions. Abraham noticed. He decided that whatever was embarrassing about their situation he would hear later. For now he intended to rejoice in Sarah's return.

*W*ith the weight of fear for Sarah's safety lifted, Abraham was jubilant. Sarah noticed the lilt in his voice and the sparkle in his eye, and she was satisfied that Hagar had not taken her place after all. Perhaps tonight, she thought, if I'm favored by the Elohim, Laughter will be conceived. She loved calling him Laughter. To already have a name made it seem much more likely that a child would be born.

With her rescue from the court of Abimelech still fresh in her mind and the news that the Elohim had stricken the court with barrenness, her faith in the impossible had grown. Had there not been men who turned out to be angels and had she not been told, "Is anything too hard for the Lord?"

She dismissed her maids and set a pot of incense burning. She pulled back the tent flaps, letting the full moon cast a soft radiance over the jars, chests, and cushions. She reached up and took down the brass mirror from the tent pole. "I don't feel old," she thought, "and I don't really look old by moonlight."

Like a young bride, she held her robe over the spiraling smoke from the incense. When it was permeated, she bent over the pot, holding fistfuls of her hair to catch the heady fragrance.

She could hear Abraham talking to his men on the other side of the tent. He spoke with such authority and dignity that men, important men, looked up to him and respected him and kings vied for his attention. She was amused and impressed by his serious demeanor, sharp wit, and austere bearing when he was with them. "But with me he is gentle and loving," she whispered in secret delight.

She leaned back on her heels and let her hair fall loose around her shoulders. At least until Hagar came he had loved only her. Now she had the recurring fear that Hagar might hold some special place in his heart. Hagar had given him a son and that made all the difference. "Dear God," she prayed, "let this be the night I finally conceive."

* * *

Abraham was able to forget Lot for a night, but the next day he was confronted by the problem. "Lot is too embarrassed to come to you," one of the servants reported.

"Is he well? Where's he been? I must see him immediately," Abraham spoke in clipped phrases, showing his frustration.

"My lord," the man said, growing fearful, "he's outside the camp with his daughters."

"Where are his servants, his tents, and his flocks?"

"My lord," the servant grew nervous, "he seems to have lost everything. Even his clothes are worn and ragged."

Abraham could not imagine Lot in such a state. Lot, the man who had always been so proud and even arrogant. The man who dressed in the finest linen, had his beard trimmed, tinted, and perfumed every day, and boasted of his adherence to fine manners. "Show me where he is. It's enough that he's alive. I feared that I would never see him again."

Abraham followed the servant through the camp, out to the tents of the shepherds. There, sitting outside one of the tents, was a man who looked faintly familiar. Abraham stopped and stared. It was indeed Lot. He was sitting hunched in an attitude of dejection. His clothes were threadbare, his feet shod with a country man's sandals made of woven reeds. His hair was long and matted.

Abraham hesitated. He didn't want to shame Lot in any way. It was obvious that Lot had been left with nothing. "Lot," Abraham said as he came forward.

Lot looked up, startled. He squinted into the sun. His mouth fell open. Instead of getting to his feet and swaggering forward to embrace his uncle as he would have done in the past, he fell to his knees and buried his face in his hands. "My uncle," he said, "for my daughters' sakes, have mercy."

Abraham reached down and lifted him to his feet. "Thanks to our God, you are safe. I was afraid I would never see you again."

"How can you say, 'Thanks to our God'? Your God brought about all this destruction. It's mere chance that I escaped."

"Not chance, Lot. All Sodom would have been spared if there had been ten righteous people in the city."

"How do you know this? Who told you this?"

"The Elohim, he told me. He said, 'Shall I not tell my friend Abraham this thing that I do?'"

"So then it was set. Fate decreed it; it was hopeless from the beginning."

Abraham sadly shook his head. "No, Lot, not hopeless. I bargained with him. He agreed to spare Sodom if he could find even ten righteous people. In the end your family was the only one rescued."

Lot was speechless. He studied his uncle, looking for some wavering in his conviction. When he found none, he began to sputter. "It would have been better for me had I died in Sodom," he blubbered. "I have nothing. I've lost everything."

"No, no," Abraham protested. "It's easy to replace things but impossible to replace family. Come, have something to eat. Let us get some clothes for you, and then I'll hear your story."

It was late in the day before Abraham was finally free to hear Lot's story. Lot asked to bring his daughters and speak with his uncle alone. Though he was now well dressed and had been fed, he had not lost his demeanor of defeat. He sank down on the cushion opposite his uncle and motioned for his daughters to sit off to one side. "My uncle," he said, "I'm grateful for your kindness. You may regret it when you've heard my story."

"I know much of your story already. It's tragic."

"Most of the tragedy we brought on ourselves."

"I don't understand."

"Mara died, you know."

"No, I didn't know. How?"

"It was her fault. The visitors told us to hurry and not look back. Mara was outside the city when she thought of a carnelian necklace she loved. She insisted on going back. I couldn't stop her. She didn't even reach the city before she was killed, covered with burning ash."

"But you and your daughters escaped."

"We barely escaped. We first went to a small town and then hid in a cave. We thought we were like Noah, the only ones left alive. That's why my daughters . . ."

Lot couldn't finish the sentence. He hung his head in embarrassment. His daughters looked at each other and finally the elder spoke. "You must understand, we thought we were the last people alive. Our fiancés would not come with us. They were lost with Sodom."

After a slight pause she went on. "It seemed important to keep life on earth alive." She was at a loss for words. She looked at the younger sister who hesitated only a moment and then spoke in a voice so low it was hard for Abraham to hear. "We lay with our own father so we might have children," she said.

"You what!" Abraham was puzzled, then astounded.

"We made him drunk, then lay with him to have children. Is that so wrong?"

Lot wiped the perspiration from his brow and shifted uneasily. "Wrong? Of course, it's wrong," he said. "Even if they thought it was their only chance to have children, it was wrong. You see how Sodom has changed us."

For the first time Abraham understood why ten righteous persons could not be found in all of Sodom. Everyone, even his nephew, was tainted. However, he saw the suffering involved and judged they had been punished enough. "I don't condone what has happened," he said finally, "but we are your family and you can depend on us."

Lot broke down and wept. His two daughters gratefully accepted the help Abraham offered and began to relax.

A week later, after Lot had recovered sufficiently, he was heard complaining, "We all know, if it hadn't been for the promises my uncle kept talking about, I wouldn't have been here. It's really my uncle's fault. And to think, none of his promises have ever come true."

* * *

Three months passed before Sarah was sure she was pregnant. She immediately wanted everyone to know. To her surprise, people looked at her with either pity or disbelief. Some were scornful that she should even imagine such a thing. "Never mind," she said, "you'll see."

As the months passed it was true that she had all the signs of being pregnant. Her stomach grew large like a ripe melon, and her breasts filled out until they looked like a young girl's. Most of all, she began to openly resent Hagar. "Hagar was a mistake," she told Abraham one evening. "If I had just waited."

"But you didn't, and now we are responsible for Hagar. We have a young boy who loves us as his parents."

Sarah tossed her head and her mouth stiffened. "We no longer need her. Once I have my own son she can have Ishmael back."

"Have Ishmael back?" Abraham said. "What are you suggesting? He's my son and I love him."

"He's not really a true son, Abraham. My son will be the son of the promise."

"Sarah, Sarah, what terrible things are you thinking?"

"It seems very simple to me. Before I found I could have a child, I needed her. Ishmael seemed the only son I could have. Now everything is different."

Abraham was astounded by her reasoning. He loved Ishmael. Ishmael was a bright boy who thrived outdoors. He remembered how the Elohim had told him that Sarah would bear a son, and it was this son by which his seed would be called and nations blessed. He struggled to remember what had been said about Ishmael. No word of covenant was mentioned, but blessings were promised and the statement was made that he would bear twelve princes.

Abraham pondered over the word princes. It was true that if Ishmael were in Egypt, he would be a prince. Pharaoh was his grandfather. "How strange," Abraham thought, "he shall be the father of princes."

There was also a sense in which he was a son of the covenant because Ishmael had been circumcised.

For the first time Abraham realized that with the birth of Sarah's child there could be conflict. He would have to be strong. He must not let Hagar or Ishmael be hurt.

The time passed quickly. Sarah gloried in every aspect of her pregnancy. She could talk of nothing else. When she first felt movement, she held both hands over her rounded stomach and waited. When she felt again the forceful push, she laughed. It was real. She was not mistaken. She was really going to be a mother, even at her age.

When the days became hot and the women came to wring out cloths in cool water to place on her head and wrists, she laughed. When she was too big and clumsy to grind the grain for her sweet cakes, she laughed. When her clothes no longer fit, she laughed. Everything was a delight. Nothing was burdensome or hard. To carry a child was infinitely wonderful, and Sarah intended to enjoy every minute of it.

"Wait until she comes to the birthing stool," the women whispered among themselves. "She won't laugh then. She won't think it is such a wonderful thing."

They were wrong. Sarah bore the hours of trauma and pain without complaint, because even they were part of her need and desire. When the small red screaming bundle was at last held up for her to see, she reached out for him. "How beautiful he is!" she cried.

As people gathered around to see the child, they asked what he was to be called. Abraham stepped forward and took the child in his arms. They all became silent, watching him, noting the look of wonder and joy on his face. "Isaac, Laughter, he is to be called Isaac," Abraham said.

Sarah looked up at Abraham with tears in her eyes as she said, "The Elohim has kept his promise and brought me laughter. Everyone who hears of this will laugh and rejoice with me. How impossible it seemed that I should give my husband a son in his old age."

That night as Abraham walked out under the stars, he felt new excitement. Sarah was a mother at last. The old curse of Ningal was broken, which proved the Elohim was stronger than the earth goddess. To promise a young virgin a child was simple, but to give a woman well past the age of childbearing a child was an astonishing miracle.

*　*　*

Sarah didn't complain when Abraham and the men of the tribe came to circumcise Isaac when he was only eight days old. "If the Elohim has seen fit to give me a child," she said, "surely I can trust him to protect him. He is a strong child."

Abraham reached down to take him from her arms, and for a moment she clung to him. "Don't be afraid," he said, "there will be many mothers after you who will cringe at such a thing. Let it be known that you were strong and trusted the Elohim."

Sarah let him go but hurried after Abraham to the tent door where she stood and wept until she heard the cry that told her the worst was over. When Isaac was brought back to her, she studied his little face for any sign of pain. When there was none, she laughed and put him to her swollen breast as a reward for bravery.

From the very first, Sarah began to shut Ishmael out. She wouldn't let him hold the baby, and she grew impatient when he wanted to show her an unusual rock formation or tell her of some adventure. In the past she had taken great pains to listen and encourage him, but now she was always too busy. Worst of all, she finally told him in a moment of impatience that she was not his mother.

"Hagar, the Egyptian, is your mother," she said and didn't notice the hurt and shock evident in Ishmael's face. He backed away and went out of the tent to hunker down in the crevasse of a great rock. He brooded and pondered and finally hated the child who had come to take his place.

When he returned to the camp, he wouldn't eat and couldn't sleep. He refused to see Hagar, and when Hagar mentioned the problem to Sarah, she was so preoccupied with the new baby, she answered, "He'll get over it. He had to know sometime."

Hagar was distraught. She had no patience with Sarah and was heard openly criticizing her in the camp. "How can she not see how she has hurt Ishmael?" she would ask.

Abraham suffered as he watched from afar. He loved Ishmael. He was proud of the boy. Everything he had ever wanted in a son was exhibited in the boy. He learned quickly. No one else could match him in physical prowess. He already had mastered the art of reading the wedge-shaped letters used to keep track of sales and purchases, but most of all he was unusually sensitive to anything spiritual.

"What will happen to Ishmael?" was Abraham's constant prayer. "The boy must not be hurt in any way by what we have done."

Gradually the realization came that at some point he would have to give Ishmael up. He would have to give him up—not just for Sarah and Isaac's sake but for Ishmael's as well. What would it do to this proud, happy boy to be displaced by a younger brother? He was the grandson of Pharaoh, and he must at some point recognize that relationship.

"In the meantime," Abraham decided, "I must teach the boy everything of importance. Most of all I must teach him all I know of the Elohim. I will have to rely on the Elohim to protect and guide him when I am not able to be there."

* * *

The birth of Isaac minimized the births of Lot's grandsons by his two daughters. To everyone's chagrin, they named the sons in such a way that no one was ever able to forget their unholy origins. The elder daughter named her son Mo-ab, "from my father," and the second daughter named her son Ben-ammi, "son of my people."

When they were circumcised by their great-uncle Abraham, an old man predicted, "These sons will be the founders of a great people. The first will be remembered as father of a people called the Moabites and the second as father of ones called Ammonites." It was usual for predictions to be made at special events, so no one thought much about what the old man said.

Only Abraham saw the small, helpless creatures and marveled. Something so small and helpless, how could it be possible for such great and momentous things to come of it? he thought.

*　*　*

The enmity between Sarah and Hagar reached a crisis on the day set aside to celebrate Isaac's weaning. Isaac was three years old, and Abraham had planned an elaborate celebration for his young son. There were magicians, story-tellers, jugglers, and musicians performing before the small boy who sat in the place of honor on his mother's lap.

Several poets chanted praise in his honor, and a singer from the town of Gerar, who usually sang for the king, composed a song especially for him. Though Isaac was too young to fully understand all that was done, he accepted the accolades as though it were perfectly natural and right that he should be so honored.

Ishmael watched from a distance with scorn. He was sixteen and could never remember such a feast or celebration being given in his honor. It also became more evident than ever that he had been supplanted by the young child. Every look of approval, every bit of praise, stabbed Ishmael to the heart. He was the elder son. "Why," he wondered, "should the birth of this child have changed everything?"

He had not intended to tease or torment Isaac, but when the two were finally together and the sweet cakes were being passed, he could not resist tell-ing the child that he was too little to have one. When the dancing started, he told Isaac he was too clumsy and then proceeded to trip him. For each offense Isaac cried and ran to tell his mother, and Sarah came with eyes blazing to scold Ishmael.

Ishmael could not endure the look of raw hatred in the eyes that had such a short time before looked at him with love and approval. To make mat-ters worse, Hagar had seen everything. She didn't approve of the way Ishmael teased Isaac, but when Sarah scolded her son before all the dignitaries, Hagar lost all patience. "Come," she said to Ishmael, "we have seen enough of this party. We don't need more of their insults."

At the same time Sarah was burning with indignation that her little son should be so tormented. As soon as the guests had gone, she cornered Abraham. "My lord, you must get rid of that slave girl."

"Slave girl, you call her a slave girl?" he said. "She's no longer your beloved handmaiden?"

That made Sarah even angrier. "Whatever she's been to me in the past is unimportant," she said.

"But Sarah," Abraham said, trying to reason with her, "Ishmael is my elder son. Nothing can change that. We must be fair."

Sarah became desperate. Her eyes flashed dangerously. Her long fingers clutched Abraham's cloak and dug into his arm. "Her son must not share with Isaac. We must not let him claim the place of firstborn." Each word was like a sword thrust. "He's not your true son. He's not the son of the promise. You must get rid of them."

"What do you mean, 'get rid of them'?" he questioned as he felt his stomach churn with fear of her answer.

"You must get rid of them. Hagar and her son must go. There will never be a moment's peace for Isaac as long as Ishmael is here."

Abraham tried to reason with her. "You are tired and distraught. Things will look different tomorrow," he said.

Sarah bristled. Her voice grew strident and harsh. "They have to go!" she screamed. "Promise me. Promise me on your father's beard that you'll send them away. I can't endure the sight of them."

"We'll sleep and discuss it tomorrow," Abraham said. "It's too late and you're tired."

"No, no, I'm not tired," she insisted, clutching his arm again and searching his face with unbridled intensity. "They have to go. If you don't drive them out, I will. I swear by our father's memory, I will drive them out."

Abraham remembered Sarah's strong action with Hagar in the past, and he realized that this time it could be worse. Sarah was so angry, she would hurt both Hagar and Ishmael. He must act fast so harm would not come to them.

"I will see to it in the morning," he promised.

"If I wake and find they are not gone, I'll handle it myself," Sarah threatened. "I'll not have my son tormented, nor will I let Ishmael steal Isaac's rightful place."

Abraham didn't sleep the whole night long. He heard the night watchmen as they made their rounds, the screeching owl, and the rustle of a small mouse getting into the new supply of grain that stood just outside the tent door. He prayed and waited. He worried and agonized, but there seemed no solution. Either he would send Hagar and Ishmael away, or Sarah would take it into her own hands. Hagar was her handmaiden. It was Sarah's right to do with her as she wished. If anything else were to be done, it would have to be done quickly.

He earnestly prayed about it, and as he hoped the answer came again and again, "Listen to whatever Sarah tells you. Don't be so disturbed about Ishmael. I will make him into a nation also because he is your son."

Abraham became resigned to a heartbreaking decision. Hagar and Ishmael must go, and they must go quickly. He must first get them out of the camp, and then he would make arrangements for them to go to Egypt.

By the first light of dawn he had a tentative plan. He wasn't pleased with it, but he couldn't think of anything else. There were no good choices.

He called Hagar and tried to explain the situation. "It would be well for Ishmael," he said, "to visit his grandfather the pharaoh as soon as it can be arranged."

Hagar had heard parts of the argument of the night before, and she realized what Abraham's decision had been. "You don't have to talk in riddles," she said. "I see how things are. It's obvious we are the ones who must go."

Abraham was finding the situation far harder than he had imagined. In the end they both knew it was impossible for her to stay. He drew a chart in the sand showing her how if she would go slightly south and east, she would come to the place of seven wells. "One of those wells is mine. My men dug it. You will find some of my people there. Stay with them until I am able to make arrangements with a caravan going to Egypt."

It wasn't more than a day's journey, and so he filled a skin with water and grabbed the first large flat loaves of bread as they came hot off the rounded clay dome of an oven. "Here, take this," he said, stacking the bread and helping her place it on her head wrapped in a scarf. "This should get you there. Remember it is the place of seven wells. My well is the seventh. Ishmael knows my shepherds, and they will welcome you."

Hagar called Ishmael, and the boy came, sullen and hurt. But he was ready to do whatever was asked of him. "You must take care of your mother,"

Abraham said, looking with pride and sadness at his young son. "You will have to make all the arrangements for staying with my shepherds until I can find a caravan going down to Egypt. You are a man now, and your mother is in your keeping."

"Will we ever see you again?" Ishmael's eyes were red and dark circled, his mouth twisted with the hurt.

For a moment Abraham could not speak. The utter pathos of this tragedy leaped out at him and threatened to crush him. He saw the years passing and the impossibility of knowing what was happening to this dear son and his beloved mother. "Elohim will bring you back in time," he said at last with great effort.

Ishmael reached out, and with a wrenching sob Abraham gathered him into his arms. "My blessing goes with you and my love surrounds you. The Elohim will be with you."

Before the sun came up Ishmael and his mother started out beside the brook of Besor. Abraham watched them go until they passed out of sight beyond the campfire into the deep shadows. "Oh, my God," he prayed, "take care of them. Let no evil thing befall them."

Having prayed, he turned back toward the camp with a heavy heart.

*T*hough Ishmael had been with his father to the place of the seven wells and thought he knew the way, he could see nothing that looked familiar when the sun came up. There was a great sameness about everything. In the distance loomed limestone ridges; close at hand sat sand dunes and loess hills swirled by the wind. An occasional acacia added a welcome sprinkling of dull green, and always there were the thornbushes that tore at their clothes.

There was no sound. A great stillness surrounded them while the sun, in stifling brilliance, wilted them. They drank freely of the water they carried, saying, "When we come to the wells, there will be plenty."

However, when nightfall came, they still had not come to the wells. They sank down exhausted beneath a gnarled terebinth and drank the last of their water. "Surely by morning," they reasoned, "we will be at the wells."

They dared not sleep at the same time. Wild animals came out at night, and the fearful djinn were said to haunt these desert places. Hagar insisted that Ishmael sleep first while she watched and then they would change places.

Ishmael had shouldered the responsibility for them both, and he was exhausted. He was suddenly the protector, and she the one needing and welcoming the protection.

"I have my sling, and I am better than most with the bow and arrow," he said proudly.

He had cautioned her about saving the water and their bread. "The desert can be cruel. Until we see the well, we won't be safe."

When the stars came out, he woke her and said they must make use of the cool night air and stars to guide them. Hagar was astonished at his knowledge. "Where have you learned so much about the stars and traveling in the desert?" she asked.

"You forget, I've gone many places with my father." She noticed Ishmeal's pride when he spoke of his father. She winced with the pain of realizing that he had not yet called her "Mother."

Closed in by the darkness she let her thoughts circle around her hurt. Sarah stole my only treasure, then tossed it off like refuse, she fumed. To be called mother by this godlike child, how wonderful, what joy. I gave away so much.

As light began to erase the stars and make long shadows of the rocks, she saw him dimly through her tears. How noble and good he is, she thought.

He stopped and motioned her to sit beneath an outcropping of rock while he prayed. She saw him spread his outer cloak over the sand, then kneel with face upturned and hands folded. She wondered what he prayed. To what god did this grandchild of the pharaoh address his prayers? He wasn't facing the rising sun as Pharaoh would have done, nor was he facing any earthly thing. It was undoubtedly the God of Abraham, the unseen, Creator God, he prayed to.

When he finished his prayers, he came and sat beside her and watched while she divided the last loaf of bread. She didn't dare look at him when she said, "The water's gone, and this is all our bread."

He didn't answer but stuffed the bread in his shirt and stood up. "There are no familiar landmarks. It's all the same. We'll have to keep to the south and head toward the east. We should soon come to my father's shepherds and his well."

There it is again, she thought. He loved his father and he loved Sarah as his mother, but I, Hagar, am nothing to him.

He was quiet and anxious as he pushed on through the heat of midmorning. The blowing sand swirled and twisted, stinging their eyes and hitting like sharp arrows. The jagged rocks pierced their sandals and cut their feet. They leaned against the wind and made little progress.

A sense of desperation hovered over Ishmael. He stopped often and looked around, climbed dunes, and gazed in all directions. She saw his face grow red and fevered. He lifted his feet with great effort, and each time he climbed a dune it was with difficulty.

Just as they were coming out onto a plateau, they heard quite distinctly the pounding of hooves and the raucous laughter of men. Hagar looked at Ishmael and smiled. "It must be our shepherds coming out to help us."

Ishmael put up his hand in warning. "Our shepherds would be on foot, and there would be the sound of animals. Let me do the talking. This could be dangerous."

As the men swung around the limestone ridge and came into view, they reined in their mules and advanced cautiously toward Hagar and Ishmael. When they came close enough, it was evident they were not going to be friendly. Their eyes were hard, and their mouths set in a hostile grimace. "Who are you and where are you going?" their leader demanded.

"I am Ishmael, son of Abraham, and I am going to his well for water."

The men broke into mocking laughter. "Abraham's well? He has no well. Go back and tell him all the wells belong to the king and we are his guards."

Ishmael drew himself up and faced them bravely. "We have no herds or cattle with us. There are only this woman and me, and we have come for water."

The men talked together, and then the leader announced, "There is no water here for strangers."

"We are not strangers," Ishmael said, trying to control his voice so they would not sense his desperation. "I am the son of Abraham who dug the seventh well. I was with him when he dug it, and I have every right to draw water."

The men's faces clouded, and their voices became harsh and their words cruel. The leader of the group unfastened a whip from his belt and cracked it in the sand at Ishmael's feet. "We are guarding all the wells. You will get no water here." With a string of curses, he turned and led his men back the way they had come.

Ishmael's face was ashen. Without saying a word, he turned and walked over to the remains of a huge tamarisk tree and sank down on the shaded side.

Hagar could see he had lost all desire to struggle. He had given up. It was useless without water. In the relentless heat no one could live long without water.

She moved off to one side, pulled her mantle up over her head, and crumpled down onto the sand. There was no longer time for angry thoughts. She was too tired and desperately thirsty. She felt dizzy and nauseated. How long does it take for one to die in this heat? she wondered. Her own death didn't matter, but to see the boy die—this lovely, splendid son—was more than she could bear.

Now it's come to this, she thought. I who was once the terror of Pharaoh's harem will die out here in this wilderness and will be eaten tonight by jackals. It is too much, too much. I'm helpless. I can't bargain or barter or steal one drop of water for me or my son.

She sat up and flung back her mantle. Sarah, what are you doing now? she thought. Are you laughing? Abraham, how could you make the choice of laughter over my son who loved you so? How could you in the end choose Sarah and her rigid bitterness over the warm love I gave you?

You said it was the Elohim who told you to send us out as Sarah demanded. So even your God rejects me.

She stretched out along the burning sand, covered her head with her mantle and finally, too weak to move, grew quiet, waiting for death. How it would come she didn't know, but its coming was sure. Perhaps an angel would come and lift her out of this shell that wrenched and choked for lack of water. How fragile a human being was after all. Even the great Pharaoh could not live without water.

How long she lay there she could never remember, but the voice that spoke to her she would never forget. It was a soft, quiet, but very distinct voice. "Hagar," it said, "do not be afraid. God heard the boy crying. You must lift him up, take him by the hand, for I will make a great nation of his descendants."

Then as she rose to go to the boy and do as the angel had commanded her, she looked down toward the valley and saw in the place where the men had been was a well. She guessed by its location it must be the seventh well, Abraham's well. The men had left, and no one was in sight.

Quickly she got the water skin and made her way down to the well. They would not die after all. She had not been rejected by Abraham's God. He had not forgotten or forsaken her. She could feel joy surging through her, strengthening her. The joy and the new strength somehow were one. With water Ishmael would live.

Gently she cooled her son's fevered brow with the water, then lifted the skin so he could drink. His eyes opened, and she could see his surprise and something more. It was as though for the first time, he was really looking at her and seeing her. With great effort he reached inside his robe and pulled out the half loaf of bread and handed it to her.

She broke off a small piece and handed the rest back to him. "Eat it all," she said. He was dazed and bewildered. He had been prepared for death and suddenly there was water, enough water to be poured over his hands and cool his brow. His parched lips were dripping with the cool, crisp water as he questioned, "How?"

Hagar laughed and sank back on her heels. "Your father's God, the

Elohim, opened my eyes and showed me the well. It was for your sake He did this thing."

Ishmael managed a wan smile. "Then do you believe in my father's God?" he asked.

For a moment she hesitated. When she spoke, it was as though she was saying something she had already worked through in her mind. "I once trusted in a small clay idol of Hathor. It may seem strange to you, but I thought she was real and could do wonderful things for me."

Ishmael was listening to her with a new awareness and understanding. "What happened to her?" he asked.

"I found she was nothing but a piece of clay. It was all in my imagination. There was no goddess, nothing but the clay image."

"How did you know?"

"I flung her away and she broke into small pieces. She was never anything but clay."

"And..."

"I learned one must be careful. Not all gods are real. Some are just clay."

Ishmael lay back with his eyes closed. She thought he was asleep and started to move. He put out his hand and stopped her. "I'm glad," he said, "that you are my mother."

Hagar thought her heart would burst. All the anger, hurt, and frustration were washed away in that one lovely word. He had called her mother.

＊ ＊ ＊

After Hagar and Ishmael left, Abraham did not have a moment's peace. He had time to think, and he realized all the things that could go wrong before Hagar and Ishmael reached the well. He told Sarah what he had done and saw that she felt no remorse. She even smiled and called him the old, tender names of endearment. She was delighted.

It was about noon when several of his chief herdsmen rode into camp. They were angry and frustrated, and the news they brought was disturbing. They told how Phicol, the commander of Abimelech's army, had seized the well Abraham had dug and claimed it as belonging to the king. "Phicol has gone to report to Abimelech but has left his men guarding the wells. Our shepherds can't water their flocks."

As soon as Abraham heard the news he realized that if his shepherds could not get near the well, neither could Ishmael and Hagar. There were no other wells or sources of water, and they would die of thirst.

"We must go at once to Abimelech," Abraham said as he began putting on his best cloak and quickly fastening it with a toggle pin.

They had sent word ahead, and the king was waiting for them when they arrived. His first words surprised Abraham. "God is with you in everything you do," he said. It was obvious that the king was remembering the curse that had fallen on him and his whole court when he took Sarah for his harem. He feared what Abraham might do with such power, and he wanted to extract a promise from him that he would not deal falsely with him or his children.

Abraham's mind was on the well and the problems it had caused. It took a few minutes for him to realize that the king was afraid of him. Perhaps the king even thought he had come on an errand of revenge.

Quickly Abraham swore that he would do nothing to harm the king or his family. Then pressing his advantage, he complained to Abimelech about the well. "They have taken a well my men and I dug," he said.

"I know nothing of this problem," the king said. "This is the first time I've heard of it."

"Then come with me to the seven wells and we'll settle this matter as friends."

The king was relieved that Abraham asked such a simple thing of him, and so they agreed to ride immediately to the site of the wells.

Abraham with his herdsmen and seven lambs arrived first at the wells.

"What are these for?" the king asked on his arrival as he pointed at the lambs.

"It is not going to be enough," Abraham said, "that we have made this agreement and treaty between us. These lambs are witness to the fact that I dug the well and it is mine."

The king agreed and further insisted that from that time on the place be called Beersheba, the well of the oath, as a constant reminder of their sworn agreement.

When the ceremony was over, the king came to the tents of Abraham's shepherds for a great feast.

After the guests had gone, Abraham asked his host if anything had been heard of his son Ishmael and Hagar. "They are here waiting to see you," the man said, clapping his hands so his servant appeared. "Bring the young man and his mother. Our lord, Abraham, wishes to see them now."

Moments later Ishmael and Hagar appeared at the tent door. They had completely recovered from their ordeal and were overjoyed to see Abraham.

Ishmael told his father everything, even to the miraculous voice that saved them by guiding Hagar to the well. He ended by proudly telling him that he had arranged for them to go in a caravan that would leave at the end of the week for Egypt.

Abraham was impressed but anxious. "Are you sure you can manage this?" he asked.

Ishmael nodded. "With the help of the Elohim I will succeed."

* * *

The next day Abraham took Ishmael and some of his herdsmen back to the well. "I am going to plant this tamarisk tree beside the well," he said. "It will give shade to the stranger who needs water, and it will be a reminder forever that this is my well."

One of his herdsmen came forward with the small shoot, and another came with a digging tool. In a short time the tree was planted, and the herdsmen went back to their work. But Abraham and Ishmael stayed at the well. "My son," Abraham said, "when you come this way and your flocks or people need water, you will know this well by the tamarisk tree beside it. Never again will you be without water in Beersheba. And when you see this well, you will be reminded of our God and his faithfulness. We will call upon him here as El Olam, the everlasting God."

Before the caravan was ready to leave, Urim appeared and asked to go with Ishmael to Egypt. "I must find Warda," he said. "I must be sure she is all right."

Ishmael welcomed the cheese maker and assured him that if his grandfather accepted him, there would be a position for the man and his cheese in the house of the pharaoh.

Urim shook his head. "I'm not intending to stay in Egypt. I don't really belong there anymore."

Abraham stayed long enough to make elaborate plans for their departure. He wanted his son to arrive before Pharaoh in a manner befitting a prince. Runners were sent on ahead, and again gifts were dispatched for Pharaoh. Nothing was left undone to assure Ishmael's acceptance.

A week later, early in the morning, the caravan left Beersheba. Part of the group had come from Hebron and others from beyond the Jordan. The large caravan would travel down to Egypt on the old route called the Way of Shur.

Hagar felt both excited and anxious. What would it be like to return to her father's house after all these years? She glanced over at her son and was reassured. Pharaoh would be proud to own this young man. All that the pharaoh had loved in his friend Abraham was now embodied in the young man who was his grandson.

Hagar looked back as the caravan began to move. The sun was just coming up, and she could see quite clearly the man she had loved so devotedly standing beside his well with some of his men. He looked suddenly old to her, and she had a feeling that she would never see him again. This part of her life was over. She had learned so much and was so different from the spunky, obnoxious young girl who had come with Sarah and Abraham from Egypt.

The last thing that was distinct and visible was the tamarisk tree, the little tree that would always stand as a welcome to her son and a reminder of the faithfulness of Abraham's God, El Olam, the Everlasting. She would probably not come back, but Ishmael was young and strong and he would be back to see his father.

Urim was gone for months, but when he came back, he brought welcome news. Pharaoh had been overjoyed to see his grandson and had immediately given him houses and lands, and Hagar had picked out an Egyptian wife for him. In time Pharaoh promised to put him in charge of all Egypt's mines and holdings in the Sinai and the Negev. "He will be a great prince," Urim predicted, "and his mother will dwell in his house in a position of honor."

At first Urim said nothing of Warda, but gradually some of the women close to Safra learned that the old man who had abducted Warda was dead. Warda had inherited all his possessions and was considered a very great and wealthy landowner in the delta.

Urim had seen that he no longer fit into her new life and so with dull determination wished her well. Then on a lighter note, he promised to send her an assortment of his best cheeses once a year. It was evident that she no longer needed him, and so he returned to Abraham's camp and to Safra.

For Abraham it was different. He felt bereft and lost. The son he had loved and cherished was gone, perhaps never to return. To make matters worse, Sarah was happier than she had been in years. "See," she said, "it's wonderful to have them gone. I should have known better than to have suggested such a thing as Hagar's bearing me a child. It was all a big mistake."

He winced with the pain of hearing her joy. He had made such wonderful plans for Ishmael. He had built so many dreams around him. Now all that was lost to him.

As time went on he also missed Hagar. He wouldn't have admitted it, but she had been responsible for his remembering some romantic ditties of his youth. She had made his heart beat faster at her touch and the sap rise in his veins like it did in trees in the spring.

However, most difficult of all was the feeling that he had lost Sarah. She no longer seemed to see him. She had very little to say to him. At times she looked right past him in her delight at every move Isaac made. The child was everything. He made up her whole world and no one else mattered. She talked about Isaac, hovered over him constantly, and worried about the least problem he might face.

What will become of my son? Abraham worried. His mother has made a toy of him. She's bound him so tightly to her that the child won't be normal. I can't even reason with her.

He not only felt that he had lost her, but he also felt that some tragedy was waiting for them in the future. He could sense it. Old women often said, "If you love something too much, the gods will snatch it away."

Of course, a child like Isaac who had been miraculously given to them by the Elohim was different. He had special protection. No evil thing could come near him because he was the child of the promise. How could the promise be worked out if anything ever happened to Isaac?

Nevertheless the feeling persisted. Sarah's love was stifling and unnatural, and no good could come of it.

*I*n the ensuing years Isaac was the delight of his father and of all who came in contact with the great man and his son. Abraham could not resist telling stories of his wit and cleverness. "He can oversee the shearers during the sheep shearing time. He's only twelve, and yet he can recognize shoddy work. He can tally our profits at the market, and he knows a good bargain without being told. He can chart the seasons by the stars, and he commands the respect of all my men. More than this, he is a good, obedient boy who gives his father no cause to worry."

Abraham didn't add that the boy was often criticized for spending so much time with his mother and for taking no interest in hunting or fighting. He threw the javelin awkwardly and almost never joined the young men in target practice with the bow and arrow. "His mother is too protective," they whispered. "She had such a hard time getting him, she doesn't want to take any chance on his getting hurt."

Sarah knew what they said but she didn't care. She wanted to be sure Isaac was never in any danger. She could not bear to think of any harm coming to him. "If he never learns to use a bow and arrow or throw a javelin well, he'll never have to fight," she said with smug satisfaction.

When Urim came to deliver his cheese a few months later, he found Abraham in his tent conferring with some of his herdsmen, and so he waited quietly, off to one side, until they were gone. "My lord," he said, "this cheese is quite delicious. I have used a new process. I think you'll like it."

Abraham nodded absentmindedly as he motioned for Urim to put the cheese on the leather mat just inside the door. "I'm sure it will be very good. You usually come earlier. Has there been some problem?"

"Not a problem, my lord. Just an unusual experience. I've been up the ridge to a festival at Bethlehem. They were harvesting their grain and giving the first cuttings to the storm god. 'The celebration of firstfruits,' they call the celebration."

Abraham was immediately interested. "What do you make of it? I'm sure you can remember coming through the land when it was dry and parched with no harvest at all."

Urim saw that he had captured his interest, and he took the liberty of squatting beside Abraham so he could reply in a whisper. "The Canaanites believe they have had no more famines because they have made many costly offerings to Ashtoreth, Baal, and Hadad."

"What do you mean by 'costly offerings'? It's obvious their celebrations and customs are more base and depraved than any in Ur or Egypt."

"They are bragging in their markets that by offering their children to the gods, they have at last won favor."

"You said 'children'? Are there many who will make such a sacrifice?" Abraham was no longer preoccupied. He was intensely interested.

"More than you can imagine."

"I suppose it's some of these people who have more children than they can feed or care for."

Urim sat toying with the fringe on his tunic. He hesitated before blurting out, "No, my lord. The children have to be the most beautiful, most loved, or they say the sacrifice is worthless. Preferably it is the firstborn like the first-fruits the god wants. The god wants their best or he will wreak vengeance on them."

Abraham didn't answer. He was deep in thought. Urim sat and waited for his response.

Abraham's thoughts had run wild. The mention of the firstfruits had done it. Abraham had been accustomed to the sacrifice of firstfruits and the firstborn of his cattle to the Elohim, not out of fear, but out of gratitude. He believed that to sacrifice of his increase was to recognize God's ownership. He owned nothing; he was a steward of all he possessed. God, the Elohim, was the real owner.

Urim grew restless. There was one question he wanted answered and he decided to just plunge in. "My lord," he said cautiously, "these gods they worship are only made of wood or stone, as you have often said. They may even be demonic beings, and these people are offering their very best to them. The Elohim is the true God, the Creator of all things. Do you think you could ever offer your son to him?"

Abraham was startled. The thought had once or twice occurred to him, but he had quickly pushed it aside. To have it voiced in such a way was shocking. He looked at Urim with annoyance. "No," he said firmly, "the Elohim has made promises to me. Isaac was given by the Elohim. He is essential if the promise is to be fulfilled."

Urim could see that he had probed too deep and was about to annoy Abraham. He had only one more observation to make, and he blurted out the words, "As I see it, the difference between worshiping the Elohim and a god like Baal is that one can't control the Elohim. We have no power over him, but their wooden and clay gods can be taken out in the field and beaten if they behave too badly after a sacrifice."

Without another question he backed to the tent door and was gone. Long after Urim left, Abraham pondered the questions Urim had voiced. It was the most frightening thing he could imagine. "Sacrifice Isaac! Impossible!" Could he love Elohim if He should ask such a thing of him? His hurt would be monstrous, but nothing compared to what Sarah would experience.

A score of pictures flashed through his mind, Sarah's delight in the little boy's first steps, her laughter when he sang the tribal songs, her pride in his quick wit, and her utter and complete joy at being a mother. "No," Abraham assured himself, "the Elohim would never ask such a thing of me."

He went further and reasoned that he had left family and friends to wander among strangers and through alien lands in answer to the Elohim's wishes. He had always given readily the best that he had whenever the Elohim had requested it. He even prided himself on being called by his neighbors "the friend of God."

It was true, as Urim had pointed out, that none of these things controlled Elohim. Their relationship was not one of control but one of trust, and he had grown to trust Elohim.

He breathed a sigh of relief. The Elohim would never ask such a thing of him. He felt better. He felt a sense of relief as though some great issue had been settled. That night he sat among his men around the fire at peace with himself and his world.

If Abraham had not grown accustomed to hearing the voice of the Elohim and recognizing it, he could have excused what happened next as a trick of his imagination. As it was, the words were distinct, and the voice, one he immediately knew. There was no doubt what had been said and who had said it. He had insisted the message be repeated lest it be some trick his mind or a demon was playing on him. It was no use. The voice was gentle and compassionate, but the message tore through his mind like a thunderbolt.

It wasn't at night or at a time when he was daydreaming or praying. It was in broad daylight with birds singing and flowers bursting with fragrance, his flocks covering the valley as far as his eye could see.

As in the past his name was called. It was personal and intimate. "Abraham," the voice said.

Abraham recognized it immediately. "Here I am," he said.

Everything became silent. The leaves of the small fig tree no longer moved, a brown lizard dodged back under a rock, a spider hung motionless in its web, and no birds crossed the sky. The whole world held its breath.

"Abraham," the voice said again, "take now your son, the son you love, Isaac, and go into the land of Moriah; and offer him there for a burnt offering upon one of the mountains I will show you."

Nothing more was said. Gradually a soft breeze began to blow, the leaves of the small fig tree moved, the lizard went on its way, and the spider continued working on its web while flocks of birds appeared in the sky. Only Abraham stood motionless. The unimaginable order had been given. His worst fear had materialized.

Abraham was unable to sleep that night. He went over and over in his mind the exact words spoken by Elohim. He tried to imagine what it would mean. What would he tell Sarah and what would he tell Isaac? He tried to picture building an altar and then placing Isaac on it. That was as far as he dared imagine. It was too impossible. He had sacrificed many animals. He had the sharpest knife.

The horror of it made him spring up from his pallet and pace the floor with his arms wrapped tightly around his chest. He went to the tent pole where his girdle hung and reached for the knife. It had been the best of its kind, and he had always been proud of it. Now he lifted it out of its holder and looked at it with loathing. He grasped the hilt and stared at the blade. What a powerful thing it was that could kill this child he loved and lay waste his dreams and hopes. He ran his hand along the blade, wondering if he could really bring himself to do this terrible thing for Elohim.

This thin, sharp blade, he thought, will slay Sarah's love for me. She would never understand. She'll hate Elohim.

Slowly and deliberately he placed the knife back in its holder and wiped his hands on his robe. If, he thought, by some chance the Elohim rescues Isaac, the lad will hate me for what I tried to do. Nothing will ever be the same. The terror he felt was worse than any he had felt facing his worst enemies.

Again and again he pictured what would happen if he ignored the request, if he went on as though Elohim had not spoken to him. He wouldn't say no. He would just ignore the whole thing. Each time he felt as though some great abyss had opened before him, he knew he would find himself alone without the guidance and relationship he had come to depend on. If, he thought, I don't do as the Elohim has asked, something fine and good in our relationship will be lost.

Then most frightening of all, he began to wonder what other terrible thing might the Elohim ask of him.

Interspersed in his struggle had been a recurring thought. It came from somewhere outside his fear and panic. The words were distinct and insistent: The Lord will provide. He heard them repeatedly as a background chorus to his tormenting thoughts. He briefly pondered what they meant. Would the Lord provide another son in Isaac's place? He wanted no other son. Isaac was the beloved, the darling of his heart.

In the end he decided he had no choice but to obey and trust the Elohim. He resolved not to discuss his decision with anyone. He knew he must not think or reason; he must simply act. He must leave as soon as possible. If he gave himself any time for reflection or let Sarah have her say, he would not be able to do this dreadful thing. To not act on what he knew to be the will of the Elohim was unthinkable. It would be as the sin of Adam, a form of rebellion, and that he could not do.

"I must leave at daybreak," he said to himself. "I will not have to explain to Sarah, and I will tell Isaac only what is necessary." With a sinking heart he realized that if Sarah even suspected what he was about to do, she would see that he was stopped.

It all seemed so unreal. He couldn't visualize doing such a thing. He couldn't imagine bearing up on the long three-day journey to Moriah, knowing what would have to happen when he arrived. How would he explain all of this to Isaac?

He slept only fitfully and rose before daybreak to gather the things he would need, the fire pot, the wood, their knapsacks holding Urim's cheese and some fresh bread. Last of all he woke up Isaac. He told the boy only that they were going on a short trip. He cringed at the trust he saw in the boy's eyes as he hurried to dress and say good-bye to his mother.

"Where are you going at this hour of the morning?" she demanded.

"I'm going with my father. I'll only be gone several days."

"What sort of trip is this that has been planned so hurriedly?"

"Something the Elohim has told him to do."

The information that the Elohim had told Abraham to make the trip terrified Sarah. She sprang up from her sleeping mat and hurried out to where Abraham was talking to two young men who were going with him. "What is this? Where are you going, and why are you taking Isaac?"

Abraham had not wanted to have to explain anything to Sarah. He had hoped they could be gone when she awoke, and others would tell her they had gone on a little trip of several days.

He could see that this would not have been possible. With a sigh he motioned for Sarah to come back into the tent and he would explain. "Sarah," he said. "It's the Elohim. He's asked this of me and I must obey."

"Asked what of you?" Sarah questioned suspiciously.

"He has asked me to take Isaac and sacrifice in the region of Mount Moriah at a place he will show me."

Abraham could see that the full import of what was to be done had not occurred to Sarah and he couldn't tell her. He could see that she was against Isaac's going as it was.

"There's no need for our son to go. He can be a part of many sacrifices right here," she said.

"But that's what the Elohim told me to do. I am to take Isaac, and so that is what I must do."

Sarah frowned. "What if some accident should happen? What if our son finds the journey too difficult?"

Abraham could see that she didn't understand and he was relieved. He must give her some encouragement for the fears she seemed to have, and so he said, "The Elohim has told me to do this and I trust Him."

"And where is the animal for the sacrifice?" she asked.

Abraham had started to leave, and now he came back and took Sarah in his arms, hoping she wouldn't see how disturbed her questions made him. "I have only the words, 'The Lord will provide,'" he said. "And I can only trust the Lord to provide."

She pulled away and looked at him with fear glinting in her eyes. "There's something strange about this. What are you doing with Isaac?"

"Don't worry, Sarah," he said, "please don't worry. It's true the Elohim told me to take my son and sacrifice him but . . ."

"Sacrifice him! Sacrifice him! How can you even think of such a thing?"

"Sarah, listen to me," he said. "I don't know what will happen. I just trust the Elohim. He will do what is best."

Sarah began to scream and cry. She clung to him so fiercely her nails dug into his flesh, "No, no!" she cried. "Not Isaac! Not my son Isaac!"

Abraham loosened her fingers and tried to reason with her, but it was useless. She backed from him, her face twisted in horror and anguish. She clawed at her hair and ripped her robe. In a frenzy she began scooping up the cold ashes from the night's fire and pouring them over her head.

Some of the women heard the commotion and came running. Abraham bade them comfort her until he returned. He turned quickly and started up the path to where Isaac and the two young servants were waiting. At the crest of the small incline he looked back and could see women from other tents running toward their tent, but he could see nothing of Sarah. "Oh, my God," he prayed, "if I am to do this thing, comfort Sarah."

The journey for Abraham was fraught with anxiety and terrors. He plodded on, putting one foot in front of the other, trying not to think. Isaac seemed not to notice but ran along exclaiming over each new bird or small dark animal. He whistled and sang with the joy of the fresh air, the sunshine, and the adventure with his father.

On the third night, Abraham was awakened by a gentle shaking of his shoulder, a whispering of his name and then the instructions, "You will see Salem tomorrow. The village threshing floor is called Moriah. You will go to the west a ways to the tallest mountain, a mountain with the face of a skull. There you will build an altar and sacrifice Isaac."

In the morning, when he arose, he remembered the instructions perfectly, but he began to doubt it was anything but his imagination until he came to the mountain with the face of a skull.

"Stay here with the donkey," he told the servants, "and the lad and I will go yonder and worship and return."

He placed the wood on Isaac's back, then fumbled around among the trappings on the donkey's back, almost hoping the knife would not be there.

A knife was a rare and costly thing. He had paid dearly for it, but now he wished with all his heart it would be lost. His hand touched the cold hardness of the metal, and he drew it out. He held the knife at arm's length, as though seeing it for the first time. It would have been so easy for the Elohim to send an angel to destroy the knife, and Isaac would be saved. Reluctantly he stuffed the knife into his belt, took the fire pot from one of the servants, and started up the steep incline.

Isaac had become quiet. He no longer dawdled along chasing butterflies and tossing rocks. It was as though he had begun puzzling over the strangeness of their journey. "Where is the lamb for the sacrifice?" he finally asked his father when they stopped for a few minutes to catch their breath.

Abraham hesitated. He could find nothing to say but to repeat the words that continually drummed in his head. "The Lord will provide," he said with a catch in his voice. He turned and started back up the hill, his steps getting slower and slower until it was obvious that something was wrong.

When they reached the top of the hill, Abraham took a long time looking for the right spot and then a great deal of time collecting stones for the altar. Isaac helped him, and seeing that Abraham was having more and more difficulty, he laid the final stones.

Abraham carefully and methodically placed the wood on the altar, then took from his belt a coil of hempen rope. Slowly he tied Isaac's hands and feet and then lifted him onto the altar. Isaac said nothing but looked at his father with calm, trusting eyes that so disturbed Abraham, he was almost turned from his purpose.

He could no longer look at his son. The trust he saw was crushing. He looked down and struggled to loosen the knife, then lifted it high and, looking up, hesitated only a moment as he felt the wrench and pain of abandonment. Elohim was not going to save him. His son, and with him all the hope and joy and meaning of life itself, was going to die. It was only a moment, but the pain he felt was akin to a whole lifetime of disappointment.

Then, just as he had lost all hope of rescue, a voice loud and jubilant cried out, "Abraham! Abraham!"

"Here I am," he whispered while his eyes strained to see where the voice was coming from and his arm trembled.

"Do not lay a hand on the boy. Do not do anything to him. Now I know that you fear God, because you have not withheld from me your son, your only son."

Through tears of joy Abraham saw a ram caught by its horns in the thicket. He lowered his arm and released Isaac. "My son," he said, "you see? The Lord has provided. We will name this place Jehovah-Jireh, the Lord provides."

* * *

Three days later, as Abraham approached the region of his tents, some of his men saw him coming and ran to meet him. When they saw Isaac, they yodeled for joy, grabbed his hands and kissed them, and kissed the hem of his garment as though he were a dignitary. Everyone talked at once. They all tried to tell of Sarah's suffering, and they asked so many questions, no one waited for answers.

The only information that was repeated was the news that for the first time in the six days Sarah had combed her hair, anointed herself with oil, and changed her clothes and was at the well.

"My son," Abraham said, "run to the well. We must not let your mother suffer one more moment of wondering how you are."

Isaac ran to do as his father asked, and the men drew back to let Abraham enter his tent alone. Abraham lifted the flap and entered Sarah's side of the tent first. He saw at a glance the awful scene of her suffering. There was the torn robe that had been her favorite. He picked it up and noticed how the ashes fell from it. He saw that all the bright-colored throws had been put away. Only Isaac's belongings were evident, as though she had clung to them in desperation. He picked up the brass bowl that had been filled with ashes and saw the untouched bread the women must have brought. "Oh Sarah," he said, "how you must have suffered. With what tortured thoughts you were tormented. Three extra days you suffered, not knowing how the lad was saved."

Jehovah-Jireh, the Lord will provide. The God who provides. How lovely it had seemed on the mountain, but how difficult it would be to explain to Sarah. It had been to him a new revelation of who his God was and how He cared for those who trusted Him.

Since leaving home six days earlier, he had eaten nothing but bread and cheese. Suddenly he became acutely aware of being hungry. Along with this awareness came the distinct recognition of a familiar odor. Quickly he pulled the heavy dividing curtain aside and stepped into his part of the tent. It was just as he had left it, except on the leather mat in front of his seating area was the old fire pot with a clay stew pot on top.

Curls of smoke drifted up from the pot, and Abraham realized it was indeed his favorite stew. He hurried over and lifted the lid to see the delicious contents. As he did so he saw that beside the pot were sitting two bowls. "It's Isaac's bowl set out by mine!" he said, holding them up. Such joy flooded through him. He laughed. "Dear Sarah," he said, holding the bowls high, "you knew nothing of what happened, but you trusted enough to set out both bowls."

He heard laughing and singing and rushed to the door of his tent in time to see Sarah coming with Isaac. The whole camp came with them. Everyone was singing and dancing in an explosion of joy. Abraham saw a new Sarah before him, and in a rush of love, he held out his arms to embrace his wife.

* * *

Urim waited until a decent time had passed before he came again with cheese and questions. "My lord," he said, shifting awkwardly from one foot to the other, "what do you make of all this? Are we to sacrifice our children now?"

Abraham was startled by the lesson Urim seemed to be gleaning from the whole experience on Mount Moriah. "No, no, Urim," he said, "we must sacrifice, for love and worship demand it. If we truly love, we want to give our best. However, the Elohim has made it clear that he does not want the firstborn of our sons. He will accept a substitute in their place."

The answer didn't satisfy the clever cheese maker. "Then why," he asked, "did the Elohim tell you to go and make the sacrifice?"

There was a long silence as Abraham pondered the question he had asked himself over and over again. Nothing was entirely clear. He had no answers that a simple man like Urim could understand. He sighed and started to take the cheese and dismiss Urim. Then seeing the eager, expectant look in Urim's eyes, he felt obliged to give an answer. "I suppose," he said, "one way of looking at it is to see that the Elohim was testing this creature that He'd made. How much love and trust was he capable of. If He was going to bless him with descendants and possessions and make him a blessing to the whole earth, He had to know just what the man was made of."

Urim's eyes grew large with reverence and wonder. "Did he tell you that?

Did he tell you all people would be blessed because of what you did?"

Abraham picked up the cheese and nodded. "Yes, Urim, He told me that and much more, much, much more."

He watched the cheese maker go and was aware of another thought that had recurred many times since the trip to Moriah. It wasn't something Urim would understand, but it was something very profound that he had learned. "Just because you get some word from the Elohim doesn't mean you should stop listening. One should never stop listening," he muttered. Listening was everything. If he had not continued to listen, if he had hurried along with the first instructions and hadn't continued to listen, he would have sacrificed Isaac needlessly.

He wished Sarah could accept and understand all that he had learned and experienced. He had been encouraged by her big step of faith in putting out the bowls, but he suspected that he hadn't heard the end of her frustration and fear.

*S*arah had learned only one lesson from the Moriah experience, and it was that Isaac was not something she owned or possessed. She no longer hovered over Isaac but tried to relax and let Abraham take over the training of this special child. To her amazement they were soon inseparable. A noticeable bond grew between them that had not been there before.

She had assumed that Isaac would resent his father, even hate him, for what had happened on Mount Moriah. Fearing his reaction, she had not dared mention the episode.

Though she had expected a change in Isaac, she was surprised to sense a change in Abraham. In the past he was willing to leave the boy in her tent when he checked on his shepherds or went hunting; now he constantly took Isaac with him. There was a new pride in Abraham when he looked at his son or mentioned him to strangers.

All this puzzled Sarah, but she could not bring herself to ask the questions that tormented her. Most of all she wanted to know what Isaac had felt and thought on that fateful trip. At the moment of decision, had Abraham faltered? Had Abraham discussed what he was about to do with his son? She had heard about the ram caught in the thicket, but what had gone before, she could not even imagine. Neither Abraham nor Isaac went into details, and she found it increasingly difficult to ask.

Years passed quickly with the same seasonal rounds of activity until one spring when Sarah lay weak and frail in a borrowed house in Hebron. At last she came to a final reckoning with the past. She had been fearful that she might die and leave Isaac without a bride. If that happened, Abraham would have to make the choice. Would this be fair to her son? Could he trust his father to pick wisely, or would Abraham again consider only the Elohim's wishes? She summoned the courage to ask the questions she had pondered so long.

Isaac had ridden up from Beersheba to spend the day with her. It was early spring and the servants had carried her couch out into an area of the courtyard where it was warm and sunny. A light rain had just fallen, leaving everything fresh and fragrant.

She looked at her son, now a strong, healthy young man, sitting so quietly beside her. She must approach the subject cautiously, not dart at it as was her usual approach. First she must broach the subject of a wife. It would be difficult to find someone who would understand their aversion to cities and their devotion to the one Creator God, the Elohim.

She realized that she had come up to Hebron to die. It was time to speak frankly, and to do that she must ask the fearful question.

"Isaac," she said, "I am concerned that I won't be here to choose your bride. Your father will have to manage."

Isaac was suddenly alert. He turned to her with an anxious, questioning look. "Don't worry, Mother," he said.

"It's not that I'm worried, but it's the mother's duty to choose a bride. If I'm not here, your father will have to make the choice."

"We are all hoping the warm spring sunshine will make you well. You must relax and stop worrying. My father can manage."

Sarah studied his fresh, honest face. "You trust your father then?"

He looked at her and a puzzled frown crossed his face. "Of course, I trust my father. He loves me. Why do you ask?"

"Isaac," she said cautiously, "I have always wondered. I never dared to ask, but now I need to know: what happened on Moriah? How did you feel, knowing your father intended to sacrifice you?"

"Is that why you wondered if I could trust my father?" At his mother's nod, Isaac looked away and seemed to be studying a spider building a web between two storage jars. When he finally spoke, it was with carefully chosen words. "I see you don't understand," he said. "For Father, it was a matter of obedience. If he trusted Elohim, he had to obey."

"To obey! He didn't have to obey!"

"If my father really trusted the Elohim and knew He had told him to do something, then don't you see, he had to obey. For me it was the same. If I trusted my father, I had to obey him that day on the altar. I didn't know about trusting the Elohim, but I trusted my father. It's really very simple. If we trust, we will obey, and if we obey, God will provide. We named the place Jehovah-Jireh, the Lord will provide."

"So that is the way it was," Sarah said at last with tears in her eyes. It was the last time Isaac saw her alive. He left her in the garden with a few of her young maids. She seemed at peace with the past and had come to a new understanding of his father's devotion to his God. She was more relaxed and even happier than Isaac had seen her in a long time.

* * *

A week later Abraham received a message that Sarah was not well and he must hurry if he wanted to see her alive. He had not imagined such a thing happening with so little warning. She had always been so vibrant, stubborn, and resilient that he could not believe she would not recover in a few days of bright spring weather. Nevertheless, he told his servants to get his donkey ready because he would need to go as quickly as possible up to Hebron.

As he rode along the worn path through the scrub and bright spring flowers, he thought of all that had happened. The time had gone so fast. He always thought he would have palaces to give her. He dreamed of orchards and vineyards. He blushed to remember that he had pictured himself king and her queen of the promised land. Could she really be dying before she saw the promises come true?

He had been too embarrassed to mention the promises lately. Although he had told her of the ram caught in the thicket, he had not told her of the message that followed, the message that he had heard at various stages in his journey. This time it had been even more distinct and forceful.

"I the Lord," the voice said, "have sworn by Myself that because you have obeyed me and have not withheld even your beloved son from Me, I will bless you with incredible blessings and multiply your descendants into countless thousands and millions like the stars or the sands along the seashore. Your descendants will conquer their enemies and be a blessing to all the nations of the earth because you have obeyed Me."

He knew the words by heart. They were etched on his mind, but he had not shared them with Sarah. Sarah was practical, even arrogantly practical. She would laugh at such promises. "I'm 127 years old," she would certainly have said, "and I have seen very little evidence of such promises being fulfilled." If he mentioned Isaac, she would surely remind him that the Elohim had demanded him back. She would have seen the ram in the thicket as a lucky happening. "What the Elohim wants Abraham will see that He gets," he had heard her say many times.

Then just as the road began to wind up to the prominence of Hebron, he became acutely aware of a very real crisis he would be facing. If it were true that Sarah was dying as the messenger had said, there was the problem of her burial. She was no doubt already worrying about it. For all the wonderful promises over the years, he had to admit, he had not a single parcel of land in which to bury Sarah. Land wasn't sold. It was carefully passed down in a family from generation to generation, and selling any part of one's inheritance was a great shame.

As he entered the gate of the courtyard, he paused and looked around. Sarah was lying on a couch that had been pulled out into the warmth of the sun. She hadn't heard him coming, and so he had a few moments to look carefully at her. He was shocked. She was obviously very weak.

"Sarah," he said as he hurried over to her side.

She reached out her hand to touch his sleeve, and he saw how feeble she had become. She tried to smile. "I suppose they told you I was dying. You should have known I wouldn't go without seeing you."

There it is, he thought. She is still making clever remarks. As he sat down beside her, she reached out for his hand, and he was surprised to find it cold and fragile.

"Our lives have gone so fast," he said. "I made so many plans."

"Things seem to be fitting into place despite our mistakes. We have our son."

"But Sarah, the land. We've never had the land. I had hoped to build such palaces for you."

She smiled. Her voice was growing weaker and she struggled to reassure him, "So much time passed and nothing seemed to happen."

"Sarah, you can't leave me now. We have so much left to do."

"I have my son and I'm content."

"Am I so wrong to want all the promises fulfilled?"

"Is the land so important to you then?"

He frowned and looked away before he spoke. He couldn't bear to see her ashen face or notice how every breath was an effort. "Sarah, if you should die," he said at last, "we have no place to bury you."

"I can't be bothered with that now," she said, smiling with a faint hint of her old spirit. "You'll have to manage."

He could see that she was a bit amused. It was Sarah's way to see some humor in a thing.

She closed her eyes. He noticed that each small effort exhausted her. He sat beside her until he knew she was asleep. Then very gently he lifted her hand and placed it on the warm woolen robe. Quietly, so as not to disturb her, he rose. Motioning to his men, he went out to search for someone in the city who would sell him a plot of land.

* * *

Hours later he returned tired and discouraged. Sarah was lying where he'd left her. She was too weak to talk but gave him a questioning look. He didn't want to frighten her but couldn't help blurting out his frustration. "Oh Sarah," he said, "I've been out all day among our neighbors trying to find one man who would sell me land. Not one, not one person, would sell me a single section of his land."

Sarah reached for his hand but said nothing. He continued, "You can't imagine how angry and disappointed I've been. In all these years I never doubted our God would give us all the land He promised, and now you're sick." He paused, too overwhelmed with emotion to continue. In desperation he blurted out the shameful situation he found himself in despite all his efforts. "I don't even own land enough to build one tomb."

Sarah, sensing his total dejection, roused herself and summoned every bit of strength she possessed. With a great effort she tried to encourage him. "Remember," she said, "when you went to sacrifice our son?"

"How could I forget?"

"You didn't see the ram until your hand was raised to slay our son."

Abraham rubbed his eyes and pushed his headpiece back. "It's true. I almost slew him."

"It seems this is Elohim's way."

"What do you mean?"

"He always waits until there's no way around or through and then He acts."

"It's true. That's how it's been. But why? Why should it always be so hard?"

Sarah patted his arm and smiled a weak, tired smile. "Don't you see? He wants you to know it's not by your wits or from your wealth but from His hand alone."

With quiet assurance she continued, "When I am gone, and you need the burial place, it will be given."

"Sarah, oh Sarah," Abraham said as he gently cradled her in his arms. Sarah didn't respond, but he felt a new and quiet peace about her. When did it happen? he wondered. When did she come to understand Elohim? He sat beside her until he knew she slept. He could see her breathing was difficult, and he worried that she would never regain consciousness.

He dared not leave, and so he sat beside her until the late afternoon. She opened her eyes only once more and seemed to recognize him but was too weak to speak. She tried to smile and then was gone.

People came crowding into the room and filled the courtyard. Isaac, Lot with his daughters, Eliazer with Urim and their burgeoning families. Tribesmen, servants, and slaves wept and spoke of things they remembered, but to each one, the question came, "Where will he bury her? After all this time he hasn't even a burial plot."

The women tried to indicate it was time to wrap the body for burial, but Abraham would not listen. Isaac insisted they let him grieve and not disturb him.

Just as Isaac said that, there was a commotion at the gate and whispers ran through the crowd. The villagers along with important men had come to pay their respects. The family and friends made way for them, and so they came to stand beside Abraham in the courtyard. He rose and looked from one to the other. They were the men of Heth who had often spent time with Abraham sitting at the gate of the city. He could see they were moved by his grief, but didn't understand his dilemma.

Abraham spread his hands in a gesture of helplessness. "As you see, I am a visitor in a foreign land, with no place to bury my dead. Please sell me a piece of ground, only one small piece of ground." His eyes moved from one to the other of the men, and he could see they were moved.

The leader, an old and much respected elder, bowed slightly and said, "Certainly, for you are an honored prince of God among us."

Another prominent old man interrupted, "We will consider it a privilege to have you choose one of the very finest sepulchres."

Abraham felt joy rising in him as he remembered Sarah's last words: "He always waits until there's no way around or through and then He acts." Abraham looked around at the men and saw they were sincere, and he bowed low before them as was the custom. He couldn't imagine what had changed their minds, but he was not going to ask questions; he was merely going to be grateful.

"Since you understand and want to help, would you ask Ephron, the son of Zohar, to sell me the cave of Mach-pelah down at the end of this field? I will of course pay the full price for it, and it will become a permanent burial place for my family."

The cave of Mach-pelah was a large cave going back into a hillside. The field in front of it was a pleasant place with old olive trees giving shade and some almonds still in bloom. The ground was bright with iris and anemones. It was a lovely place, and to the eyes of one who had spent much time in the barren Negev, it was a paradise.

Abraham insisted on paying Ephron four hundred pieces of silver so there would be no mistake that this cave and piece of land where Sarah would be buried belonged to him. The whole transaction took place at the city gate so it would be recognized as official.

It was late afternoon when Abraham returned and found the women had prepared Sarah's body and wrapped it in the finest linen for burial. It was the men's business to attend to a burial and so, carrying the precious burden on their shoulders, they wound their way out through the city gate and down to the place of the cave. Small children, villagers, and shepherds who knew Abraham followed, and women dressed in black—the city's public mourners—followed close behind, weeping and wailing and beating their breasts.

Abraham and Isaac led the way into the cave and saw the body placed on a shelf that had been carved out of the rock. It was difficult to leave, and the two men knelt and prayed and wept, reluctant to turn and face their new life without Sarah.

"We will all be brought here," Abraham said at last to Isaac. "I will be placed there beside Sarah, and you and your family will also be here. Though we have owned no place in life, our God has provided for us in death. He is faithful. He keeps His promises." Reluctantly they turned and retraced their steps.

Outside in the soft glow of the afternoon sun, they saw a large caravan approaching by the upper road. There were many young men on mules and several regally attired camels.

One stood out from the rest with its silver trappings and linen curtains, suggesting a great lady within. Beside the camels walked men holding long feathery fans, and servants carrying water skins and ebony boxes of necessities. The group at the tomb watched with amazement as the procession wound its way down to where they stood.

One mule with tasseled headpiece and silver appointments came ahead and stopped at the edge of the garden. A young man dismounted and came directly toward Abraham. "Father," he said, "I hope I have come in time."

Abraham immediately recognized Ishmael, though he was now dressed in all the regalia of an Egyptian prince. "Ishmael!" Abraham exclaimed, his voice catching with emotion. "Did you know then that Sarah died?"

"As soon as news reached me that she was ill and dying, I insisted on coming. She was my mother, a loving, indulgent mother, the first mother I knew. I had to come. Such ties are not easily broken."

Abraham was deeply touched by all that Ishmael told him. Then he asked, "And who are these you have brought with you?"

"They are my sons. All twelve have come with me to honor Sarah." At that he motioned to the young boys who had ridden up with him on their mules. The tallest and oldest was Nebaioth, the next Kedar, then Adbeel, followed by Mib-sam, Mishma, Dumah, Massa, Hadad, Tema, Jetur, Naphish, and last of all a young boy in his nurse's arms called Kedemah. Ishmael presented them all to his father and watched with pride as Abraham stretched out his hand and blessed each one.

"And the camels. Who else of such rank and importance has come with you?" Abraham asked.

"One of them carries my wife, the Egyptian my mother found for me, and the other carries my mother, Hagar."

"Even Hagar has come?"

"I must warn you, she is no longer the young woman you remember. She has become a woman of means and substance. She is the princess she was born to be."

Abraham moved toward the camel to welcome Hagar, but Ishmael detained him. "She is all the things I have said, but you must remember, much time has passed. She is still arrogant and proud but, well," he hesitated, then added, "you will see."

The camel knelt at the young driver's command. The curtains of the gilded litter gave off a subtle odor of sandalwood as they parted. Abraham looked with astonishment at the woman inside. She was thin and wrinkled and quite old, but dressed in starched and pleated linen; a golden pectoral with lapis lazuli rested heavily on her narrow shoulders. She wore an elaborate wig with the headpiece of gold with wing feathers, but no serpent at the crest. Nothing reminded him in any way of the young woman who had shared his tent and had borne him his first son.

He could think of nothing to say. She seemed elegant, foreign, and very old. It was only when he noticed her eyes, now more deeply ringed in kohl, that he had any sense of remembering. On seeing him she squinted as though pained by the bright light, then smiled, and held out one bejeweled hand. "You are quite old," she said, "not at all as I remember you."

He bowed to hide the amusement he felt. It was like the old Hagar to speak honestly.

* * *

Abraham and Isaac went with Ishmael into the cave. "I wish I could have come sooner," Ishmael said. "I would like to have given her the costly gifts that she deserved and that I can well afford."

"You hold no bitterness."

For a moment he turned away, unable to speak. "I didn't understand," he said finally. "Only later my mother explained everything."

"It is a good woman who views the mistakes of the past kindly," Abraham said.

* * *

It was a bittersweet time as they mourned for Sarah and yet renewed their almost forgotten family ties. "You must come and spend this time of mourning with us," Abraham said finally. It had softened the loneliness he was already feeling. He wanted to embrace each of these newly discovered grandsons and relish the joy of such bright, healthy children. He wanted to ask Ishmael many questions. He could see that he had prospered. He seemingly had come easily by the very things that had been promised Abraham—many sons, wide lands to administer, and amazing wealth. "You have everything and I am pleased," Abraham said at last.

"Everything," Ishmael said, "but to live in the tent of my father and learn his wisdom and faith."

As it turned out Ishmael was on his way to Hazor in the far north with a message from the pharaoh and could spend only a few days with his father and brother. When the time came for them to leave, Abraham brought the two brothers together and said, "My blood runs in both your veins equally, and my wish for you is that there will always be peace between you. Ishmael, you speak the greeting of Salaam and Isaac of Shalom but both mean peace. May there always be peace between you."

Then lifting up his eyes and stretching out his hand, he blessed Ishmael, closing with these words: "Blessed are you, oh Lord, who has blessed us and sustained us and allowed us to reach this time."

Ishmael left, promising to come again and begging Abraham to visit and instruct his grandsons in the faith. As they moved off down the road, Abraham stood looking after them as long as they were in sight. When they had disappeared around a bend in the road, he let Isaac lead him back to the house and the deserted courtyard.

He insisted they leave the city and return to the comfort of the tents as quickly as possible. He entered only partially into the old routine. He took no joy in the new lambs or the evening gathering of the men. He was silent and preoccupied so that soon everyone began to worry about him. "Why look," they said, "how Sarah's tent is still standing just the way she left it."

When Abraham heard them, he replied, "I'll leave it standing for Isaac's bride." His words made them all wonder when that would be and how it would come about.

Urim was especially concerned. He thought often of their escape from Ur and the years that had followed. He watched Abraham closely and ached to see him so alone. With these thoughts buzzing around in his head, Urim determined to find an excuse to talk to Abraham.

It was on a late afternoon some months after Sarah's death that he approached Abraham's tent with some fine rounds of smoked cheese. He had timed his visit so there would be no visitors and he could talk to Abraham alone. He stood in the tent opening and waited to be recognized and welcomed. He was surprised that Abraham spoke without even looking up from mending a leather quiver, "Urim, I see you have brought cheese, but what's on your mind?"

Urim was taken aback to realize that Abraham saw through his excuse of bringing the cheese. He hesitated and then came in and squatted down beside him and quietly watched the laborious process. His mind whirled around and over the question he wanted to ask. He knew it was bold and brash to ask such a thing, but he would have no peace until he knew.

Abraham lay the unfinished quiver on the mat and took the cheese. "How fortunate we have been all these years," he said, "to have one such as you providing us with such a delicacy."

Urim beamed and grew brave in his resolve to ask the question. "My lord," he said, "we have been on a long journey together. It has been an adventure with many promises and few answers to all your prayers and sacrifices. What do you make of it? Were you right to leave Haran and your father's home and family?"

Abraham pushed back his turban and leaned back among the cushions. He was obviously taking Urim's question very seriously. He took a long time to answer, and when he did, it was as though he was merely thinking out loud. "I was promised descendants as the stars, and I have only two sons. I was promised land, and I own only one grave site and one well. But I have been blessed above all men to have walked among kings and to have known as a friend the Elohim, the Creator God. I can now see that the Elohim is about far bigger things than I had imagined."

"I had not thought of it that way," Urim said. "Perhaps you're right. From my point of view you're a happy man."

"And you, Urim," Abraham said, "are you sorry you came along?"

Urim stood up and tucked his thumbs into his belt. "I wouldn't have missed it. Staying in Haran would have been tedious and dull compared to where I've been and all I've learned."

The cheese maker left, and Abraham had a feeling that what had been said between them encompassed everything that had happened across the years. Abraham had left Haran a brash and confident young man, eager to see God's promises fulfilled, but his understanding had been so narrow and so limited. God had a plan far grander than Abraham had ever imagined. Perhaps it would take all eternity to grasp what Elohim had in store for His children.

Look for more captivating biblical stories to come from River North and Roberta Kells Dorr.

MORE FROM ROBERTA KELLS DORR

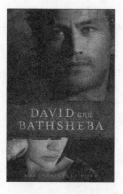

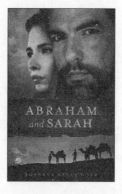

IMPACTING LIVES THROUGH THE POWER OF STORY

Thank you! We are honored that you took the time out of your busy schedule to read this book. If you enjoyed what you read, would you consider sharing the message with others?

- Write a review online at amazon.com, bn.com, goodreads.com, cbd.com.

- Recommend this book to friends in your book club, workplace, church, school, classes or small group.

- Go to facebook.com/RiverNorthFiction, "like" the page and post a comment as to what you enjoyed the most.

- Mention this book in a Facebook post, Twitter update, Pinterest pin or a blog post.

- Pick up a copy for someone you know who would be encouraged by this message.

- Subscribe to our newsletter for information on upcoming titles, inside information on discounts and promotions, and learn more about your favorite authors at RiverNorthFiction.com.

midday connection

Discover a safe place to authentically process life's journey on **Midday Connection**, hosted by Anita Lustrea and Melinda Schmidt. This live radio program is designed to encourage women with a focus on growing the whole person: body, mind, and soul. You'll grow toward spiritual freedom and personal transformation as you learn who God is and who He created us to be.

www.middayconnection.org

MOODYRADIO

Where you turn. For life.